ON THE EDGE OF
HUMANITY

BOOK 1

THE VAMPIRE NAVY SEAL SERIES

S.B. ALEXANDER

Cover designed by Hang Le
Cover copyright © 2021 by S.B. Alexander

On the Edge of Humanity
Book one: The Vampire Navy SEAL Series

First Edition: January 2013

E-book ISBN-13: 978-0-9887762-0-3
Print ISBN-13: 978-1-954888-17-3
Large Print ISBN-13: 978-1-954888-18-0

1

I was trapped in a world where I didn't belong. A world where my dad had discarded me as if I were a piece of trash. A world where danger constantly surfaced, even in places I called home. I couldn't say when I came to the decision not to be a victim anymore.

After my mother died, I spent most of my life in foster care, traipsing from one foster home to another, always wondering where I was going to sleep and what I was going to eat. Life sucked with a capital S. My only family was my twin brother, Sam. We didn't know why our father abandoned us. But if I ever got the chance to meet him, I was going to kill him.

My gypsy-style life had forced me to face all

kinds of challenges, and none were good. I hated my life, I hated school, and most of all, there were days when I hated living. I hid behind Sam, who always protected me and even fought my battles when I needed him to.

I shied away from people, especially bullies at school and one boy in particular, Blake Turner. I wished I had the courage to stand up for myself, but fourteen years of foster care had taught me the art of avoidance. I hid behind books and read constantly, trying to transport myself into another world where I was free, where I became the hero of the story I was reading. I desperately longed for a mom and dad who loved me and friends—lots of them—who supported me.

My only friend was Darcy Rose, and I wasn't even sure why she wanted to be friends with someone like me, the outcast of the school, the one they called Moonbeam because of my silver eyes. I had Blake to thank for that—he pointed it out every chance he got.

Darcy and I had first met in gym class last year after Blake tripped me during a soccer game. I'd fallen face-first into the wet mud, and Darcy ran over to help me. We'd been friends ever since. I guessed she felt sorry for me.

Tonight, I was feeling sorry for myself, but a

wave of trepidation also coursed through me. I stood alone in the kitchen, instructed by my foster mom, Hilda, to clean it up while she retired to her sewing room upstairs and her gross husband, Cliff, sat in his fat leather chair, watching TV. I was her slave, only there to do her chores—to clean her house and bow to her every need. To think I'd thought the stepmother in Cinderella was bad. I wasn't going to a ball, and midnight wasn't my deadline. I had only a few minutes to clean the kitchen before Hilda came down from her sanctuary to inspect my work. Afraid of being separated from Sam and sent to a home for girls, I obeyed.

As I wiped down the kitchen table, I contemplated what I was going to do with a full week off of school for Easter vacation. With Darcy out of town, I had to find something to keep myself occupied. I didn't want to hang around the house, enslaved to Hilda or Cliff. They would probably make me wash windows or clean their tile floors with a toothbrush, which didn't sound like fun. As I weighed my limited options, rage bubbled to the surface. While the last five foster homes had been tolerable, Hilda and Cliff's screamed danger. Sam and I had been with the Birches only for a short while, and in that time, we had followed every one of their house rules. But there was one rule I refused to obey.

Sam wasn't home yet from baseball practice, so I covered his dinner and placed it in the microwave for later.

Separating the kitchen from the family room was a paneled wall with a staircase to one side. I tiptoed over to the door and peeked up the stairs. The *rat-a-tat* of the sewing machine filtered down the staircase. I imagined Hilda was working out her own frustrations—all the better for me.

A sports announcer's voice filled the family room. I peered around the banister. Cliff's eyes were closed, his mouth hanging open.

I skulked back into the kitchen, and a floorboard squeaked in the process. I stood still for a moment and listened. The sewing machine still hummed, and Cliff began to snore.

I bit my lower lip then gave the kitchen one last glance. Satisfied it would pass muster, I grabbed the handle on the utensil drawer and pulled it open. I fished around the messy drawer until I found the corkscrew. It was stuck in the back under a bunch of plastic spoons. I gently plucked it out of its hiding spot and placed it into my sock. As I did, the creak of the stairs startled me, and my heart rate increased. I hurriedly smoothed my pant leg when Hilda walked in.

"Jo, what're you doing?" Hilda asked in a raspy voice that sounded as if she had just smoked a carton of cigarettes.

"Ma'am?" My hands were shaking, so I grabbed the towel off the counter and made it look like I was wiping them.

She glanced around and sauntered over to the refrigerator. "Where's your brother?"

"I don't know." I wasn't sure if I should move. The wine opener was digging into my ankle and on the verge of slipping out of my sock. "May I be excused?" I asked.

Hilda pulled out a can of beer and closed the refrigerator door. Her short black hair was styled into a bouffant, and thick, bushy eyebrows over-powered her brown eyes. I wanted to give her a pair of tweezers, so she could shape them.

"The kitchen looks good, so sure. It's Friday night. Do you have plans?"

My plan was to run, to get away from her and the hell I was in. "No, ma'am."

"A pretty sixteen-year-old girl like you doesn't have any friends?"

My jaw dropped. She'd called me pretty. I was shocked she had the nerve to deliver a compliment. That was a first. "My friends are heading out of town for spring break." Darcy was going on a cruise with her parents. Lucky her. She had asked me to go, but I couldn't even afford a McDonalds meal, let alone a cruise vacation.

"Are you okay, Jo?" Hilda asked.

My face must've had a blank look on it. "I need to use the bathroom."

"Well go, then. Don't let me stop you."

I walked a few steps then stopped just to be sure the wine opener wouldn't fall to the floor. With it still hanging in there, I said good night to Hilda and left.

I headed to my room, which was located down a small hallway off the family room. As soon as I closed the door, I let out a deep breath, slid down the wall, and sat on the floor. My heart raced, and I took a few deep breaths to calm my nerves. *I hate this place. Hell has to be better than this.*

I pulled out the corkscrew and touched the tip of the screw with my forefinger. I rubbed it too hard, and a tiny speck of blood surfaced. *This will do nicely.*

I suckled my finger, and a spark ignited inside me. The candied taste of that small drop of blood awakened my taste buds. My pulse quickened, then my head began to spin. *What the heck is going on? Why would blood taste as sweet as a watermelon candy?* It had always had a metallic taste to it before. *This is crazy.* I immediately wiped my finger on my jeans.

I shook my head a few times to erase the thought and surveyed my ankle. A couple of scratches tattooed the side near the bone. It was nothing to worry about. It beat getting caught by Hilda, the wicked witch of New England. The first night in the house, I'd dropped a glass of soda, and it had shattered. She yelled, berating me until I broke down in tears. Ever since then, I was careful not to awaken her evil side.

I closed my eyes, inhaled, and hugged my knees to my chest. I sat still, relishing in the quietness of the room. My life had to change. I wasn't sure I could handle two more years in foster care. But then again, I had no idea where I would go when I turned eighteen. I let out a deep sigh. I had two years to think about it—if I made it that long.

I uncurled my legs and stood up. It was almost nine o'clock, and Sam still wasn't home. I was starting to worry. But it was Friday night, and maybe he was hanging out with his best friend, Ben.

The heat kicked on, and hot air started blowing out of the floor ducts, causing my cheeks to flush. I went over and raised the window, letting in the brisk April air, which tickled my hands.

I unpacked my backpack, placing my books on top of the dresser. I looked over at the clock on the nightstand, and five minutes had ticked by. *Come on, Sam, get your butt home.* Maybe if I thought it really hard, he would come walking through the door.

With nothing else to do, I changed into a pair of blue flannel shorts patterned with black cows and a T-shirt. Then I grabbed the wine opener and a John Grisham novel I'd borrowed from the library and climbed into bed.

I didn't know if I would have to use the corkscrew, but I wanted to be prepared. I twirled it in my right hand and jabbed it in the air a few times. Maybe I should've taken a knife instead, but that would have been too risky. With my luck, I would've had more than just scratches on my ankle. I placed the corkscrew under my pillow and picked up my book. *The Street Lawyer* was just getting interesting, and I was hoping that it would keep me awake until Sam came home.

Books were my hobby, and every chance I had, I tried to escape reality by burying my nose in one. While I devoured most genres, I didn't have a penchant for the paranormal, unlike the other high school kids. They were all gaga over the latest vampire book, and it made me want to puke. The undead didn't excite me. Who would ever want to drink blood as their main meal?

I squashed the thought of blood and vampires and started reading. After two pages, my eyelids grew heavy. I shook my head, trying to stay awake, but the words became blurry. I blinked a few times. I didn't want to fall asleep. I didn't feel safe without Sam in the house.

As my head bobbed down, the aroma hit me, and my eyes popped open.

Cliff turned to close the door, stinking of booze and cigarettes. I fumbled for the light switch to turn off the bedside lamp. Maybe the darkness would give me the edge I needed for my escape.

"That's not going to help you." White specks of breadcrumbs dotted his beard, and his wiry hair was matted to his head. He inched toward the bed, opening his pocketknife.

I took a deep breath and swallowed hard, almost choking. My heart pounded against my ribs, aching to get out. Nausea rose in my throat as my breathing quickened.

My hand trembled as I flicked the light switch, sending the room into darkness. The night-light on the wall near the door turned on. *Shit!*

As I closed my eyes, I heard Sam whispering in my head. *You have to fight back, Jo. I won't always be here to protect you. You have to learn to stand up to people like Blake.* What Sam didn't know was that Blake wasn't my only tormentor.

Cliff had snuck into my room one night, filthy drunk. At first, I'd thought he was lost, but when he whispered my name, I knew he had his wits about him. Thankfully, Hilda had been looking for him, saving me from his true intentions.

I expelled the air from my lungs in tiny increments, trying to gain control. My last breath released with a cough, the heat stinging my cheeks as the blood surged through me. My inner voice screamed, *I'm dead. I know I'm dead.*

I lay there, immersed in my own quiet hell. For the past two weeks, I'd feared him and those words he whispered again: "If you tell anyone, I will kill you and your brother."

I desperately wanted to tell Sam, but I just couldn't. He'd always had a short fuse, but lately, he seemed to get mad at any little thing. Besides, Sam had been in trouble with the cops and had even spent a couple of nights in jail. I wanted to protect him from himself, but more than anything, I was afraid that we would be separated if he ended up in jail for longer—or even worse, dead. I couldn't let that happen.

Victim be damned.

Cliff's breathing grew heavier as he reached the edge of my bed. The hairs at the nape of my neck stood at attention. I grabbed the wooden handle of the corkscrew when his rough calloused hand touched my ankle.

I froze.

"Sweet Jo," he whispered, reeking of alcohol. As the heat from his breath sprayed toward me, I tried to erase the image of his jagged teeth and the crud lodged between them.

He slid his hand up my leg and air seeped under the blankets.

I gripped the corkscrew tighter, my hand shaking uncontrollably. *Do it now.*

A cold breeze blew in through the cracked window between my bed and the full-length mirror. Moonlight radiated in, casting a glow around the room. Just what I needed—more light.

With my body still as a board, I peered in the mirror, and the glint of a blade next to my leg reflected in the distance.

I closed my eyes and gasped when the cold steel blade scraped along my leg.

"Jo, I have something for you," he whispered.

I spun around, aiming for his face, but he jumped back. His left arm got in the way, and I jabbed in the corkscrew as hard as I could.

"You want to play rough, little girl?" He pulled the corkscrew from his arm and threw it to the floor. "Well, let's play."

Blood dribbled out of the stab wound, glistening in the soft light of the bedroom. *Bleed, pervert, bleed.*

My hopes were cut short when he lunged for me. I rolled off the bed, and my left elbow broke my fall. The corkscrew lay inches from me, and I reached out to grab it, but he stepped on my hand.

I looked up at him. "Fuck you!"

"Big words coming from a little girl."

"Does your wife know you rape sixteen-year-old girls? Do boys make the cut too?"

"I'll show you how I treat little girls." He grabbed me by my shoulders.

My feet dangled. I threw a left kick, connecting with his precious jewels. He let go, and I fell to the floor.

He lunged for me again with the knife pointed right at me.

My vision blurred, then a sharp pain hit me on my left side. I grabbed my rib. A sticky warmth trickled down.

"You asshole! You stabbed me!" I tried to rise, but my knees wobbled, and the pain soared through me as if he were stabbing me over and over again.

He knelt down, and his hot breath caressed my ear. "I'm not done with you yet."

As I tried to breathe, the fragrance of my own blood wafted through the air, imparting the delicious scent of vanilla. *Why does my blood smell this sweet?*

I blew out the air in my lungs and blinked a few times, hoping it was all a dream. But when I opened my eyes, the beast was still there, a smug look painting his face.

I kicked, trying to fight my way out, which only caused his insolence to grow.

"Where ya going, sweet thing?" His voice oozed with slime. "There's nowhere to run."

"If you don't get off..."

"What? What're you going to do? Kill me... with a corkscrew?" He let out an evil laugh.

He was right. I had no way to get past him. He was six feet tall and weighed two hundred and fifty pounds. I didn't have a chance in hell. He grabbed both my legs and pulled me toward him. My head hit the front of the dresser. Then he brought the knife up to my left cheek and began tracing the outline of my face.

I sucked air in and held it, afraid to move. I was sure I had one of those deer-in-headlights looks.

"You're a beautiful creature, you know. And those strikingly silver eyes of yours are—"

I spat in his face.

He wiped the spit from his mouth. "You're going to regret that."

My vision flickered in and out, and I blinked. When the haze cleared, my brother, Sam, was standing in the room with a baseball bat in his hands and a murderous expression on his face.

With the knife now pinned to my left cheek, Cliff turned his head. "Don't try it, lad, or your sister's pretty face will—"

A door slammed.

Sam gripped the bat with both hands, as if he were standing behind home plate, waiting for the pitcher. "Take the knife away from her face." His tone dripped with venom.

"Come any closer, kid, and I will carve your sister's face up. She'll look like the Bride of Frankenstein when I'm done with her."

The tip of the knife punctured my cheek, and warm liquid oozed out. I drew in a breath as I raised my hand to my face. The pain stung me as if I had just pissed off a bumblebee.

Sam lunged at Cliff.

Cliff whirled his head toward me, his eyes bulging from their sockets, and drove the knife into my cheek. Pain shot through me, and my eyes watered, the salt from my tears stinging as it seeped into the cut. I froze, trying not to scream as I bit back the pain. If I moved even a tiny bit, the blade would do more damage.

Then the bat connected with Cliff's head, sounding as if Sam had just hit a home run. Cliff shrieked so loudly that it reverberated throughout the room, and the walls vibrated. I held my breath, praying he would let go of the knife. But it was too late. He dropped his hand, pulling the knife with him, and the blade sliced through my skin.

I wailed as the blood gushed down my cheek and into my mouth. I didn't know what to process first, the pain or the fact that I liked the taste of my own blood.

I placed my hand over my cheek and stood up on wobbly legs, using the dresser as an anchor to support my body. As I glanced around the room, all I could see was Sam standing over Cliff with blood dripping down the bat.

Then Sam shouted, "Jo, don't pass out! I'll be right there."

My arms trembled. I couldn't hold myself up much longer. Blackness filled my peripheral vision. As it grew darker around me, someone squeezed my hand. "Sam?"

"It's me, Jo," he said.

Tears streamed down my cheeks. "I'm sorry, I tried... I tried to take care of myself and protect you."

He ripped off his T-shirt and placed it over my left cheek. "Shh."

"What's happening to me? The blood... I want more blood."

"Everything's going to be fine," he replied.

I vowed revenge against the disgusting beast as the light around me flickered in and out. And then it was dark.

2

My eyes fluttered open, and I blinked a few times as shivers wracked my body. The temperature in the room felt like a walk-in freezer. I wiggled my feet to wake up my toes. I couldn't tell if they had fallen asleep or if they were frostbitten under the thick layer of blankets on top of me.

I drew in a breath, the air burning my insides as it seeped deeper into my lungs. The scent of alcohol hung in the air. I tried to raise my upper body, but the pain on my left side stopped me. I tried again, lifting just my head as I scanned the room.

Two people stood at the bottom of the bed,

their backs toward me. From what I could tell, it sounded as if they were arguing.

The man in the doctor's coat said, "No, it can't be." He wore a red-and-white cap, and a sliver of a tattoo peeked out on the back of his neck just below his cap.

It appeared to be some sort of symbol, but I couldn't quite make it out. My eyes were still adjusting to my surroundings.

"I ran it three times," said the nurse in blue.

"Well, run the test again. It's impossible. Her blood type can't be AF negative." The man's voice had a velvety tone, as if I were listening to a song by Josh Groban.

"Dr. Case, I'll have her blood tested again, but the outcome will still be the same," the nurse said.

They had to be talking about me because there was no other patient in the room unless someone was on the other side of the curtain that separated the room in half. Maybe Sam was in the bed behind the curtain.

I frantically searched again. A brown door with the word "bathroom" on it appeared in the distance, and an alcove framed a small window to my left with blinds that were creased together.

Then it occurred to me—maybe Cliff was dead. Maybe he was in the bed next to me. *Oh shit!*

I tried sitting up, slowly that time, but the pain in my ribs was still there. I took in a breath, and another burning sensation slithered inside me. I touched my left side then my right. I was wrapped in a thick layer of bandages. Blood rushed to my face. The pain on my left cheek pierced through me as if the knife were slicing through me all over again. I winced, and my heart raced as if it was trying to beat an opponent to the finish line.

Suddenly, the monitor near my head accelerated and chirped frantically. The nurse approached as an object in the distance thudded to the floor. The room went silent except for the monitor, which was still belting out a fast cadence in line with my heartbeat.

A door opened. The heels of someone's shoes scuffed against the tile floor as leather rustled. A tall black man appeared around the curtain, dressed in dark-blue pants, a light-blue shirt, and a leather jacket with a badge on the outside.

"Is there a problem in here? I thought I heard a bang," the officer said as he settled near the bed, his gaze landing on the bathroom door.

I silently recited the Hail Mary, praying Sam wasn't in the room. The monitor slowly decelerated. My heartbeat slowed, and my brain screamed. *Amen.*

Why was there a cop outside the door? I didn't do anything wrong. Maybe Hilda told the cops something different. But how would she know? She didn't come to my rescue.

I closed my eyes and dipped back into my memory. The sensation of Cliff slicing the knife through my cheek sent a chill down my spine. I opened my bottom jaw and moved it side to side. As I did, the tightness eased and warm liquid seeped out. It soaked the edge of the bandage near my mouth, and a drop of blood dribbled in.

When the blood touched my tongue, visions of what happened earlier came soaring back. My mind blurred. The desire for blood overwhelmed me, and I screamed.

Everyone turned and looked at me. The cop sprinted to the bed. The doctor just walked, as if he didn't care. The EKG machine picked up speed again, and my breathing grew shallow.

"What's going on?" asked the cop.

"Please wait outside, Officer Bradley." Dr. Case's voice had a stern tone to it. "Nurse Grey, please get me two ccs of diazepam, stat."

It was weird how one minute, the doctor didn't seem to care, and in the next, he was barking out orders.

The nurse's brows lowered, and she squinted

at Dr. Case. "But doctor, you don't know how it will react—"

"Get it now, Ms. Grey!"

As I savored the drop of blood, the nurse ran out behind the cop. The doctor looked at his watch as if late for an appointment. *This dude is one weird doc!* He seemed nervous about something.

Then Dr. Case grabbed his stethoscope. "Where does it hurt, Ms. Mason?" A look of terror was etched on his face.

I was convinced that he belonged in a hospital, but not this one—one for the insane.

As I stared at the crazy doctor, I reached up to touch my face, just to be sure Cliff hadn't carved a Frankenstein look on me. All I could feel was the bandage on my left cheek and smooth skin on my right.

My insides were about to burst with the desire for blood, and the pain in my chest made me feel like I was about to explode. "Is something wrong?" I asked. I ran my fingers through my hair, and two of them got caught in between strands, which I assumed were coated with dried blood.

He knitted his eyebrows together then stepped away from the bed, his hand clenched around his stethoscope.

"Dr. Case, is there something wrong?"

"Your eyes... they're... they're changing colors. It's like a colorful storm swirling around, with silver clouds rolling in, flashes of blue and green sparking in the background. Who are you?"

I didn't know whether to laugh or cry. "What are you talking about?" He was scaring me. Between his weird mannerisms and what he had just revealed about my eyes, I was beginning to think I was in an episode of *The Twilight Zone*.

He tilted his head to the other side as if he hadn't heard me.

"Hello?" I called.

The man was frozen in place. I imagined I looked horrible with the blood and the bandages, not to mention that my hair was probably disheveled and crusty with dried blood. But something told me that wasn't what was causing his freak-out.

He stood at the bottom of the bed, fixated on me.

I wanted to throw something at him. "Where's my brother? Is he in the bed next to me? Sam? Sam, are you there?" I lifted my left arm over my head and twisted my body to reach for the curtains. The pain knocked me back down. *I really need to stop doing that.*

"The police are searching for your brother."

Dr. Case pulled back the curtain.

The bed sheets were tucked neatly in place and the pillow fluffed, waiting for the next patient. My lungs deflated.

"Your bandage will need to be changed. You must've torn a stitch," Dr. Case said.

Wow. One minute, he was acting as if he had just escaped a mental institution, and the next, he was playing a caring doctor.

He went over to the nurse's cart, dropped his head, and pulled out a bin. More of the tattoo on the back of his neck jutted below his red-and-white cap. From what I could see it looked like the letter L. The rest of it wasn't visible.

After grappling with a handful of bandages, he wheeled the cart over to me. Then he fished in the pockets of his lab coat as his gaze gravitated toward the door.

"Why is there a cop outside?" I asked.

"Ms. Mason, the police want to ask you questions about what happened tonight."

"But I didn't do anything wrong."

"It's not for me to judge. My concern is for you to heal properly."

I silently laughed. His actions didn't match his words.

"The help you need aside from that is of no

concern to me. Now turn toward me." He slowly peeled away the tape from the gauze. I flinched as he did it three more times. With my skin exposed, the warm air tickled the wound. "Just as I thought. You tore a stitch."

His hand shook as he threaded the needle. "I need you to keep still."

I was planning to, given how nervous he was.

"This will sting a bit. I'm numbing the area around the wound."

As he inserted the needle, I winced before a warm sensation flowed over the left side of my face.

When he finished stitching, I let out a sigh, thanking God that Dr. Case hadn't done more harm.

He placed a clean bandage over the cut. "You're lucky there's no major damage." He deposited the needle in a plastic bag hanging from the nurse's cart. "No sudden movements for a few days."

"Thanks." I made a mental note not to move my jaw too much. The last thing I wanted was the taste of blood filling my senses. I wanted to ask him if he knew anyone who wasn't averse to the taste, but he would probably think I was crazy and call for an orderly to wrap me in a straitjacket.

"Did you say my blood type was AF negative?"

His brown eyes widened. "The lab must have made a mistake."

Again, his expression didn't match the words rolling off his tongue. It didn't seem as though he was telling me the truth. He gathered the bandage wrapper off the nurse's cart and crumpled it in his hands.

"Is there such a type?" I asked.

"Aside from the typical A, B, O, and AB variations, there are some rare blood types in this world." He paused and took in a breath. "For example, there are people who have Pk type blood and some who have CDE blood types." His voice quivered, and he kept looking at the door. "Blood types are classified by antigens, which are specific substances on the red blood cells. There are more than six hundred other antigens that have been identified around the world. I wouldn't worry, though. You're normal."

I chuckled. The word "normal" resonated in me, and my mind trailed off. My life had never been normal. Foster homes, bullies in school, cops, attempted rape, and now this—blood fascination, eyes that change colors, and an abnormal blood type. *What's next?* As my brain belted out the last two words, a bright light blurred my vision.

Dr. Case had a penlight in his hand. "I'm going to check your eyes."

"My eye color is unusual," I said.

He gently grabbed the bottom of my left eyelid and moved the light from side to side. "You're right. Your eye color is different. But even more surprising is how it changes." He repeated the same move on my right eye.

"My eyes have always been silver. I wasn't aware they changed colors, though."

The door opened, and Nurse Grey glided in.

"Here's the diazepam, Dr. Case."

"We don't need it now," he said.

Nurse Grey looked at me then the doctor. She let out a deep sigh and placed the syringe and the sedative on top of the nurse's cart.

Dr. Case finished my eye exam. "Get some rest, Ms. Mason. I'll be back to check on you in the morning."

"What about her blood?" Nurse Grey asked as she trailed behind Dr. Case.

"Send the sample of her blood over to Patrick," Dr. Case ordered as they left.

Patrick was probably the lab guy.

Alone in the room, I poked around for the remote to lower the bed. As I plucked it out between the rail and the mattress, the door squeaked open, and the swishing of leather grew louder as the cop once again returned.

"Good evening, Ms. Mason. I'm Officer Bradley, and I need to ask you a couple of questions about this evening." He pulled out a notepad and flipped it open. "Tell me what happened to you."

I wasn't sure where to begin. I wasn't even sure if I wanted to tell him anything. But it was probably best to get it over with. "The asshole tried to rape and kill me. What more do you want to know? He's a pervert."

"What about your brother? Mrs. Birch said he tried to kill her husband."

My jaw dropped. "You're kidding, right? My brother tried to save me. Where is Sam?"

"We don't know. Mrs. Birch said he disappeared after the ambulance left the house. We need to ask him some questions too."

"Is the pervert dead?"

"No, but Mr. Birch is unconscious at the moment."

Secretly, I wanted him dead, but I didn't want my brother in jail. Cliff should have been castrated for what he tried to do to me, and I couldn't stop wondering how many others he'd tried it with before me. It figured that Hilda was blaming this on Sam and probably me.

Officer Bradley snapped his notepad closed. He produced a business card from inside his jacket pocket and left it on the table next to the bed. "If you can think of anything else or where your brother might've gone, my cell phone is listed on that card. I'll be outside until my replacement shows up."

"Why do you have to stand outside my door if I didn't do anything wrong?"

"You're in foster care, so we have to wait for the state to send someone over in the morning. It's just a formality since you don't have a guardian." He turned on his heel and left.

Anger so hot blanketed me. Hilda was accusing Sam of trying to kill her beloved, asshole husband, and the cop said the state would be there in the morning. There was no way I was going to another foster home. I would rather live on the streets than be shipped off to another stupid family.

Biting a nail, I tried to make sense of what happened. But all that kept flashing in front of me was Cliff with the knife in his hands, staring at me, telling me how beautiful I was and how he liked my silver eyes. Ugh. I hated the color.

Then another picture flashed by, and this time, my eyes were closed. My head was tilted back.

Blood flowed out of my nose into my mouth. I shook my head once. The image was still vivid. I shook my head again, and another slide flashed. Sam was swinging the bat at Cliff. I shook my head violently and mumbled, "Stop, stop, stop."

"Stop what?" a voice asked as a hand touched my forehead.

My eyes flew open. "Sam. How did you get in here?"

Sam raised a finger to his lips. "Shh. I was in the bathroom."

"This whole time?"

He bobbed his head. "We need to go."

"There's a cop outside. They're looking for you."

"No cops. Not right now. They'll throw me in jail," Sam said.

He was right. The last time my brother was in trouble, the police had been called to the school after he'd knocked out Blake Turner for pushing me up against a locker. After that incident, Blake's dad decided to press charges, and Sam spent the night in jail. That fight was nothing compared to what Sam had done to Cliff.

He rushed over to the window and peered through the blinds. Then he touched the window casing to see if it opened—no luck.

He returned to my bedside and gently touched my bandaged cheek. "Hey, are you okay? I thought I'd lost you." He let out a heavy sigh.

"I'm fine." I hiccupped, trying to swallow the emotions that were about to overwhelm me.

"They bandaged you pretty good, but you're going to have one nasty scar."

"Bad enough to scare people?" I hiccupped again. I couldn't imagine what the kids at school would say when they saw me, and I didn't even want to think of what Blake Turner would say or do.

"Hopefully. Your pretty face got you into this mess. It always does," Sam replied.

I wrinkled my nose and stuck out my tongue. "Ow!" I shouldn't have done that. I touched my left cheek just to be sure I hadn't damaged the stitches. "The cop said that they're sending someone over tomorrow from the state. I'm not going back to another foster home."

"We're not," Sam said. "We're getting out of here."

"But shouldn't you talk to the cops? We didn't do anything wrong."

"You know how that's going to go. I talk to the cops, maybe go to jail, then the state comes in, and then what? Another home, another asshole to fight off you. No way."

Sam traipsed into the bathroom and came out with a paper bag. "Here, put these on." He tipped over the bag, and a pile of clothes fell onto the hospital bed. Then he hurried to the door and peeked out.

The jeans looked new, and the sweatshirt looked as if it could fit a gorilla. I slipped on the jeans first then removed the hospital gown. I inspected the bandage around my chest. It was wrapped tightly, and I figured I would leave it for the time being. As I pulled on the sweatshirt, a hint of musky cologne drifted in, filling my senses. *This is definitely a man's sweatshirt.*

"Um... Sam, where are the shoes?"

"Sorry. You're lucky I found the clothes." He kept watch like a soldier guarding the president.

"It's cold outside. You expect me to walk in my bare feet? You're out of your mind." Glancing around the room, I didn't see anything I could use.

As I tried to do something with my hair, Sam stepped back from the door and pulled a cell phone from his jeans pocket along with a sticky note, which had a phone number on it.

When he punched the first button, a loud bang sounded in the hall, and he froze.

I tiptoed to the door, gently pulled on the handle, and peeked through a small crack. A tall man wearing a blue bandana around his head had Officer Bradley pinned up against the wall. The cop was squirming, trying to reach for his gun. Then the tall man jerked his head in my direction as if he sensed my stare. His pitch-black eyes bored into me as his mouth curled on one side, exposing a long canine tooth.

I gasped as I slammed the door. Maybe I was seeing things. I swallowed and cracked the door open again. This time, the beast was smiling, showing not just one long canine but two. I couldn't move. One of them was stained red. My brain tilted. There was something about him that screamed "predator," something far more monstrous than human. I shook my head a few times, trying to remove the cloak of fear that blanketed me. *Did I just see a man—with fangs? No, I didn't! No way. My mind is playing sick games.*

I blinked several times. When I cleared the picture from my brain, I stole another glance. The large beast of a man threw the cop down the hall. I closed the door with shaky hands as my heart slammed against my chest. *What is he?* He looked human, but there was something otherworldly about him.

"Um, Sam, we need to get out of here. Like, now." I rolled up the sleeves of the sweatshirt, blowing out all the air in my lungs.

"I know. Is it a guy wearing a blue bandana?"

"Yeah. How'd you know?" I couldn't tell Sam what I'd just seen. He would never believe me. Heck, I wasn't sure I believed myself. Maybe all the sterilizing alcohol in the air was making me hallucinate.

"After the ambulance left the house and the cops were questioning Hilda, I heard her accusing us of trying to kill that asshole, so I snuck out. When I got to the hospital, that guy was in the ER, asking which room you were in."

I didn't want to tell Sam the man looked like he had just stepped out of a vampire movie. "Why?"

"I don't know," Sam said. "You ready?"

Not in the least. But I wasn't staying there.

The noise stopped outside the door. I prayed the cop was okay and that we wouldn't run into that man—or whatever he was.

Sam peered out. "They're not there."

"What? Where'd they go?"

"We probably have a second to get out of here. Come on," Sam whispered. "Take my hand."

"Wait." I scurried over to the table, grabbed the cop's card, and shoved it in my pocket. I didn't know if I would need it, but if anything, I could contact him later to make sure he was okay.

Sam looked both ways as we left the room.

I glimpsed at the clock in the hallway. Both hands rested on the twelve. A gurney sat between my room and the next.

I turned around. The hall was empty. No cop. No nurses. No one in sight.

In the distance ahead of Sam, a red sign above the double doors spelled the way out. My heart hammered against my bruised ribs as we hurried toward the exit that seemed miles away. It was as if we were walking against the wind, pushing our way through every step.

Sam pulled me, and my body screamed in pain, my lungs burning every time I inhaled.

"Faster, Jo."

"It hurts."

Footsteps broke the silence.

I glanced back, and a shadow crept along the floor and up the wall. I didn't know if it was the cop or the bandana guy stalking our way.

"Jo, we need to run. Don't let go of my hand."

Sam squeezed my fingers as we ran through the double doors—our destination unknown, at least to me.

3

———————

Highland Memorial Hospital spanned four city blocks. It was situated in an area of the city steeped in history with opulent mansions and shingle-style homes that overlooked Mount Hope Bay.

As soon as we made it outside, the cold air stung my face, seeping into my lungs, and I gasped for breath.

An empty police car sat at the curb next to a metal post that displayed a large red-and-white No Parking sign.

The street was dark except for the light from a neon sign that hung from a medical supply building on the other side of the street. On my left, the road ended with a security fence towering at the back of the hospital. To my right, a major street intersected with a traffic light at the corner.

Sam tugged on my arm as he headed toward the traffic light. "We'll go this way."

"I can't breathe, and my feet are on fire." My bare feet were going to be frostbitten in about three minutes.

"Keep moving, and you won't feel it."

"You have shoes on. What do you care?"

"Do you want to find out what happens when that guy shows up?" Sam pointed at the door we'd just come through.

I shook my head.

"I think the place is around the corner," he said.

I had no idea what he was talking about or where we were going. My face hurt, my lungs were on fire, the bandages around my chest were constricting my airways, and my feet were stuck to the frozen ground. Running for my life wasn't exactly what I wanted to do on a Friday night.

Regardless, I prayed that we would get wherever we were going fast.

Two minutes later, we stood at the mouth of a long alley along the left side of the hospital. Sam and I both glanced behind us.

I sighed heavily—no vampire guy. Then I

silently laughed at my reference to the bandana beast. *Vampires don't exist.* The absurdity of it made my lips curl at the edges.

"Something funny?" Sam asked.

"No." I didn't want to tell him I was thinking about vampires. I had to be sure it wasn't the effect of any drugs or a dream.

Hand in hand, we began our trek into muted darkness. Several doors punctuated the side of the hospital building. The first one was marked Employees Only. A yellow light sprayed down from above the door, casting a glow over its immediate surroundings and the illuminated keypad to the left of the frame.

As we passed the first door, a noise rustled near the dumpster. I stopped, and Sam's hand slipped from mine.

"Come on, Jo," he whispered. "Keep moving." He skirted the dumpster. "It's nothing," he called.

I hurried, dodging the loosely formed ice patches that dotted the alley, letting out a screech every time my bare feet broke the thin layer of ice. As I made it to where Sam was standing, my right foot landed in an ice puddle. I squealed and jumped to a dry spot ahead of it. The pain from my ribs took over, and I almost fell. After catching a burning breath, I continued limping behind Sam.

I prayed we would get to a warm spot soon. My feet couldn't handle much more.

The second and third doors didn't say anything at all. Sam tried one then another, but both were locked.

"Why are we going back into the hospital?" I asked.

"I'm looking for where they keep the heating system," Sam said.

"Why?"

Sam waved his hand as he stood in front of a sign marked Boiler Room. "Hurry."

The door was ajar with a piece of wood holding it open. "This is it."

Sam didn't answer as he went inside with me right on his heels. Steam filtered up from the floor grates, and the hot metal machine in front of us hummed loudly.

"Head over to the desk. I'll be right back," he said before he disappeared behind the boiler.

I took a minute as the warmth of the floor helped to thaw my feet. Once they started to tingle and the blood returned, I made my way around equipment and over to the desk. The instant my eyes landed on the mug with vapor swirling out of it, my stomach growled. The aroma of caffeine prickled my senses. I was about to grab the coffee when a voice bellowed.

I jumped a freaking mile.

"I wouldn't do that, young lady," the man said as he approached.

Sam hurried around the man. "Jo, this is Neil. Do you remember him?"

"Huh? Am I supposed to?"

The man wore a navy-blue ball cap with US Navy sprawled across the front in bright-yellow letters. A small diamond earring dotted his left ear, and his starched shirt hugged his chest, revealing a muscular body. Not a bad-looking man.

"Neil Foster, the janitor of our high school. He works here at night."

I dug around in my head and couldn't place him. Besides, I'd never seen a janitor at school. "Sorry, I don't."

"How ya feeling?" Neil asked.

I shrugged. The guy wanted to chitchat while a large, fanged dude was chasing us. "Sam, what're we doing? We need to get out of here."

Sam gnawed on his bottom lip. "Neil has been helping me. I explained to him what happened at the Birches'. When the doc and nurse left your room while you were still out of it, Neil was able to distract the cop for a few minutes while I snuck in, so I could be there when you woke up."

I fidgeted with the sleeves of the sweatshirt. "Um, okay. But aren't you forgetting the dude chasing us? How do you know Neil isn't helping that guy?"

Sam inched closer to me. "Because I know Neil from school. We can trust him." He sighed. "You're right. We do need to get out of here, but where are we going to go? Do you have any ideas?" Anger laced his tone as a crease formed in between his eyebrows. Suddenly, his forest-green eyes shifted to a grayish-black, and his face turned crimson.

I stifled a gasp, covering my mouth with my right hand. *Since when do his eyes change from green to black? This is what Dr. Case must've seen when mine were changing colors.*

Nevertheless, the color change reminded me of the blue-bandana guy, and a shiver tiptoed down my spine.

Neil's baritone voice broke our staring game. "If you still want my help, we need to go."

The color of Sam's eyes slowly returned to green.

My brain was on overload as I wondered what was happening to both of us. As of late, Sam's temper was getting shorter, which could've triggered the color change. After all, my eyes had changed color after I freaked out about the blood. What wasn't clear was what was happening to us... and why.

"I found your sister some shoes." Neil handed me a pair of worn sneakers that looked like a man's size ten. The Nike logo was torn off one shoe, and the other had a rip in the toe. Neil took off his hat and rubbed his bald head. "One more thing. I just came down from the upper floors. I don't know what happened up there, but the nurses said some man came in, and he and the cop tussled. The cop ended up unconscious. The nurse thinks the man kidnapped Jo. They're checking every room. It won't be long until they make their way down here." Concern washed over him.

"Tussled" wasn't the word I would have used. What I witnessed looked more like a one-way battle between a man and a beast, with the beast beating the shit out of the cop. "Why would the guy want me?" I asked.

Neil lifted a shoulder. "I don't know, but I can at least get you out of here."

Sam raked his fingers through his shoulder-length black hair.

Suddenly, my bladder protested. "I need to use the restroom first."

Neil stabbed a finger at an opening behind me. "Make it quick."

I rushed in and took care of business. The faster we left, the easier it would be to breathe. After I washed my hands, I checked myself in the mirror. Yikes! My hair was stuck to my head, thickly matted with dried blood. My bandage was reddish-brown, and my lip was swollen on the left. "What the—"

A bang on the door jarred me away from the monster in the mirror. "Everything okay?" Sam asked. "We need to go."

Now, he wants to go. Isn't that what I've been saying all along?

When I opened the door, I found Sam standing near a lab bench, reading a sheet of paper. Neil was rummaging through a locker next to Sam.

"Zombies look better than me." I pointed to my face.

Sam chuckled, and it was the first time I'd heard him laugh in a long time. With my luck, joining in would only cause my stitches to burst.

My gaze gravitated from Sam to Neil, who was squatting with his hands buried in the locker, and I froze. On the back of Neil's neck, just below his ball cap, was a tattoo. It was some sort of symbol. It looked like a monogram constructed from the letters P and L. I wondered if Neil's tattoo was similar to the one Dr. Case had. *What would be the odds they both had the same tattoo?* An ominous prickle skittered up my legs. I was beginning to think that maybe we couldn't trust Neil.

Rising to his full height, Neil stuffed a flashlight into a blue backpack. "Let's go."

As the three of us wound our way out, a two-way radio blared above the hum of the boiler.

A minute later, the three of us were heading to Neil's car on the first floor of the garage across from the hospital. As I tried to keep with Neil and Sam, the backs of my feet sprang out of the oversized Nikes. I wasn't complaining. Big shoes were better than walking in my bare feet.

Sam's head darted from left to right, occasionally turning to scan the area behind him. Neil had his car keys in his hand, clearly ready to unlock the doors.

I shivered as a gust of wind tore through, bringing with it flakes of snow.

We passed a line of expensive cars, and each parking space had a blue sign that named the owners. Dr. Angus Silva drove a gold Porsche with dark-tinted windows. His neighbor, Dr. Lowenstein, was AWOL. I imagined he had the night off.

The next space was home to a black Corvette. As I admired the sexy curves of the sleek vehicle, my gaze landed on the license plate, which read Case-96. The blue sign above stated the car belonged to Dr. Leroy Case.

I wanted to laugh. To me, Dr. Case didn't look like a Leroy—he looked more like a nervous Nelly. I was immersed in my own thoughts when I caught a glimpse of a man in the distance, standing against a black SUV. I squinted in his direction. He was staring directly at me.

The hairs on my arms rose, and a chill crept up my legs. He wore a black knitted cap, and his face looked as if he hadn't shaven in days. Our eyes connected, and as he angled his head to one side, another chill infused me.

I turned to Sam. "Look behind me. There's a man leaning against an SUV. Is that the guy from the hospital?"

Sam peered around me. "What man?"

I spun around. The black SUV was still in its parking space, but the man was gone.

It couldn't have been the blue-bandana guy unless he had changed his bandana to a hat. No, the man I just saw wasn't as tall.

"You okay?" Sam asked.

"I swear I saw a man over there." I quickly

scanned the area and didn't see anyone. I started in the direction of the black SUV when distant sirens stopped me. Maybe that man was an undercover cop or working with the fanged dude. I ran toward Neil, lungs burning and ribs aching.

Neil pushed the key fob, and two beeps echoed. The headlights flashed on, and the interior lights illuminated.

I climbed into the backseat of Neil's red four-door Dodge Ram truck, and the buttery leather seats immediately sucked me in. Sam slid into the front as Neil started the truck.

As Neil began to wheel out, I sighed and propped my head against the backseat. Once on the road, the streets were deserted as we traveled north on Robeson.

Safe for the moment, I closed my eyes, drifting off, lulled by the hum of the tires. My body relaxed as the heat from the truck's vents warmed the air. What a screwed-up two days it had been. I wondered how my life had spiraled so far out of control. It seemed that danger lurked in every dark corner, waiting to jump out at me, and I shuddered to imagine what was next.

As the truck moved, I opened my eyes and stared out the window. A soft blanket of snow covered the budding trees that dotted the road's edge, not unusual for early April in New England. I took another mental snapshot of the passing landscape. We were driving toward the Fall River State Forest. *Where is Neil taking us?* I started tapping my foot underneath Sam's seat.

The Fall River State Forest was an area of town that no one wanted to be in after dark, on the outskirts of the city with only a couple of main roads leading into and out of the forest.

I peered around Sam's seat and out the windshield. Neil had the high beams on, and the lights irradiated the piles of snowdrifts along the road embankments. Every now and then, a pair of yellow eyes glowed and peeked through the trees.

"Is this Blossom Road?" I asked.

"Yep. We're almost on the other side," Neil replied.

"Where are you taking us?" I leaned forward, so I could hear him over U2 blaring on the stereo.

He turned down the volume. "My parents have a place they're not using in Westport. You guys can hunker down there for the night."

"Westport?" I kicked Sam's seat again.

"What're you doing?" Sam turned around. "Stop worrying." His tone was lethal.

"Yeah, right. Coming from my brother, whose

middle name is 'Paranoid.' How're we going to get back?"

"Get back to where? We're not going back to Hilda's. We'll need to figure out our next move in the morning."

Sam was right. I wasn't going anywhere near Hilda or the hospital, not with that creepy fanged dude lurking around.

"I'll be staying not too far from you. I'll pick you up in the morning, and I can help with whatever you need," Neil offered.

Oh, I bet he could. I still didn't trust him. I was curious about why he was helping us.

"Why're you so nervous, Jo?" Sam asked. "You've been listening to all that nonsense at school about murders taking place in the forest?"

"Well, it's true, isn't it? They did happen."

Sam and Neil just looked at each other. They knew I was right.

Sometime in the midseventies, a brutal murder took place on the reservation—the police found a fifteen-year-old girl tied to a tree. Ever since, the state forest had been the site of several other crimes. High school kids were always having weekend parties there. On Monday mornings, the school courtyard constantly buzzed about how great the parties had been.

I sat back and hoped that our final destination would be better than spending it in the hospital or being chased by some predator with long teeth. But something didn't feel right—why would the janitor of our school help us?

John Mayer belted out, "Your Body is a Wonderland." I silently chuckled as I listened to the lyrics. The one thing I knew was that my body was not a wonderland. In fact, when I looked in the mirror earlier, I saw a wasteland.

Before long, the vehicle slowed, and we were turning onto a driveway. Neil shifted the truck into park. The neighborhood had several homes along one side of the street. Each one looked empty. But it was one o'clock in the morning and difficult to get a clear idea of the area with the blowing snow.

As I hopped out, a For Sale sign on the front porch caught my eye. Just beyond the sign, beneath the bare bulb of the porch light, a plaque was nailed to the wall. My jaw hit the ground.

Foster and Sons Funeral Home, est. 1962.

I took a hesitant step forward, but Sam grabbed my arm. "Not yet," he whispered.

It was evident that Sam was not comfortable with the choice.

"Why here, Neil?" I asked.

"Well, for one, it's a good distance from the

hospital. Besides, nobody will find you here, and it has heat and electricity."

I bet no one would find us, which was what I was afraid of. The newspaper headlines would read, "Dead Bodies of Twin Siblings Found in Abandoned Funeral Home." I gulped. "A funeral home?"

"Better than the alternative, right?" Neil walked up the front steps.

I didn't know what was better, a foster home or sleeping with the dead.

The tall streetlights lining the edges of the sidewalks lit up the surrounding area. A local park dominated the block across the street with an ice rink covered in a thin layer of snow.

Sam and I were taking mental snapshots of the area when Neil waved to us.

"Sam. Jo," he called, "we need to get inside."

The funeral home sat on a corner lot with a path from the sidewalk to the front porch, which led visitors to the main entrance.

Sam trudged along the driveway while I circled around the front of the truck.

"Sam, where are you going?" I asked.

My brother had a suspicious nature about him, and sometimes it drove me nuts. I couldn't complain, though. His doubtful nature kept us out of trouble most of the time.

"I'll be right there," he said.

When I reached the door, Sam came up the path, planting his footprints in the virgin snow.

"So, Mr. Paranoia, are you satisfied?" I asked.

"For now," he replied.

4

The funeral home had a large foyer, which I imagined had welcomed guests at one time or another, but dust hung in the air and tickled my nose. I sneezed once then again.

"Bless you," Sam said.

A worn Oriental carpet runner covered the dusty wood floor and clashed with the chintzy flowered wallpaper. As we stood there, taking it all in, a spitting and rattling noise resounded.

"What's that?" I turned to Sam.

"Sounds like Neil's tinkering with the heater."

I went over to a sofa table butted against the wall next to a set of double doors. A black book lay open, its pages filled with signatures. *These must be entries from the last wake or funeral.* A slight chill caressed my skin, and I closed the book. As I did, more dust bunnies flew into the air. I sneezed again then dragged the back of my hand across my nose as I made my way toward Sam, who was sitting on a red loveseat.

"Don't sit too fast unless you want more crap up your nose," he warned.

Heeding Sam's advice, I eased down onto the velvet cushion. Slowly, I leaned back and rested my head against the couch then released a loud sigh, which echoed in the small room. "Now what?"

"Sleep," Sam replied as he kicked out his legs and propped his back against the couch.

Sleep would have been great, but I couldn't relax. Bandana guy was stuck in my head—I hoped that he was still looking for us somewhere near the hospital. And spending the night in a funeral home wasn't high on my list of favorite things to do. In fact, it was creepy. I tapped my foot as we waited for Neil to emerge from wherever he was.

"Jo, stop it," Sam said.

"What?"

"Your foot. You do that when you get nervous. It drives me crazy, especially now."

Pursing my lips, I jumped up. I needed to do something. My mind wasn't allowing me to relax.

Curious about what lay behind the doors in front of me, I decided to check it out.

Once inside, I rooted around along the wall, found the light switch, and flicked on the lights. The room came to life. Centered against the back wall was a closed, shiny white coffin. A chill infused my whole body. *If this place has been vacant for over a year, what is a coffin doing in this room? Is there a dead person in it?* Not wanting to linger or even think about it, I switched off the light and scurried out. I had a feeling that nightmares were in my future.

"Anything interesting in there?" Sam asked as he leaned his elbows on his knees.

"Nope." I sat in my original spot.

Another fifteen minutes passed before Neil came back. "I managed to get the heat on."

Sam jumped to his feet.

I didn't move. After sitting for a few minutes, my body had grown stiff. My ribs throbbed as if someone whacked me with a sledgehammer a few times.

Neil rubbed the back of his neck. "It should work through the night. Let me show you around. Then you guys can get some rest."

Sam extended his hand and pulled me upright. We followed Neil to a set of stairs leading to the second floor. We passed two more viewing rooms on our way down the hall, which had their doors open but were empty—no coffins, thank God. The thought of dead people brought back the image of the man with the long canine teeth at the hospital. *Yep, I'm definitely going to have nightmares tonight.*

At the end of the hallway, we climbed a set of stairs to the top floor.

Neil waved us in. "You can crash in my dad's old office."

We entered the room to find two floral couches sitting adjacent to one another. A large cherry-wood desk, a bookcase that traveled the length of one wall, and a pair of dark-red velvet curtains hung from the window, making it look like blood was streaming down. *Blood.* That conjured up all kinds of images, but none more potent than the tingle in my stomach. I wanted to slap myself. *Stop thinking about all these terrifying things.*

Neil extended his hand to Sam. "Here's a spare key in case you need it. I'll be back first thing in the morning with some food. Oh, and one more thing. Take this." He gave Sam three twenty-dollar bills. "There's a variety store a block north of here. It opens early in the morning. Get her something that fits better."

As he headed out, I caught a better glimpse of

the tattoo on his neck. The capital letter P was superimposed on top of the letter L, with a red diagonal ring circling the black monogram letters. The ring reminded me of the planet Saturn's outer band.

"I'll see you in the morning," Neil said as he padded down the stairs.

A few minutes later, the front door shut, and the lock clicked. His truck engine roared to life. Then silence.

Sam jumped onto one couch, and dust flew in the air.

Ugh. I covered my nose so I wouldn't sneeze. "Did you notice the tattoo on Neil's neck?"

Sam got comfortable, closing his eyes. "Uh-huh," he mumbled.

I settled on the other sofa. "What do you suppose it is?"

"Not now, Jo. I'm tired."

"Do you think he's working with the guy chasing us?"

"No."

"Well, I don't trust him," I persisted.

"I do. All right?" Sam took in a deep breath, and within seconds, he was snoring.

"Sam?"

His snoring grew louder.

Sam had the right idea, but sleep evaded me. I was still curious about whether the tattoo had any meaning. As I waited for sleep to take over, the wind began to howl. Between the snoring and the howling, the heater sputtered. It was like listening to an orchestra.

After a few minutes, the orchestra muted, and the pounding of my pulse thudding in my ears accompanied a list of questions scrolling across the darkness. *Where are we going to go? Is the cop okay? Why is someone with long canines chasing us? Who is Neil? Why would a complete stranger help us?*

As I pondered the answers to these questions, the noises around me faded, and a hot breeze caressed my neck, lulling me to sleep.

I AWOKE the following day with a crick in my neck that prevented me from moving it to the left. I eased my head from side to side to loosen it. The cracks reverberated in my ears, and I shivered. I hated that sound. I inhaled, taking inventory of my body. The intake of air still burned, and the pain in my ribs seemed more intense than it had the night before. I imagined it was going to take a while for my body to heal.

The other couch was empty.

A loud bang sounded, and I jumped off the couch, holding on to my midsection as I ran out of the room. I peered over the banister. "Sam?"

He appeared from under the stairs and tilted his head up. "I'm trying to get this stupid heater to work. I'll be up in a minute."

I shuffled back into the office and over to the window. I pulled aside one of the curtain panels and peered out. The freshly fallen snow blanketed the trees, roads, and surrounding homes. The park across the street showed no signs of life, but then again, its barren appearance matched the still life in the neighborhood. The gray sky threatened as if it were about to deliver its second strike of snowfall.

I captured a nail in between my teeth, wondering what we were going to do. We couldn't stay there. Well, I didn't want to stay there. Even in daylight, the place gave me the willies. Then I lightly touched my left cheek. The bandage was dry, but my face ached. Since I couldn't do anything about my bruises, I turned my attention from my poor-me syndrome to the office space.

Five enormous bookshelves paneled the right wall. Each book was stacked neatly against the other. I was about to check out the titles when the hallway stairs creaked before Sam stalked in.

"Heater is working," he said just as warm air blew through the room.

"What time is it?"

He looked at his watch. "Six."

Ugh! I'd tossed and turned all night, afraid to sleep not only because of the macabre images of the man chasing us, but because my bruises and cuts were too painful to put pressure on. Plus, I'd had the feeling that someone had been watching us while we slept.

I crossed my arms over my chest. "What now?"

Joining me by the window, he combed his fingers through his matted hair. "Well, we can't stay here."

I wouldn't have been the least bit disappointed if we never came back. "What was your first clue? The coffin in the room downstairs?"

He reared back. "There's a coffin?"

"Well, we're in a funeral home."

He rolled his eyes. "Yeah, an abandoned one."

"You think there's a dead body in it?"

"Okay, okay. All the more reason to get out of here. And we need to get some help," he said.

"Again, what's your first clue?"

He narrowed his green eyes my way. "Jo, don't get smart."

"Anyone with a blue bandana walking around out there?" I meant it rhetorically. I hadn't seen anyone out there a minute before. Still, the hairs on my arms rose as I waited for his answer.

He shook his head. "I don't think so."

"Well, what're we going to do?" I shuddered a breath.

If we went back to the hospital, we could be accused of beating up the cop and running. Besides, the cops still wanted to question Sam about the incident with Cliff—he wasn't out of the woods yet with the law. So the hospital was out of the question.

I chewed the inside of my right cheek and sat in the leather desk chair.

Sam moved over to the couch. "I thought we could get Ben's dad to help us."

My eyes widened. "Mr. Jackson? You're kidding, right?"

"He'll understand. We don't have anyone besides Neil, and I don't want to stay here. This place is creepy."

It was downright terrifying. But I wasn't so sure Mr. Jackson would understand. He might have been the high school principal, but there had been a lot of crazy shit going on with us in the last two days that I couldn't even wrap my mind around. "I'm not so sure."

Sam rubbed his hands on his dirty jeans. "He just needs to look at you."

I was afraid to. Frankenstein's monster looked better than I did. "How can he help? He can't keep that animal from finding us, and the cops are probably looking for us too. Maybe they think we beat Officer Bradley."

He scrubbed a hand along his jaw. "Jo. You heard Neil. The nurses saw the whole thing. How can we be blamed for that?"

I still didn't trust the cops, although Officer Bradley had seemed nice. As I thought about him, I couldn't erase the image of his feet dangling in the air while that beast strangled him. *I hope he's okay.*

Sam pushed to his feet and paced.

I thought about Mr. Jackson. He'd always been kind to me, especially when Blake and I ended up in his office. Sam wouldn't do anything he didn't feel was right. And I desperately needed a shower.

He came to an abrupt halt as he regarded me with horror stamped in his eyes. "Jo, is that blood on your neck?"

"What!" I grabbed the right side.

"No, the other side." Sam rushed to my rescue. "Stand up. Tilt your head to your right."

"Is it blood?" My voice quivered as an image of fangs flashed in my mind.

Sam scratched my neck. "Did someone bite you last night?"

"Shut up!" I punched his arm. "Well?"

"There are two holes...." Sam's lips curled at the sides.

"No way!" I rubbed my hand over my neck. The skin was smooth and dry.

He held his hand out, laughing. "It's just the red lint from that nasty couch. It was stuck to your neck."

"You're a jerk sometimes." I took a step forward with my heart in my throat.

"I'm sorry. I couldn't help it. You should've seen the look on your face. I know how much you like vampires."

At the mere mention of the word, I shivered. "Listen. I didn't want to tell you, but the guy at the hospital, the one chasing us... um, I don't know how to tell you this."

"Just say it. It can't be that bad."

He had no idea.

"When I opened the door and saw the bandana guy squeezing the air out of the cop, he smiled at me."

He pinched his eyebrows. "So what? He smiled at you. You know how men are around you."

I knew all too well.

"I'm trying to tell you that the guy had these long canine teeth. One of them even had blood on it. I think he bit the cop."

Sam gave me a nonplussed look. "Have you been sneaking around and reading vampire books? Do you hear yourself?"

I threw up my hands. "Fine. Don't believe me. I know what I saw. And I didn't say he was a vampire. He just had these long creepy-looking teeth and really black eyes. Plus, he was huge. Like seven feet tall. You didn't see him strangling that cop." I plopped down in the chair and touched the left side of my neck. A flurry of panic surfaced. Someone had been in the room while we slept. I could feel it.

"Well, hopefully, he's long gone," he said.

I hoped and prayed I would never see that man again. As it was, I was going to have nightmares for the rest of my life.

Sam pulled out the money from the pocket of his jeans. "I'm going to that store Neil said was down the street and getting us something to eat."

I shook my head. "No way."

"We need food." Sam touched his stomach.

"No. Don't leave me here alone. Isn't there a refrigerator downstairs?"

"Yeah, so? If there's food in it, it's probably nasty. I'll check, but if not, I'm going to the store."

Before I could protest, Sam was out the door.

I held back a frustrated scream. After a beat I decided to distract myself and check out the books. Reading the spines, I trailed my fingers along the edges of the leather-bound covers. It looked as if Neil's dad had a specific filing system. Each shelf was dedicated to particular authors. Shirley Jackson and Mark Twain commandeered one shelf, while another displayed books by two of my favorite authors, Stephen King and Edgar Allan Poe.

One shelf had a line of books on embalming. My fingers landed on a book titled *The Embalming Process*. Curious, I pulled it out and skimmed the opening pages. One chapter was dedicated to arterial embalming. I read through the first few lines as the author explained how blood and interstitial fluids were...

I didn't get past the word *blood*. Then it dawned on me. Maybe somewhere in the sea of books, I might find something on blood types. I inserted the embalming book back into its home then knelt down and scanned the line of books on the bottom shelf. One caught my attention—*The Science Behind Vampires*. I swallowed a screech—*vampires? Here we go again. The word "blood" and now "vampires." I can't seem to get away from them.*

My hands trembled as I removed the book slowly from its resting spot next to *The Vampire's Life*. I didn't know there was a science to vampires. Surely, they only existed in the pages of fiction novels. The books spun in front of me, and my vision blurred. A chill rippled up my arms. I grabbed both books and sat on the couch.

I opened *The Science Behind Vampires* first and scanned the list on the contents page. The title of the first chapter? "Creating a Vampire." My gaze stilled when I read the title of chapter two, "Blood Thirst." I immediately flipped to it. I took a deep breath and began reading.

Vampires require a large intake of iron. The iron helps to gather oxygen from the lungs then provides it to all the other body tissues. Since blood has a high iron content, it's a great source of food for vampires, which is why they need it to survive. When vampires are low on iron, their hunger surfaces, and they crave blood. Older vampires know how to control their hunger.

They've learned to drink only what is needed to survive.

A wild laugh broke out in my head. I thought I was seeing vampires, and now I was reading about vampires, not to mention how my own blood had tasted like candy. I swore. Someone was trying to tell me something.

I reread the page. *Huh? Are my iron levels low? Is that the reason why I craved blood? Does it mean I'm a vampire?* I laughed nervously, the sound stifled. *Me, a vampire? Yeah, right.*

A warm breeze grazed my neck, and I let out a low scream.

Sam snagged the book from me. "Scary stuff in the vampire book?"

"Hey, give it back. I'm not finished reading."

"You hate vampires. Wait. You think you're seeing vampires, and now you're reading about them." He touched my forehead. "Nope, your temperature feels human. You're not cold-blooded." Then he read the title of the book out loud. "*The Science Behind Vampires,*" he intoned. "Did you learn anything?"

"I learned how to turn you into a vampire," I teased.

"Yeah? How?"

My playfulness vanished. "Seriously, Sam. Aren't you experiencing any weird changes?"

"Yeah. But that doesn't mean I'm a vampire." He laughed nervously.

"I'm learning that I like the taste of—"

"Taste of what?" He eased down next to me.

"You know?"

Sam's gaze was glued to the cover of *The Science Behind Vampires*. He wasn't laughing anymore. He had to process information before he weighed in on a topic unless it involved an immediate physical reaction, then he never hesitated. I hated when he didn't speak. It always made me feel like I was crazy or he didn't believe me.

"I know because you told me." He raised his head, and a tear pooled in his left eye. "You don't remember?"

I shook my head.

"One of the last things you said to me before you passed out the other night... 'I want more blood.'" He swallowed. "My heart skipped a thousand beats when you said that to me. After I-I... swung the bat at Cliff, blood spattered everywhere. Some of it sprayed on my face and into my mouth. I tried to spit it out, but it tasted... peppery. A sudden urge exploded inside me." Sam let out a loud sigh as if he'd just released the weight of the world from his shoulders.

My taste buds perked up as he described the spiciness of the blood. Funny, I'd found it sweet. *Focus, focus.*

Silence filled the room for what seemed like an eternity. I cleared my throat. "Did you know your eyes changed color?"

Nodding, he roughed a hand through his hair. "The other day, I got into a scuffle with an ump. He called me out for stealing second base. We were nose to nose, yelling, when all of a sudden, he stopped. It wasn't until Ben came over to calm me down that I found out why—he asked me why my eyes were changing colors. Of course, Ben thought that was the coolest thing." Sam regarded me briefly before he pushed to his feet and ambled over to the window.

A sharp pain stung my chest as I studied him. A shadow outlined his eyes, making him look as if he had risen this morning out of one of the coffins in the funeral home. Stubble dotted his face just beneath his broad cheekbones. He looked as if he had aged ten years. His Pink Floyd T-shirt showed every muscle as if he'd outgrown it overnight.

"Dr. Case said my blood type was AF negative."

"Yeah, I heard that conversation," Sam said in a low voice.

"Do you think that means anything?"

"Well, we're not aliens or anything." He continued to gaze out the window.

"Since we're twins, wouldn't we have the same blood type?"

"I don't know."

He turned his gaze from the window to me. "I found some bottles of water and a box of crackers."

I stood and snagged a bottle of water off the desk.

Sam came around and hugged me. "We'll figure this out. I promise."

Sam always made me feel safe. I hated that he carried so much weight around with him. I knew a lot of his anxiety stemmed from me. He was constantly bailing me out of challenging situations only to get himself in trouble. He had been my guardian angel. I vowed to myself from that day forward, I would shoulder some of the load in our relationship—at least, I would try.

I wrapped my arms around him and squeezed as hard as I could. Tears cascaded down my face as he tightened his hold. After a few seconds, he let go. I patted my eyes with the sleeve of my sweat-shirt then grabbed a few crackers.

"I called Ben," Sam said.

"And?" I bit into one cracker.

"His dad is out of town. He said we could crash there tonight, and we can talk to Mr. Jackson when he gets home tomorrow. He went to a principals' conference or something for the weekend."

"How're we getting there?"

"Taxi," Sam said. "I've already called."

We finished all the water and the box of crackers. Before leaving the room, I took both books on vampires and followed Sam downstairs.

No question, we were better off at Ben's than at the funeral home, but I wasn't sure if Mr. Jackson would be as understanding as Sam thought. By the same time tomorrow, Sam and I could be on our way to yet another foster home—or jail.

5

I rummaged around in a downstairs closet and found a pair of boots and a sweater to replace the beat-up Nikes and gorilla sweatshirt. Sam wrote Neil a note thanking him for his help and letting him know about the clothes I borrowed, adding that I would return them the first chance I got. He signed the bottom, saying he would see him at school next week.

The cab was parked in the driveway when I walked out the front door.

The cold air stung my cheeks as I descended the front porch. I scanned the neighborhood, and my gaze drifted toward the park. A handful of kids were ice-skating while their parents lingered nearby, wrapped in blankets, watching them. At the far end of the parking lot, my gaze landed on a black SUV. I stopped midstride, trying to get a better view, but I slipped off the last step and landed face-first in the soft snow. *Shit!* I planted my palms on the wet, cold ground, pushed off, and got up. I spit out a mouthful of ice crystals when Sam touched my shoulder.

"Did you forget how to walk?"

I glared at him as we made our way to the cab idling in the driveway. I focused on the park, searching for the SUV, but as we slid into the back seat, I couldn't see it anymore. It probably wasn't worth telling Sam. He was already paranoid, and he would just think I was crazy. After all, anyone could have been driving a black SUV.

The cabby looked at me through the rearview mirror. "Where to, folks?"

"Riverside," Sam replied. "Twenty-two Ash Street."

The driver pressed a button on the meter bolted to the dashboard. The cab hadn't moved an inch, and the meter had already charged us two dollars and fifty cents.

Once we were on the road, the cab accelerated down the street. We passed several boarded-up homes with a For Sale sign staked to the ground in every yard. A homeless man slept on the porch of one of the empty dwellings, his shopping cart full of trash bags parked at the foot of the steps. Another residence had a car sitting on its rims in the driveway. Two young men leaned against it, sharing a paper bag of who knew what. The entire neighborhood looked as if the world had died in that part of town.

We crossed over the main intersection, and the tenor of the area changed. The cars parked in driveways had tires attached. I spotted a man through his bay window, sitting in his chair and reading the paper. Smoke trickled out of several chimneys. The world on this side was alive and thriving.

I tossed a look out the back window, curious to see if one road could split the same city into two different worlds, but a maroon car followed, blocking my view of the neighborhood we'd just left behind. I was about to turn my head when the maroon car went down a side street, and a black SUV came into view. My muscles tensed as I slid Sam a sideways glance.

"What's wrong?" he whispered.

"I think the car behind is following us."

Sam turned and looked. "Hey, man, can you pull into that gas station up ahead?" he asked the cabby.

"I thought you—"

"I just need to run in and get something," Sam said.

The cab rolled into the gas station and parked in front of the store. Sam grabbed the handle on the door but didn't move.

I watched the black SUV drive past the gas station.

"It's gone," I whispered.

Sam jumped out and ran into the store. A few minutes later, he walked out with a bag of donuts and two sodas.

"Do you think someone followed us last night?" I asked softly, snagging a donut.

"I don't know." Sam opened a bottle of soda.

The rest of the cab ride, Sam's radar seemed on high alert. He constantly scanned the area as the cab driver dodged through neighborhoods and side streets.

Before long, the scenery outside the window melded into a wooded landscape. Snow-covered trees lined the road as it narrowed and curved back and forth.

We were traveling through the state forest. It certainly appeared different in the daytime. The yellow pairs of eyes I had seen the night before were no longer peering out between the trees. Today, the edge of the roadside was dotted with small paw prints that disappeared into the forest.

When we exited, the cab rolled to a stop at the corner of Caran and Hamlet Street. We were just on the outskirts of the Highlands, not far from Ben's house. He lived in Riverside, a small community within the Highland area of Fall River. The neighborhood overlooked Mount Hope Bay, home to the Riverside Black Sox, a major-league baseball team that had won the World Series for the past two years. Half of the Black Sox players lived in the Highlands. In fact, Ben and his dad, Travis Jackson, lived next door to the starting catcher for the Black Sox, Buster Greene.

Sam practically lived at Ben's after school during baseball season, hoping he would get a chance to meet the infamous Buster Greene.

I think I had been to Ben's three times during the past year. The first time was for Ben's birthday party. The second was to pay my respects when his mother died, and the last was at Thanksgiving.

Sam and Ben were best friends, which always surprised me. They had met under tense circumstances at school one day when I sort of introduced them to each other.

I had met Ben in space science class on my first day of high school. I was late to class that day, and by the time I walked into the planetarium, there was only one seat left. With no other choice, I sat next to a redheaded kid with pimples and freckles.

"Hi. I'm Ben." He'd smiled widely and extended his hand.

I didn't know what to say. I'd never made friends with boys in school. My experience with them was nonexistent. Boys bullied me. So I ignored him as I slunk into the chair.

When the lights went out, the teacher instructed the class to lean back and gaze up at the fake sky. As the rest of us sat and looked up at the stars, his stare bored into me. When class ended, Ben followed me out and seemed angry that I had ignored his friendly gesture.

"Hey," he'd said. "You never told me your name."

As Ben kept talking, I kept walking, still ignoring him. He grabbed my arm and whirled me around in the middle of the hallway. I looked around to see all the kids staring at us. At that moment, I thought, *Not again—another new school, another bully. Why can't I catch a break?* I didn't get a chance to say anything to him. Sam had shown up the moment Ben touched my arm.

"You have a problem, buddy?" Sam had blurted out.

"Who the hell are you?" Ben had countered.

At the time, Ben stood a head taller than Sam, but that didn't matter. Sam had fought off men bigger than Ben.

"Don't lay a hand on her again!" Sam had shouted.

"And what if I do? Are you going to stop me?" Ben's pale face had glowed bright red.

"Sam, don't do this," I'd pleaded.

"Is this your boyfriend?" Ben had asked me.

When Ben blurted out the word "boyfriend," Sam threw the first punch.

Ever since that first day of ninth grade, Sam and Ben had been best friends.

The cab driver turned onto Ash Street, severing my trip down memory lane. Tall ash trees lined the road, creating a beautiful snow tunnel. I couldn't help but remember Ben bragging that the white ash trees were why the Black Sox players chose that neighborhood—they felt connected to the energy the trees released. Not to mention, they thought it was a superstitious sign because baseball bats were made from the timber of the ash tree, which in their minds was their four-leaf clovers.

The cab parked in front of 22 Ash Street.

"Twenty-five dollars," the cabby demanded.

Sam handed the cabby forty bucks. "Just give me a ten back."

The cab driver handed Sam two five-dollar bills. "Thanks, man."

"No problem," Sam replied.

After we both got out, Sam did a quick scan up and down the street before we made our way up the snow-covered walkway. No sooner than we reached for the doorbell, the door opened.

Ben's full lips parted, and a radiant white smile greeted us. His hair was no longer red. It had changed to a cinnamon color with red streaks through the top as though he'd had it profession-ally highlighted. His sideburns were neatly trimmed, and like Sam, he had dimpled cheeks that made the girls at school giddy when he walked by.

"Hey there." Ben gave me a bear hug.

"Ow. My ribs, please?"

"Sorry," Ben whispered.

Sam had one foot inside the door when the crunch of tires rolling over the snow-covered street broke the quiet of the morning air. I caught a glimpse of the nose of an SUV before it came into full view, complete with blue-and-red lights on top. My heart dropped to my knees. It wasn't a black SUV, but it still conjured up a picture of a jail cell.

Sam pushed me deeper into the house. We both jumped into the living room to the right. The bay window had no curtains, which meant we were on display like mannequins in a high-end clothing store.

Sam moved to one side of the window, out of view. I plastered myself against the wall on the other side while Ben's dog, Lucy, trotted in and started barking. She was a small dog and looked like either a Shih Tzu or a Maltese. She had big brown eyes and reminded me of an Ewok from *Star Wars*. I bent down to pet her in the hope that she would stop barking.

Sam gasped. His expression was frozen like he'd seen a ghost.

"What's wrong?"

He shook his head as if he didn't want to tell me.

"Sam, tell me!"

He put his finger to his lips, and the doorbell rang.

My heartbeat shifted into gear and went from zero to a hundred in a matter of seconds. I held my breath, silently reciting the Lord's Prayer. *I just hope that jail is better than foster care.*

"No, Officer, my dad isn't home. Is there something I can do for you?" Ben's voice was soft.

"No, son. Your dad had a problem at school the other day. I was in the neighborhood and wanted to see what the outcome was. I'll catch up with him next week," the officer said.

"Okay, I'll let him know you came by, Officer Wilkins."

"Have a nice day, son."

"You too," replied Ben.

After the front door closed, I slid down the wall and sat in a crouched position with my face in my hands. Sam grunted and collapsed next to me.

"You okay?" I asked.

He raked a hand through his hair and popped his head back against the wall.

Ben sauntered in and eased down onto the brown fabric sofa opposite the bay window. Lucy followed then jumped onto his lap.

"Josie, you look horrible."

I snarled. "Don't call me that. And thanks for the words of endearment."

"Hey, man, is there someplace we can shower?" Sam asked.

"Follow me, amigos." Ben rose from the couch.

As I padded down the stairs, an orange scent filtered up the staircase. When I approached the bottom, a light came on. In front of me, a sea of sports trinkets, paintings, signed jerseys, footballs and baseballs filled the room. The place was a shrine to all things sports.

The pictures of the Black Sox when they won their first World Series hung on one wall. On another hung signed photos from Cal Wilson, the quarterback for the Cowboys. The only area of the room without pictures or trinkets was the wall with the TV. Not surprisingly, the TV was a fifty-five-inch flat-screen, and in front of it was a black leather sectional sofa—it screamed man cave.

I trailed my hand over the back of it as I walked around to the front, thankful that it wasn't floral or dusty. The soft, buttery leather reminded me of Neil's truck and sucked me in as soon as I sat down. While Sam and Ben talked at the bar behind the couch, I placed my head on the pillow, curled my legs under me, and closed my eyes.

I awoke a couple of hours later to Sam and Ben shouting at the television. The Boston Bruins were playing the New York Rangers. The game was tied, two all. As I glanced at the TV, the hockey puck slid into the net, and the Bruins scored, sending Ben and Sam flying in the air, body bumping each other.

"So this is what you do when girls aren't around?" I asked.

"Sorry, Josie... I mean Jo. We didn't mean to wake you," Ben said.

"Shower?" I asked.

"Why don't you use my bathroom upstairs?" Ben replied. "It's quiet. Plus, you can have some privacy."

That would be nice. I stretched, then yawned. When I did, my mouth stretched too far. My hand flew to the left side of my face and pressed my fingers against the bandage.

"What's wrong, Jo?" Sam's eyes popped wide.

"I think it's bleeding again."

"Move your hand," Sam ordered.

I did as he said then squeezed my eyes together, afraid I'd torn a stitch.

"Stop squinting." Sam pulled one of the ends of the gauze from my skin. "Ben, do you have any antiseptic?"

Ben scurried out.

"I can't get blood in my mouth. I would rather not be tempted to crave—"

"Crave what?" Ben returned and handed Sam a bottle of peroxide. "Here's the cotton."

Shit! I didn't hear him walk back into the room. Sam stepped on my toe.

"I'm starving," I said quickly. "I've had a craving for pizza for days now."

"I'll order pizza, then," Ben said.

Sam wiped the dried blood from my stitches with cotton saturated in peroxide. It stung for a second, but then fresh air swept over it, and it tingled. He didn't find any new blood leaking out, and as I climbed the stairs to the third floor, I prayed it would stay that way.

6

The two-story colonial house, which sat atop one of the highest hills in the neighborhood, had a beautiful view of the city below. The surrounding homes, similar in style, boasted large yards with pristine, manicured lawns.

For the past year, since the death of Mrs. Jackson, Ben and his dad had been living like bachelors, but Ben's bedroom was spotless. The tops of the dressers and the nightstand were dust-free, as though a housekeeper had just cleaned. The blankets on the bed were tucked in, the pillows fluffed and standing at attention against the headboard. Like the man cave, the walls sported Ben's favorite players from the Riverside Black Sox, and on the wall between the two windows, a picture depicted a naval fighter jet flying in the distance against an orange sky.

The view from the window of Mount Hope Bay took my breath away. Over the course of the day, the graying sky gave way, and the sun made its appearance. As the sun slowly disappeared into the western horizon, I combed my fingers through my wet hair then twisted my neck a few times, the cracking sound pounding in my ears. The pressure from the hot shower had pummeled my muscles, which helped relax the crick I had in my neck. With a decent night's sleep, I was hoping I would feel even better the next day.

Since Mr. Jackson would be home on Monday afternoon, Sam and I needed to be prepared to explain what had happened at Cliff's the other night. I wasn't sure what we were going to say or how he was going to react. I hoped the end result wouldn't lead to another foster home.

The clock on Ben's nightstand blinked six p.m., and my stomach growled. I was brushing my hair when the doorbell rang.

"Thank you." Ben's voice echoed up the stairs.

It must be the pizza.

I grabbed my shoes and peeked into the mirror one last time. The dried blood that had glued my hair together earlier was gone, and the zombie look was history. I flipped off the bathroom light when the smell of pizza filtered into the room. I was about to walk out when Ben's laptop caught my attention. *Maybe I can find information about blood cravings and blood types on the Internet.*

I opened the laptop then wiggled my finger on the trackpad, and the screen brightened. A website flashed on the screen—United States Navy SEAL program. I glanced up at the fighter jets on the wall. I wasn't aware he wanted to join the Navy. He'd always bragged about playing professional baseball for the Black Sox one day. I made a mental note to ask Ben about it later.

Instead of clicking out of the website, I clicked on the file button at the top of the screen. I didn't want to lose Ben's place. A drop-down menu popped up, and I clicked on New Tab, which brought up a blank screen. Then I typed "people who crave blood" in the search bar. I grabbed the laptop off the dresser and sat down on the bed. The bar at the bottom of the screen indicated it was thinking. A few seconds later, a list of websites scrolled down the screen.

The first website on the list was *The Myth About Vampires*. Every website listed had the word *vampire* in it. I didn't see anything about humans craving blood. I decided to change my keywords in the search bar to "blood type AF negative." While I waited, I caught a glimpse of an envelope sitting on Ben's nightstand. I leaned over to get a better visual—the return address was the United States Navy. Interesting. Ben was only a sophomore in high school. *Why would the Navy be interested in recruiting Ben at sixteen years old?*

The screen flashed, and several websites appeared with the names of local blood banks in different cities around the country. I raised an eyebrow when I read "rare blood types." I clicked on the web address, and a PDF document opened. The report listed many blood types such as Pk, Ko, and Hy negative. Dr. Case had been right. There were several rare blood types, but none in the report that matched my AF negative.

A deep-seated dull pain throbbed in my temples. I needed food, and my growling stomach confirmed it. I clicked out of the website and placed the computer back on top of the dresser when a car door slammed. I scampered over to the window, the dull pain shifting to a sharper one. *Mr. Jackson?* My hunger pangs turned into angry butterflies. I began pacing when the front door opened then closed.

"Ben. Ben," Mr. Jackson called.

The door to the room was cracked open, so I tiptoed over to it.

"Dad, you're home early." Ben sounded winded.

"The last two lectures didn't interest me. I figured I could get home and hang out with you for a couple days while we're both on spring break."

"Um, Dad? I don't want you to freak out."

"Son, what's wrong? Did something happen?" Mr. Jackson asked.

"Sam and Jo are here," Ben said.

Mr. Jackson let out a deep breath. "Is that all? You scared me. It's fine, son. You know I like Sam."

"But the thing is, Dad... um...."

"Spit it out," Mr. Jackson said.

Ben sounded afraid to tell his dad about me. He didn't have to. I rolled back my shoulders and headed downstairs.

Mr. Jackson stood in the foyer, wearing a New England Patriots ball cap that shadowed his unshaven face. When his gaze rounded on me, his chestnut-colored eyes blinked a few times. But when I drew closer, his eyes grew as large as golf balls.

Ben grimaced as if bracing for the firestorm that his father was about to deliver.

Mr. Jackson fixed his gaze on Ben then on me. "What happened?"

At that moment, Sam appeared at the edge of the banister. He'd pulled his hair into a low ponytail. "Mr. Jackson, we can explain."

He stabbed a finger behind Ben. "You sure will. Kitchen. Now. All of you."

His hardened tone sent a shiver up my spine and reminded me of those times I'd sat in his office, waiting for him to yell at Blake and me.

Sam grabbed my arm before I could follow Ben and Mr. Jackson. "I got this."

Nerves knotted in my stomach as Sam and I joined the Jacksons. The minute I stepped over the threshold from the hall into the brightly lit kitchen, my eyes started burning. I opened and closed them a few times, trying to clear them, but it didn't help. I blinked a few more times, but it was no use. My eyes were on fire, as if someone had stuck a hot fireplace poker in them and held it there. I covered them with both hands.

"What's wrong?" Sam whispered.

"I don't know. My eyes hurt."

He grabbed my arm and guided me to a barstool at the island that served as the kitchen table.

"Just give me a minute. I think it's from the shampoo." I blinked a few more times.

Then Ben handed me a wet paper towel. The coolness of it eased the burning sensation.

Mr. Jackson crossed his arms over his chest as he leaned against the sink. "Well, let's have it."

"Sir, you know Jo and I have been in foster care," Sam said. "Well, about a month ago, we moved to a new foster home. Mr. and Mrs. Birch seemed to be okay, but I wasn't home much because of baseball practice." Sam regarded me before he continued. "On Friday night, Ben and I grabbed a bite to eat after practice and hung out. When I got home, I heard Jo shouting. I ran to her room and saw that creep Mr. Birch attacking her. I got my baseball bat and hit him, but not before he stabbed her a few times." Sam had a tear rolling down his cheek.

I blinked away a tear as well.

Ben gaped from his spot beside his dad. I guessed Sam hadn't clued him in.

"Where was Mrs. Birch when all this was happening?" Mr. Jackson asked.

"I'm not sure," Sam replied. "Mrs. Birch couldn't have been in the house. Otherwise, there's no way she wouldn't have heard Jo shouting."

Mr. Jackson scrubbed a hand down his face. "Jo, how're you doing?" he asked in a soft tone.

I didn't know what to say. It was hard to find the words to articulate just how I felt or what was happening to me or that I might be a vampire. "Fine."

"So what happened after you hit Mr. Birch?" Mr. Jackson asked.

Sam slid onto the stool next to me. "Mrs. Birch showed up. She called the ambulance. I wanted to go to the hospital with Jo, but the cops wouldn't let me. So I managed to get out of the house while they were asking Mrs. Birch questions."

Mr. Jackson removed his ball cap. "And they're still looking for you?"

"Don't know," Sam replied.

The silence grew thick as Mr. Jackson regarded Sam and me. Sam and I hadn't talked earlier about what we were going to say to Mr. Jackson. We didn't expect him to be home so soon. I was curious if Sam would tell him about the guy chasing us. Or how Neil, the janitor, his employee, helped us. But after a beat, Sam didn't continue.

"I talked to the... cop." My voice quivered on the last word.

"And?" Mr. Jackson's dark eyebrows lifted.

"I think Mrs. Birch is accusing us of trying to kill her husband."

Mr. Jackson set his hat on the counter beside him. Then he ran a hand through his thick dark hair. "You think?"

Adults were always so quick to blame the kids.

"We didn't get a chance to hang around," Sam said.

"Why not?" Mr. Jackson asked in an unyielding tone.

Sam's forehead creased as he looked to me for permission to tell Mr. Jackson more. I nodded.

"When I got to the hospital, there was a guy asking for Jo's room. I've never seen the guy before." Sam paused and dropped his gaze to the counter. "When I was in Jo's hospital room, we heard noises outside the door. Jo peeked out and saw the same man that I'd seen in the ER earlier. He was fighting with the cop. We managed to get out of the hospital before we found out what he wanted with us."

"You don't know why he's chasing you?" Mr. Jackson asked.

"No, sir."

Ben was quiet as he listened intently.

Mr. Jackson pursed his lips. "Let me see if I have this right. Mr. Birch stabbed Jo, then you hit him with a bat. Jo ends up in the hospital and is questioned by the cops. While at the hospital, you see a man in the ER asking for Jo. Then Jo witnesses this same man fighting with a police officer outside the hospital room. Then you two run out of the hospital and end up here at my house." Mr. Jackson glared between Sam and me. "Is that accurate?"

Sam bobbed his head.

"Is there anything else?" Mr. Jackson asked.

"No, sir," Sam replied.

Mr. Jackson sighed. "Why did you come here?" He gave me the impression he wasn't convinced with Sam's story.

I didn't expect him to understand everything, but I was the walking wounded, and it seemed like that should have been proof enough.

Sam placed a gentle hand on my leg. "Mr. Jackson, we have no one, no family whatsoever. We have no one to help us. You know I've been in trouble with the law before. The last time the cops showed up at school, they threw me in jail. I couldn't let that happen with my sister in the hospital. I did what I believed was right for us, and I was hoping you could help."

"Son, there are a lot of holes in your story. If

you want me to help you—if I even can, that is—you need to tell me the truth."

I clenched my teeth. "It's the truth. The pervert tried to rape me. Sam did the only thing he could to get the fat jerk off me. We didn't do anything wrong." I covered my face in my hands as tears began to fall.

Sam squeezed my leg and whispered. "Calm down. You don't want your eyes giving you away."

I didn't care. I was the one who Cliff had tried to molest, not Sam. Besides, Ben knew about Sam's eyes changing colors. But he was right. It would be hard to explain to Mr. Jackson.

"Mr. Jackson, please. Can you help? If not, Jo and I will leave," Sam pleaded.

"Dad?" Ben cut in. "Can you call Chief Garrett? Maybe he can help? Look at her. They're telling the truth."

Mr. Jackson rounded his angry gaze on his son. "To tell him what? I'm hiding two runaways that he's probably looking for?" He waggled his head, scratching his chin. "Let me think."

I silently thanked Ben. I didn't want to tell Mr. Jackson anything else. I didn't want to recount every detail, every step we took. I just wanted to forget the past two days had ever happened.

7

After a restless night, I woke up on Monday morning, praying Mr. Jackson would help us and call his friend, Chief Garrett. I'd slept on the leather couch in the basement while Sam had crashed in a sleeping bag on the floor in Ben's room.

I padded up the stairs as Sam's voice filtered down.

"I'm sorry we involved you and Ben. I didn't know what else to do with some guy chasing us. We didn't have a choice but to run," Sam said.

I had my hand on the doorknob when Lucy started barking. *Busted.* I walked out and followed the hallway into the kitchen. The sun glared through the window over the sink, causing me to squint. My eyes burned, but not as severely as they had the night before.

Sam was sitting on a high-back barstool, and Mr. Jackson was holding a coffee cup and leaning against the sink. The coffee aroma imbued the kitchen, and even though I didn't drink coffee, I suddenly wanted a cup.

As I stepped up to the bar, Mr. Jackson placed his coffee cup on the counter near the sink. "Good morning, Jo." His curly brown hair was wet, his face clean-shaven.

"Morning, Mr. Jackson."

"Let me see your face." He grabbed my chin with his forefinger and thumb and tilted up my head. When he removed one edge of the bandage, his eyes went wide. Then he gently placed the bandage against my skin.

I stood frozen, unsure what he was trying to accomplish. Maybe he was looking for confirmation that I actually had a cut on my cheek. Well, it wasn't a cut—it was more like a gash. Or maybe he thought it would make it easier for him to speak with Chief Garrett.

I slid onto a stool and regarded Sam. We couldn't read each other's minds, but his creased forehead spoke volumes. He appeared to be just as confused as I was about Mr. Jackson inspecting my wound.

We both sat in silence, afraid to say anything else to Mr. Jackson. I hoped and prayed we could stay with Ben and his dad. My body was too sore to run again. But if it meant staying out of another foster home, I would have left immediately.

A cell phone rang and vibrated on the kitchen counter. Mr. Jackson tapped on the screen.

I nudged Sam and whispered, "You think—"

He flicked his head toward Mr. Jackson then raised a finger to his lips.

"Chief Garrett, how are you? Thanks for returning my call. I know you're extremely busy."

Sam and I sat quietly, listening.

When Mr. Jackson finished his conversation with Chief Garrett, he refilled his coffee cup. Carefully, he added two spoons of sugar before stirring it.

I held my breath and tapped my foot on the bottom of the stool. The pesky butterflies had awoken early, too, and fluttered around in my stomach.

Then Mr. Jackson cleared his throat, and as if on cue, I stopped tapping my foot. Every muscle in my body tensed.

"I don't know how to say this," he said.

My chest tightened. *This can't be good.*

"You kids are lucky. First, Mr. Birch is going to be fine. He's claiming that Jo was the one to come on to him and that he's innocent."

My jaw practically slammed on the granite surface. *Lucky? Far from it.* Rage began to boil deep down inside me. *Who did that weirdo think he was, accusing me of coming on to him?* I shivered at the thought of the disgusting beast. Revenge would be sweet one day.

Sam placed his hand on my leg. "Ignore it."

"Easy for you to say," I snapped. "You weren't stabbed, and no one was trying to—"

"Okay, kids. Listen. Chief Garrett doesn't believe Mr. Birch at all. As long as Mr. Birch doesn't press charges, then you two should be off the hook. That's the good news."

How is that good news? I've just been accused of coming on to a man who tried to kill me. What an asshole!

"Now the bad."

He must mean worse—what he just told us is bad.

"Sam, you'll have to give a statement to the police. I know you and the law have had a tumultuous relationship, but you *will* speak with them. Do you understand?" His tone permitted no argument.

"Yes, sir."

"Third, Chief Garrett has left both of you in my custody. I will be your guardian until the state can make sense of what's going on."

I drew my eyebrows in and looked at Mr. Jackson.

"Jo, do you have a question?"

"What about the guy who was chasing us? And is the cop okay?"

I couldn't get the image of the cop hanging in the air by the grip of an animal that looked ready to sink his teeth into his prey.

Mr. Jackson commandeered a stool across from us. He rubbed his eyes, letting out a deep breath. "Officer Bradley is in a coma. He was beaten pretty badly. The police are searching for his attacker."

I gasped as my hand flew to my mouth. Sam rubbed the back of his neck.

My mind spun to make sense of what that guy could have wanted with Sam or me. A chill crawled up my arms as I recalled those pitch-black eyes staring back at me, not to mention his teeth. I wasn't sure if Mr. Jackson was done talking or if there might be more. I held my breath, afraid to speak or move. My heart ached for Officer Bradley. I knew Sam didn't like cops, but Officer Bradley was a human being who didn't deserve to get beat up like that.

"Chief Garrett would also like to speak to both of you about this man. He'll be here this afternoon. Now, some ground rules while you're living in this house. I don't take kindly to deceit. I know, Sam, you were doing what you thought was best for you and Jo, but once you left the hospital, you should've called the police. I'm also upset with you bringing Ben into this situation. He's not yet over his mother's death. He doesn't need more drama in his life right now."

I knew Mr. Jackson was a nice man, and as principal of our high school, he was usually fair in handing out punishment. But we weren't at school, and our problems were far worse than Blake and me getting into a fight. A cop was in a coma because a man was chasing us. *What if the man finds us here? What will he do to Mr. Jackson and Ben?* Suddenly, I didn't want to stay. I didn't want to be responsible for someone else's life.

"We're sorry, Mr. Jackson," I said in a soft voice.

"I don't want you two leaving this house until school begins next Monday. It's too dangerous." A muscle in his jaw ticked.

"Thank you, sir," Sam said with a sigh. "I know

you don't have to help us. My sister and I really appreciate it."

He wagged his finger in between us. "If anything happens to Ben, I'm holding both of you responsible."

My heart sank. I would hold myself responsible if anything happened to Ben.

At three that afternoon, Chief Garrett had knocked on the door. Mr. Jackson and Ben had left to run some errands while Chief Garrett spoke to Sam and me.

Sam and I sat together on the couch in the living room, and Chief Garrett occupied a winged-back chair near the bay window.

He crossed a fat leg over the other and pushed the gold wire-rimmed glasses up higher on his nose. "Well, which one of you wants to start?"

"I already explained my side to Officer Bradley," I said.

His features pinched, causing the underside of his eyes to wrinkle. "Young lady, do you think Officer Bradley can tell me what happened? You do know he's in a coma."

Heat stung my cheeks and I began tapping my foot against the couch. *Stupid me. I'm an idiot.*

Sam grabbed my hand. "Sir, we didn't do anything wrong. I was trying to save my sister from

Mr. Birch. When I got to the hospital, a man showed up, and for some reason, he was asking where my sister's room was. A few hours later, the man is outside the hospital room, fighting with the cop. That's all we know."

The chief stared at us, his glance shifting between Sam and me. "What did this man look like?"

"He's a tall, big dude, wearing a blue bandana around his head," Sam replied.

"And has pitch-black eyes," I piped up. I debated whether to tell him about the man's supposed fangs and how they were stained with blood, but I decided that the chief would only have me committed.

"You haven't found him?" Sam asked.

"No, son, we haven't. I was hoping you could tell me more. Why is this guy chasing you, and what does he want?"

Those were my questions too.

"We never saw him before yesterday," Sam said.

Chief Garrett regarded my brother with questions swimming in his brown eyes. "Why did you run from the house?"

"I wanted to be with my sister. I couldn't leave her alone." He squeezed my hand.

"Did you come here directly from the hospital?" He glared at each of us in turn.

I gnawed on my bottom lip and dropped my gaze, afraid to look at the chief.

"Sort of," Sam said. "When we left the hospital, we ran. We ended up at the high school and hid in the dugout until yesterday morning." Sam's voice was confident, and he didn't waver when he spoke.

What? I didn't dare look at the chief. I slid a sideways glance at Sam, who was still staring at the stocky man in the chair.

"Jo, can you look at me?" Chief Garrett asked. "Is that true?"

Sam nudged me.

I wasn't a good liar. I imagined Sam had a reason to lie, but I didn't know why. Still, I'd always followed his lead. Besides, I was sure he had a good reason.

Sam squeezed my hand harder.

Slowly, I eyed the chief. "Yes, sir," I managed to squeak out, hoping I sounded confident as my brother.

Chief Garrett studied us intently, clearly trying to read Sam more than me. My heart pounded, and I prayed he couldn't hear it from across the room. Then he unfolded his bulky body from the chair. "I know where to find you if we have any more questions. Tell Mr. Jackson we'll be in touch." He nodded. "You two, be safe." Then he left.

I let out a heavy sigh. "Why did you lie?" I punched Sam in the arm.

"He didn't need to know any more right now. If I told him about Neil and the funeral home, he would've hauled us down to the station and then... more questions. Besides, you need to get some rest and heal."

"Do you think he bought our story?"

"I don't know. But Mr. Jackson isn't going to let us leave here, so let's be thankful we have a place to stay for now."

I didn't like lying to the cops, but Sam had a point. It would've meant tons more questions. I just wanted this whole thing to be over with. Except for Neil and the funeral home, Sam had told the truth.

"What's happening to us?" I mumbled.

"I wish I could answer that," he said.

I wished he could too.

8

The rest of the week was quiet. I had a chance to sleep for more than four consecutive hours, which I hadn't done in a long time. Mr. Jackson worked in his office in the garage—although he'd claimed he would hang out with us, he never did. He visited the Birches and was able to get all our belongings, including Sam's baseball gear, which he worried about.

While my wounds were healing, I was a little concerned about the cut on my cheek. A scar was inevitable, as was being ridiculed by Blake Turner. He was going to have a field day with me when we returned to school. I shuddered just thinking about what he would say when I ran into him at school next week. I planned to be ready.

Sam kept his anger in check, which meant that his eyes didn't change colors. Fresh blood wasn't on any of the menus, so I wasn't tempted to test my resolve for the sticky red stuff. I was beginning to think it had just been a weird one-time thing.

Since Sam and I weren't allowed to leave the house, Mr. Jackson had given us homework in math and English. He had crafted some exercises that he'd said would help us when we returned to school. As Sam and I studied in the mornings, Ben trotted off to baseball practice, which irritated Sam. But it was a price that he admitted was better than another foster home, staying on the run, or jail.

After Chief Garrett questioned us, he and Mr. Jackson had a long conversation. They agreed that it would be best for Sam to attend an anger management course at school. Sam was required to report to Mr. Bale during second period on Monday morning when school was back in session.

Officer Bradley came out of his coma but was still in the intensive care unit. I made a mental note to ask Mr. Jackson if I could go see him.

Chief Garrett didn't have any news about catching the fanged bandana dude. I prayed I never saw that guy again.

On Friday, Mr. Jackson gave Sam and me a list

of chores, including detailed instructions about completing all the items on the list by the end of the weekend.

By Sunday, the April snow had melted, and the weather had warmed. The smell of lilac trees permeated the air. Sam and I had cleaned out all the flower beds and trimmed the rose bushes in the yard. I had never worked in a yard before, and within one hour of pruning roses, my hands had tiny punctures from where the thorns had broken my skin, but thankfully, no blood surfaced. I thought staying with Mr. Jackson was going to be easy—not a chance.

We completed every task on the list by early afternoon. Afterward, Mr. Jackson made us clean out the garage. I couldn't believe all the sports crap Ben had accumulated over the years. Once we gathered everything into a pile, Mr. Jackson hauled it off to Goodwill.

I breathed a sigh of relief when the sun finally dipped below the horizon. Around six in the evening, I climbed the stairs to my new temporary bedroom, just down the hall from Ben's. A hot shower and a pillow sounded like heaven.

Unlike the sports dungeon in the basement, my new room had windows with sheer curtains. While it didn't have a view of the bay like the one

I'd witnessed from Ben's window, it didn't matter. What mattered most was that I didn't have to share a room or a bunk bed with anyone.

My nerves propelled me awake early on Monday morning. After a stretch and a yawn, I sauntered into the bathroom and started the shower. While the water warmed up, I checked myself in the mirror. I didn't look as gruesome as a week before, though the stitches didn't compliment my appearance. My eyes were still silver. I said a silent prayer that they would stay that way today.

Regardless, I couldn't help but think of what stupid comments Blake would have if I bumped into him. He was the only one who picked on me for my eye color, which I never understood.

"Your black hair and silver eyes are a lethal combination," Ben had said. "It's like you're looking into a mirror. People can see their own reflections which can be creepy. Blake probably hates the way he looks and blames it on you."

Ben might have been right, but I had a potential scar to add to the list. Whatever Blake's motives, I wasn't dealing with him anymore.

After a quick shower, I traipsed into the bedroom with a towel knotted around me. The cool air caused me to shiver. I pulled open the top dresser drawer and surveyed my choices of what to wear. I didn't have a lot of outfits like the other girls in school. I had two pairs of old jeans and one pair of new skinny jeans, which Mr. Jackson was kind enough to buy me when he saw how little I had. I decided to go with the layered look and donned a white tank top under a long-sleeved pink Henley and my new jeans. I loved the boots I borrowed from the funeral home, which looked great with my outfit. I brushed my hair and grabbed my backpack. Then with a sigh, I made my way toward the door to face what the day had in store for me.

Mr. Jackson was reading the paper, and Sam and Ben were eating cereal at the bar when I walked in the kitchen a few minutes later.

Ben's brows lifted at the same time he let out a low whistle.

Sam growled and punched Ben in the arm. "That's my sister, dude."

"Now, boys," Mr. Jackson said. "Jo, you look nice."

"Thank you," I said, grabbing a bowl and spoon from the dish rack then sat on the remaining stool next to Mr. Jackson.

The boys were eating Raisin Nut Bran—not my favorite, but I wasn't particular about what I ate. In foster care, I'd quickly learned to eat what was given to me, whether I liked it or not. That morning, I had a few choices, and Raisin Nut Bran was not on my list. I picked up the box of Lucky Charms and poured a heaping mound into my bowl. My mouth watered in anticipation of that first bite with the sweet marshmallows soaked in milk.

As I savored my sugary cereal, Mr. Jackson cleared his throat.

"Jo, I had some time to think about your situation." He went over to the sink and washed his coffee cup.

Sam and Ben jerked their heads up at the same time.

I scrunched my nose, bracing myself for whatever he had in store.

Mr. Jackson set the cup in the dish rack. "You need to know what to do when someone tries to attack you. You need to learn how to protect yourself. Just like your brother needs to learn to control his anger."

While I was relieved to hear it wasn't about my eyes changing colors, I still had no idea where the conversation was going.

"Therefore, I want you to see Coach Welles

after school. He has a program dedicated to helping young ladies learn the art of aikido."

Sounds like the name of a wolf out of the Alaskan wilderness.

Mr. Jackson seemed to read my mind. "Coach Welles will go through the history of aikido."

"But Mr. Jackson?" I protested.

My body was healing, and it didn't hurt to breathe, but it was still bruised. There was no way I could do anything physical yet.

"No buts, Jo. I know you're still sore. Coach will go easy on you."

Sam and Ben started laughing. I glared daggers at them.

"Boys, no need to laugh. I will add chores to your list."

"Dad," Ben protested.

"Ben, I don't want to hear it," Mr. Jackson intoned. Then he looked at me. "Jo, are we clear?"

"Yes, sir."

"Good. I need to run. I have to be in early. I want all of you to go directly to school. No sidetracking. Chief Garrett hasn't caught that man yet. Ben, report to me when you get there. I want to make sure you kids get in safely."

"We'll be fine, Dad," Ben said.

"I know, son. That's why the officer outside will

make sure you get to school." He patted Ben on the shoulder before he walked out.

Ben's face turned crimson.

"Your dad is paranoid," Sam said.

"Let's go. The cruiser leaves in fifteen." Ben had a hint of anger in his voice.

I couldn't figure out why he was angry. His face looked as red as the school colors. Maybe he was embarrassed. I didn't know what the big deal was. At least we would get there safely. Besides, if Ben saw that dude who was chasing us, he would take a step back and run too.

Sam and Ben dumped their dishes into the sink and scattered to gather their baseball gear. I sat alone in the kitchen, contemplating what Coach Welles would make me do after school. What a way to start my day.

I was eager to get to school. Before spring break, Darcy and I had planned to meet at our usual spot in the courtyard on our first day back. I wanted to spend a few minutes catching up with her and hearing all about her cruise vacation.

As we left, I wondered if Sam had thought about what he would say to Neil if he saw him at school. We hadn't heard from him, not that I was expecting to.

9

Durfee High School, located in the Highlands area of Fall River, boasted about its academic and sports programs. Three thousand students from all over the city attended the school.

When we arrived, the parking lot bustled with cars and kids hanging out, talking to one another. The cop car that followed us was far enough back, so no one really noticed, which was good. On the ride over, Ben kept griping about the cop car on our tail. He was worried kids would laugh at us. I thought he was acting like a drama king. Then again, I knew firsthand some kids could be mean.

I opened the door and muttered to myself, "Here goes nothing." I jumped out of the car, lifted my backpack over my shoulder, and started toward the building.

"Jo?" Sam called.

I turned and walked backward. "I need to meet Darcy."

Sam hiked his backpack over his shoulder. "Wait a second."

I huffed as I dropped my backpack on the ground near a blue Honda.

A few yards away, groups of students gathered in their own circles, talking and whispering—I imagined about spring break. As I waited for Sam, I couldn't help but overhear two boys talking behind the Honda.

The taller one wore a black ball cap with the bill facing backward. A skull and crossbones were embroidered in white stitching on the edge of his hat.

The shorter boy had his back to me. His name, McDonald, was stitched on his sweatshirt above the number seventeen.

"Dude, did you hear? They found a red four-door pickup in the state forest with a mangled body inside. I mean, like, an animal attacked him or something," Skull and Crossbones said.

"Shut up. Who was it?" McDonald asked.

"My dad knows Officer Wilkins. I overheard

him telling my dad the truck was registered to the janitor of our school," the taller one replied.

My knees buckled. I used the blue car as an anchor to hold me up, trying to catch my breath. *Did I just hear him correctly? Was it Neil? Maybe that's why we haven't heard from him. Oh my God! Maybe the bandana dude killed him.* Then something else occurred to me. *Were we followed the other night? If so, was it the man in the hospital garage standing next to the black SUV?* My mind was doing somersaults when Sam snapped his fingers.

Sam snapped his fingers. "Hey? Is my sister in there?"

"What's wrong with her?" Ben asked.

"I think she saw a ghost."

I blinked to find Sam and Ben with wide eyes and fear on their faces.

"Her eyes are changing colors like yours, Sam. Is that a genetic thing? It's cool as shit," Ben rambled.

"Jo, what's going on?" Sam asked.

"Um, can I talk to you alone?" I looked at Ben. "Brother-sister thing."

Ben picked up his sports bag and flung his backpack around his shoulders. "No problem, sweets. I need to tell my dad we made it safely, so he doesn't have a cow. Sam, I'll meet you in the locker room in twenty. Jo, love the eye thing you got going on." He drew an imaginary circle around his eyes with his forefinger. "The green-blue color suits you." Then he trekked towards the school building.

"My eyes are changing?" I asked.

"What happened?" Sam ignored my question.

I scanned the parking lot. The cop car that had followed us to school was parked at the front entrance. The two boys who had been standing behind the Honda were gone.

"I overheard these two boys talking, and—"

"You're upset because you heard two boys talking? Look, I've to get to the baseball meeting before school starts."

I swallowed hard. "Neil is dead."

All the blood rushed out of Sam's face as he dropped his sports bag and crouched to his knees.

"What're we going to do?" I asked.

He popped up. "We don't know for sure if it's true, right?"

"The boy said Officer Wilkins told his dad. Office Wilkins, Sam. The same guy that was at Ben's last week just after we got there. Remember?"

Sam glanced up at the gray sky. "Classes start in twenty minutes. We'll talk at lunch."

"That's it?" I hauled my bag over my shoulder.

"What do you want to do? Go identify the body?" Sam picked up his sports bag.

"Something. What if the cops find out we were with him? Do you think the bandana man had anything to do with it?"

"I don't have time for this right now," he snapped.

"Hey, I'm not the one to blame here," I said.

We trampled through the dewy grass in silence. Usually, a security guard stood at the gate, but I didn't see anyone. Most of the students had dispersed from the parking lot, except for a few talking on their cell phones. Mr. Jackson had a strict policy that prohibited anyone from using a cell phone during school hours unless it was an emergency. Otherwise, any student caught with one ringing, vibrating, or texting during class would receive a pink slip for detention.

When we reached the main entrance, Sam said, "I'm sorry I snapped. I'll see you at lunch, okay? And keep the whole emotional eye thing under control."

Sam and I had speculated that any heightened emotions such as anger caused our eyes to change colors. We didn't know why, but we agreed to try and chill about things. With the news about Neil, I couldn't promise him or even myself that I would stay calm.

The day wasn't beginning the way I had planned. I was as superstitious as those Black Sox players. I believed things happened in threes, whether good or bad. If the first incident was bad, the next two would be too. The news about Neil was terrible. If anyone knew Neil helped us, Sam and I would be in more trouble—worse than what had happened with Cliff. We could be accused of murder.

The bell was about to ring. So I climbed the steps two at a time to the second floor, and when I reached the top, I had to catch my breath. My ribs were throbbing, but not as badly as a week ago. With three minutes to spare, I scurried to my locker near my first period history class. Thank God. I grabbed the books I needed for morning classes, slammed the door, and clicked the lock in place.

When I entered the classroom, students were chatting in small groups around the room, and Mr. Zielinski was seated at his desk, his nose buried in a large, thick book. I made my way to my seat, which was in the last row near the windows. I had just bent over to pull my history book out of my bag when someone pinched my arm.

"Ow," I screeched as I jerked my head up.

Darcy Rose, my best friend, stood in front of me. Her golden-blond hair spilled over her shoulders, and her gold-speckled mascara glinted in the light from the classroom window.

"Whoa! What the heck happened to you?" she asked.

I had totally forgotten about meeting Darcy. *Shit!*

"Spill, woman." She had one hand on her hip and the other wrapped around her bag.

"I'm sorry. I got caught up talking to Sam."

"That's not what I mean." She pointed to my face. "It looks like someone was trying to carve you up for dinner."

"Ha ha. After class."

"No. Now." She raised her voice.

"Hush." I didn't want to draw attention to myself, but she would make a scene if I didn't say something. "I promise, after class. The bell is about to ring."

She huffed and plopped down in front of me.

Darcy took the title of drama queen to a whole different level. In my book, she was drama squared. While she was my best friend, and best friends were supposed to keep secrets, she still tended to gossip or let things slip.

The bell rang. Mr. Zee, as he liked to be called, closed the classroom door. He didn't waste any time as he handed out a quiz. *I didn't study a thing.*

I grabbed a pencil out of my backpack when Darcy handed me a note.

"You have fifteen minutes. Begin," he said.

The sea of heads in the class lowered their gazes and began scribbling.

I opened the note. *Where's Ben?* was written in big letters. Darcy had a thing for Ben. She'd yearned to go out with him since we'd started school in the fall. Her words: "Who's the Greek god? I think I'm in love."

Ben had a small following of girls from all grades hanging out at his baseball games and cheering him on, and now, he had Darcy.

I folded the note then stuffed it into my jeans pocket. I scribbled my name on the top of the page and scanned the quiz. Most of it was multiple-choice except for the last question, which was an essay.

Since we were studying the Civil War, the essay question asked us to describe President Lincoln and the Confederate forces at Fort Sumter in a paragraph or two. I unpacked my memory, trying to think about Mr. Zee's lecture on President Lincoln—no luck. I couldn't recall anything on the topic. I answered all the multiple-choice then wrote the first word for the essay when Mr. Zee called time.

"Pass your quizzes forward."

I sighed. I was sure Mr. Zee would be disappointed with me for not answering the last one.

As soon as he collected the quizzes, Darcy turned around. "Well?"

"Gee, you're irritating."

"Are you going to spill or not?"

"When the bell rings." I narrowed my eyes.

Mr. Zee spent the rest of the class polling us about the quiz. I drifted off, thinking about Neil and hoping he wasn't dead. A pattern seemed to be forming. Everyone around me was getting hurt —first, Officer Bradley, and now, Neil. *Who's next?* As I combed through my brain, trying to come up with some sort of theory, the bell rang, jarring me back to reality.

I rose from my seat and joined the other kids filing out and realized that Ben had never made it to history. *It must've been one hell of a baseball meeting.*

I pushed my way out of the classroom, but Darcy got tangled in the crowd. My next period was study hall, but I had about ten minutes before class.

I leaned against a locker outside the room, waiting for Darcy, when Ben walked up.

"There you are," Ben said.

I lifted my eyebrows. "The meeting took the whole period?"

"Yep. It got kind of heated," he said.

"What happened?"

"Nothing. You know guys," Ben said.

I honestly don't. Boys, guys, whatever—not in my vocabulary.

"Jack Powell, our pitcher, was being his same old self—an ass. The meeting got heated, so Coach Welles gave us a free pass for first period. Nice, huh?" He wore a grin from ear to ear.

"Jocks get away with murder," I said. "Is Sam on his way to anger management?"

Ben nodded.

I'm sure Sam is thrilled to spend the next period learning how to control his anger. I hope he doesn't lose it during class.

Darcy made it through the tangled web of students and planted herself directly in front of me. She didn't acknowledge Ben. Obviously, she was pissed. "Spill, and spill now!"

"You haven't told her yet?" Ben asked as he let out a low whistle.

"Like I've had time, and oh yeah, let me call up

Darcy on some cruise ship in the Caribbean. Are you insane?"

Ben raised his hands and leaned back against the lockers.

"We don't have much time, so I'll spare you the details." I didn't realize I was touching my left cheek until Darcy grabbed my hand.

"Jo, focus."

"Cliff tried to rape me at knifepoint, and I fought back." It was the second time I'd said it out loud. The first time, I cried, but it felt like a fifty-pound weight fell off my shoulders that time.

"He *what*? That motherf—"

"Easy, Darcy," Ben said.

She clenched her fists, ready to do battle. "I hope the bastard looks worse than you."

Darcy was an Aries and held true to her astrological fire sign. Her powerful expression of energy and her impulsiveness had gotten her into trouble many times, especially with people of authority.

I loved her like a sister, but her impatience drove me crazy.

"You better give her something," Ben whispered.

He was right. She wasn't going to let up.

"I'm not ready to dish on the details. We have

to get to class, anyway. And you know the halls have ears."

She stuck her finger at me. "You owe me, then. After school, we'll go to my house and hang out. My mom won't be home until nine tonight. Deal?"

"I can't go right after school." I wrinkled my nose.

"Why not?" Darcy asked. Redness surfaced on her tanned cheeks.

"I have to go and see Coach Welles."

"Are you trying out for the baseball team?" she asked.

"It's something Mr. Jackson wants me to do," I said.

Ben chuckled. He seemed to think the exchange between Darcy and me was cool. I turned and extended my arm, but he caught it before I could punch him.

"You don't want to do that, love."

"Oh, but I do." I nodded.

"Hello. What's with the 'love' and 'I do' shit?" Darcy stuck her hand on her hip and raised her brows. "Explain. Mr. Jackson wants you to do what?"

"You better tell her," Ben said.

"Yes, you better tell me." Darcy's voice teetered on the edge of screaming.

I glared at him. "Mr. Jackson feels it's a good idea for me to learn how to protect myself. I have to take self-defense classes with Coach Welles after school."

I didn't want to tell Darcy about the guy chasing us or Neil or anything else. It was too risky around that place. With my luck, Blake was hiding in the shadows.

"Shut up! All you need to know about self-defense is to kick where it hurts, if you know what I mean." She pointed down below her belt.

I wasn't ready to tell her that her way didn't work, and when I'd kicked Cliff between the legs, he'd stabbed me in the ribs.

We had only a few minutes before the bell, so we barreled our way through the crowd.

Darcy looped her arm through mine. "You can come over after your self-defense class, then."

"I'll check with Mr. Jackson first," I said.

Sam and I were confined to the house for the time being, but I didn't want to ruin her day and tell her it wasn't going to happen. She wasn't the kind of girl that took "no" lightly.

"Mr. Jackson? Do you have to run everything by him now?" she asked.

"Sam and I are living with Ben. So... yeah."

"Get out!" Her mouth fell open. "You're living

with Ben?" She raised her right thumb and flicked it in his direction.

I nodded.

"You bitch!"

"Jealous, are we?" I asked.

"Then maybe we should hang out at Ben's tonight?" She smiled wide and nodded her head a few times.

God only knew what was going through that brain of hers.

10

After study hall, I said goodbye to Ben and Darcy and made my way to math class. The corridors buzzed with students walking in opposite directions, similar to a two-way street. I stopped and waited for an opening to squeeze into the far lane. A tall redheaded kid stopped to let me through, and I slid between two cheerleaders who were all decked out in their red-and-black uniform skirts. The cheerleading coach wanted to keep the old seventies uniform style, which meant saddle shoes and bobby socks.

The blonde behind me said, "Watch where you're going, Moonbeam."

It was a good thing she couldn't see my face. I rolled my eyes and ignored her. The wannabe blonde in front of me stopped short, and my head hit her backpack.

She turned. "Oh, it's the school idiot. Walk much?"

I knew better than to open my mouth. The exchange of words wouldn't end well. "Sorry," I mumbled.

She resumed walking, and her friend moved in front of me. Both of them turned into the planetarium. I picked up my pace and continued to my history of math class.

I had my head down as I rounded the corner and bumped into something hard. At first, I thought I'd walked into a wall, but then a hand palmed my head.

I glanced up and found yellowish-brown eyes peering down at me—Blake Turner. It was like looking into the eyes of a wolf.

Shit!

An evil grin was etched on his face. "Well, lookie here. Who is this? Or should I say *what* is this? Moonbeam, you just keep getting scarier and scarier every time I see you." Blake placed his hand on my right shoulder.

That corkscrew would have come in handy.

"Did you try and have some plastic surgery over spring break to make yourself look pretty or something?" He let out a deep grunt and laughed, which reminded me of Cliff. "You realize it didn't work. Nothing will work on you, Moonbeam. You can't change creepy."

I tried to keep my emotions in check, but it was too late. My hands began shaking. I was sure my irises were changing colors as I balled my hands into fists. I wanted to punch him squarely in the crotch. But any altercations with Blake would land me in Mr. Jackson's office, and that wasn't part of my plan. The fact he was my new guardian wouldn't make him go any easier on me—just the opposite. I didn't want to sit through detention.

"Did they slice out your tongue too?" Blake asked.

I had to get around Pimple Face and to class, but he wasn't going to let me move. My fate was sealed. *I should accept the consequences of my actions now.*

I glanced around the hall. One student had his head buried in his locker. The other slammed her locker shut then walked down the hall in the opposite direction.

"I'm late for class," I said.

"Don't let me stop you." He swung his right arm in a wide arc, motioning me to go.

I stepped to my left to get around him. He followed, blocking my passage. I slid to my right, and he mimicked my move again.

"You're an asshole," I said.

His hard eyes drilled into me. I thought steam was going to come out of his nostrils. I moved to my left again and caught a glimpse of his hand in midair, heading for my face. I ducked under his arm. When I looked back, his cheeks had turned five shades of red, and his lips were pinched together into a thin line. He stood there like a bull in an arena, waiting to attack his opponent.

Now would be a great time to get to class. My inner voice told me to run, but my legs wouldn't move, and my heart pounded against my bruised ribs.

I took one step forward, and as I did, Blake took three steps toward me. I took another step and turned to run, but he grabbed me by the arm and threw me against a locker.

"Asshole? No one calls me an asshole, bitch."

His nose was an inch from mine. The spray of his spit hit my face, and his breath smelled of onions.

A flash of Cliff came screaming into view, causing my veins to throb, rage percolating. Without thinking, I grabbed Blake by his crotch and twisted my hand one way then the other before I let go.

He dropped to his knees. His backpack fell off his shoulder, and tears pooled in his eyes.

I bent over. "Asshole, asshole, asshole."

Then I adjusted my backpack, turned, and ran through the crowd of students that had gathered in the hall. Some of them had their phones out, snapping pictures. With my luck, the headline was going to read "Weird Creepy Girl Attacks Jock." I couldn't worry about that. I was already late for class.

I pulled the door open, trying to catch my breath.

"You're late, Ms. Mason," Ms. Costner said. "Come in and take your seat." She nodded as she regarded me with a stern expression.

"I'm sorry. The halls were packed today," I lied.

Her blue eyes softened. "Don't let it happen again."

Ms. Costner had always taught algebra and trigonometry—the history of math was a new class.

I slid into the seat of the metal desk, inhaling and exhaling so that my breathing would get back to normal. My theory on events happening in threes was proving to be true: Neil then Blake. I was afraid to ask myself what was next.

Ms. Costner cleared her throat as she was opening her *History of Math* book. "Let's talk about Pythagoras."

Some of the students in class moaned. I slouched in my chair. My breathing was just about back to normal, but my hands still shook as I opened my book, tearing a page in the process.

"Pythagoras was not only a great mathematician but also a Greek philosopher. His teachings influenced a number of great people, such as Socrates and Euclid." She looked around the room then continued. "Pythagoras believed the universe was divided into three worlds."

I perked up when I heard the word "three." An electrical charge swirled around me.

"There's only one world, Ms. Costner!" a boy at the back of the room shouted.

"One that you know, Henry. But ask yourself, how many other worlds are in this universe?" She walked around to the front of her desk, shifted her stance, and leaned against it. "The first world he believed existed was the *Supreme World*, which, according to Pythagoras, was the supreme mind."

I raised my shaky hand.

"Yes, Jo?"

"The Supreme Mind? I don't understand." I asked.

"God, you idiot!" a boy shouted from the other side of the classroom.

I jerked my head and glowered in his direction. His eyes grew wide, and he dropped his head.

Oh, crap. My eyes aren't back to normal.

"Pythagoras believed that man was separate except for his soul. We'll spend some time discussing the Supreme Mind after your assignments are turned in next week." She jotted down something in her notebook. "Let's continue. The second world Pythagoras believed existed was the *Superior World*. This world was home to immortals. Now—"

"Yeah, vampires and werewolves!" a third boy near the window shouted.

The class erupted in laughter.

My body went rigid when I heard the word "vampires," and now she was talking about immortals. *Eerie!*

"Frank, one more outburst, and you'll be sent to the principal's office."

Frank's wild-eyed expression indicated he was afraid, but of whom—the principal or Ms. Costner, whose unblinking eyes projected a murderous expression? After a long pause, the class lowered their heads.

She scanned the room. "The third world was known as the *Inferior World*. Would anyone like to guess which world Pythagoras was speaking of?"

The girl seated in front of me raised her hand.

"Yes, Karrie?"

"Our world?" Karrie guessed.

"That's correct. The Inferior World, as Pythagoras outlined, was the home of mortals, man, animals, and all the things you students think are important—material things. The point of all this is that Pythagoras wasn't just a mathematician, he..."

I doodled in my notebook as she continued her lecture on Pythagoras. I drew three circles. Underneath each one, I wrote *Supreme, Superior, and Inferior,* respectively. In the circle marked *Superior,* I scribbled the words "blood" and "vampires." I wondered what a world of immortals would look like.

The overhead speaker blared and jarred me back to the mortal world. The static from the speaker filled the classroom, and I winced. It was worse than someone dragging their nails on a chalkboard. If anyone had been asleep, they were awake now.

The person on the other end banged on the microphone.

"Ms. Costner, this is Gail. Mr. Jackson would like to see Jo Mason in his office right away."

I froze. *That damn Blake Turner ratted me out.* On the other hand, maybe the cell phone pictures had already gone viral. Everyone looked at me. If they didn't see my face before, they certainly did now. A prickly heat rose inside me, and my muscles tensed.

Ms. Costner pushed a speaker button located on the wall near the door. "She'll be down in a few minutes."

Then the speaker was silent, and my heart picked up a rhythm I was sure everyone could hear. I was in trouble... again.

11

———

The principal's office was located in the administration wing of the main building, near the entrance of the school. It took at least fifteen minutes to get from the math wing to the admin building. As usual, banners and signs for the latest school event peppered the walls. Since it was April, the school's dance committee was preparing for the annual May dance. They'd voted for a costume ball set in 1700 as a tribute to the late Mrs. Elise Jordan, who had been chair of the English department for over twenty years.

I wrapped my hands around both straps of my backpack, wondering what it would be like to attend a school dance. Last year's theme had been a sock hop, and Darcy had said it was like being on an episode of *Happy Days*. Boys had dressed up as Fonzie, and the girls had worn three-quarter-length dresses with saddle shoes. Dressing in costume would certainly beat the hand-me-downs I wore every day. But I wouldn't be going to any dance, and I didn't have any money to buy a fancy outfit or costume, anyway.

I reached the doorway between the math and history wings, intent on getting to my destination as quickly as possible.

"Jo. Yo, Jo. Wait up," a familiar voice said.

I turned around, and Darcy was walking down the hall. I stopped and waited for her to catch up.

"Where're you going?" she asked.

"I got called to the principal's office."

"Yikes. What'd you do? Let me guess. You got into it with Blake again, huh?"

My jaw dropped. "Is it going around school?" I twisted my lips and crinkled my nose.

"Yep. It's viral. I like that you're coming out of your shell."

Sweat dotted my forehead. I kept thinking of how I would explain to Mr. Jackson that I'd grabbed Blake's crotch. First day back at school, and I was already called to the office. I had a feeling he was going to add to my punishment list —probably a Ms. Manners class.

She must've seen the look on my face. "Don't worry. You're living with Mr. Jackson, so I'm sure he'll go easy on you."

"Believe me, Mr. Jackson can be just as scary at his house as he is at school." I stabbed a thumb behind me. "I'm late. Where are you off to?"

"Guidance counselor. My mom wants me to talk to Mr. Grant about Boston College." She shrugged her shoulders. "She's so set on me going to BC—you know, her alma mater."

Darcy's future was planned. Her parents had decided which schools she could apply to and which were off-limits. Her mother taught at the local community college, and her father was some big CEO of a law firm in Boston. He commuted every now and then, but most of the time, he stayed at their apartment in the city and drove home on Friday nights.

I wished college was my only worry. It sure as hell wasn't my top priority. Plus, I couldn't picture myself going to college. I was lucky if I made it through a day. If the events of the past week were any indication of how my future looked, I was in deep trouble. Besides, I needed to find out who I was before I could decide on my future.

Darcy and I didn't talk much about where we would be when we grew up. We were both still trying to find our way in this world. At least she had parents to guide and help her, although she was more interested in boys than college. I wanted to share with her all the details and events of my horrible week but couldn't. What would I say? "Hey, Darcy, I like the taste of blood. You should try it."

Since we were going in the same direction, Darcy slid her right hand through my left arm.

"So, are you going to the dance this year?" I asked.

"Maybe. You should go."

"I don't do dances," I said.

"Come on. It'd be fun. I can do your makeup —" Suddenly, she stopped walking.

"What is it?" I asked, my body jerking forward.

"I had a thought." She winged up her brows and smiled wide. "I can be Ben's date, and you can be Jack's date. You know he's hot. His soft, brown curls are always falling in his face, and his teal-blue eyes just do something to a girl's body." She sighed and placed a hand over her heart. "Plus, I know how you like boys with brown hair and blue eyes."

"Jack Powell? The pitcher of the baseball team? Crazy idea." I shook my head. "No way."

"Why not?"

"Are you looking at me? Do you see this cut on my face?"

I had to agree with her. Jack was hot with broad shoulders, a strong jaw, and a bad-boy look that could melt butter. I'd never been on a date in my life. I wouldn't even know what to do.

"The cut will heal by then," she said.

"He doesn't even know who I am."

"We can change—"

"Jo?" Gail, Mr. Jackson's secretary, hurried toward us. "Mr. Jackson needs to see you. *Now!*"

Gail was never uptight and always had a calm voice, but she seemed panicked.

Darcy and I exchanged a surprised look.

"Yes, ma'am," I said.

Two minutes later, Darcy and I were in the administrative offices, a large quad-like area. In the middle stood a counter where students checked in for the appointments. Surrounding the counter, were offices for attendance and absentee, the guidance counselor, and the enrollment and grading office.

After a quick hug, we said our goodbyes with Darcy wishing me luck.

I had a feeling I was going to need more than luck.

Mr. Jackson's office was located down a hallway

and tucked away from the hub of activity. Gail typed frantically on the keyboard and barely looked up when I approached.

She must've sprinted back to her desk.

With the tilt of her head, she said, "Go on in, Jo. He's waiting for you."

Nerves swirled in my stomach as my hands trembled. I desperately wished Sam was next to me. I replayed the fight with Blake in my head. When I came to the part where I grabbed Blake in the... I shuddered. *I don't go around grabbing guys in the crotch. I don't know what got into me.* Maybe Sam's rage was rubbing off.

I placed my backpack on the floor and gave myself a mental pep talk.

"Jo, go in, already." Gail had stopped typing.

Here goes nothing.

Two men in military uniforms stood in front of a bookcase in Mr. Jackson's office. Their black berets tucked under their left arms. While another military man sat in a chair in front of the desk.

I didn't know it took military men to discipline a sixteen-year-old girl who grabbed a boy's crotch.

"Jo, please come in and sit down." Mr. Jackson pointed to the empty chair next to the man in fatigues.

My knees locked in place as my mind scrambled to understand why military men were in Mr. Jackson's office and what they wanted with me. I looked at Mr. Jackson as he lowered his gaze—something was wrong.

The military man in the chair stood. His young-looking face was clean-shaven, and his cobalt-blue eyes were tucked under his thick, dark lashes as he waved his hand to the empty chair beside him. "Please, have a seat," Blue Eyes said.

My heart fluttered as I swung my gaze from Blue Eyes to the other two guards.

Like Blue Eyes, they wore black leather boots laced up over their pants and T-shirts disappeared into their green fatigues. Their eyes were frozen on some object in the distance, as if they were guarding a king's palace.

On a quiet exhale, I shuffled over to the empty chair.

"Jo, this is Lieutenant Webb London. He's here to discuss a personal matter with you and Sam. We're waiting on Sam," Mr. Jackson said.

I sat down as question after question bombarded me. What personal matter? What could the military want with us? Are they here to question us about Neil?

Gail came in. "Mr. Jackson, can I have a word?"

As soon as Mr. Jackson left, silence filled the

room. The electricity in the air prickled my skin. This wasn't about my fight with Blake. No, it was more serious than that.

My heart beat rapidly as I stared out the massive window that overlooked the football field. A class stood on the green carpet, jumping in the air and clapping their hands over their heads as Coach Welles inspected everyone's form. I wondered if Coach was going to make me do jumping jacks after school for my self-defense classes.

Blue Eyes cleared his throat. "Jo, I'm currently in charge of a Navy SEAL team known as the Jupiter Sentinels. As Mr. Jackson mentioned, my name is Lieutenant London. But you can call me Webb."

His soft expression made my stomach flutter, seemingly quieting the nerves that were running rampant through me.

"And your name is supposed to mean something?" I asked.

"Jo, I—"

Mr. Jackson returned, stroking his newish goatee. I thought it looked good on him, but Ben disagreed.

"Is Sam on his way?" I asked.

Mr. Jackson bit the bottom of his lip as he settled at the window behind his desk. "I'm afraid we have a problem. Sam didn't show up to his history class."

My pulse quickened. Maybe he was still in Mr. Bale's anger-management class or with Coach Welles. No, Coach Welles was out on the field, and Sam wasn't in the crowd. It was only third period. Then my heart fell to the floor. *Did the bandana dude show up at school?*

"Maybe he's with Ben." My voice trembled.

"Ben is on his way," Mr. Jackson said.

I didn't want to panic. I was trying to be calm, but my body said otherwise. I tapped my foot against the chair. *Don't panic. It's nothing.*

Lieutenant Webb or whatever his name was went over to one of his guards and whispered something in his ear. Then both guards marched out of the room when Ben hurried in.

"Hey, Dad. What's up?" Ben sized up the military men. "Who are these guys?" He pointed to the two disappearing guards then to the lieutenant.

"This is Lieutenant London, son. He's here to speak with Sam and Jo about a private matter. Do you know where Sam is?"

Ben knitted his brow. "Isn't he in history during this period?"

"No. I checked. He wasn't in his last class, either. We've checked the school grounds. I have security doing another search."

A dull pain started to form at the base of my skull.

Ben tucked his hands into his jean pockets. "Sorry, Dad. The last time I saw Sam was at our baseball meeting first thing this morning. After that, Sam was talking to a couple of people—one kid named McDonald and then the janitor. I was going to be late for my class, so I hightailed it out of the locker room."

"You mean Neil, the janitor?" I asked.

Mr. Jackson angled his head. "Who?"

Tears threatened. "Neil. Isn't that the janitor's name?"

"Sorry, I don't know that name," Mr. Jackson said.

I gripped the arms of the chair. "Neil Foster is the janitor here. He also works at the hospital at night. He helped us at the hospital."

"You're not making sense," Mr. Jackson said.

"Neil is tall, with a bald head and a tattoo on the back of his neck." I bit a nail while tapping my foot.

"Excuse me," Lieutenant London interrupted. "I'll be right back." The door closed behind him.

"Jo, Arlan Summit is the janitor of this school

and has been for the past few years. He's not bald, either." Mr. Jackson had a confused look on his face, which scared me.

"Is… Mr. Summit in school today?" I asked.

"He is. I saw him in the locker room this morning," Ben said.

None of this was making sense. *Who is Neil Foster? How would Sam know Neil from school?* I dropped my head into my hands. Maybe Sam went back to the funeral home to find Neil. I took a deep breath in the hope that my superstition about threes didn't include Sam.

"Do you think that guy was chasing—" I lifted my head when Lieutenant London returned.

"Mr. Jackson, may I have a word with Jo alone?" he asked.

"Hey, are you guys SEALs? Like the Navy ones?" Ben asked with a hint of excitement in his voice. "I want—"

"Sure. Take as long as you need. Ben, let's go." Mr. Jackson placed his hands on Ben's shoulders. "I'll check with security again. I'll be back in about thirty minutes."

Once Lieutenant London and I were alone, the electrical charge I felt earlier returned. I wondered if it emanated from him.

He leaned against the desk directly in front of

me. "First, I have a team of folks searching for your brother. Between Mr. Jackson's security and my team, we should be able to uncover some clues as to Sam's whereabouts." His voice sounded confident, but his bleak expression said something different—whether angry or worried, I couldn't tell. Whatever it was, it made my pulse race.

His two guards entered then nodded at Webb as they resumed their position three feet behind me.

Crossing one ankle over the other, he regarded me with those blue eyes that had a way of making my stomach flutter. "I came here today to speak to you and Sam about your father, Steven Mason. Now, it seems with this recent news of Sam being MIA, our suspicions of what we didn't want to happen have been confirmed."

I scanned his tall, lean body. His wavy brown hair was tucked behind his ears. It seemed a bit long for a military man, but what did I know? My knowledge of the military was minimal. What I did know stemmed from watching movies like *Top Gun*. I had no idea what he was talking about and certainly didn't understand the military lingo.

As if he could read my mind, he continued. "I know I'm not making much sense. Let me explain.

I work for your father. I've worked for your father for the past twelve years."

Twelve years? This guy doesn't look a day over twenty-one.

"We've planned for this day," he said.

I knitted my eyebrows together. "You've planned for this? What does that mean?"

"I know you're confused."

"I'm not confused. I know I don't have a father. I know my brother isn't in school. And I know I don't care for you or the two goons standing behind me." Rage boiled within me. Undoubtedly, my eyes would show it, but I didn't care. I stood, and Lieutenant London grabbed my wrist.

"Jo, I'm not here to hurt you or your brother. And I know you have no reason to trust me, but please just listen." His tone was even.

He was right that I didn't trust him. He could have been working with the guy that was chasing us.

He let go of my wrist, raised his hand to my chin and gently tilted my head to my right. His touch sent a prickly heat scattering through me. *There's that feeling again.*

"With the exception of that two-inch cut, you look every bit like your father." He lowered his hand. "Sit, please? Let me explain. I think you'll want to hear what I have to say. After that, you can leave if you want to."

I'm not just going to leave. I'm going to run like hell. I eased into the chair and kept my eyes glued to his.

"How did you get that gash on your face?" A red ring of fire rimmed the outer edges of his cobalt-blue eyes as he spoke.

"I'd rather not talk about it."

"Your father isn't going to be pleased." He examined every facial feature as if he were taking snapshots of my face.

My mouth fell open. "Pleased? Why would he even care? Where's he been for fourteen years? Where is he now?"

Webb regarded his men before addressing me. "About a week ago, your father went missing. In fact, he went missing when we got word that you had some sort of accident and landed in the hospital. Up until that day, we hadn't been able to find you and Sam."

My body went numb. All the blood rushed to my feet. I didn't know how to process it. The person I cared for most was missing. A team of military men was at my school, telling me my father was missing too. Not to mention, all the other crap that had happened in the past week.

"I told you, I don't care about a man I don't know. Unless you can help me find my brother, I don't want to hear about a man you say is my father. He's not here, so he doesn't care. Don't make it sound like he does."

Webb glanced behind me as if looking for help on how to respond.

I tossed a look over my shoulder to find the guards weren't staring straight ahead. No, they were both looking at me. They had their names embroidered on their shirts. The one on the right was Tripp, and the other guard was Sloan. Their berets each had a gold emblem with "Jupiter Sentinels" embroidered on it. On one side of their belts, each had a cell phone clipped on, and from the opposite side dangled a leather object that looked like some type of police baton.

I swallowed thickly as I considered Webb. When I did, the vein in his neck caused my pulse to quicken. I counted each beat as it pumped blood through his body.

Suddenly, my upper gums ached. The lust for blood overwhelmed me. Panic stole my breath. *Oh my God, what is happening to me?*

I rose, but the muscles in my legs instantly relaxed. A wave of warmth swept over me, and I fell gently back into the chair. It was a feeling I couldn't quite discern.

What just happened? I felt groggy, as if I had just taken a sleeping pill. My eyelids were heavy. I blinked several times in succession to keep them from closing.

I glowered at Lieutenant London. "What are you doing to me?"

"Tripp." He nodded.

A hand touched my shoulder. I flicked my head up, and Tripp's bronze eyes were peering down at me. As his hand squeezed my shoulder blade, his eyes slowly changed to a deep coal black with a red ring circling the outer edges. All of sudden, the groggy feeling dissipated. Tripp's eyes returned to their bronze color as he let go of my shoulder and stepped back.

Whoa! I wondered if the immortal world did exist, as Ms. Costner had explained. Maybe Pythagoras was right about that three-world theory. I sat in limbo between two of them, the Inferior and the Superior. "Who are you guys? You're not the military."

"We're just like you," Webb replied as if I should know what he meant.

I moistened my lips then bit the bottom one. "Like me?"

"Yes, Jo." He paused and nodded at his guards. "A natural-born vampire."

I stopped breathing. My jaw dropped. *Did he just say "vampire"? It's not possible. Vampires don't exist.*

Suddenly, I was more alone than ever.

12

A fire raced through my limbs, trying to process this new information. Webb had said the word "vampire" and not just that, but "natural-born vampire."

I desperately wanted to run—to find somewhere to hide. I squeezed my eyes shut as tears threatened to spill. I desperately needed Sam.

A hand touched my arm, jarring from the haze I was in. "Jo?" Webb whispered in my ear. His voice was velvety and smooth, awakening my limbs, causing me to twitch.

Tilting his strong jaw, he studied me through those mile-long lashes, which only served to make me fidget once again.

The walls of Mr. Jackson's office seemed to be

closing in. I couldn't get the word "natural-born vampire" out of my head. I took in a gulp of air then swallowed. "What do you mean by 'natural-born'...?" The word was caught in the back of my throat.

Until a week ago, I had never picked up a book about vampires or anything related to one. They just plain freaked me out. But now, the images of the books in the funeral home were swimming before me. I even had two of the books in my backpack, which was sitting somewhere. Between the books, the fanged man outside the hospital room, and hearing Webb speak about vampires as if it was the most natural thing in the world, I pinched myself, making sure I wasn't dreaming.

"Vampire," Webb intoned. "Jo, you're not a vampire yet. Right now, you only carry the gene. Those of us who are born with the vampire gene are normal mortals up to the time we choose not to be. However, at the age of sixteen or thereabouts, your body will start to go through what we call *vampire puberty* in preparation for the change." He dipped his head, gesturing at Tripp, who was beside Webb with hands cupped below his belt.

I wanted to scream and laugh all at the same time.

"For example, Jo," Tripp started to say in a deep but gentle voice. "For me, my gums started hurting when I was fifteen. I reached puberty early. Then, at seventeen, I discovered I liked the taste of blood."

Like Webb, Tripp didn't look a day over twenty-one. His sandy-blond hair was cut short with the sides shaved just above the ears.

"One of the first things that usually happens is your eyes change colors," Webb said. "You'll notice this when your emotional state alters in some way. But all this depends on your genetic makeup." Webb flicked his head at Tripp. "He craved blood to the point it became a drug for him."

My brain couldn't wrap itself around that idea that blood was a drug or any of what they were saying. Yet he just described me. My eyes were changing colors. I craved blood, and my gums had started aching a few minutes ago. I didn't know if I should be relieved that I wasn't crazy or panicked by the idea that I had a thirst for blood—or even worse, that I might be a vampire.

I squirmed in my seat. "You said I wasn't a vampire yet. Will I be?" I held my breath, not sure I wanted to know the answer. My inner voice kept telling me to get out of there and run as far away as possible.

"That depends," Webb replied. "Some people choose to cross over. Others are forced to become one."

I didn't like the latter part of his response. With my luck, I was going to be forced. "It doesn't happen naturally?" I bit the inside of my cheek, hoping he would say no.

The door squeaked open, and Mr. Jackson entered. "I'm sorry. I need to get some keys out of my desk."

"We're through here for now. Any luck finding Sam?" Webb asked Mr. Jackson.

We were far from through. In fact, we hadn't even scratched the surface. We had a lot to talk about. I still had a ton of questions.

I was curious what Mr. Jackson would think if he knew I was a... natural-born vampire. The words "crazy," "loony," and "nuts" popped into my head. He undoubtedly would call his friend Chief Garrett and have me committed.

Mr. Jackson fished around in the top desk drawer. "No. Manny, my head of security, checked all the places Sam was supposed to be during school this morning. The only person we haven't questioned yet is this McDonald kid that Ben saw Sam speaking to. His dad picked him up just before second period for a dental appointment."

That's right. I'd forgotten about McDonald, the kid in the parking lot this morning—the one talking with his friend about the janitor being dead.

"Is this McDonald student returning to school today?" Webb asked.

Mr. Jackson dangled the keys he'd pulled out of his drawer. "Not sure. I'll have Gail contact his parents."

"I know it's still during school hours, but I would like to take Jo back to headquarters, if that's all right with you?" Webb requested.

I stiffened. "I'm not going with you. I need to find Sam."

"Jo, we're not done with our conversation. Plus, I would like to give Mr. Jackson back his office. We can continue where we left off. My team will have more information for me on their progress with finding Sam," he replied.

He gave Tripp a commanding stare. Then Tripp left.

Mr. Jackson pocketed the keys as he knelt near my chair, placing his hand on mine.

"Jo, it's best if you go with Lieutenant London. His team has the resources to help us. Will you be okay? If not, you don't have to go."

I choked back tears. It was the first time that an adult was giving me a choice. I'd always been pushed around and told what to do. No one had ever asked me what I wanted or what I thought. Mr. Jackson acted as an actual father figure, not one who wanted something except an answer, which was new to me.

I leaned down and whispered, "What if these guys are with the man who was chasing us?"

"They're not. I had them checked out while you were in here talking with them," he whispered back. "I'll notify Lieutenant London if I find any hint of Sam or where he might be. Okay?" His voice rose above a whisper.

I wasn't sure if going with the Jupiter Sentinels was the right thing to do or even if I could trust them, but if Mr. Jackson trusted them, I figured it would be okay. Besides, I had to do something other than wait around. If Sam were in my shoes, he would be out there looking for me. I had to help in some way. If I could get more information from Webb about who I was, maybe it would lead to Sam.

"Lieutenant, we'll talk later," Mr. Jackson said.

"I can drop Jo off at your place this afternoon, if that's all right?" Webb removed his beret from his back pocket.

"That would be great. Jo, do you need to stop at your locker before you leave?" Mr. Jackson asked.

"No, sir." I rose from the chair, and my knees wobbled. I guessed I'd been sitting for too long without moving. Regardless, I grabbed the arm of the chair to steady my balance as I inhaled then exhaled. *I can do this. I need to do this to find Sam.*

Once I was steady on two feet, I searched the room for my backpack but didn't see it. Then I remembered I had left it outside the office. Webb followed my line of sight, picked up my bag, and slung it over his shoulder. I guessed that was my cue to hurry up.

I thanked Mr. Jackson for all his help then walked out and right into Darcy.

She threw her arms around me. "Hey, are you okay? I ran into Ben when I was leaving Mr. Grant's office. He told me about Sam." She gave me a fierce hug.

Tears were threatening to overflow. If I started crying, I was afraid I wasn't going to stop. I had to be strong. I had to fight. "I'm fine." My voice was quiet and sounded strangely distant.

She released me. "Bull. You're not fine. I know you. You're as fragile as they come."

"Thanks for the vote of confidence, friend." I skewered a look her way.

She peeked around me. "Who's the hunk in fatigues?" Her lips were curled at the ends, and, if I wasn't mistaken, I could hear her heart racing. Sometimes, her attention span was the size of an ant's, constantly shifting from one subject to another.

"He's too old for you."

"He's barely over twenty, if I had to guess," she shot back. "Are you leaving with him?"

I nodded.

"How do I get on that train?" She was still sizing up Webb.

I snapped my fingers. "Focus, Darcy."

"Sorry." She shook her head a few times. "Why are you going with Gorgeous Brownie Locks?"

"He might be able to help find Sam. He came here to speak to me and Sam about—"

Webb gently touched my arm. "Let's go, Jo."

I raised my eyebrows at Darcy and shrugged. "I should be back at Mr. Jackson's later."

"Don't worry, girl. Sam will show up," she said.

As Webb escorted me out, I prayed that Darcy was right, but my intuition was screaming at me— something was very wrong.

13

The halls were buzzing with students inside and out. In the courtyard, kids were seated at benches, eating their lunches. The thought of food made my stomach perk up. I wondered if natural-born vampires could still eat human food when they became vampires or if they were restricted to just... blood. That thought made my stomach churn, but I wasn't sure if that was a good thing or not.

Once outside, a small ray of sunshine shone through the thin clouds, and I came to a screeching halt.

"What's wrong?" Webb asked.

I furrowed my brows. "The sun's out."

"So? Keep moving," he commanded.

"Aren't vampires sensitive to the sun, or it burns them, or something like that?"

"You read too many myths. I need you to keep walking." His voice had a nervous tone to it as he nudged me.

I resumed putting one foot in front of the other. Up ahead, standing next to a black sedan with tinted windows, was Tripp. He was holding the handle on the back door.

Webb nodded.

Boy, they did a lot of nodding and little talking. *How do they know what the other is saying? Can they mind speak or something since they're vampires?*

Webb scanned the area with mechanical precision, all while touching my elbow, ensuring he didn't lose physical contact with me. I guessed he was cautious since Sam had gone missing, but I was sure it was also the military order of business to be as guarded as he could be.

As we got closer to the car, Tripp opened the door and jerked up his head. Webb snapped his head to the left in the same direction.

I followed suit but didn't see anything. Several trees obstructed my view, but I was hanging out with vampires. I assumed their auditory and sensory perceptions were heightened. Then again, Webb had said not to believe everything I'd read about vampires. Little did he know that I'd barely read a thing about them. My knowledge of vampires stemmed from listening to Darcy and the other kids at school who were gaga over the undead creatures.

"We need to walk faster, Jo." He pressed on his ear and said, "Make sure Sloan has the car in gear."

"What's wrong?" I asked.

I couldn't figure out what they were worried about. A school security guard stood motionless at his post near the gate. It didn't appear that he heard anything.

"Where are they?" Webb asked.

I didn't know if he was talking to me, but when I looked at Webb, his head was forward, eyes fixed on Tripp. Then I shifted my glance slightly. A small plastic device was embedded in Webb's ear.

So that's how they talk to one another.

"Shit!" he said.

We were steps from the car when Webb ripped my backpack off his shoulder and threw it at Tripp. He barely caught it. I was about to protest when Webb palmed my head and guided me into the car.

"In! Now, Jo!" His voice was curt, words clipped.

Webb slid in next to me. Tripp slung my backpack onto Webb's lap. He shut the back door then jumped into the front seat.

"Go! Go!" Tripp told Sloan.

Sloan hit the gas, and the car jerked forward.

The security guard shouted, but I couldn't hear him. He probably didn't like the way Sloan peeled out of the parking space. I knew I didn't. I wouldn't be surprised if I got whiplash.

"What're you guys so nervous about?" I asked as I glanced out the back window. I didn't see any cars behind us.

"Charlie two, come in," Tripp called.

"Charlie two, go," a man's voice blared through the car speaker.

"We got a bogie. We'll head them off at Crest and Skylark. It's deserted in that part of town. Send backup to meet us there," Tripp rattled into a speaker located somewhere in the car.

"Alpha one, ETA?" said the voice on the other end of the speaker.

"Twelve," Tripp returned.

"Ten-four. Team engaged and en route. Charlie two out."

Sloan was speeding through neighborhood side streets, barely pausing at stop signs.

I closed my eyes and prayed that I would at

least make it alive to wherever they were taking me. I prayed that I would see Sam again.

I was beginning to think I should have stayed with Mr. Jackson. My stomach churned as if piranhas were swimming around. Between the road bumps and the quick jerks of the car, I was about to lose the Lucky Charms I had eaten for breakfast. When I opened my eyes, the trees along the sides of the road were passing like blips on a radar screen.

Webb sat calmly, watching the road, and I couldn't help but think how he wasn't ready to puke. Upon closer inspection, his skin had a sun-kissed glow, which I found odd given he was a vampire. They were supposed to be pale.

"Is there a problem, Jo?" Webb asked. "You know it's impolite to stare."

I grabbed my backpack off his lap, unzipped the inner compartment, and rummaged around in the bottom until I found the package of Pop-Tarts that I had taken from Mr. Jackson's house that morning. I had to eat something to settle my nerves. I was so focused on ripping open the wrapper that I hurriedly set my backpack between Webb and me when it fell to the floor. The book I borrowed from the funeral home, *The Science Be-*

hind Vampires, fell out. *Shoot!* I rushed to pick it up, but Webb grabbed it first.

Before he could say anything, I blurted out, "I'm doing research for my literature class. We're studying the occult. I had to choose a topic." *Geez, I sound like a babbling idiot.*

"How appropriate, then." Webb handed the book back to me.

I shoved it into my backpack as fast as I could when Sloan slammed on the brakes. The forward motion propelled me headfirst into the back of Sloan's seat.

"Get down, Jo," Webb shouted.

"I am down," I snapped. My head was spinning.

"Stay down, then," Webb said before he jumped out.

"Take the car around," Tripp ordered as he hopped out as well.

"Charlie two, come in," Sloan said in a calm tone.

"Charlie two, go."

"Where's backup? We're at Crest and Skylark."

"Two minutes out. They had a problem at Fifth and Main."

The speaker went silent. My heart raced as adrenaline surged through me.

As Sloan turned a corner, I gaped over my shoulder as Webb's foot connected with a man's face. The guy fell to the ground, but within a second, he jumped to his feet as if he wasn't even hurt. Webb's opponent raised his elbow and swung, hitting the bottom of Webb's chin. His head bounced back then forward. The man's other elbow lifted. Then they disappeared from my view as the car rounded the side street.

Sloan parked the sedan. "Jo, keep the doors locked and stay in the car," he instructed. "I'll be at the corner. You'll be able to see me the entire time. Backup should be here shortly." Then he climbed out and pressed the key fob and locked me in.

I watched him jog to the corner with his hand at his side, holding the brown leather baton. Then I scanned the area quickly. The building across the street had several broken windows. Just beyond the building on the same side sat an empty lot surrounded by a crinkled chain-link fence. When I looked in Sloan's direction, my heart stopped beating—he was gone.

I snapped my head around, searching every corner and space. But the street was deserted. Daylight dimmed as a set of dark cumulus clouds rolled in. The wind picked up, accompanied by a sound like a can rolling along the pavement out-side the car door.

A loud bang jarred my attention forward. Shards of glass from the windshield flew at me, splattering against my face. I threw my hands up to block the debris, but it was too late. I gently patted the bottom of my chin and searched the area around my face. I let out a deep breath, thankful that the glass didn't stick in my Cliff-in-flicted wound. The area around my mouth wasn't so lucky.

I grabbed the door handle and pulled. But the door wouldn't open. I pushed the automatic lock button—nothing happened. I tried the handle again—no luck. *Shit! Shit! Shit!*

Warm fluid trickled down from my upper lip, on the brink of slipping into my mouth. The aroma of the blood caused hunger to stir within me. I patted my mouth with my fingers then stared at the burgundy stain. I inhaled, taking in the sweet fragrance. I was about to taste my candied blood when a light reflected off the rearview mir-ror. I jerked up my head and caught an image of a girl with red dots peppering her chin, as if she had just broken out with chickenpox. *Is that me? It can't be.* The person staring back didn't have silver eyes. She didn't even have the blue-green eyes Ben had described. The face in the mirror had black eyes with a ring of fire circling the outer edges.

I was just moving closer to the mirror when the side window shattered. I threw my arms over my head, then the door opened. A large hand reached in and grabbed me. I squirmed, kicking my way out of the car. He wrapped his arm around my waist and lifted me.

I craned my neck, trying to steal a look at my attacker. The man holding me wore a blue bandana over his head. I screamed.

"Be still," he said.

"It's you!" I shouted. "You were at the hospital. What did you do to my brother?" I asked, wriggling.

"I said be still!"

I clutched his hand with both of mine, and the nail of my pinky finger got caught in a gold ring he wore. When my gaze landed on the engraved insignia, I gasped.

The symbol matched the tattoo that Neil had had on his neck. Before I could process it, my attacker shook me.

I kicked and wiggled, trying to break free.

"Stop moving," he growled.

"No. What did you do with my brother?"

He reached into his pocket and produced a syringe. He tried to uncap it with the hand that had me in a vice grip. I tried to snag it, but he jerked it out of my way. The needle was two inches in length and looked like something a veterinarian would use on a horse.

"Oh no. You're not sticking me with that," I shouted.

"Stop moving, will you?" He adjusted his grip on my body, squeezing my waist tighter.

"You're hurting me!" I kicked and lifted my arms behind me, ready to scratch his face, but I couldn't turn my body well enough to do any damage.

"Let her go, Jonah," a familiar voice called.

I snapped my head around. Webb stood ten feet in front of us. He grabbed the leather baton strapped to his belt and removed it. It looked like the same device that Tripp and Sloan wore on their belts, only Webb's contraption was red.

A click echoed around us as Webb engaged the thin baton device as a blade emerged from its housing. At the base of the blade, a piece of metal extended perpendicular to the handle. Another click sounded, and as if in slow motion, the flat-edge knife extended into a three-foot sword. It whistled as metal slid across metal, snapping the blades into place. Webb held on to the grip with two hands and pointed it into the air. The double-edged blade glistened, projecting a blue hue around the edges.

My mouth gaped open as the sword came to life. My heart pounded against my chest. I knew Webb wasn't going to hurt me, but the thug who held me was holding a horse needle, ready to stab me. Jonah, or whoever he was, grunted a few times as he wrestled with something, but I couldn't see what.

Webb was motionless. *What the heck is he waiting for? This goon to stab me?* Then Jonah loosened his grip. I tilted my head to see what he was doing. As I did, he blew something out of his mouth. The plastic tip that covered the needle rolled off the pavement into the street.

Webb took one step forward.

"Don't do it, London," Jonah ordered, "or I'll stick her with this. You know what'll happen."

"Happen?" I asked. My adrenaline was at an all-time high as my pulse flew off the charts. A spark fired, and I bristled.

Fear and rage propelled me forward. I couldn't wait for Webb to make his move. This goon was going to use me as a pincushion. I twisted, kicked, and pulled on the hand that was wrapped around me.

Jonah squeezed tighter, cutting off the circulation in my stomach.

I looked at Webb, trying to speak but couldn't.

Webb stalked slowly toward us as Jonah edged backward.

I fixated on Webb. His eyes were no longer blue but had turned pitch-black, and his fangs had descended. I was mesmerized. I didn't realize until now how real the whole vampire thing was. He looked fearless with the sword in his hands, fangs exposed.

He dropped his left hand from the grip of the sword, raised it parallel to the ground, then lowered it. His lips were moving, but the words were inaudible.

I furrowed my brows and shook my head.

"Down, now!" he shouted.

I bent over as Jonah squeezed me tighter, stealing the air from my lungs. As my head bobbed, my chin hit his hand, and a piece of glass pushed in deeper.

I stifled a scream.

Without thinking, I bit his hand as hard as I could.

"You little witch!" Jonah barked as he released his grip.

I fell to the pavement, rolled off into the thin

layer of grass that edged the sidewalk, and scurried to my feet.

I plastered myself against a tree, breathing hard as Webb glided toward Jonah. He had both hands on the grip of his sword again, with the blade angled upward, ready to strike.

Jonah threw the syringe down then removed a dagger from a side pocket of his cargo pants. He gripped it so that the tip of the blade and his forearm were facing Webb.

I stared at the two, wondering how it would end. Just as Webb raised his sword, his opponent fell to the ground.

Snapping my head to the left, I sucked in a deep breath. It couldn't be.

My gaze shifted between the guy with the baseball bat and Jonah, who was already on his feet, his dagger aimed at Ben.

Webb wielded his sword at Jonah, missing him by an inch as Jonah lunged for Ben.

I screamed and ran toward Ben. I was inches from him when Webb grabbed me.

"No. Get back," he snapped.

"Jonah, it's our fight, not his," Webb said as he flicked his head at Ben.

Jonah whirled around with his fangs bared.

My head spun. This whole scene was too surreal. I didn't understand why vampires were chasing Sam and me. I couldn't even comprehend what they wanted with us.

Webb swung his sword, and the blade whistled as it sliced through the air. Jonah raised his right leg in some type of karate kick and knocked the sword out of Webb's hands. It was Jonah and his dagger against Webb, who was now weaponless.

As the two vampires fought, their karate moves sent the brawl into the middle of the street.

"You okay?" I asked Ben

He stood motionless and wide-eyed.

I slapped his face. "Ben, snap out of it."

He regarded me absently before focusing again on the two vampires in the street.

A black Jeep rounded the corner then screeched to a halt. A man and a woman jumped out. Both wore the same style uniforms as Webb, so I assumed they were both Jupiter Sentinels. Tripp and Sloan emerged from behind the Jeep.

The woman pulled a gun from its holster. The man with her had a crossbow in his hands. Tripp and Sloan carried swords, the blades extended and ready for battle.

The four Sentinels surrounded Webb and Jonah.

"You don't have a chance," Webb said as he lunged at Jonah.

"Olivia, now," Tripp called.

She pulled the trigger, and Jonah dropped to his knees, his body jerking on the way down. It wasn't a gun—it was a Taser. The metal strings stuck to the large vampire as smoke erupted from his body. When Jonah was down, Sloan reached out with gloved hands, grabbed Jonah's arms, twisted them behind his back, and secured two-inch metal shackles around his wrists. As he squeezed them together, a small amount of smoke erupted from underneath, as if his wrists were on fire. I guessed they would need something sturdier and more lethal than ordinary handcuffs to hold a vampire.

Sloan gripped his prisoner's arm before depositing him into Olivia's Jeep.

Webb retrieved his sword from the sidewalk, retracted it, then clipped it to his belt. "Why were you two late?" Webb barked as he straightened his uniform. "This better be good."

"Sir, one of the Plutariums sideswiped us back at Fifth Street. It was like they knew our route," Olivia explained.

"Return to headquarters and prepare the meeting room," Webb ordered.

"Yes, sir," Olivia replied. She withdrew her cell phone and pushed a few buttons while taking long strides over to her Jeep, her partner in tow.

"Tripp?" Webb waved his right hand. "Radio command and let them know we have another human returning with us."

Tripp nodded and traipsed off toward the sedan that we drove in.

Ben was sitting on the grassy edge of the sidewalk with his head in his hands.

I didn't blame him. All this was freaking me out too. While I'd had some time to process it back in Mr. Jackson's office, hearing about it and seeing it were two completely different things.

I touched Ben's arm. "Hey, you okay?"

"What's going on?" His voice was stifled. "Who are these people?"

"They're military. They call themselves the Jupiter Sentinels. Some Navy SEAL team."

"They're not Navy SEALs. They're va—"

"I know."

I couldn't say anything else. I couldn't bring myself to tell him I might be one of them. I had to give him time to process all of this. I'm not sure I believed it myself.

Webb picked up the needle that Jonah was

going to use on me. "Ben, you'll need to come with us. We can take you home later today."

Ben didn't move.

I had no idea what lay ahead. What I did know was I needed someone other than vampires to accompany me. Plus, I wanted to make sure nothing happened to Ben.

"Ben, come on. You can keep me company. It's bad enough without Sam. Then Webb will take both of us back to your house." I grabbed his hand. "Do this for me and Sam. Please?"

Nodding, he pushed to his feet.

I slid into the car first, and Ben followed. Webb climbed in on the other side of me. Sloan was behind the wheel, while Tripp sat in the front seat. I hoped that Sloan's driving would be better this time unless we were ambushed again. Olivia and her partner were in the Jeep ahead of us, sitting idle with the prisoner in the back.

I wasn't sure what happened to the guy Webb had fought with earlier. There had to be a few of them. *What did Olivia call them?* I gnawed the inside of my lip, struggling to remember, hoping it would come to me.

As the car moved, Ben leaned back and closed his eyes.

I wanted to steal a look at Webb and pepper

him with questions. But one, I was afraid he would snap at me again, and two, I knew he wouldn't answer.

So I kept my eyes forward and found Sloan's green-eyed gaze staring at me in the rearview mirror.

"Sir, do you want me to alert Dr. Vieira that he needs to prep the room?" Sloan asked.

My eyebrows lifted. "Prep the room? Who died?"

"Your face is a mess, Jo," Webb replied.

Has my zombie look returned? I couldn't seem to get away from it. Maybe Blake was right when he said, "You can't change creepy."

"What else is new?" I muttered.

Sighing, I mimicked Ben and closed my eyes. Nausea threatened in the pit of my stomach. I didn't want to think about all the scars that would crisscross my face. Out of nowhere, I remembered the name Olivia had used for the attacker.

My eyes flew open, and I blurted out, "What does 'Plutariums' mean?"

"Not for discussion," Webb said in a snide tone.

Again, I knew he wouldn't answer, but I wanted to ask anyway. "What was that guy going to inject me with?"

Webb kept his attention straight ahead. "Again, not for discussion."

"I think he kidnapped Sam." I said as a matter of fact.

"What makes you think that?" Webb asked.

"He was the guy who was outside my hospital room. The one who put the cop in a coma."

All eyes were on me, except Ben's.

I must've said something interesting or hit a nerve.

Webb pinned me with a hard look before a sudden wave of fog flowed through me. He was doing that thing again with his eyes.

I shook my head and broke eye contact with him. "Stop it. I know you're doing something to make me dizzy. I get it—you don't want to talk about it."

"We're almost there, sir," Tripp announced, breaking the tension.

I crossed my arms over my chest. Webb wasn't going to tell me a whole lot, which was fine for the time being. I wasn't about to give up.

14

The car stopped at the gate to the Jupiter Sentinels' headquarters. Two security guards manned the first entrance. Two more sentries stood outside their posts ahead of another gate.

We drove through both after the guards searched the car—not once, but twice. Camouflage-patterned buildings dotted both sides of the road as it twisted and turned. The cement structures blended well with an assortment of evergreen and deciduous trees that towered over them.

When we rounded the last curve, an old building emerged. A dilapidated sign hung from its hinges, indicating that the site had once belonged to Stafford Textiles. The brick edifice was four stories high and flanked by two similar buildings. All three had a black iron fence lining the rooftops with guards patrolling the perimeters. Each carried large guns, watching for any threats below. I felt like I was entering a maximum security prison, especially given the iron bars covering the windows.

Stationed at the entrance of the steel double doors were four guards, each armed with a full-length sword strapped to his belt, a knife holstered at his waist, and an extremely large gun hanging from his shoulder.

Ben had his head pressed against the window. Tripp wrote something on a notepad. Webb, as usual, stared straight ahead. I wrapped my hand around the top handle of my backpack and began to tap my foot.

Webb placed his hand on my knee. "You don't have to be nervous."

Easy for you to say. You're not the one freaking out. You don't have a brother missing... And yeah, you just told me that I'm on the verge of becoming a vampire.

"Do you think your team will have news about Sam?" I asked. "Maybe Jonah will tell you where he is."

"I doubt that," Webb replied.

"Why? Just threaten him with that horse needle. Maybe then he'll tell you," I countered.

Tripp laughed.

I regarded Ben. "How are you doing?"

He shrugged. For Ben not to speak suggested that he wasn't processing very well. He'd thought my eyes changing colors was cool, but vampires? Probably not so much.

After Sloan parked in front of the building, all of us got out.

"Things will be fine. They're not going to hurt us," I said to Ben at my side.

"I know. It's just...."

"Let's concentrate on finding Sam," I said.

Two of the guards stood at attention while holding open the ten-foot steel doors. I wasn't sure I was ready. I wasn't ready to believe Webb and the whole natural-born vampire thing, even though a lot of what Tripp and Webb had described had my name written all over it. Plus, it was hard not to believe in vampires when I'd witnessed Webb's fangs in action, along with his opponent's.

I scanned the surrounding area. Olivia's Jeep was nowhere to be found, and I wondered where they'd taken Jonah. The building was large enough to house a small city of people, and I imagined the place had a jail for criminal vampires or whatever they called them in the vampire world. Something told me I was about to learn more about the creatures than I ever wanted to know.

As soon as I strode across the threshold, chills peppered my arms. As I peered over my shoulder, I had an eerie feeling that I was saying goodbye to a world I hated but entering into a one I wasn't ready for.

The air was brisk inside, and the atmosphere had a tinge of sterility. In front of me, a circular desk was centered in the entryway of the Jupiter Sentinels' headquarters. A petite woman sat behind the desk with a phone headset on, talking to someone on the other end. Just beyond the desk was a set of elevators, guarded by two armed sentinels, and above the silver doors hung a plaque with the following message:

Jupiter Sentinels
A SEAL Team Community
We protect the Superior World from all enemies,
human and non-human, and uphold the laws of our
existence. We strive to shield and protect the Inferior
World from those who seek harm upon them.

MY HEART STOPPED. I had to read it again because I couldn't believe it—Pythagoras was right with his theory about three worlds. A part of me was beginning to believe that maybe Ms. Costner wasn't even human.

The squeaking sound of the doors sliding against the floor jarred me out of my trance, and as the steel doors closed behind me, I cringed.

Ben touched my shoulder. "Here we are."

"Yep, here we are," I repeated.

"Now what?" he asked.

"No clue."

Ben took in his surroundings. "Do you think they know where Sam is?"

"I hope so," I said. "Why did you follow us, anyway? If your dad finds out...."

"I wanted to help. Sam is my best friend and like a brother to me."

"Well, you sure stepped in vampire shit."

"So did you," Ben countered.

I sighed, puffing out my cheeks. "You don't know the half of it." *I* didn't even want to know.

The elevator doors opened, and a short, squat man wearing a white lab coat ambled out. With his hands in his pockets and a stethoscope wrapped around his neck, he scrutinized Ben and me through his thick, black-rimmed, square glasses. Embroidered on his coat at chest level was the name Dr. Vieira.

"He's gunning for you, Jo," Ben said.

I snorted. "He could be coming for you. He might have orders from the fearless leader, Webb, to put you in a straitjacket or maybe erase your memory."

Ben paled. "Not funny, girl."

I wasn't kidding, but I wouldn't tell Ben that. Webb might have had something planned for Ben, since he was human. I was still human, and Blue Eyes might have had plans for me as well.

Dr. Vieira cleared his throat. "Oh my. You look awful."

Ben chuckled. "You do, you know."

I slapped Ben's arm. "You want to stay human? Or should I ask Webb to turn you into a vampire?"

Dr. Vieira reached out with a stiff hand. "Jo, it's so nice to finally meet you. My name is Dr. Damon Vieira. I'm the resident doctor for the Jupiter Sentinels."

I was curious if he was a vampire too.

"You look just like your father," he said as we shook hands.

"Your father? They know your dad?" Shock rode Ben's tone.

"Let's get you cleaned up. Follow me." He flicked his head toward the elevators. "The medical facility is on the fourth floor." He nodded to the guards, and one of them pushed the elevator button.

I tossed a look over my shoulder. Webb and Tripp were engrossed in some heated discussion near the entrance—Webb didn't budge when the elevator dinged.

I tugged on Ben's arm to follow me.

Dr. Vieira held the elevator door, his glare urging us to hurry.

"Do you think it's safe?" Ben asked.

I tucked strands of my black hair behind my ear. "We'll find out, won't we?"

Once we were in the elevator, Dr. Vieira focused on his phone as his fingers danced across the buttons.

"Is your dad... you know... a...?" Ben asked.

I shrugged. I didn't have enough information about my so-called father to answer Ben's question. Besides, I didn't want to know. My father had abandoned Sam and me a long time ago. To me, he was dead. My life was Sam and no one else.

Two minutes later Dr. Vieira was escorting us

down a long hallway and then another until we reached a steel door. On the side of it, a small box glowed, and Dr. Vieira pressed a button. When a beep sounded, he positioned his eyes directly opposite the translucent bar on the top of the panel. After another beep, the steel door slid open.

"Follow me," Dr. Vieira said.

Ben and I did as we were told as chills crept up my arms. The lights above illuminated as we traveled down another long corridor. At the end, Dr. Vieira pushed open a set of double doors. It reminded me of when Sam and I escaped from Highland Memorial—only this time, I was entering, not exiting. It was a long shot, but maybe Sam would sneak in and rescue me again.

The inside of the clinic didn't look anything like a hospital. The large, open room was divided into two areas. Against the left wall was a gray metal box with a slatted roller door. Above it was a hooded vent. A stainless-steel bench lined both sides of the metal box. In front of it, a black lab bench traveled the length of the room with small openings on each end for access to the area between the two structures. A refrigerator and a sink lined the back wall, and cabinets were to the right, ending at an entrance.

We followed Dr. Vieira, passing four desks on

our right. A beep sounded before a computer screen on one of the desks came to life. After several other beeps, a printer next to the computer sprang into action.

"We'll go into that back room, near the cabinets," Dr. Vieira said, pointing to his right.

Once inside, Dr. Vieira instructed me to sit on the leather bench that had white paper on it while Ben stood next me.

Dr. Vieira proceeded to wash his hands at the sink in the room before donning a pair of nitrile gloves. Then he picked up the tweezers from an assortment of medical instruments that were laid out on a paper towel on the counter adjacent to the sink.

"This might hurt," he said. He lightly grabbed my chin and tilted my head back. "Don't move."

He plucked the first shard of glass embedded in my upper lip, just under my nose, and dropped it into a metal bin. The sound of the glass hitting metal made Ben jump.

Dr. Vieira removed four more pieces, which claimed the area below my bottom lip. Then he cleaned up the dried blood on my face. "I'm surprised the glass from the windshield did this to you. Normally, it wouldn't. All cars have safety glass to prevent major injuries," Dr. Vieira explained.

That might have been true, but he didn't see the force Jonah had put behind breaking the glass.

"Your stitches are dissolving nicely. Whoever sewed you up did a great job. You might not have a scar."

"Really? No scar?" Excitement filtered through in my voice. In a week that had consisted of attempted rape and finding out that vampires were real, it was the best news. No scar meant I could cross it off the bully list.

"I said you *might not* have a scar," Dr. Vieira repeated.

It didn't matter. It was exciting news. I made a mental note to find Dr. Case and thank him.

"The puncture holes are superficial, so they'll heal. You won't see any scars from the glass."

I silently shouted for joy. Maybe things were looking up. Maybe Webb would have good news about Sam.

Dr. Vieira finished cleaning my face. "I need to get a small amount of blood from you."

"Uh, why?" I asked.

"Just precaution. We need to ensure there are no infections. You've been through a lot. Since I can't get your records from the hospital, I need to verify that everything is okay."

It couldn't hurt. After all, I wasn't so sure about Dr. Case. Who was he, really? Besides, I needed to know if my blood type *was* actually AF negative.

Dr. Vieira gathered all the necessary tools to take a sample of my blood. Then he tied a rubber band around my left arm, just above the crease of my elbow. He patted the vein with two fingers. A second later, the vein pulsed into view. As he extracted my blood, his eyes changed from golden brown to black.

My vision blurred for a second.

He stared at me. His dark-black eyes had the same tint of red in them as mine had earlier... or maybe as they did now.

"Hey, man, the vial is full. Dr. Vieira, blood is leaking out!" Ben shouted.

I blinked.

"I'm so sorry. I don't know what got into me," Dr. Vieira said.

"I do, man. You're a vampire, and you're hungry," Ben replied. "You're not touching her, so don't even think about it." He regarded me. "What's going on? I thought your eyes changed from silver to blue-green. Now, they change to black? Are you... one of...?" He flicked his thumb at Dr. Vieira.

"No." I shook my head. "I don't know."

Ben's horrified expression returned, and he paled as he moved as far away from me as he could. Maybe part of him was starting to put the pieces together. Maybe he could fill me in if he figured it out.

Dr. Vieira was quiet as he placed a cotton ball under a Band-Aid on my arm. He washed and dried his hands. "Let's go. I'll escort you to Lieutenant London's office."

Ben kept his distance as we made our way back to the elevators as though he was frightened of me. I couldn't blame him.

"Are you one of them?" A hint of disgust laced Ben's voice.

"I told you, I don't know. I don't know if my dad is, either. All I know is I carry some sort of stupid vampire gene, which makes my eyes change colors. But right now, I'm still human. Do you have a problem with that?" Anger surged through me. I couldn't help that I had been born with an inhuman gene.

Ben raked his fingers through his hair then let out a deep sigh.

I tempered my anger. Again, I couldn't blame

him. "I'm not contagious. If you can't handle this, then I'm sure Webb can take you home, but I would like you to stay. I need another human to help me through this, and Sam needs both of us."

Ben stabbed a thumb at Dr. Vieira who was waiting for us at the end of hall. "Look, I don't agree with the whole vampire thing. While these guys seem nice and all, I don't want them sinking their teeth into me. I don't even want them near you. You don't even know for sure who these guys really are or if they're telling the truth about who you are. Until we know more, I'm not letting you out of my sight."

"Do you think you're going to keep vampires off you and me with a baseball bat?" I asked, trying to lighten the mood a little.

"Whatever works." His mouth curled up on one side, a dimple showing.

My heart fluttered slightly. "Mm-hmm. We saw how that went today." I smiled.

"Let's go." Dr. Vieira's voice echoed down the hall.

15

Webb's office was located on the second floor. As we rode the elevator down, my mind drifted, and I thought of my brother. Maybe he'd gone back to the funeral home looking for Neil. Then again, he would need a car to do that. My gut was telling me Jonah had something to do with Sam's disappearance.

"Jo?" Ben called.

The elevator doors had opened. Blinking, I shook off the thoughts of Sam lying in some ditch in the state forest and joined Ben. His cinnamon crop brightened beneath the LED lights in the hall.

Voices hummed nearby. A phone rang in the distance, and electricity floated in the air. I tried to discern the tingling feeling I kept experiencing. Maybe it had something to do with vampires. Maybe they emitted an electrical charge.

"In here." Dr. Vieira guided us into Webb's office.

With the phone to his ear, Webb stood near a small window adjacent to two bookcases with his back to us. He'd changed from his green fatigues to a black uniform. His cargo pants were tucked inside his boots and the leather sword strapped to his belt with the blade inside, hiding for his next victim.

Ben beelined it for the couch in the small sitting area while I glanced around. A credenza abutted the wall behind the desk. Several pictures, depicting a naval aircraft carrier, a drone airplane, two fighter jets, and a picture of the Pentagon dotted the walls along with a plaque with the same message as the one downstairs.

"Yes, sir," Webb said before lowering his phone and turning to face us.

I took in a big breath. I wasn't sure whether it was the way he looked at me or because he might have news about Sam that affected me so strongly.

He retrieved a coffee cup off his desk and cradled it in his hands. "Thanks, Dr. Vieira. I'll take it from here."

Is that blood in his cup? I inhaled. *Yep, it sure is.* Hunger pains surfaced, and I moistened my lips.

Dr. Vieira was about to leave when Webb called his name. "Dr. Vieira, take this." He handed Dr. Vieira the coffee cup.

Webb might have sensed my hunger. He looked at me with narrowed eyes. "Have a seat." He held out his hand, motioning me to join Ben who had his feet up on the coffee table.

I sat beside Ben while Webb commandeered one of the chairs opposite us.

"Ben, I've spoken to your father." Webb rested his elbows on his knees. "He's agreed to let you spend the night here at the compound. We should be able to get both of you to school in the morning. The barracks are on the third floor along with the mess hall. There are restrooms on each floor, with the exception of the fourth. That floor is off limits unless you're accompanied by Dr. Vieira."

I didn't care about the layout of the building. "What about Sam? Did you question Jonah?"

"We'll get to that in just a second," Webb replied. "Ben, Tripp is going to escort you to the mess hall. You can get something to eat. I need to speak with Jo for a few minutes."

Ben straightened. "I'm not leaving her alone with you. I saw what Dr. Vieira almost did."

Webb furrowed his brow.

"I want him to stay," I said. In fact, I needed Ben to stay. I needed a human to keep things real, to keep my sanity. I wasn't sure how much more I could handle. The secret was out. Ben had witnessed the vampires in action, so whatever else Webb had to say or tell me shouldn't surprise Ben.

Webb shifted his gaze between Ben and me, his brow still knitted as he contemplated my request. "Ben, you've seen a lot in the past couple of hours. I imagine you're struggling with the reality of it all. Sometimes, it's hard for humans to process vampires being in the mortal world. Regardless, I can't have you broadcasting the fact that vampires exist. The military has measures in place to prevent humans from doing so."

I drew in a breath as an eerie feeling washed over me. They were going to do something terrible to Ben. I could feel it in my bones.

Ben froze.

"Your dad told me that you're interested in joining the Navy SEALs. Is that true?" Webb asked.

Ben's eyes were unblinking. "If I can't make it in the major leagues, then, yes, I'm very interested in the Navy SEAL program."

Webb scrapped a hand across his jaw. "Well, this may be your taste of what's to come."

Ben blew out a breath. "I don't understand."

"How much do you know about the SEAL program?" Webb asked.

"I know that they go on secret missions and do all kinds of cool stuff," Ben replied.

That's right. I'd been on his computer the week before. Ben had been researching the SEAL program. I also recalled the letter from the navy on his nightstand, although I hadn't read what it said.

Webb smiled. "And why are you interested in the SEAL program?"

"Because I want to fight and protect my country. I feel that I can rid the world of the really bad people who want to kill us," Ben said proudly.

"Let me guess. Like SEAL Team Six did with Osama bin Laden?"

"Well, yeah."

Webb considered Ben. "Just about every kid in America has your dream. But only the toughest recruits make it through SEAL training. You have to be tough, physically and mentally... and I want to emphasize *mentally*. I can see your physical attributes might not be a problem, but with what I witnessed today, you're far from having the mental capability to withstand what it takes to be a SEAL."

I was amazed and confused as to whether Webb was trying to help Ben or scare him. I also couldn't make out if Ben was shocked at Webb's honesty or at the words Webb had delivered.

"You know nothing about me," Ben said.

Webb sat back. "Son, I know plenty. Do you think I would've let you in this facility, not knowing who you were or who your dad was? I know you were born on June eighth, sixteen years ago, to Travis and Victoria Jackson. I know your mother died last year of breast cancer."

Ben pushed out a shoulder. "So what? All that's public record."

"I also know you've been in trouble with the law and that police Chief Ron Garrett overlooked your little incident because he went to high school with your dad."

A muscle ticked in Ben's jaw. "Hey, that record was sealed and locked in Chief Garrett's office. No one's supposed to know about that."

My jaw came unhinged. "What did you do, Ben?"

"Nothing." He squeezed his hands together, rubbing one thumb over the other.

"Ben?" I nudged him.

He sighed heavily. "When my mother was going through chemo, I was… let's just say I wasn't happy. I had to attend some stupid political function for Mayor Edwards with my dad. The mayor said something to me, and I attacked him. The cops came in, and I was hauled down to the police station. That's it."

My eyes bugged out. Ben needed anger management, just like Sam. Maybe that was the reason Mr. Jackson had set up a class on anger management at school. I breathed a sigh of relief. The way Webb had set up the scene seemed far worse than what Ben had just told us.

"So, you got mad." I looked at Ben then glanced at Webb. "He got mad. What's the big deal?"

"Right now, there is no big deal. But Ben, as long as you're in this building, you will do as I say, and that means you obey my team as well. As I mentioned earlier, you've seen things that humans such as yourself could never imagine. And if you're serious about becoming a SEAL, now would be a good time to practice the secrecy that SEALs live by. We don't tolerate people who don't abide by the rules of the military… and more importantly, our code of ethics as SEALs. Our missions are covert, which means secrecy is the highest priority. Any violations of the rules and regulations will result in death."

Ben gasped. "SEALs don't kill their own team members."

Webb dipped his chin. "You're correct. SEALs don't kill their own, but my team is unique. Only a handful of humans know we exist. As you are aware, we aren't your normal SEAL team, which is why any breach of our existence or rules can only lead to death. Do you understand me?"

Ben's cheeks flushed crimson. I imagined he was still embarrassed at having to explain his run-in with the law, but he listened intently to every word that rolled off Webb's tongue. His expression shuddered through excitement and seriousness and ended up stolid as Webb explained the consequences.

Webb, on the other hand, I couldn't read. "Ben, do you understand?" Webb repeated.

Ben rose from the couch and paced the floor in front of the desk.

"Answer him," I begged.

He kept pacing with his hands in his jean pockets.

My heart raced. If Ben didn't agree, the Sentinels were going to kill him. I couldn't let that happen. He was family, Sam's best friend. Plus, there would be no way to tell Mr. Jackson that his son was dead. No, the only answer had to be yes. He had to agree to the rules that Webb laid out. "Ben? Say something," I pleaded.

"I'm not sure I can. How can I agree to something I don't know anything about? I don't know the rules, the laws, or any of the regulations. I'm not sure I even believe this vampire crap." Ben stopped pacing. "I would do anything for you and Sam. But I believe in a world where we live to grow old, have families, and then die." His voice quivered.

"You have to agree. You and your dad are like family. Sam's your best friend. Please, Ben."

Ben pinned me with daggers. "Would you?"

"I don't know that I have a choice." My voice wavered.

Webb plucked his phone from a pocket in his cargo pants, punched some keys, and waited. "Tripp, my office."

A second later, Tripp stalked in. "Sir?"

"Please take Ben upstairs," Webb commanded.

I swallowed hard. Tears pooled, threatening to spill over.

"Ben, let's go," Tripp said.

"*No!* You... you can't do this. Webb, you can't. Let him go. Please."

"Humans aren't ready to know that vampires exist," Webb said.

Tripp grabbed Ben by the arm and escorted him out of the room.

A blanket of fear washed over me. For the second time that day, my human existence shifted, and all those in it were disappearing, one by one.

16

An hour had passed, and I was pacing and biting my nails in front of the couch. Webb had left me in his office alone while he addressed some issue in the building. I prayed the issue didn't involve Ben. I prayed harder that Ben was okay. I started to tear up when Webb came in.

"How could you?" I ran over to him with my fingers balled into a fist, ready to swing.

He clamped down on my hand, strong and powerful. A seed of hatred sprouted, and my stomach clenched. I suddenly hated him. He had sentenced Ben to death.

"You need to calm down," he said in a tone that permitted no argument. He steered me to the couch. "Sit."

"I'm not a dog."

"I said to sit down." His nostrils flared.

It was the first time I detected a little impatience from the blue-eyed vampire. I was finally seeing the real side of Lieutenant Webb London. I crossed my arms over my chest then plopped onto the couch,

"You're a little dramatic," he said as frustration washed over him.

"What? You told Ben that if he didn't agree to keep a secret, you'd kill him. And you think *I'm* dramatic?"

He laughed and sank down on the cushion next to me. "Ben is the least of my worries."

"Oh, that's right. My father is more important to you." I pulled my knees into my chest.

He laughed again. He was an irritating vampire that I wanted to beat to a pulp. My brother was missing, Ben's neck was on the chopping block, and this annoying, blue-eyed creature was more worried about a man I didn't know and didn't care about.

Hours had passed since we'd arrived, and I hadn't seen any signs of Webb or his team doing anything to find my brother. Given all the security around the place, it was going to be hard to get out, but I had to try. I had to do something to find Sam.

He inched closer, his movement swift. "You're correct. Your father is important to me and to this team. But I haven't spent the last twelve years helping my best friend search for his children only to let your brother die or kill his friend. I'm not the monster you think I am."

His musky scent tickled my nose, and my stomach did a somersault. I lowered my head to my knees, refusing to look at him.

When he tucked a strand of hair behind my ear, chills rippled up my spine. I couldn't quite figure out why I kept having weird light-headed feelings every time he looked at me or touched me. He was handsome, but I'd never had any interest in dating or guys for that matter. Not like Darcy did.

"Look at me, Jo."

"No. You'll only try to mesmerize me or whatever you vampires do."

"It's called *compelling*. Vampires can compel humans to believe what we want them to believe. We in essence scramble their thoughts. We can even do it to some of the weaker vampires."

"So why have you been trying to compel me?"

"I haven't. I've been trying to calm you. You were so nervous in Mr. Jackson's office. Your heart was pumping as fast as it could. I was trying to ease your nerves so we could talk, so you would listen." He inhaled deeply. "I overdid it, so Tripp stepped in to prevent you from passing out."

I kept telling myself that none of what was happening was real. Maybe the more I said it, the more they would become human.

"You see, Jo, vampires have unique abilities. Not all of us have the same ones. For example, Tripp can relax people by the way he touches them."

I braced myself, not sure I wanted to know what Webb's special ability was. I raised my head. "And yours?"

"I can create a telepathic connection with another vampire."

I thought back to Mr. Jackson's office and how Webb kept nodding to his guards. He must've been speaking to them that way.

"Does that work on humans?" I prayed that he would say no. The thought of him getting into my head scared the shit out of me. I didn't want to hear his voice in my head. It was bad enough that I was becoming a ball of mush around him.

"It's been known to work on a select few of those with the vampire gene who haven't crossed over, but no, telepathy doesn't work on humans.

Basically, you're walking a fine line between being human and becoming a vampire."

I didn't know whether to be more worried that Webb might be able to get in my head or that I was on the verge of becoming a vampire. Either way, I wished the fine line that I was supposedly walking would lead me out of that building and away from this whole sordid situation. "I carry the vampire gene. So what?" The words spilled past my lips as if I was a spoiled brat. But I didn't care.

A muscle in his jaw ticked. "I explained earlier today that some people choose to become immortal, while others don't have a choice." He paused and dropped his gaze.

"Are you saying I don't?" I held my breath.

"I'm not sure yet. But I hope you do have a choice," he replied.

Despite how confused I was or how clouded my brain was about vampires existing, my choice was easy. There was no way I wanted to become a vampire. While some days, I wanted to die, today wasn't one of them. "What's the big deal?"

His vibrant blue eyes penetrated through me as though he was trying to get in my head. "In my world, we don't like to force those with the vampire gene to choose between mortality and immortality. Like the human world, we have laws—lots of them. But the one we honor and protect the most is the right to choose between my world and the human world. As you heard Ben say, he believes in growing old. Some people who carry the vampire gene want to experience that—they want to grow old. They want to be as human as they can be. When your destiny doesn't give you a choice..." His voice was sullen, and he sounded as if he had never had a choice.

I wanted to find my way, to escape the world I was trapped in. I wanted to be free to make my own decisions. But not as a vampire.

Yet I had one burning question that I needed answered. "You become a vampire, how?"

Webb shifted his position. "Since you carry the vampire gene, the only way for you to become immortal is to drink a pint of your father's blood."

A chill crawled up the back of my neck and pinched me hard. "So, you don't become a vampire by another one biting you?"

The corners of his mouth curled. "Didn't I tell you not to believe everything you read? If I were to bite you now, all I would do is either satisfy my hunger or drain you of all your blood."

I unfolded my legs and scooted away from him. As I blinked, I thought I saw him lick his lips.

He was a pretty vampire, but I didn't want to be his snack.

"Don't worry. I know how to control my hunger."

Suddenly, I wasn't so sure because his eyes changed slightly, and flecks of red dotted his cobalt-blue eyes.

"A pint, huh? And then..." I snapped my fingers. "I materialize into a vampire?"

He ignored me. "It's a complicated process, and I'm not going into the details."

Anger rose, stinging my cheeks. "Then how do you expect me to believe anything you say? I don't know even know why I'm here. You say I carry the vampire gene and my father is missing. I don't know where Sam is or if he's dead. And that's just the beginning of my long list of what's happening in my world. Oh, and I'm sitting here next to a vampire, worried if I'm going to be his snack."

Webb pushed to his feet.

The tension eased, but my rage still simmered. He stood on the other side of the coffee table and scratched his neck. I assumed he was trying to keep his anger at bay.

"I want to get out of here. I want to go back to Mr. Jackson's house—now," I said.

Jerking his head slightly, he flared his nostrils

again as his eyes slowly turned black. If he wasn't angry before, he sure was now. "You've seen evidence that vampires exist. That's enough for you to believe something. You're not here so that I can convince you to trust me. You're here so that you don't end up missing like your brother. And you need to stop being a brat and listen to what I tell you. I'll explain things when necessary—and only when necessary." His hard tone matched his eyes as he glared at me.

I just pissed off a vampire. Great.

Taking a breath, he sat on the coffee table in front of me. "Your father has to be a vampire in order for you to become one. The vampire blood, his blood, is essential in the crossover process. Once you reach the age of sixteen, your father starts to store his blood. Once a month, he replenishes the old with the new until you and Sam make the decision about whether you will stay human or become a vampire. Your father wants you to have a say in your future, in your life. But his blood is also stored for emergencies."

I wanted to laugh. My father hadn't been around for fourteen years. Why would he care what Sam and I wanted? If he did, he wouldn't have dumped us in the foster system.

"A father's blood is like a precious and rare

gem." Webb's voice softened. "It should be guarded at all times. If your dad or your dad's blood were to fall into the hands of his enemies, they would destroy him and any of his stored blood. You would never get a chance—"

"What makes you think I want to be a vampire?"

He stared at me for a long second before he continued. "Your father's enemies don't want more vampires like him. Your dad is a very powerful immortal. His enemies believe that you and your brother are a threat to their plan, especially when they're fighting for control."

A knock on the door sounded, before Sloan came in. "A word, Lieutenant?"

"I'll be right back," Webb said to me before he and Sloan left.

I blew out all the air in my lungs. *Whoa.* I couldn't believe what he'd just said. My father—a powerful immortal. Whatever that truly meant. Plus, my dad had enemies. Maybe those enemies were responsible for Sam's disappearance. Not to mention, drinking a pint of blood—was he kidding? Sure, I was drawn to the sticky liquid for some reason. But drinking it like a tall glass of milk—no way.

Suddenly, I felt as though a freight train was

barreling down the tracks and I was stuck between the rails, struggling to break free.

"Get up and walk around. Shake it off," I muttered out loud. "I'm dreaming. I'm dreaming," I repeated over and over.

Once on my feet, I twisted my neck in one direction then the other. Then I rubbed my eyes and blinked a few times to adjust my vision. When I did, a picture on one of the bookcases caught my attention. Two people in green fatigues stood smiling together with a crystal-blue ocean spanning the background.

I zeroed in on the man to the left of Webb, and my mouth fell open. If I wasn't mistaken, the man beside Webb was Sam. His long black hair was tied back. His emerald-green eyes sparkled, and his smile was as endearing as Sam's. I was about to grab the picture when my gaze landed on another next to it. My pulse sped up as I studied the two little kids in the picture. *Is that Sam and me?* If it was, we seemed happy as we sat on a beach, building sandcastles.

I ran a hand over the picture and muttered, "Sam, where are you? Please, please, be all right. I will find you."

"That's your father in the other picture," Webb said.

I flinched. I didn't hear him come in. "And this one?" I pointed to the one with the two little kids.

"That picture was taken when you and Sam were two years old, just before your mother died."

My mother? I bit my bottom lip. I didn't even want to think about her. My life during the past week was enough to process. I wasn't ready to learn about my father, let alone my mother. I closed my eyes and inhaled. Webb had given me enough of a family-history lesson to last a lifetime. But something told me he wasn't finished yet.

"You should eat. It's getting late," Webb said.

The gray light that spilled in from the small window didn't give me any indication of the time of day. There wasn't a clock in the room, but my stomach was a little queasy, which I had assumed was due to nerves, but since Webb mentioned eating, it sounded like a good idea.

He waved his hand at the door. "Let's go up to the mess hall. Dinner isn't until five, but we can find a snack."

"Um, I do have more questions."

"We have plenty of time later," Webb replied.

My intuition was telling me that if I wanted answers, I would have to search for them on my own.

17

The mess hall on the third floor made the cafeteria at school look like a run-down diner. The stainless-steel refrigerator had three doors on top and two that pulled out on the bottom. The tables were all set for dinner, complete with cloth napkins, like a high-end restaurant.

Two long islands lined the right side of the mess hall, not fitting the atmosphere or design of the expansive room. Each had a granite countertop with barstools tucked underneath. Behind them was a small selection of liquor bottles neatly stacked from the bottom shelf to the top. They probably wouldn't let me drink any of it, though I imagined something strong would have helped my nerves.

Webb pushed in a swinging door to what I assumed was the kitchen. "I'll see if the cook can make us a light snack."

I was thirsty, and since liquor wasn't one of my choices, I checked the refrigerator. Two rows of colorful juice boxes in orange, blue, green, and black sat neatly under the sprinkle of the refrigerator light. I plucked an orange one from the shelf and surveyed the small box that had a plastic straw secured to the side of it. The words Orange Cream were imprinted across the top edge. *This sounds tasty.*

I inserted the straw through the foil spout on top then drew in a long sip. The sweetness of the orange-and-vanilla combination made my taste buds tingle, but the thickness of the liquid made my stomach clench. This wasn't juice. The consistency was more like a milkshake.

My stomach started to churn, and bile rose in the back of my throat. I swallowed then inhaled, becoming suddenly dizzy. Maybe I was dehydrated. I grabbed another orange box and went through the same procedure, though I sipped the second one slowly rather than downing it. The room began to spin.

"Jo, what are you doing?" Webb yelled. "Put that down. You *can't* drink that!"

I snapped my head up to find a look of horror plastered on his face. His eyes suddenly turned black. Not a good sign.

"Put *down* the juice box." His voice was hard and scary.

My mind agreed with him, but my hands didn't. "This isn't juice." I looked at the blurry words printed on the box.

"I know, Jo. It's *blood*!"

I stood frozen in place with the straw in my mouth, still sipping the... *what?*

"Dr. Vieira, I need you down in the mess hall, *now!*" Webb yelled into his phone. He guided me to a chair. "How do you feel?"

"Fine. What's all the fuss? I'm just drinking..." *Oh my God! Is this my father's blood? Am I going to turn into a vampire?* The room spun faster. My stomach decided it didn't like the blood. I dropped the box, grabbed my stomach, and bent over.

Webb snatched a trash can from somewhere. "In here." He placed the container at my feet.

I heaved the contents of my stomach into it. My hair fell in front of me as sweat beaded on my face and forehead. The first round was painful, as if I had just completed fifty sit-ups. I burped, and as soon as I did, the second round began. Webb gathered my hair behind me and held it.

"What happened?" Dr. Vieira asked. "Ah, I see."

I couldn't tell what he saw. He probably figured it out from the orange boxes on the floor.

"Will she be okay? Or will this mess up our plan?" Webb whispered.

"What plan?" My voice echoed from the trash can. Him and that damn plan, whatever it was.

"No, she'll be fine. She's eliminated most of it. Only a very small amount will be absorbed into her system, but it shouldn't do any harm," Dr. Vieira explained. "Make sure she eats something bland for dinner."

"Did I just drink my father's blood?" My heart raced.

"You told her?" Dr. Vieira sounded concerned.

"We don't have much time. She needs to know," Webb said.

"Then it begins. I'm almost finished with her tests. They may be ready by this evening," Dr. Vieira said.

With my hands glued to the rim of the trash can, I lifted my head. "Tests?" I shifted my blurry gaze between Webb and Dr. Vieira.

They both wore unblinking expressions.

"I get it. A need to know basis, right?" I asked.

"Let's go back to my office. You can lie down for a bit," Webb said.

"I want to see Ben. That's if you"—I stuck my head in the trash can, waiting, but it was a false alarm—"didn't kill him yet."

"What is she talking about?" Dr. Vieira asked.

Webb's heavy footsteps faded as he went over to the bar with his phone at his ear. "Nothing."

I sat motionless, trying to still the dizziness that clouded my head while I thought of Ben, wondering if Webb had actually killed him.

"Dr. Vieira, do you know if Ben…"

Before I could finish, Webb was grabbing my arm. "Let's go."

Dr. Vieira helped me to stand. "Make sure you eat something light at dinner, Jo."

As Webb ushered me out, I willed my stomach to begin its third round. I desperately wanted to puke on his shiny military boots.

Olivia was waiting for us in the hall. "Sir, you requested me?"

"Escort Jo to the ladies' room then return her to my office," Webb ordered.

I snarled. "Hey, I'm not some postal package who needs to be returned to sender."

This man is irritating with a capital I.

Webb flicked his head to the side, and Olivia returned his command with a nod.

Like Webb, Olivia was dressed in black cargo pants and laced-up boots. She wore a black golf shirt, which disappeared into her trousers, and her weapons were strapped to her belt. I focused on her sword, which had a black leather handle with a silver plate with words engraved on it. I squinted, but the words were too small to make out. I wondered, though, whether there was any significance to the different-colored handles. I remembered Sloan's sword as having a brown handle, but Webb's was red.

Once inside the restroom, my stomach tightened. I covered my mouth as I ran to the sink. I was a little disappointed that it took until then to vomit.

"How many boxes did you drink?" Olivia asked.

I held up two fingers as I continued to puke.

"No wonder. A human can't handle a spoonful without getting sick, let alone eight ounces of blood," she replied.

After my stomach settled, I puffed out my cheeks and straightened.

"Here." Olivia handed me a paper towel.

I turned on the faucet and examined myself in

the mirror. Yikes! I looked like death. My bangs were stuck to my forehead, and my chin was marked where the glass had punctured the skin. I needed a long shower, although no amount of water would change my appearance in an instant.

As she handed me a paper towel, her brown-eyed gaze was glued to my face.

"Is something wrong?" Aside from how deathly I look.

"You look just like—"

"I know, like my father. How many times am I going to hear that today?" I rolled my eyes, and the room spun. My stomach gave way. I jerked my head toward the sink, but not quickly enough. The contents of my stomach sprayed onto Olivia's shirt.

I hugged the sink and heaved again. I inhaled deeply and waited a few seconds before I even moved. "I'm sorry. It tasted good, but my stomach sure doesn't think so."

She removed her shirt then ran the water over the area I'd soiled. "Which kind did you try?"

"The Orange Cream."

"Not my favorite. The one in the black box is a peppered flavor with some other spices in it. That's mine."

She reminded me of something Sam had said at the funeral home, which seemed ages ago. He had mentioned that when he got blood in his mouth, it tasted like pepper to him. I desperately missed him.

After she'd finished rinsing her shirt, I tracked her movements to the air dryer, and I couldn't help but stare. She wore a white tank top that was perfectly fitted to her body, showing a hint of six-pack abs. Her sculpted biceps rippled along her arms as she rubbed her shirt under the dryer. When she turned to face me, the front of her left shoulder exposed a tattoo that appeared to be the number four written in calligraphy style. If the vertical stem had been removed, it would look like the number two.

"Your tattoo. Does it stand for something?" I asked.

She glanced down. "Oh, that. It's nothing."

"What does it mean?" My stomach gurgled, echoing in the room. "Sorry."

"Do you have to throw up again?" she asked.

"I don't know. But stay back."

She smiled. "It's the symbol for Jupiter. We're the Jupiter Sentinels, and this sort of brands us into the group. Every vampire recruit that makes it through SEAL training is imprinted with a symbol of their SEAL team."

"Neil has a symbol on the back of his neck in the shape of—" I froze.

His was a monogram, as well, with the letter P... and did his symbol stand for the Plutariums? If so, then he was one of the bad guys, which could mean he kidnapped Sam.

She arched her brow. "Neil? Who's Neil?"

I wasn't sure if I should tell her. But it was only a tattoo.

"Some guy I met at the hospital. He had a tattoo on the back of his neck. Not like yours, but it looked like the symbol that's engraved on that ring Jonah was wearing."

She flinched. Her hands shook slightly as she buttoned the top of her golf shirt.

My stomach talked back, and I leaned over the sink. While I waited for the vomit to rise, my mind raced. The pieces of an extremely complex puzzle were falling into place, but little was making sense. A few seconds ticked by. I burped then hiccupped. A complete mess, I splashed water on my face and played with my bangs, but it was useless. The monster look would have to do for the time being.

"We should get you back to Webb's office," she said.

My stomach settled, and the gurgling had stopped, but a cloud of haze floated around me.

No sooner than we were out in the chilly hall, my knees buckled. Cool air whistled past my ear as I landed on my right shoulder before my head hit the tile floor. Then everything around me faded.

I awoke on the couch in Webb's office. I lifted my head, but it felt like a weight was pressed against my forehead, pushing me back down. A sharp pain throbbed just above my right ear. I inserted my fingers into my mouth, searching my gums for fangs. I sighed heavily, relieved that I didn't find any pointy teeth. My hands roamed over my body, seeking what I didn't know. Aside from fangs, I wasn't sure what other physical changes vampires experienced.

"Are you like a magnet for trouble?" a familiar voice asked.

Excitement stirred as I sat up.

Ben grinned from his spot in the chair across from me.

Webb hadn't killed him. "You're alive?" I sounded like a squealing girl at a Justin Bieber concert.

"Why wouldn't I be?"

"Oh, because Webb was supposed to kill you for not agreeing to... you know."

Ben shook his head. "Jo, I couldn't do that to you or Sam, even if you could be one of them.

Anyway, I'm glad Webb had Tripp take me upstairs. I needed time to process all this. This vampire stuff is heavy. Tripp explained some things to me and showed me around the compound. The SEAL team members in this building are mostly vampires, but a couple of them are human. I had a chance to talk to one of them. While I'm not completely comfortable with vampires, it was good to hear what another human had to say."

I was relieved that Ben sounded a bit more relaxed. Maybe his vibe would wear off on me.

"And Tripp showed me the weapons room. It looks like something out of a James Bond movie. It's some cool shit." Ben's eyes glistened as he talked.

"Do you hear yourself? A couple of hours ago, you were no way about this vampire crap. You meet a few vampires, talk to a human, see a bunch of weapons, and now you're into it?"

"Not completely. But I decided at least to listen. The human guy said something that made me think. 'You can't change how you're born.' Honestly, all this scares the shit out of me. You kind of scare me. But I'm not going to abandon a friend."

Tears filled my eyes. "You know, I was freaking out, thinking the worst. While I want to strangle you, I'd rather strangle him," I whispered as I flicked my head at Webb, who was sitting at his desk shuffling papers.

I rose from the couch then fell back down.

Ben jumped up from his chair and sat next to me. "You okay? Is it from that snack? How did it taste?"

"Who told you?" Not that it mattered.

He nodded at Webb, who was engrossed, reading something from a white sheet of paper. *What else did Webb tell Ben?*

"You're not a vampire, Jo." Ben started laughing.

"When I am one, you will be my first victim." I licked my lips.

"Let's hope that doesn't happen." Ben lost the playfulness in his tone.

I wasn't sure what Tripp had explained to Ben, either, but I wasn't ready to tell him what I had learned from Webb.

Webb came over and stood behind the empty chair. "Okay, you two."

"I guess I should thank you for not... well, thank you," I said to Webb.

"Ben is part of this now. He's going to help us as much as he can," Webb replied.

Surprise flitted through me at the sudden change Webb had regarding Ben.

Ben beamed. "I'm going to be one of your bodyguards."

"You?" I chuckled.

He straightened and tensed. "Why not me? I swing a mean baseball bat."

"We've been through this. You know how that turned out," I reminded him.

"Can you two get along or not?" Webb asked.

Ben nodded. I wanted to be a smart-ass but decided against it and nodded.

"Good. Now that we agree, we'll head back up to the mess hall. After dinner, you two will meet me in the war room. Tripp will show you where it is."

Ben and I exchanged a surprised look. I had no idea what a war room was or why I would need to be there. I wasn't at war with anyone, at least not yet.

After we left the mess hall, Tripp wanted to use the stairs instead of the elevator, which had a group in front of it, waiting to board. Ben and I followed the tall, muscular vampire to another hallway, which pitched down to the back of the building, before taking the stairs to the second floor.

A strange odor hung in the air. It smelled like a cross between blood and vinegar, and the tanginess made my eyes water. I grabbed the banister before stepping off the last riser, and my hand landed on a sticky, red substance. I wiped my hand on my jeans and lingered for a brief second. I couldn't help but wonder what had happened in there.

"We're going to be late. Move," Tripp commanded.

His hand urged me through the door on the second floor.

Ben leaned against the wall with his hands in his pockets, looking bored out of his mind. "What's with the tortoise walk?"

I had the urge to flip him off, but instead I ignored him as Tripp led the way.

"Not talking to me now?" Ben asked.

I shook my head.

"What did I do?" Ben prodded.

I raised my finger to my lips. During dinner, Ben and I had argued. He teased me about the juice incident, wanting to know how the blood tasted. In my book, he'd been rude for asking all those questions in front of Tripp, who'd seemed uncomfortable with the conversation. My patience was walking a tightrope, and at any moment, I was going to unleash my anger.

"Are we in church?" Ben whispered.

I clenched my jaw. "God, you can be just as annoying as Darcy."

"Watch your tongue," Ben replied in a somewhat sarcastic tone.

Tripp pivoted on his heel and wagged his finger between Ben and me. "When we get into the war room, you two will sit in the back row next to me. You will not speak a word. You're there to listen, and that's it. If I hear you two arguing, I will personally lock both of you up for the night. Are we clear?"

Later, I was going to follow through on my promise and kill Ben. I'd spent more time around him than ever in the past week, and I didn't know he could be so annoying.

The war room was lit up like an airport runway, and the brightness blinded me for a second when I entered a minute later. The chairs rose in a pattern similar to an amphitheater, with elongated steps cutting through two sections and leading down to a large conference table. On top were a couple of books and a stack of papers. Behind the table, a movie screen hung from the ceiling.

Tripp directed Ben and me to the last row, which butted up against the back wall. I thought Tripp was going to sit between us so Ben and I wouldn't talk, but he took the aisle seat and instructed me to sit in the middle.

Several people were already chatting in the rows below us. I scanned the room and didn't see Webb, but Olivia, her partner from earlier, and Sloan were seated in the front row, directly below us. Dr. Vieira came in from a side door adjacent to the movie screen with a binder in his hand. He ambled up to the conference table, set the binder down before thumbing through the pages.

Tripp stoically looked straight ahead, and Ben had his feet up on the chair in front of him, leaning back. I tapped his leg, and he just glared at me.

"Feet down, Ben," Tripp commanded.

Ben obeyed, straightening before we both exchanged a scowl.

Webb had entered and stood by Dr. Vieira, who was reading something in the binder. According to the clock on the wall in the far-left corner, it was 6:59. The people seated wore black military uniforms similar to the one Webb had on. Other than Ben and me, there was one other person in civilian clothes, a woman who sat in the far section on the other side of the aisle in the front row. She wore a gray pantsuit, and her brown hair was in a bun.

When the large hand on the clock slid to the twelve, Webb cleared his throat. "Okay, settle down," Webb boomed, his voice filling the room.

The chatter stopped as if someone had slammed on the brakes.

Then Webb pointed a remote at the projector, and a slide appeared on the screen.

The word "Agenda" was at the top followed by "Breakdown at Crest and Skylark." Item number two—"Endotoxin." Three had the names "Dr. Patrick Mason and Edmund Rain."

My eyes rested on the names, and I began tapping my foot.

Tripp placed his hand on my knee. "You don't need to be nervous."

Easier said than done. I'd been through hell in the past week, but that wasn't what had me on edge.

I leaned in. "Is Patrick Mason any relation?"

"It will all be explained shortly," Tripp said.

I continued to tap my foot as I read item number four, "Plutariums."

"What's with the planet names around here?" Ben asked.

I shrugged. I wanted to know the answer to that one too—even the tattoos were still a mystery to me. Olivia did explain why she had hers, but she didn't elaborate as to why the vampires had to be branded.

Number five on the list was "Update and New Information." Excitement stirred as goose bumps peppered my arms. Maybe Webb had some news about Sam.

The last two bullet points were "Plan for Tomorrow" and "Wrap Up." After reading the list, I had a feeling we were going to be there all night.

Webb shifted his gaze between the audience and the screen. "Tonight, we'll recap the events of the past few days and look at the path forward. First, I want to make everyone aware that we have two civilians in the room. In case you're not aware, one of them is Commander Mason's daughter, Jo, who is sitting next to Petty Officer Tripp. The other is Ben Jackson, a friend of the Masons." He pointed in our direction.

A sea of vamps looked at me.

"You're famous," Ben said. "The daughter of a commander and a Navy SEAL. Wow, impressive. But the vampire thing? Not so much."

I dropped my gaze and ignored him.

Tripp whispered, "Breathe. They need to know who you are. It's pertinent to the mission."

As I returned my attention to Webb, I spied the pretty lady in gray staring at me. Her burgundy lips pronounced her pale features, and her eyes were a deep blue. Her gaze lingered on me for a beat before she shifted her position forward.

Webb continued as he stood stoic, commanding the room like a born leader. "The breakdown at Crest and Skylark can't happen anymore. Brock and Fehherty were ambushed as if the Plutariums knew their route. I'm not sure how this happened, but while we're looking for both Commander Mason and his son, Sam, it is imperative that we pay attention to detail. Every one of you has been trained not to be complacent. We cannot for one second let our guard down. They're becoming stronger as the days go on, and their army is getting larger as well. Is that clear?"

The room vibrated as the group of vampires all said in unison, "Yes, sir."

Webb bobbed his head as he interlaced his fingers in front of him. "Second, the Plutariums now have access to an endotoxin, which Dr. Vieira will discuss in a second. I want each of you to pay close attention to what this toxin can do. But before we talk about the toxin"—the screen flashed, and a picture of two men appeared—"I want to make sure everyone is aware of these two men."

The one on the left was tall with short, slicked-back brown hair and a blue long-sleeved button-down shirt, which accentuated his sky-blue eyes. The other was slightly taller and wore a short black military haircut.

"The man on the right, as most of you know, is Edmund Rain. He was part of our team four years ago. The other is Dr. Patrick Mason. He's a renowned genetic scientist and was recently recruited by the Plutariums." Webb scanned the room. "He's also Commander Mason's half-brother."

The audience drew in a collective breath, sucking in all the air in the room.

I inhaled, and my throat tightened as if someone was choking me.

"Your uncle bats for the enemy?" Ben sounded shocked.

I shrugged. I didn't even know I had an uncle, but it was sounding that way.

"We'll discuss their status in a minute, but first, let's talk about the toxin. Dr. Vieira, the floor is yours." Webb nodded at Dr. Vieira then took a seat.

"Thank you, Lieutenant London." Dr. Vieira fiddled with the computer until a picture of a needle appeared on the screen.

It looked a lot like the horse needle Jonah had tried to stab me with.

Dr. Vieira pointed at the screen. "This needle was confiscated at Crest and Skylark earlier today. One of the Plutariums, who managed to grab Jo Mason, was going to use this on her. The contents of the needle contained an endotoxin, which is a bacterium. A couple of key points on what this substance can do." He paused and took a sip of water.

The entire audience stilled, waiting for Dr. Vieira's next words.

"Once this toxin enters your bloodstream," he continued, "it can cause the blood to coagulate, causing a host of issues. Most importantly, it leads to blood poisoning when the toxin settles in and attacks the DNA and white blood cells. While most of you in this room may be immune to something like this, some of the younger folks may not be. However, if this needle had been used on Jo Mason, it would certainly have ended our mission, or at least in part made our mission more challenging. This is a lethal weapon, folks. We don't want to mess around with it." Dr. Vieira clicked a button on the remote.

The next photo depicted a row of body bags on the ground in front of a brick wall.

The vamps rustled in their seats and adjusted their positions as if nervous.

"This is getting weird." Ben grabbed my hand.

I agreed. But I wouldn't have said "weird." It was getting spooky.

Dr. Vieira sighed. "Our sources within the human government tell us that the missing-persons rate for the city has doubled over this time last year. In fact, their phones have been ringing off the hook with humans disappearing. Our own government has also documented an increase in missing vampires during the last few weeks. We speculate that the Plutariums and Dr. Mason have something to do with all this. Our government has confiscated these bodies and is running autopsies on them. We'll have more information during tomorrow's meeting." Dr. Vieira took another sip of water.

I had two questions nagging me. What did Dr. Vieira mean by if the needle had been used on me it would've ended their mission? And why am I so vital to what happened?

Webb took control of the projector as Dr. Vieira sat down. The screen went blank.

Ben let go of me and placed his hand in his lap. "This is some deep shit."

I agreed. But unfortunately, I was part of that deep shit.

"If you have any questions about this toxin, see Dr. Vieira after the meeting," Webb said. "Now, back to Edmund and Dr. Mason. We discussed this in our meeting last week, but it begs repeating here. The natural-born vampire population is dwindling, and some vampires in our community believe that the world needs vamps as part of the evolution of life. With that said, we have many problems with this belief, but two that are important to our short and long-term missions." Webb paced in front of the screen.

"Let's start with the bigger issue and drill down. We know that the Plutariums are building an army so they can infiltrate the government and rise to power. But we've learned recently that the Plutariums want to engineer a vampire army. And with our race fading, they've hired Dr. Mason to fabricate a serum to do just that. But before Dr. Mason develops a way to change humans who don't carry the vampire gene into vampires, he's taking care of the low-hanging fruit first and experimenting on himself. It will be the ultimate test to prove to the Plutariums that this can be done." He took a breath. "We also know that Patrick wants revenge against his half-brother for a host of personal reasons, which we won't discuss here. Whether Patrick is successful or not, we have a few problems on our hands." Webb opened a red folder, shuffled the contents around, and pulled out a piece of paper.

My mouth fell open. *This is the guy partly responsible for trying to kill me? My own uncle?* First, my father threw Sam and me away like pieces of trash, and now, I had an uncle trying to permanently dispose of me. Blood rushed to my face. My muscles tensed, bracing for Webb's next words.

"We believe that Patrick has figured out that he needs his half-brother's blood to have any chance of becoming immortal, which means he needs Commander Mason alive. In addition, we have it on good authority that Patrick will also need the DNA, blood, and marrow of a male family member to run his experiments." Webb glanced in my direction.

A chill skittered up my arms.

"Sir?" A guy seated in the section over from us raised his hand.

"Yes, Thatch?"

"Do we know if Edmund has the commander in custody?"

"We don't," Webb replied.

"Lieutenant?" Another vamp who was seated in the section over from me spoke. "Since the commander is family, wouldn't Patrick just need to drink his brother's blood? Wouldn't that complete one of their plans?"

Webb shook his head. "It's not as easy as you drinking your father's blood. There are a lot of problems pointing against Patrick being successful. The first is that Commander Mason and Patrick are from different mothers. We know the elder Mason was a vamp, but we also know he's dead—the second problem. We don't know if Patrick and the commander have the same blood type, which is important to the change—third problem. Aside from all this, the most important thing to consider is the genetics. Natural-born vampires are sired by a male vampire who mates with a human female. But that human female must have a blood type of Vel negative, which is a very rare blood type. And we don't know if Patrick even carries the vampire gene." Webb sipped from a cup on the table.

"I feel like we're in medical school," Ben whispered.

This was Genetics 101. I didn't know what to process first. I was trying to understand the last part of what Webb said about the blood type of the human female, which meant my mother had a rare blood type. I was starting to relax a little. I wasn't the only weird one carrying rare genes.

While the blood types were one thing, I couldn't get my head around the idea of vampires and humans mating. I shook my head, trying to clear it. Sam was the topic, not the mating of vampires.

I gave Tripp a sidelong glance. "Is Webb

talking about Sam? Is he the male family member?" I held my breath.

Tripp lifted a shoulder. "I don't know. Let's listen."

Webb tucked a hand in his pants pocket. "Given what we discussed, we don't know if Patrick will be successful in genetically engineering a blood serum, but one thing's for sure: he's one of the best in his field in this country, so let's not forget that. If anyone can do this, it will be him. Any more questions before I move on?"

Two vamps raised their hands at the same time. Webb called on some dude named Talon first.

"You mentioned that the Plutariums want to build an army. Change humans into vampires. Is that even possible? It sounds like cloning if you ask me."

Webb's blue eyes glinted beneath the overhead lights. "I can't answer that. What I can share with everyone, which is common knowledge to the medical community, is that Dr. Mason has had a medical breakthrough in taking a rat and changing that rat's genetic features. While this is far from changing a human into a vampire, we need to be cautious. We'll discuss it further as we gather more information."

I was about to raise my hand and ask about the male donor when Webb pointed to the other vamp who was next in line to ask a question. "Sanderson?"

"Do we suspect that Commander Mason is the male donor?" Sanderson asked.

"Thank you," I muttered.

"We believe that the Plutariums have—" Webb looked directly at me, or so I thought.

Tripp grabbed my hand.

"We believe... it's Sam Mason, the commander's son," Webb said.

The blood rushed to my feet.

19

Webb focused his attention in our direction. Tripp shook his head. I imagined Webb asked if I was okay through his telepathic connection.

"Let's take a fifteen-minute break and be back here at eight sharp," Webb said to the crowd.

Some of the vampires filed out of the room, while a few hung out talking. One had cornered Dr. Vieira, probably to chat about that needle.

I covered my face with my hands, and tears began to fall as confusion clouded my brain.

A hand touched my back. "Jo, they don't know for sure if it's Sam. Webb said he *believed*. He didn't say it *was* Sam," Ben said in a soft voice.

"Webb wants to talk to us," Tripp said. "Ben, take her arm."

I stood and wiped my nose with the back of my hand. "I can walk."

Tripp led us down the wide steps to the bottom of the meeting room. A door to the right of the conference table was open, and light trickled out.

"In here." Tripp pointed to the door and waited for Ben and me to go ahead of him.

"Have a seat, both of you." Webb waved a hand at a table and metal chairs, which were the only items in the dimly lit room.

Ben and I sat while Tripp stood at the door with his arms crossed.

"Jo, I'm sorry you had to hear about Sam in there. We don't know for sure if your Uncle Patrick has Sam or not. We're speculating. But it's a realization that we have to consider." Webb bit his bottom lip.

"But why Sam?" Ben asked. "Why not their father?"

Webb's Adam apple bobbed. "The Plutariums could very well have both of them. We can't confirm the validity of what we suspect because the Plutariums' compound is just as heavily guarded as our own. Remember what I explained. It's not as easy as Patrick drinking the commander's blood." Webb regarded me with soft blue eyes. "What we suspect—and Dr. Vieira is researching this—is that Patrick needs the DNA of a family member who has not *yet* become a vampire. He will need to isolate Sam's adolescent vampire gene to study and test. Plus, he will need Sam's blood to extract the white blood cells and then the marrow. I know this is a lot of information and probably doesn't make sense, but the bottom line is if Patrick can study Sam's genetic makeup, then Patrick is halfway to reaching his goal." Webb sat back in his chair.

My stomach twisted into a knot of nerves as my heart hurt for my brother. "What else does he need?"

"He will need to use a vampire's blood to create the serum," Tripp said. "And that blood has to come from a family member. One key element, though, is that Patrick's blood type has to match your dad's blood type." Tripp had moved away from the door to stand next to Ben.

"So that's why we think he has both your dad and Sam," Webb added.

I blew out all the air in my lungs. I was still a little hazy from Tripp's medicinal touch.

"Can't you just put together a team and break into their compound?" Ben shoved his hands through his cinnamon-colored locks. "You're SEALs. That's what you guys do."

"Sure, we could. But we don't think Sam is at their compound," Tripp said.

"That would be too easy. The Plutariums are waiting for us to do just that. However, they could have Commander Mason there," Webb explained.

"Then where's Sam?" Ben asked.

Webb blew out a breath. "We don't know. We're checking a few places we suspect, but we haven't been able to confirm anything yet." Webb sounded tired.

"Why separate the two?" I asked.

"Remember I told you that your father is a very powerful vampire?" Webb asked.

I nodded.

"Well, they would need to lock him up at their place in a very secure room and keep him sedated until they needed him."

Ben fidgeted in his seat. "A little lost here. What do you mean by 'powerful'?"

I was just as lost as Ben.

Webb pushed to his feet. "His mental abilities far outweigh any other living vampire. When they cross over, all vampires go through physical changes, and when they emerge on the other side, they're stronger, their eyesight is ten times sharper, and their hearing is better than the canine species. But we also inherit one or two unique mental acuities, such as the ability to compel humans or speak to other vampires through a telepathic connection. Those are just a couple of examples." Webb walked around the room with his head down as if he was struggling or stalling.

Then Webb and Tripp exchanged a knowing look before Tripp nodded.

I was beginning to hate the telepathy thing.

Ben stared at Webb, clearly waiting for him to speak.

Webb grabbed the back of his neck. "There are no other vampires that we know of who have more than two mental acuities—other than Commander Mason. He not only has the ability to do what we can, but he also has a unique psychic strength that no other vampire has—he can *read minds*. He can get in your head and read your thoughts. This ability is something that the Plutariums are concerned about. They think Commander Mason will discover the ins and outs of their plan."

I bounced my knee. "So why not just kill my father? Then they wouldn't have to worry about him reading anything. Why go through all this trouble of blood serums and kidnapping my brother?"

Webb clasped his hands in front of him and began pacing. It seemed he wasn't ready to answer any of my questions. As I waited for him to speak, I thought of how easily I could kill my father. Better yet, maybe I could take a contract out on his head. Then all of this would be over with. Although, with Sam missing, it probably wasn't a good idea.

"Edmund Rain," Webb said, jarring me from my sinister thoughts, "the leader of the Plutariums, is a twisted individual. He and your father go way back and, at one time, were best friends. Well, Edmund got mixed up with the wrong people and was dishonorably discharged. He believes your father betrayed him. Now, he wants revenge—not only against your father but the government as well. Killing your father would be too easy. Vampires settle their scores by making their enemies suffer for a long time before ending their lives. Edmund knows if he's caught committing any crimes, our vampire laws are strict. The penalty could be as high as death. He has a plan. Knowing Edmund, he's going to make your father's life a living hell. If he's successful with creating a vampire army, he'll kill your father and his whole family. Until then, we have our work cut out for us."

I couldn't believe what I was hearing. I was a pawn. It seemed the Sentinels were using me as their sacrificial lamb, while Sam was being used as one by the Plutariums. Foster care was looking better by the minute.

Ben stood, rubbing his chin. A small amount of facial hair had grown in since we left for school this morning. "Back to Sam. How are we going to find him?"

It seemed clear that Ben didn't care about my father or his enemies. He wanted to find Sam. I wanted to jump up and hug him. But I was also surprised at how serious and in control he seemed. During the last few hours, I'd seen his emotions rise and fall between shock, horror, excitement, and anger. Bravery was new.

"We've been looking," Tripp said. "Our team has been following the Plutariums. Understand, though, that it doesn't take long for them to figure out what we're doing. Vampire senses are strong and sharp, so it's hard to catch them off their game."

"We need... to..." Webb scrubbed a hand over his face, seemingly struggling for words.

"Sir, do you want me to explain?" Tripp asked.

Webb shook his head. "No." He took a deep breath and knelt on one knee in front of me. "Jo?"

I didn't know whether to laugh or cry. The gesture looked as if he was about to propose. He had one hand on his knee as he looked up at me through his long, dark lashes. I tried to ferret out his thoughts, but the doleful expression etched on his face spoke volumes. I grabbed the seat of the metal chair as my heart raced, and blood snaked through every pore in me.

He raised his hand from his knee and placed it on mine. His touch sent a spark through me, slowing my heartbeat. My emotions were scrambled, as if a mixture of fear and anticipation were fighting each other for control.

I dropped my head. He touched the bottom of my chin and tilted it up. Our eyes met, and my body trembled. I squeezed the chair tighter, bracing for the dreadful news.

"Hey, man, don't touch her," Ben said sharply.

Webb snapped up his head and glared at Ben. His eyes vacillated from blue to black. After the incident with Dr. Vieira, I imagined Ben wasn't too trusting of the vampires in the building.

I uncurled my fingers from around the chair and gently touched Webb's face. He turned his gaze toward me. Tripp grabbed Ben and pulled him away from my chair.

"What is it?" I whispered, hands shaking.

Clearing his throat, Webb closed his hand over mine. "Jo, I need you to be prepared for something. When we spoke in my office, I mentioned to you about choices, about choosing our path. Do you remember?" His eyes were pitch-black with a hint of red dots inside.

I nodded, afraid to speak but thankful he held my hand.

"If we do find your brother, he may be on his... deathbed. Meaning, for us to save him, he will need your blood to survive."

Save him? Deathbed? My hand trembled beneath Webb's, while the other one gripped the metal chair, holding on to it for dear life. I surveyed each of the men in the room. Tripp had his head tilted a fraction, looking at me. Ben was staring at me with a pained expression, and Webb watched as if searching for a green light from me so he could continue.

"My blood? You mean transfusion?" I asked. "I can share some of my blood with him." I prayed Webb wouldn't let go of my hand. I was afraid the rest of my body would start shaking, and I wouldn't be able to stop. Suddenly, I longed for

Tripp to hold me, calm me with his magical ability.

"I'm not sure you understand, Jo. What I mean is, Sam will need your *vampire* blood to survive," Webb whispered.

My body went numb. I sat statue still and couldn't move. I probably looked as pale as the white tile floor beneath my feet. *Forget my suspicions about things happening in threes. No, the universe is spitting out terrible, horrible things in tens.*

"We don't know for sure if it will come to that, but you do need to be prepared. You have a choice," Tripp chimed in.

I reared back. "I don't... don't... even know what that means. Are you saying that I need to become a... vampire... to save my brother?"

Webb gave me a slight nod. "It may come to that. We're trying to find Sam first and confirm his physical state. We want you to be prepared to make the decision as soon as we know. It will take at least twenty-four to forty-eight hours for you to make the transition. This is strictly your decision."

Tears spilled and flowed freely down my cheeks. Wrapping my head around the fact that vampires were real was one thing. Asking me to become one was an entirely different story. The thought of immortality was nauseating. I couldn't imagine walking around Earth for eternity. I had a life—maybe not a perfect one, but I believed the future held promise for me, for Sam. Now, my world was turned completely upside down, and I didn't know which way to go.

20

The news Webb had delivered in the war room still had my body trembling. My mind seemed frozen as tendrils of fear and confusion snaked through, altering my vision. Tripp had escorted Ben and me to the barracks on the third floor, but I didn't remember leaving the war room. I wasn't even sure if we had ridden the elevator or taken the stairs. The past two hours were no more than a blur. All I kept thinking about was how screwed up my life had become in such a short time.

For every minute that ticked by, I took in a deeper breath, bracing for the next earthquake to rumble my way, to ruin my day and my life. I flipped through the events of the last week, looking for something, anything to help me, to give me a clue or a sign of why all this was happening to me. I didn't understand how becoming a vampire could save Sam.

I'd listened to everything Webb explained, but I didn't want to believe any of it. Maybe I was dreaming. Maybe I was in a coma from Cliff's attack, and my mind was playing out its own movie while I lay comatose in a hospital bed.

Cold air streamed in as a door opened in the distance. A beautiful woman walked toward me, her brown hair fanned behind her while her navy-blue eyes sparkled beneath the glow of the hallway lights. Maybe she was an angel sent down from heaven to take me away.

As she approached, a hint of cinnamon filled the air. My instinct was to run. I glanced behind me for an escape route. There was a door at the other end of the mile-long hallway, but I didn't have time. She would have been in front of me before I could turn.

I scanned the hall for Ben and Tripp. They were here a moment before. I turned my head, and the pretty lady was getting closer. I dug my nails into the softer skin of my palm. Maybe, if I was dreaming, the sensation would propel me to wake. At least it might tell me if I was still alive, still human. All of sudden, a small amount of blood surfaced, and the warm fluid trickled down the length of my ring finger. I peered up, and the brown-haired lady stopped midstride. Her eyes changed from navy blue to black. *Not good.*

I examined my hand and the blood dripped slowly off my fingertip and tumbled to the white tile floor. Its scent overpowered the cinnamon aroma of the brown-haired woman standing directly in front of me.

Before I could react, she gently grabbed my hand and pressed two of her fingers to mine. "Child, what did you do?" Her voice was soft and soothing as she searched through one of the pockets of her cargo pants. Her skin glowed under the light layer of pink blush that painted her high cheekbones. Her lips were full with a tinge of neutral-colored gloss. "You know you shouldn't draw blood in a building full of vampires."

That last word slapped me in the face. My eyelashes fluttered. "Who are you?" My voice was raspy as if I had chain-smoked two packs of cigarettes.

"Let's get you to your room." She placed a tissue she'd found in her pants over my hand. "Hold this on it until the bleeding stops." Then she waved her hand forward. "Follow me. We'll get you settled for tonight."

I didn't move. "What happened to Ben?" Then I realized this was the woman in the gray pantsuit who had been in the front row in the war room.

"Child, follow me. You'll be staying in this wing of the building." She pointed to a door in the distance that read Women Only. "Once we get you settled, you can speak to Ben."

The restroom sign poked out up ahead, but I couldn't find a door that read Men Only. Ben was the only person who made me feel that vampires weren't real.

"It's okay." The woman must've sensed my anxiety as her soft voice echoed in the hallway. "I promise you can see Ben in a few minutes, but I need to get you out of this hallway, especially with your finger oozing blood."

She was right, of course. It didn't want to be a vampire's after-dinner snack.

She pulled a two-way radio from her side pocket. "Tripp, come in."

The radio crackled.

"Go." Tripp's voice came through the radio.

"I found her. We're in the barracks."

"Ten-four," Tripp said.

I followed her through the door into the

women's quarters. The room was set up with couches, large plush chairs in the center, and bedroom doors that dotted the walls surrounding the lounge area.

"In here." She flicked on the light as I entered the room on the left side of the lounge. "You know, I'm sorry. I should've introduced myself. But the blood dripping earlier was a little distracting." Her eyes returned to their normal blue color as she smiled.

In the brighter light of the bedroom, she reminded me of Webb. Her features were strikingly similar with her deep-blue eyes and full lips that accentuated a perfect smile.

"I'm Kate, Webb's sister." She extended her arm.

Her hands were clammy as we exchanged a weak handshake.

"Were you the one in the war room this evening?" I asked.

"Yes, I was in my civilian clothes. I had just returned from an appointment and barely made it to the meeting." She raised her eyebrows and bit her lip at the same time. "Webb would have had my you-know-what on a platter if I was late or missed that meeting."

I had no idea what she was talking about, but

her last comment seemed to assume that I knew her brother well. He'd irritated me a few times, but I wasn't in any position to agree with her yet.

"I'm sorry—I don't know much about your brother."

"You will. And when you do, we'll talk. Enough of my brother. I have to say that your father will be pleased you're safe."

I was saddened to hear how easily she dismissed her brother. I would give anything to have Sam there with me, so we could argue back and forth. Suddenly, a shiver crept up my back, and my legs wobbled. I dropped down on the twin bed.

"You're probably tired, and here I am, rambling. The restrooms are down the hall. There's water in the refrigerator." She flicked her thumb at the door. "My room is on the opposite side of the quad if you need anything."

"Can I see Ben now?" I blew out a breath.

"I'll let Tripp know. He'll send Ben up. I'll see you in the morning." She turned on her heel and left, closing the door behind her.

The room, like the lobby, had a cold, sterile feel to it with minimal furniture—a bed, a small dresser, and a high-backed wooden chair. The only light in the room sprayed down from the recessed lighting above me.

My backpack rested against the bed pillow. The last place I remembered carrying it to was the medical facility. I assumed Dr. Vieira had brought it down. I pulled it toward me and unzipped the back compartment. All of my books and my sweater were still tucked inside. I pulled out my black button-down cardigan and slipped it on then grabbed the *Science Behind Vampires* book. *Maybe if I read a few chapters, it will help me understand the vampire world a bit more.* I rubbed my hand over the picture of the microscope on the cover.

A knock startled me before the door opened and Ben sauntered in, his six-foot frame seemingly too big for the room. "Hey. There you are." he said with a hint of relief in his voice as he sat beside me. "What happened to you? Tripp and I were talking as we climbed the stairs. When we reached the top, you weren't there." Ben's brandy-infused eyes searched mine.

"I don't know. I was standing in an empty hallway, and all of sudden, a brown-haired lady found me."

"Is it that lady out there?" He nodded toward the door.

I nodded. "That's Webb's sister, Kate." I lowered my gaze to my book.

"What's that?" Ben snatched the book from me and fanned the pages. "Where'd you get this? Did Dr. Vieira give this to you?" His voice dropped an octave.

I shook my head. "I got it from the place Sam and I stayed that night."

"Jo, you're not considering what I think you are." Ben's voice wavered.

"What if... I am?" I didn't take my eyes off the book.

"I know you love Sam, but you can't just become a vampire. It's insane. We can find him. This book isn't going to tell you anything about all this shit." He waved his hand around the room. "Think about what you would be doing. Do you want to walk around this planet forever? That's not who you are."

"How do you know who I am, when I don't even know?" I pointed to my chest. "You've been sheltered by your dad and given everything you ever wanted. You've always had a family, a beautiful house, things that I've never had. My life... is Sam." My voice shook.

Ben touched my hand, and a tingling sensation danced across my skin. It was as if he had injected me with some kind of magic. "My life has sucked since my mother died. My outlet has always been hanging out with Sam. Having him around as a brother has been the best thing for me. And now you. I don't want to lose you too." Ben gently raised my chin, and he stared at me with a silky warmness that made my heart skip a beat.

He talked as if Sam was already dead.

He lightly rubbed the left side of my cheek with the back of his fingers, and a thread of excitement weaved through the knots in my stomach. My breath hitched. I sat frozen on the bed with his warm hand touching me. A prickly heat rose, stinging my face, and I couldn't look away. I hoped Ben couldn't hear my heart pounding against my ribs. *What kind of feeling is this?* I'd always thought Ben was handsome, but I didn't like him in a boyfriend kind of way. For some odd reason, my body didn't seem to agree.

I pulled away, stood, swallowed, and took in a deep breath. It was the same feeling I had when Webb placed a strand of my hair behind my ear, only stronger. Maybe it was all the vampire puberty messing with me. It had to be.

"What's wrong, Jo?" he asked.

I leaned up against the door. "We need to get out of here. I'm tired of being surrounded by cement walls and sterile furnishings. Besides, I feel helpless that I can't do anything to find Sam." It was sort of a lie, but I did truly ache to get out of that building. I didn't want to deal with trying to unpack my emotions. I had to stay focused on finding Sam.

"Yeah, me too." Ben said, his voice barely a whisper.

Silence thickened the room, and it suffocated me. Ben had his head down. *Did I just hurt his feelings by pulling away?* I wanted to ask him, but I was afraid of his answer.

I dragged my back down the length of the door and relaxed on the floor. "Did Tripp tell you what we're doing tomorrow? Are we going to school?"

He kept staring at the book, which was still in his hands.

"Ben?"

He shook his head. "I'm sorry. I was thinking about my mother."

My cheeks suddenly flushed with embarrassment. It made sense. I was an idiot to think Ben liked me. Boys didn't like me. They chastised me. I hated myself to even think I was pretty enough for someone like Ben... or any boy, for that matter.

"Yes, we're going back to my house, but I'm not sure about school. Tripp just said he was taking us to get some clothes. My dad isn't going to let me miss school again. I'm not sure what to tell him." He sighed.

"You don't have to tell him anything. We'll go back to your house, shower, and change. Then you can go to school."

I didn't want to be alone with all the vamps, but Ben was right. Mr. Jackson was strict when it came to school. I was hoping the alpha vampire, Webb, would be okay with me going to school. Something told me Webb wasn't going to allow it, even if someone had seen Sam.

"I'm not leaving you alone," Ben said.

"A few hours ago, you were afraid of me." I pulled my knees to my chest.

"We talked about this already. I'm your body-guard, remember?" He dropped his elbows to his knees and leaned forward.

I smiled then flinched.

Ben rose. "What's wrong?" He threw the book on the bed.

"Nothing. I haven't smiled in a long time, and it hurts." I raised my left hand to my cheek.

Ben sauntered over, his lips curled at the ends, displaying the deep dimples against his strong jaw. At that moment, my heart started racing. I suddenly knew why the girls in school went giddy when he walked into a room.

Damn the vampire puberty!

Ben sidled up next to me on the floor. I closed my eyes and dropped my head to my knees. The small room became quiet again, except for my pounding pulse echoing in my ears, which I hoped he couldn't hear. I was keenly aware of how close we were. A thin line of white tile separated my body from his. *Snap out of it. This is crazy.* All this vampire-gene crap was messing with my body. Not only was I going to kill my father for leaving me in a foster home, but I had another reason to add to the list—vampire genes.

"So, I have my baseball bat ready for tomorrow," Ben whispered.

I peeked at him. He had his knees raised to his chest, head resting in the palm of his left hand, eyes wide with a wolfish grin on his face.

"Let's hope you won't have to use it." I silently prayed tomorrow would be a better day, but my Spidey sense was telling me otherwise.

21

———————

After Ben left my room, I lay awake in the dark. The silence of the night gave me a chance to think. There were too many emotions and decisions to puzzle through. All of it swirled around in my brain, making my head hurt... and one made my body numb. Webb had said I needed to be ready to make a decision, *but is it truly a decision to save Sam's life?* In my mind, it was more of a decision of whether I wanted to kill myself—my humanity. More than anything, I wanted to save my brother, but I was less sure about changing from human to vampire.

While I had several questions about the physical changes, the struggle for me was immortality. *Does God intend for a species to live on this planet for-*

ever? I will be stuck in a world where time passed and people changed, but will I be physically the same? Will I be sixteen forever? I couldn't fathom it.

The next morning, I stared at Kate as we rode the elevator down to the lobby, admiring her taste in clothes. She had a pair of black jeans painted on her five-foot-six frame and her military boots laced up over her calves. A long pink silk sweater flowed behind her, a white camisole poking out from underneath. My hands gravitated to my head, and I began fidgeting with my bangs.

"Jo, you look fine," Kate said.

I didn't think so. She looked as if she'd just walked out of a hair-and-makeup appointment.

The elevator door opened, and we stepped out at the same time. The lobby was as cold as it had been the day before, and the same petite receptionist sat behind the circular desk. Ben was perched on a bench alongside the left wall. Webb and Tripp were talking near the desk, and two military men stood sentinel at the exit door. A shiver ran through me when I thought about how my world had shifted when I'd walked through that large steel contraption yesterday. I hoped my world wouldn't shift again today. I hoped we would find Sam before I had to make my decision. I shook my head. I didn't want to think about myself. The day's focus was trying to find Sam.

"Jo, over here," Ben called.

Webb and Tripp stared at me, and suddenly I felt self-conscious. The scar on my face seemed to burn under their scrutiny. I looked like something out of a horror show. I kept my head down while I headed toward Ben.

"Hey," Ben said. "You—"

"Don't even say it," I snapped.

"Say what? I was just going to ask you if you slept okay. No sense in getting all huffy." Ben scooted away from me and to the other end of the bench.

I plopped down on the leather bench. "I'm sorry. I didn't really sleep." I was about to check the time when I spied Webb.

He strutted over with his cell phone in one hand and a red folder in the other. His shoulder-length hair was wet and tucked behind his ears. "Good morning." His woodsy scent triggered the dormant butterflies that were sitting idle in my stomach. Heat rose and pinched my cheeks. I swore he was wearing a particular type of pheromone to drive me insane. *Focus, focus, focus.*

"Have you thought about what we discussed yesterday, Jo?" he asked.

The flutters in my stomach stopped as I reared back. I was faced with a life-changing decision, and this arrogant vampire thought that—poof—overnight, I would make a choice? I wanted to attack him, to beat and shake him into reality. I was beginning to think that maybe, just maybe, to die as a human had to be paradise compared to becoming an insensitive vampire. "When are we leaving?"

"Don't avoid the question. I need to know where you are in making a decision. We need to plan." His voice had a slight growl to it as he placed his phone in its holster.

I know where I am in my head, and it's definitely not anywhere near vampires. "Are you serious? You can't think—"

"Sir, the car is out front," Tripp called.

I was thankful for the interruption. I hoped Webb would leave me alone, but his glare promised otherwise.

"She's not joining your ranks," Ben blurted out as he slid closer to me on the bench.

Webb froze, his pupils slowly changing to a sea of black as he glowered at Ben. "My patience is wearing thin with you, son. I told you yesterday—my compound, my rules. If you interfere again, you will not return here or see Jo again." He stepped toward Ben, pointing his finger. "We're dealing with people's lives, and right now, yours doesn't mean anything to me," he said brusquely.

Whoa! Wait one second. Who does he think he is, using me as a threat?

I slowly let out the air in my lungs.

Tripp rushed over and stepped between Ben and Webb. "Sir? Sir?" He pushed Webb back. "Lieutenant London?"

Webb raked his hands through his hair as rage jumped off him.

Ben glared at Webb. "You're right. We're dealing with people's lives, and Jo's is one of them. So *you* need to lay off!"

My jaw came unhinged as my eyebrows drew together. Ben was so screwed. He must want to die. I wanted to slap him back to reality. We were in vampire territory, and he was being a total moron by trying to stand up to the leader of the pack.

Ben rose.

Tripp whirled around. "You need to stay where you are," he commanded.

Ben took a step toward Tripp. My heart pounded.

In a flash, Tripp flew at Ben, pushing him down on the bench. Ben landed so hard his head hit the back of the wall with a thud.

I gasped, covering my mouth with both hands. If Ben didn't have a concussion after that hit, he would be a lucky boy.

Kate touched my arm. "Come with me, Jo."

I couldn't move. My eyes widened as Webb and Tripp surrounded Ben.

"Jo?" Kate's voice was stern but soft.

I followed her to the exit door, glancing over my shoulder the whole time. I appreciated her pulling me away, but I was extremely worried about Ben. Two strong vampires were hovering over him, doing God-knew-what to him.

In an instant, the two guards at the door ran past me, swords in their hands.

"Listen, Jo. Look at me." She touched my face.

"No. I'm worried about Ben. Can't this wait?" I kept my gaze glued to the scene playing out—four vampires to one human wasn't a good match for Ben. It was evident that he didn't stand a chance, but I didn't know if they would hurt him.

Kate seemed to read my mind. "Webb isn't going to harm him."

"How do you know?"

"Let me give you some advice. I know you don't know my brother that well, but everything he's doing is for you, your brother, and your father."

I tore my attention away from the commotion

in the distance. "What about Ben? Can't Webb help him?"

She tucked strands of her brown hair behind her ear. "Ben has been extremely rude, lashing out at my brother. From what I understand, that wasn't the first time. Webb has a lot of patience, but right now, he's under a lot of pressure to find Sam and your father."

She was right. Ben had started it. His moodiness was going to get him killed.

"Jo, listen to me. Webb has a heart, and this whole thing hits too close to home for him. So please, do as he says. He knows what he's doing."

I choked back a laugh. I thought vampires couldn't feel things like emotions—they were supposed to be cold, emotionless creatures, not caring about anything or anyone. Kate made it sound like Webb was... human.

I knew little of vampires, and Webb had said I shouldn't believe everything I read in books. I guess the books I had in my possession were useless. I could ask, but I didn't want to. I wanted to find my brother. I wanted him back alive and human.

I crossed my arms over my chest. "He wants me to make a life-changing decision, like, right now. I can't do that." I tried to look over at Ben just to be sure Webb wasn't killing him, but I couldn't see anything with the four vampires in my way.

She gave me a sad smile. "Believe me when I say I know how hard this is for you. But time is of the essence. Webb might not have told you that. He was probably trying to give you some space, but we really don't have much time. *You* don't have much time. It's better if you make the decision and come to terms with it. If you don't make it soon, like today, then we can't plan accordingly."

I pinched my eyebrows together. I had no idea what she was talking about. I heard what she said, but my brain didn't process any of it. "Why do I have to make a decision right now? What if we find Sam?"

The guards dragged Ben to the exit.

I started to follow Ben when she grabbed my arm. "Not so fast. Ben is fine. They're taking him out to the car."

"But—"

She blinked, and her navy-blue eyes had changed to light gray. "No. I haven't finished speaking with you. If we find Sam, all that's lost is your time in deciding. But it's better if Dr. Vieira prepares"—a tear filled the bottom edge of her left eye—"for you to shed your human existence. Trust me, it's better if you can come to grips with whatever decision you make. But either way, you need to decide today." She brushed my bangs away from my eyes, and the tear trickled down her cheek.

I stared at some picture on the wall in the distance. My stomach had been doing a queasy tap dance since the guards removed Ben from the building. But at Kate's words, my head started spinning. *Shed your human existence.* The queasiness turned into slow and steady nausea creeping up the back of my throat. There was no way I was going to shed anything, not that day.

22

Once I was in the car, fear crept in as I thought about what Kate had said. The inside air was suffocating me, so I pushed the button to open the window. A brisk breeze played with my hair as I leaned out, trying to wash away the claustrophobia and, I hoped, the events of the past week.

The side streets were quiet with few cars on the road. Ben lived a couple of miles from the Jupiter Sentinels' compound, so we didn't have far to go. The scenery suddenly changed when we crossed over South Main Street. We were no longer in the mill district. Three-story tenements dotted the streets, and chain-link fences wrapped around each property, securing the tenants inside.

The sidewalks were deserted except for a couple walking their dog.

I pulled in my head. Ben was resting his elbow on the portable console that separated us in the back seat. His chin was propped up in his hand as he stared out the other window. Tripp's left hand was at twelve o'clock on the steering wheel, and his right arm rested on the console. He seemed relaxed after trying to keep Lieutenant London from killing Ben. I couldn't see Sloan's face, as he sat in front of me, but it sounded as if he was texting or something. Webb had stayed behind to do whatever it was he did as the leader of the Sentinels, which was probably a smart thing for all of us, especially Ben.

After several stop signs and a few traffic lights, Tripp made a right turn onto Rock Street, where we slowly passed the former Durfee High School building. I had always admired its Renaissance architecture—it looked more like an Old World church than a high school. It was a historic landmark, erected high on the hilltop in the middle of the city. Anyone traveling into Fall River from the west could see the clock tower from the other side of the Braga Bridge.

Tripp made a few more turns, and we were traveling east on President Avenue. Olivia's Jeep was a few blocks behind us. The radio crackled when Tripp stopped at a red light.

"Alpha One, come in," Olivia called.

Sloan pushed the button on the radio. "Go, Echo Three."

"Thirty minutes, then you're out," she commanded.

"Ten-four."

I had planned on taking a long shower and staying a while. I had no desire to return to the cement-and-steel prison.

"Jo and Ben? We need to get in and out. Get what you need then back to the car," Tripp instructed.

I tapped Ben on the arm. "Do you think your dad will be home?"

Ben glanced at his watch. "Probably not." His voice was sullen.

He'd been quiet since we got in the car. He seemed a bit uneasy. I couldn't blame him. I would be, too, if Webb had almost ripped off my head. Nevertheless, I imagined Ben was regretting ever getting involved in the first place.

I certainly didn't want to be here or know anything about vampires, either. Surely, Mr. Jackson was worried about us.

"Webb spoke to Mr. Jackson this morning. I believe he's at school," Sloan piped in.

I wanted to tell Sloan it was impolite to eavesdrop. But one pissed-off vampire was enough.

The car turned onto Ash Street. The trees rustled with the light breeze. We passed Ben's neighbor, Buster Greene, who was picking up his newspaper in the driveway. He stared at us as we drove by. I wondered why he was even home. Baseball season had already started, and usually, he was on the road a lot, according to Ben. Maybe he had a few home games this week.

Buster's house faded behind the trees as Tripp pulled into Ben's driveway alongside his Ford Explorer. I wondered how his car had gotten back there—it had been parked at Crest and Skylark the day before, where the fight had broken out. Ben and I looked at each other. As if he knew what I was thinking, he shrugged. He opened the back door and stuck one foot out.

"Not yet," Sloan snapped.

Tripp's head jerked up, adjusting the rearview mirror.

Oh no! Not again. The last time Tripp's head jerked up like that was the day before, at school, when he'd sensed danger. I held my breath.

A car stopped at the curb in front of the house.

Tripp glanced over his left shoulder. "Okay, we're clear."

Olivia climbed out of her Jeep and scanned the area with mechanical precision, as if she had been programmed with a computer chip, then walked toward the left side of the house. Her partner, whose name I'd found out was Fehherty, backed the car up, disappearing from our view.

As if on cue, Sloan got out and went around to the right side of Ben's beautiful home.

After Tripp gave the all clear, he reminded Ben and me we had thirty minutes.

Ben bolted out of the car and stalked up to his front door. I hurried to catch up to him.

Once we were inside, Lucy came barreling down the hall, wagging her tail.

"Hey, girl. How're you?" Ben asked in a high-pitched voice.

"We only have a few minutes, Ben," I said.

Ben picked up Lucy. "I don't care how long we have. I'm taking my time. I don't want to go back to that dungeon and deal with more crap from the vamps. I'm going to school."

"How're you going to get by our bodyguards?"

"Shh." He put his index finger to his lips and looked around as if he was about to tell me a big secret. "Dad? You home?" Ben called out.

"Sloan said he was at school," I reminded him.

Just in case, we didn't move, waiting for any signs of Mr. Jackson.

Ben shook his head. "He's not here. He would've heard us by now."

Tripp glided in through the front door and glared at us. "We need to stay on track." He pointed to the watch on his right wrist.

"It's not like we have vampire speed," I muttered.

"I heard that, Jo," Tripp growled.

Ignoring Tripp, I padded up the stairs, thinking about a much-needed shower, but hesitated when I reached my room. Ben was staring at me as though he wanted to say something. After a long second, he broke eye contact and walked into his room.

I couldn't tell what was going through his mind except my heart had skipped a beat.

Blowing out the air in my lungs, I rushed into my room and flopped on the bed. Then I grabbed a pillow, buried my face in it, and screamed. My feelings were all over the scale. One minute, my body tingled, and in the next, fear coursed through me, followed by pain. I couldn't make sense of anything. The emotional faucet opened, and tears poured out. I kept telling myself to be strong and stay focused, but I wasn't sure how much more vampire excitement I could handle. I wiped my eyes with a corner of the pillowcase, stood, and headed into the bathroom.

I stood under the hot spray and examined my body. The stitches on my cheek were all but gone except for one just below my eye. The stab wound under my left breast was still sore to the touch, but not as painful as a week before.

After I finished showering, I toweled off. I didn't have time to dry my hair, so I brushed it, gathered it into a ponytail, then wrapped a band around it. I braved a quick glance in the mirror, hoping my appearance had graduated from zombie to halfway-decent-looking human. Satisfied I was presentable, I changed into a clean pair of jeans and another long-sleeved Henley in red. As I laced up my boots, a loud bang echoed in the house, followed by glass shattering.

I jerked up my head, held my breath, and listened. Another loud bang sounded, but it was more like someone chopping wood. I quickly laced my other boot then grabbed a few clothing items and shoved them into my backpack when a knock startled me.

"Jo?" Ben whispered. "Jo, you in there?"

Relieved it was Ben, I opened the door. "What's going on?" I peeked into the hall.

"I think those Pluto vamps followed us." He extended his hand, motioning for me to take it.

"Wait." I hurried to get my backpack, and when I turned, I plowed right into Ben's muscular frame. "Geez. Give a girl some space, would you?"

His gaze bored into me as he grabbed my hand. "Come on."

This time, his touch didn't spark any type of tingling sensations. I wanted to scream again. Maybe the night before had been a fluke, or maybe my nerves and adrenaline were masking my vampire hormones.

We rushed down the hall, passing Ben's room where Lucy was crying and scratching to get out. My heart broke for the adorable dog.

But Lucy became a distant memory when it sounded as if a lamp broke somewhere in the house.

Ben came to an abrupt halt at the top of the steps, causing me to plow right into the bulging backpack he had strapped to him.

I rubbed my nose where it made contact. I really needed to pay more attention. My nerves were going to get me hurt or into trouble. "How are we getting out of here?"

He paced in short furious strides as the grunting sounds grew louder and closer.

We needed to get out quickly. I didn't want to be used as a pincushion. I'd escaped the day before, but I wasn't so sure I would be so lucky again, even with Jonah locked up. Somehow, I didn't think that mattered.

"Ben?"

"I'm thinking," he whispered.

"You don't have time to think," I murmured. I wanted to shout at him. I was tired of being chased and told what to do. "Do you have the keys to your car?"

He shook his head. "I left my keys in the car when I saw that dude about to stab you with a needle the size of a yardstick. It was all I could do to put the car in park and shut it off."

Something banged against the wall near the stairs. I jumped and let out a little screech. If Ben wasn't going to move, I had to. We would be vamp meat before we could blink. I wrapped the other strap of my backpack over my left shoulder and adjusted it so I had equal weight on both sides. Then I grabbed the railing and stepped down onto the first stair.

"What're you doing?" Ben ran over to me.

"We can't stay up here. We're cornered."

He raked his hand through his wet cinnamon hair. "Let me go ahead of you." He jumped down, landing softly onto the second step then the third. Then he waved his hand.

I took in a deep breath and followed, but not too close in case he knocked me out with his backpack.

Ben bent over the railing, peered down the hall before straightening.

"What's wrong? Is it Tripp?"

The banging stopped.

Where are Tripp and Sloan? I prayed they were okay and that they were close by.

"I need to get my spare keys," Ben whispered. "They should be on the key rack in the kitchen."

Great. Nothing like walking into a vampire's nest.

Ben peered over the railing one more time. "Okay, the coast is clear. Let's go."

I didn't move. The house was chillingly quiet. *Where did the vamps go?* A minute before, it had sounded as if they were in the hallway.

"Come on." Ben signaled with his hand.

I ran down the rest of the stairs behind Ben. He headed in the direction of the kitchen while I peeked into the living room.

My pulse quickened when I found the wood coffee table was broken into pieces. Then my heart hammered against my sore ribs when I saw Ben frozen at the basement door.

"What's wrong?" I whispered.

Ben slid his hand through the crack in the door, eased it open, then slowly pointed to his ear as he listened.

I couldn't hear anything, but I could smell something. I inhaled deeply. A sweet incense drifted in the air and my mouth watered.

Ben's eyes grew wide. "What?"

I could feel my eyebrows drawing down. "I smell blood. Lots of it."

"How do you... never mind. I didn't hear anyone downstairs. I'll get my keys. You stay here."

I couldn't move anyway. The smell of blood had me frozen. Suddenly, it was driving me crazy. My head began spinning, and my veins burned like they were on fire. I needed fresh air.

I was about to turn when I spied a hand reaching around the other side of the kitchen en-trance and grabbed Ben's wrist. Then his body jerked forward before he disappeared into the kitchen. "Jo, run!" he shouted.

My brain froze. If I ran outside, I would prob-ably have run right into a swarm of Plutariums. If I stayed there, I would be vamp meat anyway. Either way, I was screwed. *Where are Tripp, Sloan, and Olivia?*

My mind told me to get out of the house, but my feet had something different in mind. Before I knew it, I was running into the kitchen.

I rounded the corner and tried to stop, but my feet kept going, sliding as if I was skating on ice. I looked down, and the floor was covered in blood. I extended my arms to balance myself. I plowed right into a black-haired vamp leaning against the kitchen island with one ankle crossed over the other, examining the hilt of a dagger between his hands.

I pushed, using his hard chest as a springboard to force myself away from him. The dagger he held thudded to the floor. I lost my balance as the weight of my backpack threatened to pull me backward. Trying to stay upright, I swung my arms, thrashing at the air as if trying not to drown. I bent slightly forward and nearly fell face-first into the pond of blood.

I dug my heels into the floor as an anchor to keep my legs from extending outward. My arms hung parallel to the floor as if I was on a balance beam. Slowly, I placed both my hands on my knees and pushed up, straightening my upper torso. When I was certain I was safe from swimming in the pool of blood, I blew out all the air in my lungs.

"Bravo, Jo." The black-haired vamp clapped. "That took some skill."

His dagger lay on the floor, the blade gleaming.

Whose blood is on the floor? Oh my God, is it Tripp's blood? He was the only Sentinel in the house with us. A sudden pang of anger welled up in me. I wanted to punch the smug vampire standing in front of me.

"Who the heck are you? And what did you do to Tripp?"

"Now, now. Slow down. One question at a time, my dear."

"I'm not your dear, creep."

"Jo, maybe tone it down a bit. He has a knife," Ben said in a low voice.

The vamp glared at Ben. "It's a dagger. Get your weapons straight, kid." Then the vamp turned to me. "Yes, Jo. You should listen to your boyfriend here." He flicked his thumb toward Ben. "My name is Fernando, and I'm pleased to finally meet you, Jo." He sounded as though I was some sort of celebrity.

Far from it.

Regardless, Ben seemed frozen where he stood. The key holder dangled near his head. All he had to do was grab his car keys and run. On the other hand, the sticky, slick substance beneath my feet kept me rooted in place. If I ran, the blood would claim me before the cocky vampire did. Plus, the smell of it had my head spinning.

Ben looked at Fernando then at me.

Fernando glowered. "I know what you're thinking. Don't even try it, boy."

"*Run!*" I mouthed to Ben.

Ben took one step to his right when a thud sounded in the room. My heart jumped out of my chest.

Ben had a look of sheer terror on his face. The dagger stuck straight out of the wall just half an inch from his head.

I gasped. "Ben, *run!*"

Ben grabbed a handful of keys from the hook and sprinted out of the kitchen.

"I don't care about him. You know I'm here for you, sweet thing," the smug vamp said.

"Fuck you, asshole."

"My, my. I do have a feisty one on my hands. I like a challenge, you know."

I slid my left foot back then my right, using the blood to my advantage. *Maybe I can lure Fernando into the puddle of blood and see if he could stand without falling.* I kept my eyes trained on him as I inched back toward the hallway.

Angling his head to one side, he grinned. "You're not going to get away from me, sweet thing."

"Humph, watch me, asshole."

I was hoping the boots I wore would have some traction on the bottom. With the adrenaline pumping through me at warp speed, I spun on my heel, glided a few feet, then ran. I made it to the front door when Fernando grabbed me by my ponytail.

I reached around with both hands, trying to get him off me, but he only pulled harder. "Let me go," I screamed. "You're hurting me."

He grunted, dragging me into the entryway. "Sweetheart, the last thing I want to do is hurt you, but you gave me no choice."

"Let me go," I repeated as my muscles tensed.

"Only if you cooperate." He whirled me around so we were facing each other.

Terror coursed through me as I widened my eyes.

He was holding a dagger ready to plunge the blade into me. "I will use this on you, and I won't hesitate, either." He pointed the tip of the dagger at my cheek. "Like the person who already branded you did."

Fantastic! Another asshole who needs a knife to threaten a sixteen-year-old girl who is half his size and with only human strength. I was beginning to think having vampire strength wouldn't be such a terrible idea. "Fine. What do you want, then? You want to kill me? You want to inject me with some horse needle? Or...."

Out of the corner of my eye, I caught a glimpse of Ben with a baseball bat in his hands at the other end of the hallway.

I scrambled to think of a distraction so Fernando wouldn't hear or smell Ben. But it was no use.

The vamp moved in a blur and was ready to annihilate Ben.

I tapped Fernando on the shoulder. "Um, sir."

He gave me a fleeting look and growled. His fangs had descended, and his eyes were liquid coal.

We were so screwed. Ben and this vampire were about to go head-to-head in a battle that Ben couldn't win, even with a baseball bat.

"Sir, forget him. You're here for me, right? Let him go, and I'll go with you."

He ignored me, his dagger ready to drive

into Ben.

"Seriously, asshole," I shouted, "take me! You said Ben means nothing to you. Besides, how can he hurt you? He's human."

Lines dented Ben's forehead. "What are you doing, Jo? You can't go with him. Are you nuts?"

"Yeah, Jo. What are you doing?" Fernando mimicked.

I had to convince this angry vampire I was serious, even though I wasn't. I had to lure him away so Ben wouldn't get hurt.

"But I want to go with him. Maybe I'll see Sam. I can help him," I said in a soft voice, hoping Fernando would believe I was sincere. But, while I was trying to lie, I realized that maybe I was right. Maybe I would see Sam and *could* help him.

Fernando stepped to the side, his back toward the living room. I assumed he did that just to keep his eyes on us.

"You're not going with this dude," Ben said with both hands securely around the baseball bat, his knuckles reddish white.

"Who're you to tell me what I can do?" I fired back.

Fernando watched us in quiet fascination. "This is quite amusing. You human teenagers are very dramatic."

I wanted to laugh. This vamp didn't know what the word "dramatic" meant. He was the one being dramatic, with his daggers and fangs.

Ben inched forward, shaking his head. "I can't let you do this, Jo."

"Boy, I wouldn't come any closer. She's already told you she doesn't want you." Fernando chuckled.

I glowered at Fernando who upon closer scrutiny was dressed in all black. "Stay out of this, asshole."

He snarled. "Sweetheart, I told you my name is Fernando, and if you call me 'asshole' one more time—"

At that moment, Ben swung the bat, made contact with the vampire's head, and knocked him to the floor.

"Run, Jo. *Now!*" Ben commanded.

I bolted out and jumped the porch steps two at a time, then ran toward Ben and Tripp's cars. I scanned the street, looking for any sign of Tripp, Olivia, Sloan, and Fehherty. The neighborhood was dead quiet—not even the birds were singing.

They had to be around somewhere. Fernando couldn't have taken out four strong military vampires, not with the weapons they had strapped to their uniforms.

"Come on, come on," I said into the cool spring air. I tapped my foot frantically on the concrete. "Hurry up, Ben," I whispered to myself.

Then I remembered Olivia's Jeep. Fehherty had moved it out of sight.

I stalked down the driveway when Ben shouted, "Get in the car."

Before I could pivot, Ben peeled out of his driveway. When he reached me, he slowed, leaned over and opened the passenger door. But the car was moving too fast for me to hop in.

"Slow down!" I yelled.

"Just jump in the fucking car, Jo!"

As I was about to dive in, I caught a glimpse of Fernando staggering out the front door, holding his head, a bloodthirsty expression plastered on his face.

"Get in! Get in!" Ben's voice cracked as the car picked up speed.

"Ben, slow down," I shouted again.

I had half my body inside and half out when Fernando flew through the air and landed on the hood. The vehicle jerked, I lost my footing, and the car dragged me down the driveway as I held on. Then Ben slammed on the brakes, and Fernando's body slid off the hood onto the pavement while my head hit the bottom of the door.

"Come on, Jo. Get in the car—hurry!" Ben was frantic.

I'm going to kill someone today, and it might be Ben. After I was safely in the passenger seat, my heart raced like a sprinter toward the finish line.

I clutched my chest as I kept my eyes focused on Fernando's body, which lay motionless next to Tripp's car. I wasn't sure if he was dead, but I didn't think a fall like that would kill a vampire.

The car fishtailed out of the driveway as Ben shifted gears then floored it. We sped down the street, passing Olivia's Jeep, but neither Olivia nor Fehherty was anywhere in sight.

"Where're Tripp and Sloan?" I asked.

"No clue. Don't care right now."

"Ben, slow down. There's a stop sign ahead," I shouted.

The car decelerated, and out of nowhere, someone fell on the hood. The dent from Fernando only got deeper when the flying brute landed on the Explorer. Ben slammed on the brakes, and the vampire flew off and skidded across the pavement in front of us. My body jerked forward, my hands plastered against the dashboard keeping me from going through the windshield. Then Olivia appeared out of the blue, her eyes pitch-black and fangs in full view. She bent down, hoisted up the new vamp, then threw him onto the lawn of the corner house.

Ben and I watched in amazement as the broad-shoulder vamp, who Olivia had just planted into the grass, stood up as if nothing fazed him.

"Do these vamps ever die?" Ben asked.

"I don't know."

"Uh-oh." Ben was looking in the rearview mirror.

I gaped behind me to find Tripp was in a dead sprint toward us. "Ben, maybe we should wait for him."

"Are you insane? I'm not hanging around." He slammed on the gas.

The car bucked. I grabbed the seat belt and strapped myself in. We had just crested a hill when the front of the car rose in the air.

"Shit. Tripp's on the back," Ben bellowed.

I craned my neck to see that Tripp had both hands on the trunk and was pulling the car toward him. "We really need to stop." I braced my hand on the dashboard.

"Look, the safest place for us right now is any-where but here," Ben said calmly.

The engine revved and sounded as if Tripp were holding back a wild lion.

I closed my eyes and said a silent prayer. I

didn't want to hurt Tripp, but maybe Ben was right. Maybe we weren't safe around them. In a flash, the front of the car dropped, the engine whined, and we pitched forward.

I stole a look behind me. Tripp had his cell phone at his ear, probably calling Lieutenant London.

I said another prayer, thanking God it wasn't Tripp's blood on the floor in the kitchen. We'd just passed Olivia fighting the brute, who I assumed was a Plutarium. That left Fehherty and Sloan. The last time I saw Sloan, he'd disappeared around the back of the house, while Fehherty had stayed in the Jeep.

I covered my mouth and shook my head a few times. I didn't have time to worry about Sloan or Fehherty. Ben and I needed to stay alive. Besides, I wasn't ready to be a prisoner again.

Ben kept checking the rearview mirror. "Where should we go?"

I thought about it for a minute. With the vampires behind us, we had our chance to search for Sam without vampires breathing down our necks, especially Lieutenant London. We were free for the moment.

I was determined to take full advantage of it.

23

Ben and I made our way through the state forest. I hadn't told Ben yet where we were going. I really didn't want to go back to the funeral home. It was creepy, and all signs suggested that Neil was a Plutarium, given the tattoo on the back of his neck. But if Sam had been looking for Neil, he might've tried to go back to the funeral home. I didn't have a clue how to get there, though. It had been dark the other night when Neil drove Sam and me to it. The only landmark I could remember was the park, but that wasn't going to help me.

"Okay, we're in Westport. Where to now?" Ben asked.

"Foster's Funeral Home," I replied.

"What?" Ben snapped his head toward me. "A funeral home? Why?"

I didn't know if Sam had told Ben anything about our hospital escape, how we hid in a funeral home for a night, or that we were running from a large man who turned out to be a vampire. Given his surprised reaction, it didn't appear so. Besides, it wasn't as if I was releasing any top secret information. Heck, the sheer knowledge that vampires existed was certainly classified as top secret, and Ben already had that in his arsenal.

I sighed. "The night I landed in the hospital, a bunch of weird things started to happen. When Sam—"

"Jo, *weird* isn't the word for what happened to you."

I rolled my eyes. I didn't disagree, but Ben annoyed me by cutting me off midsentence. He had done that a couple of times the day before too. "Anyway, when we were in the hospital room, Sam was trying to find a way we could get around the cop. The one in the coma. Anyway, we heard banging and grunting, so I peeked out the door, and there was this tall dude with a blue bandana and pitch-black eyes. He had the cop pinned against the wall by the throat. Well, that was

Jonah, the one you hit with a baseball bat at Crest and Skylark. Remember?"

The car slowed to a crawl. It was as if Ben was in a trance. I was learning that he was moodier than an athlete on steroids. At that thought, I flinched. Maybe he was. He had great physical form, sculpted arms, and a broad chest, not to mention that he was one of the best players on the high school baseball team. His batting average was .385, and he constantly hit home runs.

"What happened next?" he asked.

I peeked at the speedometer, and the needle fluctuated between twenty and twenty-five miles per hour. The speed limit was forty. "Are you going to go any faster?"

Ben checked the rearview mirror. "There's no one behind us. Go on."

I had to think for a second. "Oh... then Sam and I somehow made it out and ended up in the hospital's boiler room. That's where we met Neil Foster. Sam was convinced Neil was the janitor at our school. Neil drove us to his parents' funeral home for the night. But in school last week, I over-heard two boys talking about a red truck and a dead body the police found in the forest." I paused to moisten my lips.

"Whose body was it?"

I shrugged. "Not sure. But one boy mentioned the red truck the police found was registered to the janitor of our school. At least, that's what the police told his dad. I relayed what I'd overheard to Sam, and he said we would talk about it at lunch. But we never made it to lunch. I assumed when Sam didn't show up in your dad's office, he was trying to find Neil. Then Webb showed up, and you know the rest."

"My dad told you that Arlan is the janitor, not Neil."

"But that's what I don't understand. Sam knew Neil, like they were best friends. Sam even told me he trusted him."

Ben slapped his hand down on the console, making me jump. "You know, Arlan has a couple of dudes that come in occasionally to help out when we have practice or a ballgame. Maybe this Neil guy is part of Arlan's crew."

"But it still doesn't add up. I get how Jonah fits into the picture, but I don't understand how Neil fits." I shook my head. "Jonah was chasing us. Neil was helping us, or at least I think he was, but he also seems to be one of them."

"You think Sam went to the funeral home, looking for Neil?" Ben asked.

"I don't know. It's the only place I can think of that Sam might go." My body trembled.

"You okay?"

"Yeah. There was always something about the funeral home that gave me the creeps."

"Well, duh. It's a funeral home. You know, with dead people?"

I dropped my head into my hands. Just the mention of Sam and dead people didn't mesh well. I sensed Ben was trying to make light of the situation, but he had a smart-ass streak as well.

"Hey. I'm sorry. I... didn't—"

I raised my head. "What if Sam is—"

"He's not. Don't even think that," Ben said. "We'll check it out and see what we find. By the way, is Neil part of the fang gang?"

"Huh?"

"You know." Ben sucked in his lower lip and pulled back his upper one, making his teeth protrude. "Get it?"

I arched an eyebrow. "You're weird. I'm not sure. He has a tattoo on the back of his neck. Some type of symbol with the letters P and L. It's the same symbol that Jonah has engraved on his ring. I think it stands for Plutarium."

"I still don't get the whole planet thing, either." Ben flipped on the right blinker as he wheeled onto a side street then stopped along an embankment of low brush and bushes.

"Are we lost?" I asked.

"Um... not exactly sure where you want me to go."

A roof peeked out in the distance. The street had several tall maple trees, which dominated the wooded area along the side of the road. The hair at the nape of my neck rose as the trees rustled in the wind, and a shiver skidded up my arms. *Odd.*

I turned my head slightly to find a black SUV approaching from behind, slowly moving in our direction. My heart sank.

"What's wrong, Jo?" Ben asked. "Did you see a ghost?"

I flicked my thumb over my shoulder. "You could say that. The SUV behind us. It looks like the same vehicle that I think followed Sam and me last week on the way to your house."

Ben adjusted the rearview mirror. "A lot of people own black SUVs."

"That may be true." I let out a deep sigh even though my intuition was screaming to run.

The SUV inched past us. I was sure they could see us, but the dark-tinted windows kept us blinded from them.

Ben shifted into gear and eased onto the road,

following the SUV. "See? Nothing to worry about. If they were vamps, they would've been out of that car so fast, we'd be vamp meat."

He may have been right, but my heart still hammered against my sternum.

"Come on, buddy, move," Ben called. "Is this guy going to a funeral?"

I laughed nervously. Maybe we were going to a funeral, and the car in front of us was leading us to it—maybe it was our funeral.

My pulse went into overdrive. I had a fleeting thought that we probably should've stayed with the Sentinels. They were irritating and intimidating, but their presence might have been better than the potential nest of trouble we were driving into.

Ben tapped his right hand on the steering wheel. I imagined he was trying to release some of his nervous energy. I hadn't told him about the mysterious man leaning against a black SUV in the hospital garage. I had forgotten all about it.

"You're still pale. Did you see something else?" he asked.

I shook my head. "It's probably nothing."

"Nothing? I recently found out that vampires are real. What else is there?"

"I just remembered something from the night

when Sam and I left the hospital. It involves the car in front of us."

Ben slammed on the brakes, and the car jerked.

"What the heck are you doing?" I shouted. "Are you trying to kill me?"

"You're telling me the car in front of us or one like it was also... what? At the hospital the night you left?"

I bobbed my head. "There was a person in the hospital garage, leaning against a black SUV that night. I think the same person followed Sam and me the morning we took a cab to your house." I peeked at him through the corner of my eye.

He raised his eyebrows, practically reaching his hairline.

"Um, Ben, do you think you should pull over?"

"So who are they?" he asked as the car accelerated slightly.

"I don't know. But it's good we're behind them. It might be nothing."

"Let's hope so." Ben began tapping the steering wheel again, more loudly than before.

Between his impatience and, I imagined, his nervousness, I prayed he wouldn't explode. He kept his gaze straight ahead, staring at the vehicle in front of us.

We rounded a curve, and a stop sign stood sentinel ahead. The leading car's brake lights illuminated, and Ben tapped his brakes, almost stopping the car, keeping his distance.

I gnawed the inside of my cheek, praying that the chills that skated up my spine and down my arms were all for nothing.

"Do you know how to get to the funeral home?" Ben asked in a shaky voice.

I didn't take my eyes off the road. "Not sure, but I don't think it's that far outside the state forest. I remember some big park across the street from it."

He snapped his head toward me. "Park? You're kidding, right?"

"No. Why?"

"There's only one park in Westport, and it's in the worst part of town."

Bingo! I remembered thinking how Neil had dumped Sam and me in a trashy part of town with shady-looking people and abandoned homes. "Do you know how to get there?"

"Yep, but it's not a place I want to hang out in, even during the day. Gee, you're full of all kinds of scary info, aren't you?"

I swallowed thickly. "It can't be any worse than what we've been through already."

The SUV stopped at the stop sign ahead of us.

"Is there another road you can take?" I asked.

"There is. But not until we get past this stop sign."

I sucked in some air, waiting for the vehicle in front of us to move.

"The area has a couple of gangs, and there's a lot of drugs in that part of town. You think the vamps are bad? Let's hope we don't run into any of the gang members." Ben kept his focus on the black SUV.

Great! It was just my luck that more drama would be added to the day.

Then their right blinker flashed. The green sign on the corner read Fall River – 15, and an arrow pointed to the right. The black SUV turned, and Ben and I released a huge sigh at the same time, as if someone had pumped a load of air into the car.

The Explorer rolled to a stop. Ben looked both ways before crossing the intersection.

Every ounce of tension disintegrated from my body, and I let out another deep breath. "See, it was nothing," I squeaked.

"Maybe." Ben relaxed against his seat.

As we made our way to the park, I couldn't help but think of Sam. We had to find him before Webb asked me again about my decision. I stared at the dented hood of the Explorer. My mind was a medley of confusion, fear, and anticipation of what lay ahead. Several questions peppered my thoughts. *Will we find Sam? Can I overlook the fact that vampires exist? Or that my father is a powerful vampire? If I don't change into a vampire, how much longer will I crave blood? Will vampire puberty ever go away?* Not only was I trapped in a world where I didn't belong, I was trapped inside myself, inside my pseudo-vampire body, complete with blood cravings and emotions I couldn't make sense of. I closed my eyes and inhaled, trying to release the rising tension that began to itch inside me.

"We're almost there," Ben said.

I blinked a few times, and rows of abandoned, boarded-up three-story homes came into view, making for a gloomy landscape, exactly the way it was a week ago—with one exception. There were no homeless people sleeping on the porches. The neighborhood was deserted. It looked as if we were driving through a ghost town. Not even the gangs Ben spoke of were anywhere in sight.

"The home should be up ahead," I said, pointing to my right.

"What's wrong?" Ben asked.

"Nothing. Why?"

"Your eyes are black. You're not vamping out on me, are you?"

"No. I was thinking about Sam. My emotions just got the best of me, that's all. Besides, I'm not a vampire."

"It'd better stay that way," he replied.

He had no idea how much I agreed with him. "Let's focus on Sam." I didn't want to talk about me.

The park came into view on our left.

The car slowed as Ben pumped the brakes, surveying his surroundings. "This place gives me the willies. Where is everyone? It looks like we're crawling into some kind of horror movie."

"Just imagine sleeping in the funeral home. In this neighborhood," I added.

After Ben parked in front of the home, I slid out and admired the Victorian style with its wrap-around porch and the pyramid pitched roof, which I hadn't gotten the chance to see the other night. I'd acquired an appreciation for old-style architecture thanks to Mr. Zee, my history teacher. He'd spent the entire last semester teaching us the history of Fall River. Part of the class was dedicated to the different architectural styles of the homes and buildings in the area. Aside from the paint chipping off the shingles, the funeral home was the best-looking structure in the neighborhood.

"So what now?" Ben scanned the park. "It doesn't look like anyone's here."

I started walking up the path to the front porch when Ben grabbed me. "What?" I practically snapped at him.

"How're we getting in? What's our plan?" Trepidation laced his tone.

I wasn't thinking about any of that. I just wanted to see if Sam was inside. "Look, we don't have much time. We'll do a quick check. That's it. Okay?"

"I don't like this," he said as he followed behind me.

Up to that point, Ben had been on an emotional rollercoaster, wavering between fear, anger, disgust, and acceptance and ending with bravado toward the vampires, even standing up to the alpha vamp. But his bravery turned into mush—about a funeral home.

The wooden steps creaked as I climbed, sending my nerves into overdrive, even more so when I found the front door ajar. But what had me stopping short was the scent drifting out. I covered my mouth and nose with my hand.

"What's wrong?" Ben asked as he sidled up to me.

Suddenly, my gums began hurting, and I winced. The addict in me took over, and I wasn't sure I could control myself. The urge to drink blood overwhelmed me. My gums began throbbing, and I had this overwhelming need to release the fangs I didn't have—*or do I?* I dipped my fingers into my mouth and searched my gums but found nothing.

"Gee whiz, Jo, it looks like you're about to pass out." Ben threw his arm around my back. "Sit over there." He motioned to a loveseat on the porch.

Wiping my hands on my jeans, I shook my head and slid out from under his arm. I needed to get away from him. While I didn't have fangs, I still didn't trust myself. "No, I'm fine. I mean, I'll be fine. Let's get this over with."

A puzzled look washed over him. "You sure? We don't have to do this."

Get a hold of yourself, I repeated silently in my head. But the smell of blood wafting out drove me crazy, drawing me inside. I wanted to scream, to run, to get as far away from Ben and this place as I could.

Propping up my courage, I walked into the funeral home, the smell of dried blood and decay washing over me. I sensed that something had happened in there recently.

The sound of Ben's heartbeat echoed as he approached from behind, his blood raging through his veins. I turned and watched the vein in his neck pulsing with every heartbeat. Taking in a quiet breath, I stood deathly still, making sure I had control of myself.

"It stinks in here," he said in a nasally tone.

He had no idea what the smell was doing to me.

"Why don't you check out the rooms down here, and I'll check the rooms upstairs?" he said. "We'll meet back here in a few."

"No. I'll go upstairs." Before Ben could protest, I disappeared around the corner. The smell dissipated a bit as I climbed, taking the steps two at a time. My mind wandered as pictures of the body bags Dr. Vieira had shown us flashed before me. I had a feverish feeling that some of those killings took place here.

At the top of the landing, I surveyed the hallway. One of the three rooms had its door closed. I walked over to the white-paneled aperture of the room Sam and I had slept in, swallowing down my nerves. I counted to three before I grabbed the doorknob, praying I wouldn't find Sam's body.

The second I opened the door, the pungent stench hit me like an F5 tornado. I gagged as I covered my nose. It seemed someone had doused the room in vinegar trying to cover the underlying scent of blood.

I rolled back my shoulders as I entered. The room was in shambles. A curtain rod had come loose, and the curtain panel hung at an angle, ready to fall off. The large assortment of books that had been neatly tucked into the bookshelves was a cyclone of piles spread around as if someone had been hunting for a lost treasure. But I didn't see a body or my brother for that matter.

As relief coursed through me, I stepped carefully as I went over to one stack and knelt in front of a book that had its pages splayed. I picked it up with my free hand and turned it over. My eyes bulged when I read the title, *Vampire Genetics*. I sat on my heels and released the hold on my nose, fascinated by the topic that someone would write about vampire genetics. I mean, vampires were one thing, but I wasn't aware that someone had actually documented it. Then again, my knowledge of the history of the vampire species was only one week old, and that knowledge was a tiny speck on the radar.

I grabbed the book. I had to get out of there, or

I was going to puke. Just as I was about to leave, a car door slammed. Excitement stirred. Maybe it was Neil, and he had Sam with him.

I rushed over to the window and peeked around the panel. But the only car I saw was the one Ben and I came here in. I shifted my gaze out to the park, where a few die-hard runners were jogging around the melted pond. Maybe I was hearing things. I was ready to leave once again when I spotted something familiar on the red couch.

As I headed in that direction over the scattered mess, I couldn't help but smile as the memory of Sam teasing me came to mind. How he'd pretended I'd had blood on my neck, as if a vampire had bitten me. As it turned out, it had been the red velvet lint from the couch.

But my smile quickly faded when I found a balled up red T-shirt on the couch. I dropped the book and picked up the T-shirt. Dried blood splattered the front just below the words Got Milk? Tears streamed down my face. Sam had been there. It was the T-shirt he'd worn to school the day before.

No. No. No.

I couldn't breathe, even more so when I pivoted on wobbly legs and my gaze landed on a very familiar face.

"What... what are *you* doing here?" I asked as my eyes widened.

"Is that any way to greet your doctor?" Dr. Case asked with a sinister smile.

My brain scrambled, trying to make sense of why he was at a funeral home.

"I've noticed you're healing well." His gaze roamed my body. "Your stitches are gone. I have to say, I do good work."

I touched the new scar on my left cheek and returned the gesture, sizing him up as he leaned against the doorjamb. He wore a black button-down shirt that hung loosely over his blue jeans. The last time I saw him, he'd had on one of those surgical caps. Today, his dark, wavy brown hair hung loosely just above his ears, and his brown eyes were alight with pleasure.

"What do you want?" I asked.

"I'm here for you," Dr. Case replied with malice.

"Get in line," I blurted out. I wasn't sure what he was talking about, but a tingling of menace prickled my skin.

"I see you found something?" His thin lips were curled at the edges.

"Do you have something to do with this?" I held up Sam's T-shirt.

His half smile indicated he did.

As if the trees parted and light shone through, I remembered the tattoo on the back of his neck. I couldn't see all of it when I'd first met him, but a puzzle piece snapped into place. "You're one of them." My body tensed, and I squeezed Sam's shirt.

"You need to be more specific, Jo," Dr. Case said as he pushed off the doorframe and came toward me.

I edged back, and my left foot slipped. I fell onto a pile of books, straight down on my butt. Books, picture frames, and boxes surrounded me as I tried to stand. The box I used as an anchor was too squishy and collapsed, causing my right hand to puncture it. Panic set in.

Before I could make my next move, Dr. Case yanked me by the left arm. The force of his strength sent fear whistling through my veins. He wasn't helping me. He was hurting me.

Why do I always get myself into this kind of mess? Why won't people leave me alone? As he pulled me out of the mountain of books, my hand came free, and I swung my arm around and punched him in the stomach.

His smug smile vanished, replaced with a murderous expression. He squeezed my arm tighter and dragged me toward the door.

"Where's Ben?" I screamed.

"He's not going to hear you," Dr. Case said through gritted teeth.

All the blood rushed to my feet. "You better not—"

"Or?" He stopped dragging me, his hand still wrapped around my left arm as he glared at me. "You and I are going downstairs to have a chat. If you stay calm, we'll get through this relatively quickly."

I had no clue what he wanted. Whatever it was sounded ominous. I swallowed down my nerves and tried to think of something fast.

"Are we going to stay here and ogle each other, or are we going downstairs to dance?" I asked.

He began pulling me again, but his grip was slightly weaker. "You really are a smart-ass. Figures for a teenager."

I jerked my arm away, and with lightning speed, he grabbed hold of my throat. *Maybe he is a vamp.*

I clawed at his hands, but his grip only tightened. So I did the one thing that had worked for me before with Cliff and Blake. I jabbed my knee into his crotch, not once, but twice.

He released me immediately and planted his hands between his legs. "You little bitch." His voice was strained.

I ran out for my life, gagging, trying to get oxygen back into my lungs. At the bottom of the stairs, I peered around the banister, still massaging my neck. The door to the basement was ajar. A dank smell wafted through the crack, and my stomach lurched.

My Spidey sense warned me not to go down there, but I had to find Ben.

Praying, I said out loud, "God help me."

"God isn't going to help you," Dr. Case said at my back.

Blowing out a breath, I pivoted to find Dr. Case standing at the base of the banister. I was screwed. As we stared at each other, I weighed my options. My only option was the basement, and I wasn't sure if there was an exit to the backyard, unless I kicked him in the balls again. Then I could run by him and out the front door.

"Go ahead. Run. Run down there." He flicked his chin toward the basement door.

I took one step back, keeping my focus on him. Then dug deep for courage and ran toward the basement door. Shrieking, I came to an abrupt halt on the top step as I latched onto the sawed-off railing, which prevented me from plunging to my death.

Where are the rest of the stairs? A light glowed from below. Ben's voice echoed, sounding muffled. *How did he get down there?*

Before I could react, Dr. Case wrapped one arm around my waist and the other around my mouth, dragging me down the hallway before throwing me into the front viewing room. I stumbled across the floor and landed inches from the open coffin.

I quickly crawled in the other direction, trying to get as far away from the ghastly thing as I could. I rested my head against the sill of the stained-glass window, thinking about my next move. I had no recourse as Dr. Case closed us in, jamming a chair under the doorknob. It was Dr. Case and me, and my stomach knotted.

He stalked toward me. "I'm not going to hurt you, Jo. I only want to talk."

I scrambled to my feet and hurried to the other side of the room. "Then talk."

He followed. "You want to tango. Interesting."

"I'm not sure what a Plutarium wants with me. I have nothing to offer." I kept dodging him, slipping from his grip every now and then. It was as if we were playing tag in the schoolyard.

He tucked his hands in his pockets and came to a stop in the middle of the room. "So you figured it out, did you?"

"Figured what out?" I didn't want to give away how much I knew.

He stared at me intently, his gaze menacing.

I rested against a sidewall, waiting for him to make a move.

He cocked his head to one side. "You really do look like him."

"Who? Sam? Of course I do. We're twins," I shot back.

Okay, we weren't identical in features, but we shared a lot of the same qualities. We both had black hair. The same shape lips, average-size nose, and, as I learned last week, we had a lot of the same physical changes going on. The only difference that I was aware of other than gender was the color of our eyes. Mine were silver, and Sam had forest-green eyes.

"I wasn't talking about Sam. I was talking about your father."

My jaw dropped as I slowly slid down the wall and dropped my head into my hands.

Who doesn't know my father? I wanted to raise

my hand like a little schoolgirl and shout, "I don't know my father. Am I the only one?" My desire to kill or mangle my absent dad was growing stronger as hours and days passed. I raised my head.

"I want to help you," Dr. Case said.

I jerked up my head to find him towering over with his hand extended.

"Get away from me," I snapped.

"I know he abandoned you. I can tell by your expression that you're not fond of him, either."

I shook my head. "You don't know anything."

"I'm not playing cat and mouse with you any-more." Before I could move, he was lifting me up and into his arms. "I don't have time for this."

"Put me down." I squirmed, trying to get free as he carried me to the coffin. Fear so strong stole my breath. "There's no way I'm getting in that!" I shouted.

He placed me inside the coffin, then closed the bottom half and knelt on the makeshift altar in front of it.

I jolted upright. "You're fucking crazy." I struggled to open the bottom half. "Get me out of this thing right now!" I screamed at the top of my lungs.

Dr. Case rose, pushed me back down, reached

over me, and placed his hand on the top cover. With one hand on the lid and his other hand on my chest, he said, "I'll close this and walk away. I just want to talk."

"Fuck you!"

"You leave me no choice. Besides, it will be better this way—tit for tat." Then he lowered the lid.

"No. Don't!" I begged. "I'll listen. What did you mean by tit for tat? Please, Dr. Case, open the lid."

He raised the lid slightly and glared down at me. "This is revenge for your father killing my sister." As he released his hand, the lid slammed shut.

"You're an asshole. I'm going to kill you!" I shouted, but my voice was muffled.

"Keep talking. Expend all your air. It'll make for a quicker death."

As I lay in the dark satin enclosure, my body shook uncontrollably as my claustrophobia kicked in. I took the deepest breath I could as tears streamed down my face. It was my father's fault. Everything bad in my life was the result of something my father did: foster care, vampires, and now this crazy doctor who wanted revenge.

I hated the man responsible for me being born.

"Dr. Case? Dr. Case? Are you out there? I'm sorry," I called. I closed my eyes and listened.

Only silence. Dead silence. *Did he leave?*

I banged and kicked, hoping he was still in the room. I screamed several times, but it was useless. "Stay calm," I muttered.

The more I tried to quiet my nerves, the faster my heart rate sped, ramming against my rib cage. *Boom. Boom. Boom.* I swore it was about to fly out of my chest.

"Please, God, let me get out of here. I've been a good girl. It's the bad people around me who treat me like this. Please help me," I said into the morbid darkness.

My breathing became shallow, and my eyelids grew heavy.

I didn't want to die before I found Sam.

24

A pain seared through my chest as if a heavy weight pressed against it. A man's voice filled the air, counting from one to five. I couldn't breathe through my nose. Someone or something pinched my nostrils together. Then a hand gently grabbed my mouth, and hot air entered as if someone were trying to kiss me. My chest heaved with every breath that entered my lungs. My eyes fluttered open then closed.

"Where's Dr. Vieira?" a familiar man's voice asked.

"Jo?" A hand tapped my cheek then pulled my left eyelid open. "Jo. Wake up." He tapped my cheek again.

I opened my eyes, and a blanket of haze

clouded my vision. I blinked several times and the room spun as if I was riding a merry-go-round.

My abdominal muscles contracted, then an intense pressure gripped my stomach. Vomit threatened, creeping up into the back of my throat. After several contractions, the pain eased, giving way to clear liquid filling my mouth, seeping out, and dripping down my neck.

"Sit her up. Now," a different male voice commanded. His voice was familiar too.

A hand slipped under my back and raised me forward. Then another hand grabbed hold of my wrist and pressed fingers on it.

"Her pulse is weak. We need to get her to the infirmary, but I don't want to move her just yet," the first voice said. "Olivia, get me a bottle of water from the van."

As if a pressure relief valve opened, I grabbed my stomach and heaved again, soaking my jeans. The dizziness slowed, and the room righted itself. I drew in a breath and oriented my vision.

Tripp stood to my left, watching Dr. Vieira, who was kneeling over me and touching my wrist. Webb sat on his heels on my right, holding my back for support.

"Where's Ben?" I asked Webb.

"He's fine," Webb replied.

I sighed, relieved that Ben was okay. "How long was I in the..." I couldn't bring myself to say it.

"We're not sure. But it couldn't have been longer than two hours, or you'd be dead," Dr. Vieira replied.

"What happened?" Webb asked, regarding me with concern swimming in his blue eyes.

"Why don't you ask, Dr. Case? Where is he?" I asked.

"He's on his way to the prison on base." Webb pushed to his feet. "Dr. Vieira, can we get her out of here now?"

Dr. Vieira rose and grabbed the water bottle from Olivia who had walked in. "Her pulse is stronger. Let's get her into the van. The fresh air might help." Dr. Vieira handed me the water. "Here. I want you to finish two bottles of water before you get back to headquarters. There's more in the van."

As Tripp and Webb gently eased me upright, the walls around me rushed in, and I staggered. Before I could take another step, Tripp picked me up and cradled me in his arms.

I was grateful it was Tripp. Maybe his touch would ease the dizziness. At the very least, he would calm me. As he carried me out, I spotted

Webb examining the ghastly coffin. For what? I wasn't sure.

Olivia picked up a small object from the altar before turning it over several times. Then she handed it to Webb.

"Watch your head," Tripp said as he carried me through the doorway to the sitting area.

I pressed my cheek on his shoulder. "I'm sorry."

"You shouldn't have run," Tripp said. "You could've gotten yourself killed." The muscle in his jaw ticked. "You scared the crap out of us." He sounded worried.

I had a hard time believing he was concerned about me. After all, Dr. Vieira's message in the war room the night before had been clear. I was essential to the outcome of their mission.

"You mean vampires get scared?" I asked with a hint of a smile.

"I see you're feeling better," he said.

I wasn't, but I couldn't pass up the chance to talk with Tripp. The only time he usually spoke was when he yelled at Ben and me or told me what to do. Engaging in an actual, normal conversation with him was unusual.

"Is Sloan okay?" I was afraid of his answer.

Tripp set me down on one of the seats in the

back of the van. "He lost a lot of blood, but he'll be fine."

"Where's Ben?" My voice broke.

He strapped me in, not saying a word.

"Tripp, any news on Sam?"

He stood at attention outside the van, watching and waiting for the rest of the team to emerge.

As if hours passed, he finally said, "I'll let Lieutenant London answer your questions."

An eerie feeling zipped through me. If they didn't have news on Sam, Tripp would've said no. He wouldn't have hesitated.

I shuddered, wondering whether it was good news or bad.

I HATED walking through those large steel doors again. I loathed everything about the Sentinels' Headquarters, from the cement structure and the stark white floors to the whole draconian vibe. Only the thought of news about Sam and making sure Ben was okay propelled me into the cold reception area.

On the drive over, I had kept quiet, thinking through what Dr. Case had mentioned about my estranged father killing Dr. Case's sister. I found trouble around every corner because of my father and was beginning to rack up quite the list of enemies thanks to Commander Steven Mason.

I sifted through the events during the past couple of weeks, trying to understand what Dr. Case's role had been in helping the Plutariums. *Is he a vampire? Is he the one who'd started my life on its road to hell?* Then, as if someone had splashed icy water in my face, it hit me. Dr. Case had told the nurse that night to send my blood sample to Patrick. *Was he referring to my Uncle Patrick, the great genetic scientist? Did Dr. Case know then that I was the daughter of Steven Mason? Was he the one following me in the black SUV?*

Cold air rushed past me, and I looked up to see Kate, who ran over and wrapped her arms around me.

"Lord, child, what did you do? You look pale. Let's get you up to Dr. Vieira's facility."

She should have been asking Dr. Case what he did. "Is Ben here?" I asked.

"He's in the medical wing." She guided me toward the elevator. "We have a surprise for you." Her eyes were alight with excitement, turning from blue to light gray.

I was learning that any emotional change in the vampires caused their eye color to change, as if their irises were mood rings, shining vibrantly one minute and turning darker the next. Since I carried the vampire gene, I wondered how often mine were shifting.

She stabbed the button adjacent to the elevator doors. "So, do you want to know what your surprise is?" she asked eagerly.

"No. I'm not ready for any surprises, unless you're going to tell me Sam is here and he's alive. I'm not sure I could handle anything else."

Her expression turned sullen.

I didn't care that I seemed to have hurt her feelings. I'd been locked in a coffin and left to die by a Plutarium doctor who claimed my father had killed his sister. Plus, I'd almost been taken by Fernando, another Plutarium vampire, who'd come close to killing Ben.

Five minutes later, we were on the mile-long trek to the medical facility. The only sound I could hear was my heart banging against my ribs. I drank the two bottles of water, as Dr. Vieira had instructed, but it didn't quite quell the dizziness. My body was sluggish, my eyelids were heavy, and I longed to lie down and sleep.

With each step, my body grew more painful. The white walls and never-ending hallways made it seem like a psychedelic black-and-white maze.

When we reached the double doors to the medical facility, Kate pressed a button on a metal panel, waited for the beep, then positioned her eyes over the clear bar at the top of the box.

"You ready?" she asked apprehensively.

"Ready for what?" She was scaring me.

She extended her delicate hand. "It's okay. You can see Ben," she said.

Despite the bad feeling I had, I placed my hand in hers, and together, we entered the infirmary.

Once inside, I rushed in, only to stop cold. I had no idea where Ben was.

"Over there." Kate pointed to a windowed room on the right.

The minute I laid eyes on Ben lying in a hospital bed, pain clutched my chest. I sucked in air when I spotted the bandages that covered his throat. *Did he get bitten by a vampire?*

Ben's chest rose and fell as the machine pumped oxygen into his lungs.

Webb had told me Ben was fine. He wasn't fine. I rushed up to his bedside and grabbed his hand as tears burned my eyes.

"He's in a light coma," a man's voice cut in between the beeping heart monitor and the whirr of the ventilator.

Surprised, I jerked my head, looking around the room. I'd been so fixated on Ben; I didn't even know there was someone else in the room.

A man with long black hair and forest-green eyes sat in the chair in the far-right corner.

My mouth fell open as I scanned his features.

He looked exactly like Sam. There was no mistaking that the man in the chair was my estranged father, Commander Steven Mason.

I wanted to go over and punch him, beat him, even kill him for all that he'd put Sam and me through in sixteen years. He had left Sam and me to grow up in filthy foster homes with perverted foster dads. He never told us that we carried a gene that would change our lives forever. I'd been beaten up, chased, almost kidnapped, locked in a coffin to die slowly, and told that I might have to shed my human existence.

Killing him might be too kind.

He stared at me, not saying a word. He had one leg crossed over the other. His hands grasped the edges of the arms on the chair as if he'd been bracing for the human storm that just blew into the room.

I glared back. His face was unshaven, and patches of dried blood or dirt dotted his cheeks.

His clothes were ragged, and dark circles punctuated his eyes, as if he hadn't slept in weeks.

I had always thought that I would run to him and beat him until... but standing in the same room, feet away from him, my body couldn't move. My boots were glued to the floor.

I swallowed several times, biting my lower lip. I shifted my gaze from the man in the corner to Ben, whose breathing was steady. The monitor indicated his heart was still beating. I inhaled and was about to speak when the door behind me slammed shut. Suddenly, the walls around me closed in, and a blanket of claustrophobia covered me.

"Jo." His voice was smooth and deep and exactly like Sam's.

My emotions went into overdrive. Tears pooled, and one escaped to slide down my right cheek. I closed my eyes, and a few more tumbled out. I thought the Plutariums had kidnapped him —*what is he doing here?*

I blinked a few times, trying not to bumble and cry like a teenager. "Where's Sam?" I glared at him through clouded eyes.

"I'm sorry. Please forgive me."

"No. You don't have any right to ask for that. You don't know what I've been through. You don't know anything about me. You're a rotten father. You deserve an award for being the worst father in history."

He rose from the chair, collected a large yellow envelope from the table near the door, then ambled over to me.

I scrunched my nose at the stench oozing off him. He smelled like he had just crawled out of a dumpster.

He studied me, hard and intense. "You're correct. I don't have the right. At least, not now. But I would like to show you something. Would you come with me so we can talk privately?"

I checked on Ben. At least he was still breathing.

"Ben should be fine. Please." My father held the door open, pleading with his eyes.

I struggled to decide whether to listen to him or not. Maybe he had news about Sam. I gave Ben one last look and brushed past my father and out into the lab.

Webb, Kate, and Dr. Vieira were standing against the black lab bench on the opposite side of the room. They were reading papers that were strewn across the counter. I suspected they were going over their mission, which I prayed was to find Sam.

My father ushered me into an office in the back corner of the facility. Once inside, he waved his hand at a leather sofa. "Have a seat."

I did as he commanded, admiring the gray décor, plush carpeting, and Dr. Vieira's diploma from Harvard and several awards from various medical and research organizations.

My father sat on the other end of the couch with the yellow envelope on his lap.

A beat of silence stretched between us as he raked his hands through his oily hair. His eyes were no longer the deep forest green I witnessed in Ben's room. They had changed to a lighter green right when they were on the verge of shifting to black.

Something is wrong.

He masked his worry with a weak smile. "I understand that Webb has explained to you a small amount of our family history and genetics."

"I thought you were kidnapped by the Plutariums."

"The Plutariums never kidnapped me."

I narrowed my eyes. "Then where were you?" Webb probably knew but hadn't told me because it was classified and on a need to know basis, which was usually how Webb answered my questions.

"It's not important." He tightened his lips.

Anger rose to pinch my cheeks. "Yes, it is. You were supposed to be with Sam."

He let out a deep breath, irritation leaking out as if I were keeping him from some other pressing matter. "Very well, then." He rubbed his hands over his face. "There's so much to tell you, and we don't have time."

He appears out of nowhere, asks for my forgiveness, wants to talk, and doesn't have time. Once again, I wanted to kill him.

As if he could sense my anger, he said, "When I got word you were in the hospital, I rushed there to see you. I'd been looking for you and Sam for years. And when I found out where you were, I had to—" He stood and walked to Dr. Vieira's desk, gripping the envelope as if it had top secret information in it.

Under the microscope of my glare, he ran his free hand through his beard. "I knew it was a risk, showing up at the hospital. But I had to make sure... I thought you were dead. Then the Plutariums got in the way. They got to you before I could because of Dr. Case. So I called in a favor from a friend of mine." He sat down in the desk chair. "After following you for a week, the situation got a little out of control, and we lost a soldier in a fight.

After that, I wasn't sure what the Plutariums' next move would be. I knew they were after me, but with you and Sam in the picture, the game changed. I had to do everything I could to lure them away from you. So I headed out of the city with a group of Plutariums following me. At first, they thought both of you were with me. Then last Monday, something changed."

I was immobilized as he told his story. While I understood how Dr. Case fit into the jigsaw puzzle, and I knew about Patrick needing my father's blood, I didn't understand why it took me landing in a hospital for my father to find me. Not to mention wondering who his friend was. "Monday was our first day back at school from spring vacation. That's when Sam disappeared," I said.

"I realize that now," he whispered.

"So, was it you in the black SUV?"

He nodded.

"And were you standing in the garage when—"

"Yes."

I cocked my head. "Is Neil Foster the friend, the guy who died?"

"I can't answer that."

He didn't have to. Neil had been helping us that night, and I couldn't stop wondering if he was dead. But if Neil was part of the Plutariums, then why would he help the Sentinels?

"Webb told me that Patrick needed Sam's DNA. Is that true? Is he using Sam for his lab tests?" I asked.

He came over to sit next to me with the envelope still clutched in his hand. "While Patrick does need my blood, his success hinges on a lot of things. I believe Webb explained it to you. But Sam was just in the wrong place at the wrong time. Patrick found the Holy Grail in Sam. He's a smart individual, and he's using Sam to study our family genetics. And if I know my brother, he will extract and study as much data as he can, even if it means killing Sam."

I hated the way he articulated those last words, which seemed to roll off his tongue with ease.

I let out a deep breath. "But how did the Plutariums get into school to kidnap Sam?"

"I don't know. We thought we had time to get in there on Monday morning, take both of you out, and bring you back here. But Webb and his team were too late. When I found out that Sam was missing, I came back to help." He slid a finger through the underside of the envelope flap. "I need to show you something. And... and... I need you to stay calm." He slipped his hand into the envelope. "Will you try and stay calm?"

Tension snaked through me as he spoke. Whatever was in that envelope, it didn't sound good.

He pulled out an eight-by-ten picture and stared at it. He lifted his gaze then handed it to me. I reached over and took hold of it, but my father held onto it for a second more, as if frightened that I might die from looking at the picture.

The minute I zeroed in on the photo, my pulse quickened, thudding in my ears like a kick drum.

This can't be. It can't be Sam. No! No! No! I flung the picture across the room and started crying, the tears flowing furiously down my face. "I hate you!" I yelled between sobs.

My father rubbed my back with one hand, while the other tried to wipe away my tears.

"Get away from me! This is all your fault. You're responsible for every horrible thing that has happened to us. Now, Sam is dead on a bench, locked in a glass room, with tubes in him." I jerked my arm away. I wanted to stand, but my body trembled, and I couldn't control my crying.

"Jo, please calm down."

"Calm down! Sam is the only family I've ever known, the only one who has taken care of me and protected me from bullies at school, foster parents, and every other danger thrown at me. If it wasn't for Sam, I'd be dead." My tears intensified, and I shuddered violently. "You're a bastard. Why? Why did you leave us?"

"I want to explain. But not now. You're in no emotional state to listen. Plus, we'll have time to talk later." He tried to pull me toward him, but I moved back.

"There won't be a later. I hate you," I spat.

I waited too long to decide. *This is my fault. Sam is dead because of me.* I was a terrible sister. I stood on wobbly legs.

"Wait. We're not done talking." My father grabbed my wrist.

"We have nothing left to talk about. My brother is dead because of you. You're not my father." I glared daggers at him, hiccupping from all the crying.

"I didn't show you that picture as a sign that Sam is dead. I've been trying to tell you that he's not dead—but we don't have much time. Sam is at a point now that the only way to bring him back is for you to save him."

I swallowed air and collapsed onto the couch.

"Please listen," my father said as he wiped my tears with a stinky cloth he pulled out of his pants.

"How do you know he's not dead?"

"It's not important how I know. What's important is that we discuss how we're going to bring Sam home."

Here we go. It's all about the mission. My father, the vampire SEAL—mission before family. "That's simple. You're here now. And Webb said that Sam needs to drink your blood."

"Yes, that would be true if he wasn't on his deathbed. I'm afraid too much of his blood has been lost. Besides, it's not that simple."

"Yes, it is. You're his father. Webb said that we needed to drink your blood to change. So rescue Sam with your blood."

He went over to retrieve the picture I'd thrown across the room. "Look closely at this photo." My dad placed it on my lap.

I turned my head. I didn't want to see Sam like that. It shattered my heart into a million pieces.

"Jo, I'm not asking. I'm telling you. Look at the photo. I know I haven't been around to help you through life, and I'm not going to give you excuses. Please believe me when I say I don't want you or Sam to live the life of a vampire. But sometimes, life doesn't give us choices. Sometimes, we have to do things we don't like to save our family." His voice was deep and commanding.

"Webb said I had choices, that I could make my own choice." My voice cracked.

"I know what Webb told you. In case you're forgetting, he also told you that Sam would need *your* vampire blood to survive. Don't lie to me. I know you're upset, but don't put your brother in harm's way just to get out of this. We don't have time for your teenage antics." My father's tone shifted to a low growl.

I wasn't trying to lie to him. I was incensed because he had left us all those years ago and felt betrayed that he waited until my brother was on his deathbed to show up. "Okay, so what if he did?"

His eyes suddenly changed from green to black with a rim of silver pooling at the edges. He took in a deep breath, raked his hands through his black shoulder-length hair, and cleared his throat. "Do you think that Webb wanted to be a vampire?" The cushion dipped beside me as he sat down. "Webb didn't have a choice," he said softly. "He was put in a similar situation. The only reason he is who he is today was to save his twin sister, Kate. Their father couldn't save her."

"What are you talking about?" I asked. "They're twins?"

I knew they resembled each other—they had the same color eyes and hair—but I hadn't been around them long enough for it to register. Besides, I had my own hell to deal with.

"Years ago, when the Mafia became a popular organization here in the United States, Webb's father was a Mafia boss, head of one of the most powerful families in Boston. What the world—including other Mafia families—didn't know was that Mr. and Mrs. London were vampires. Webb and Kate were still human at the time, but they carried the vampire gene. Per the Mafia and who they were, Mr. London had several illegal activities going on within his organization. When crime and smuggling got out of control, law enforcement stepped in to watch all the Mafia families very closely." My dad shifted his position on the couch, taking the picture from me.

My crying had stopped, but my body still trembled. I thought of Tripp and his calming abilities and wished he was holding me. I had an inkling that the story wasn't going to end well—at least not for me.

My dad scanned the picture of Sam then cleared his throat. "Kate and Webb were twenty years old then. They had each decided humanity was more important than immortality. They struggled with their decision for years. But things went horribly wrong for them. Not long after they made their decision to stay human, their father hired a lieutenant to take charge of one of his smuggling rings. The young man, only a few years older than the twins, fell in love with Kate. As their relationship grew, the young man started to notice odd things about the family. Even though Kate was human, her senses were heightened, and she had to live with some of the vampire qualities that came with carrying the gene. The young man started to notice. He got suspicious of the family and started taking pictures and jotting observations in a notebook. But Mr. London also grew suspicious of the young man and had him followed one day. Turned out that the young man who was in love with Kate was also working undercover for law enforcement. Mr. London went to confront the man, but instead found his daughter lying in a pool of her own blood. She had been stabbed several times."

I covered my mouth with my left hand.

My father continued. "Mr. London knew the only way to save her was for her to drink his blood. Since she was unconscious, he forced his blood into her. They waited hours to see if she would change, but nothing happened. They tried another pint, but still nothing. Webb was so distraught, he needed to do something. He wanted to save his sister more than anything, even if it meant his life for hers. So he changed. He became a vampire. He didn't know if it would work, but he had to try. Across twenty-four hours, Webb fed Kate his blood, and Kate woke up as a vampire hours later."

I rubbed my eyes. "I don't understand. How did Webb know to do that? And what was different about his blood and his father's?"

"Webb didn't know. He just did it. He was desperate to save his sister."

Unlike me, who is struggling to save her brother.

He let out a long sigh. "After that incident, the family went into hiding. They left the country and moved to Mrs. London's family estate in Ireland. It was there that they did a lot of research and paid doctors to study their genetic makeup. The family started documenting the research in journals and books to help other vampire families in case this ever happened to them. What they found was that once the vampire-human patient, those who carry the gene, loses over forty percent of their body's blood, they've passed the point of no return—in essence, death. The only person who can save them or change them into a vampire, however you want to look at it, is a family member who has all the right genetics. Their DNA matched perfectly."

I thought about the book I had in my hand earlier, *Vampire Genetics*. I should've brought it with me. "You believe that Sam and I have the right genetic makeup?"

"You're fraternal twins, so yes, there is a chance. I know it's a risk. Our situation may not be the same. It will depend on how well your genetics match with Sam's, but Dr. Vieira has been working around the clock to find out. He has your blood sample as well as Sam's."

I closed my eyes and shook my head. "How did he get a sample of Sam's blood?"

"Not for discussion. We've wasted too much time already."

"Wait, I still don't get it. How come I can drink your blood and change, but Sam can't?"

"Dr. Vieira can explain it better than me, but Sam is going to need a specific enzyme and an enormous intake of iron, which helps to make the hemoglobin necessary for carrying the oxygen from the lungs to the body tissue. New vampires need a large amount of iron. More importantly, as Sam's twin, you should carry the specific enzyme needed to infuse his cells and bone marrow. He's lost too much of both. Since I'm old, my body doesn't produce a high amount anymore. You're healthy and require little to make the change. My blood will only help him through you.

"Look, Jo, there are a lot of medical things happening here. There are classes and books dedicated to this. Patrick is well aware of all this, which is why he tried to poison you—so you can't save your brother. Revenge is what he's striving for here." He paused and raked his gaze over my face. "If he's successful, it may help his bigger goal to build an army for the Plutariums."

I blew out all the air in my lungs. I couldn't believe what I was hearing. Maybe I was still in the coffin, dreaming or hallucinating.

"I'm not going to force you into a specific choice, but you need to decide immediately. You've had plenty of time... too much time. As the days progress, Sam loses more blood and marrow. His kidneys are shutting down, and—"

"Wait, how do you know this? You know where he is?"

He nodded. "I'm going to leave you alone for a few minutes. I need to make sure Dr. Vieira has completed all the blood work and tests and that everything matches." He walked to the door and paused. "Jo, I'm sorry. I really didn't want to meet you under these circumstances, and I certainly didn't want your choices to be pressured like this." He gave me one long look then left.

Mary, Mother of God. My mind flipped in several directions from all the medical jargon. Questions piled on top of each other. However, two took center stage. *How does my father know where Sam is? How did he get that picture and his blood?*

I picked up the picture of Sam from the cushion and studied his lifeless body, tears forming again as I prayed he wasn't in a lot of pain. I rubbed my hand over it, and thoughts surfaced of us playing in the schoolyard. We were young, and he had been teaching me how to play base-ball. He would throw the ball to me, and I would swing, missing it. He'd throw it again, and again, I would swing and miss. We did this for hours until I had finally sent the ball soaring into the outfield. He had been so excited and proud of me—which in the current moment, I imagined he wouldn't be. *What kind of sister am I?* He'd always protected me. He'd always been there for me, and I knew without any doubt he would die for me. *Why can't I make the damn decision to save him?*

I was rubbing my eyes when a knock sounded before Kate glided in.

"Are you okay?" she asked.

"No. I hate my life. I keep hoping that I'm in a coma, and at any minute, I'm going to snap out of it." I cradled my head in my hands.

The cushion dipped beside me. "Sweetie, I can't say I know what you're going through because I don't." She rubbed a hand up and down my back. "I'm extremely glad that Webb did what he did for me, even if we both didn't want this life. Nevertheless, if it weren't for him, I wouldn't be here right now. While eternity sounds depressing, I am thankful that I get to spend it with him."

I lifted my head. "I'm an awful sister." Tears flowed down my cheeks.

She gave me a sad smile as her blue eyes filled with tears. "I know it can't be an easy decision for you, but I'll leave you with one last thought. Put yourself in Sam's shoes. What if the roles were reversed? Would he do whatever it took to save you? Would you want him to? You know Sam better than anyone. Don't let this vampire life scare you. Make your decision based on what's best for you and Sam. If death is best for him, then so be it. If living with your brother and doing something to change this world for the better is best, then maybe immortality is the path you take." Standing, she blinked away a tear. "We're here for you. All of us." She flicked her hand in the direction of the lab. "You're not alone."

After she left, I sifted through everything my father had explained and Kate's advice. While her words of wisdom were comforting, I still wasn't at ease with the decision I had to make. As the weight of the world rested heavily on me, I tried to put myself in Sam's shoes. But I was only a teenager, and the vampires were asking me to make a godlike decision. It wasn't fair. I should have been in school, doing homework, going to school dances, and hanging out with friends. Instead, I was sitting in a secret compound in an alternate world, making life-changing decisions for Sam and me.

Without another thought, I stood, wiped my eyes, took a deep breath, and shuffled to the door.

God help me for what I'm about to do.

25

───────────

When I emerged from the office, four sets of eyes stared at me. My father had a horrified look on his face, and I wondered whether he could read my mind. Webb appeared nervous, fidgeting with a syringe, and Kate and Dr. Vieira appeared calm.

Kate ran over to me and, as usual, put her arm around mine. "What have you decided, dear?"

I waited until we approached Webb, my father, and Dr. Vieira, all of whom were standing near the lab bench on the far side of the room. After skirting a couple of desks and a table, I closed my eyes and said a silent prayer. *Here goes nothing.*

"I've made my decision," I whispered, dropping my gaze to the floor as my hands began to shake.

Before I could get the words to roll off my tongue, my father grabbed me, and I craned my neck up.

Confusion flickered in his green eyes. "Please, Jo. Tell me your answer is yes."

I had thought he could read my mind, but I was wrong.

A tear slid down my cheek as my father's grip became stronger. Then my body began trembling. *Get a grip. They'll understand.*

"Honey," my father's tone cracked. "It's okay."

"I... I..."

His forest-green eyes were shifting as I stared at him. He reminded me so much of Sam that a pain pierced my heart.

Then, as if the devil grabbed hold of my mind and twisted it, I said, "If I regret this, then I vow to kill all of you." My mouth hung open as I finished the sentence.

Kate leaned in. "Is that a yes?"

Did I just say that? I bent over and dropped to my knees.

My father pulled me to my feet and wrapped his arms around me. "We'll get through this. I know life hasn't been good for you, but given the chance, I'll make it up to you." Remorse soaked through his words.

I stood cocooned in his arms, his warmth wrapped around me, the tension seeping from every pore. Maybe part of me wanted his love and acceptance. I wasn't sure how he could make up for the last fourteen years, but I was willing to give him a chance... if we could save Sam.

He let go of me. "Thank you, Jo. I promise I'll do everything in my power to bring Sam back."

I blew out a breath and wiped my eyes with the back of my hand—*now what?* I stole a glance at Webb. His eyes were wide, his eyebrows raised as if shocked by my answer.

Hell, I was dumbfounded by my answer.

Dr. Vieira slipped on his lab coat. "Jo, please follow me. We have much work to do."

Once Dr. Vieira spoke, my dad, Webb, and Kate scattered as if they had work to do as well. I imagined they did.

"Can I see Ben one last time?" I pleaded.

"You have two minutes," he said.

I hurried into Ben's room. His unconscious body was still attached to a machine helping him with every breath.

Grabbing Ben's hand, I said, "If you can hear me, I want to tell you how sorry I am for getting you into this mess. I hope that the next time I see you, you'll be talking and irritating me like you were for the last few days. Whatever happens, I want you to know that I'm grateful for everything you did to help me. You were the best bodyguard-slash-friend a girl could have." I squeezed his hand then rushed out.

Dr. Vieira was waiting for me, seemingly eager to get the show started. "I have the room ready. We'll be using the one next to my office."

"Does this mean that my blood type and all the other genetic things match up with Sam's like my father said it should?" I asked.

His loafers clicked along the tiled floor. "It's a perfect match."

I bit a nail. "So, how did you get Sam's blood?"

"That's classified."

Great. No one is going to tell me anything. "Can you at least tell me what I'm going to go through?"

Dr. Vieira stopped in front of the room and waved his hand, gesturing for me to go in. "In due time."

My pulse quickened when I entered. Was I making the right decision? Would the process hurt? And so many other questions.

I dropped down on the twin bed that was surrounded by a heart monitor, an IV stand, a blood pressure device, and a defibrillator. Off to one side was a table with needles, syringes, a stethoscope, and several empty vials. The setup was far from comforting.

"There's sweatpants and a T-shirt on the chair in the corner. Change into them. I'll be back in five minutes, and we'll get started."

Once I was alone, I couldn't get my heart to stop racing. I took in a deep breath then another. Again, I had to ask myself if I were making the right decision. Part of me said yes, but another screamed no. I didn't know which one to listen to, but I couldn't waver anymore. I'd analyzed the whys and why nots, had put myself in Sam's shoes, and had thought through how Sam would react to his new vampire life and what he would do for me. Each time, I kept hearing Sam's voice in my head: *you have to take care of yourself, Jo.* I didn't know if Sam wanted a life of immortality, but he would do anything to save me. Still, to take away his humanity shouldn't be my decision.

I stared at the door, debating whether to run—a last chance to save my soul.

The air inside became suffocating. I looked up at the ceiling for some sort of sign. While I wanted to run, a voice inside me kept telling me, *Sam needs you.*

I mustered up all the courage I could find and changed into the sweatpants and the T-shirt before I collapsed into the chair. The plush, oversized recliner swallowed me as I leaned back and closed my eyes. I started to drift off when Dr. Vieira cleared his throat.

Opening my eyes, I sat up straighter.

Dr. Vieira was holding a clipboard, and my dad had a glass container with red liquid in it. I imagined it was his blood.

Dr. Vieira and my dad exchanged looks, and my father nodded. I guessed Dr. Vieira was waiting for him to give the command.

"The first part of this is simple," Dr. Vieira said. "I'll prep you by inserting an IV, attaching the nodes for the heart monitor, then setting up the blood pressure machine. Second, you'll be giving me twenty percent of your system's blood. This will help with vomiting and allow room for the blood you'll drink and for regenerating more of the mixture between your dad's blood and your own. Then you'll drink the pint of blood that your father is holding." Dr. Vieira stared at me, clearly waiting for me to do or say something.

"Okay. But you know, I'll just puke it up like I did when I drank the box of blood."

My father gave Dr. Vieira a puzzled look, but Dr. Vieira ignored him.

"I know, but that's what the IV solution is for. It'll help keep the fluids in you, and it also has a solution to slow down the vomiting," Dr. Vieira explained.

My heart was ramming against my rib cage. I would rather have been listening to Ms. Costner tell us about Pythagoras and his three worlds than be in a room with some vampire doctor lecturing me on the origins of his species.

Dr. Vieira set his clipboard down on the table with the syringes. "After that, we wait. The process should take twenty-four to no more than forty-eight hours. It will all depend on how your body reacts to all this. The test results show that you and Sam match perfectly and that your father is your biological father. Are we clear?"

What does he want me to say? Yes, I can't wait to have fangs and drink blood? I nodded.

"Jo, I'll be here the entire time," my father added.

How appropriate. The man from hell was going to watch me go through hell—yippee. "Um, physical changes?" I asked.

Dr. Vieira switched on the heart monitor. "Without getting technical, dizziness, stomach pain, maybe some feeling of claustrophobia. Your body may feel itchy, and you'll more than likely experience head and gum pain. There are a lot of internal changes taking place, and each person is different in the way they experience and feel it. So are you ready?"

I laughed nervously. I was ready, but not to become part of the undead society so much as to run to the other end of the Earth, away from vampires. As if by magic, my legs unfolded, and I stood, eyeing the door as though it was my salvation.

My father shook his head. "Don't do it, young lady. You made your decision. I'll be here with you every step of the way."

I sighed and walked over to Dr. Vieira—I didn't want to be near my father. Sure, his hug earlier and the tears he'd shed had comforted me, but that didn't mean he was out of the woods just yet. Plus, I suspected he was trying everything he could to make this easy for me, and there was nothing easy about it. My humanity was about to be stripped.

I reluctantly climbed into bed and laid my head back onto the pillow. Dr. Vieira started inserting needles into my hand and arm. Then he wrapped the blood pressure pad around my other arm while my dad pulled off the backing from the self-adhesive pads and pressed them onto my chest. The heart monitor came to life, and I was reminded of the day I'd awoken in the hospital a week before. It was the first time I had ever been in a hospital and where my life had changed forever.

With all the needles, electrodes, and machines working, my father poured his blood into a tall glass then set it on the table. The heart monitor chirped nonstop. Sweat peppered my forehead, and the blood pressure machine beeped. The smell of blood filtered through the air, and my nostrils flared, the scent making my tongue tingle. My mouth suddenly became dry.

"It'll be okay. Breathe," Dr. Vieira whispered. "I want you to squeeze this tube, so the blood pumps into the bag. I need two bags."

My father regarded Dr. Vieira. "Is she okay?"

"Your daughter, I believe, has been experiencing some early signs. You know, the normal ones that teenagers of vampire descent go through. Hers seem to be stronger than most, which may speed up the change."

I almost laughed. There was that word again, "normal." It wasn't normal. Nothing about it was normal.

I lay there, watching the blood flow into the

bag, and thought about Sam as I silently recited the Lord's Prayer, hoping it would help both of us.

Forty-five minutes later, Dr. Vieira had two pints of my human blood. It was time to drink. I sat up and the room spun. My pulse was in over-drive, and I hadn't even touched the blood. I was hosed.

Dr. Vieira sat beside me. "I want you to drink it slowly. If you drink it too fast, you'll pass out." Then he nodded to my father, who placed the tall glass of blood in my hands.

I stared at it, trying to drum up the courage to bring it to my lips, the aroma prickling my senses. My brain didn't follow suit.

My father inserted a straw.

Yeah, that's not going to help me.

I took a deep breath, covered the straw with my lips, closed my eyes, and sucked. The first sip exploded in my mouth, the texture thick. The taste was sweet with a hint of salt. Dr. Vieira told me to drink it slowly, but all of sudden, I wanted to drain the glass. I began sucking on the straw as quickly I could. My cheeks caved in as I savored every mouthful. Suddenly, the glass was yanked from my hands.

I opened my eyes in protest.

"Slow down. Do you want to get sick?" my father asked.

Like a baby attached to her bottle, I snagged the glass back from him. "I feel fine."

Horror etched lines in Dr. Vieira's forehead.

I almost wanted to laugh, but there was nothing funny about this process. Not to mention, my head hurt as if I had brain freeze from sucking in an ice-cold milkshake.

Dr. Vieira examined the monitor. "How are you feeling?"

"Just a little light-headed." I raised the glass and sipped again through the straw, more slowly than before. I had a feeling I was going to be a crazed vampire, always wanting blood. "What happens after the change? Will I always crave blood like this?"

Dr. Vieira exchanged a knowing look with my father.

"That will depend, honey. It might be tough for you, or it might be easy. It's hard to tell. Some newborns have a constant craving, so we need to watch them closely. Take certain precautions. Others seem to moderate their intake better and not crave it as much," my father explained.

That wasn't exactly a straight answer. In fact, it sounded a bit like gibberish to me.

I sipped the rest of the glass and wanted more.

My father, who was sitting on the edge of the other twin bed, studied me. I couldn't tell if he was amazed, frightened, or in shock about my reaction to the blood. I imagined he was probably determining what kind of vampire I would be. I had the same question, but I wasn't ready for the answer.

I handed the glass to Dr. Vieira. "Now what?"

"We wait. Do you feel the need to throw up?"

The dizziness had waned. My stomach wasn't upset, which I imagined was a good sign. Maybe whatever Dr. Vieira put in my IV was helping the queasiness. "I do feel a little tired."

Setting the glass on the table, Dr. Vieira scribbled on his clipboard. Then he proceeded to listen to my heart before moving the scope around my stomach. When he finished, he made more notes on his clipboard.

"Did you hear anything?" I asked.

"No. Everything seems normal." He looked at his watch. "I need to step out. Why don't you try to sleep? Your father will be here with you in case you need something. I'll return in a couple of hours."

"When I wake up, will I have changed?"

"We'll see. It's hard to tell." He turned to my father. "Commander, may I speak to you outside?"

After they left, I stared at the ceiling, wondering how long it would take to lose my humanity. Or maybe the process wouldn't work. Maybe when I woke up I would still be human.

MY EYES POPPED OPEN. I grabbed my stomach and curled myself into a ball. My insides burned with every organ inside me screaming to get out. My whole body cramped and tightened from my sternum down to my legs. Sweat ran down my back and the sides of my face.

What was happening to me?

I closed my eyes then opened them again. A noise beeped beside me, a loud noise that had me cringing in pain. I moved my hands from my stomach to my ears, trying to quell the loud sound that was driving me insane. Then another intense cramp wracked my insides. My stomach lurched and I heaved, but nothing came out. Something cold touched my forehead. I looked up, but my blurred vision didn't allow me to see who was next to me.

I squeezed my eyes shut. "Please make the sound stop—please." I pressed my hands against my ears.

"Jo? This is Dr. Vieira. Do you know where you are?"

I struggled to see the man standing over me. I knew his voice and the name, but I couldn't see him. I blinked a few more times, trying to clear the haze that covered my eyes. When I opened them, Dr. Vieira was peering down at me.

The pain ramped up again, grabbing hold of my stomach more intensely. I shifted my hands from my head to my abdomen. A fire rushed through my veins, and suddenly, my throat burned.

"What's happening to me?" I screamed.

Dr. Vieira wiped my face with a cold compress. "Jo, you're going through the change."

"Make the pain go away. Please!" I cried.

The burning intensified, snaking through every organ and vein inside me, itching for release. I closed and opened my eyes then closed them again, the light above me burning like I was touching the sun. "The light. Make it go away."

"Jo, can you hear me? Honey, it's me, your dad. Only a little while longer, and the pain will subside." He rubbed my sweat-soaked back.

The pain diminished, and I took in a breath. The sweet smell of cinnamon hit me. The aroma intensified as a familiar female voice filled the room.

"How is she?" Kate asked.

"Not now. You shouldn't be in here," Dr. Vieira said.

"We're twelve hours into it. She just woke up. She should fall back to sleep soon," my father explained.

I didn't want to fall asleep—I wanted someone to kill me. I lay in bed, frozen in a fetal position as the pain ramped up again and nausea swept over me. I heaved, but like before, nothing came out.

My father lifted me and positioned me over the side of the bed. I opened my eyes, and the room was darker. The beeping noise had stopped, but my eardrums still vibrated. The only sound echoing in my ears was my father's heartbeat. I counted the beats as he held me.

"My throat. It's burning," I whispered.

"That's normal. It's a vampire's thirst," Dr. Vieira said.

As he said the word 'vampire,' a cluster of cramps gripped me, spreading throughout my body, each one more intense than the last.

"When can you give her blood?" my father asked.

"When her fever breaks. I inserted a mild sedative into her IV. She's probably through the worst of it, so it shouldn't stop the final process."

There is a final step? I can't take any more of this pain. I pray the last step doesn't kill me.

My father eased me back down onto the bed. The heaving had stopped. I curled up and held onto my stomach for dear life, afraid it was going to disintegrate. "Can I have some water?" I asked.

Dr. Vieira held a cup in front of me while I lifted my head. I sipped through the straw as the water seeped down, cooling the parched skin at the back of my throat.

I dropped onto the pillow and resumed my fetal position. The pain had dulled, and for the moment, I could relax.

God help me. I didn't know if vampires believed in God, but I needed to believe he existed, even in the world I was about to enter.

I LOOKED up to find the sky dotted with bright, twinkling diamonds, as if someone had sprinkled fairy dust and it had stuck to the background. *Where am I? Am I in the planetarium at school?* My gaze roamed from side to side. A blanket of sand stretched for miles in both directions. *No, this isn't school.* A stream of water ran by just beyond the sandy carpet I was sitting on.

I rose and walked to the edge, stepping into a cool stream of liquid that tickled my toes. I turned, and thick, dense trees filled in the landscape behind me. It appeared I was on a beach—a deserted one. The bright moon shone down, its reflection dancing on the water. I took two steps into the stream, looking down through the crystal-clear water and at the sand glistening beneath it. I inhaled the fresh, clean air, reveling in the beauty that surrounded me, and made a wish as my gaze roamed the horizon. As I stepped farther into the sparkling water, an electrical charge skimmed up my legs, and my body shivered. My chest tightened as if someone had wrapped a rope around me and pulled it tight. Every sense and shiver told me to go back, get out of the water, but as if a magnet drew me to it, I kept walking into the stream, which was only ankle deep.

The farther I walked, the stronger the force, pulling me forward. I continued my journey, stepping slowly into the velvety sand. The breeze played with my hair, and for the first time in my life a true sense of freedom washed over me.

My vision was sharp as if it had been altered,

enhancing every detail of the sandy floor beneath the crystal-clear water.

A soothing sound sang in the distance. A soft breeze blew, and the sweet aroma of honeysuckle tickled my nose. As I waded through the stream, the splash of water grew louder, piercing my eardrums. The water around me became turbulent, and the clear liquid turned red. My pulse quickened as fear blanketed me. Danger lurked ahead, but I couldn't stop.

I kept walking, stepping slowly through the red water, which became darker the closer I got to the waterfall. I willed my feet to stop, throwing my arms out in front of me, trying to balance myself. My right foot hit a rock, sending me over the edge into the blackness below.

As I soared downward, my body relaxed, allowing the world below to swallow me. I was no longer afraid. It was as if my destiny were pulling me down into my new world—the Superior world.

All the inhibitions that had suffocated me were melting away one by one, leaving the Inferior world behind. I inhaled, taking in the salt from the red water that sprayed on me as if the fairies had released their magic dust. As I got closer to my destiny, the cloying scent of jasmine and lavender filled the air. I closed my eyes, bracing for impact, when my body began to slow as if someone applied brakes. A slow burn crawled up the back of my throat, and suddenly, I couldn't breathe.

I sat up and grabbed my throat, choking, gasping for air.

"Jo. It's all right. I'm here."

I opened my eyes. "Sam, is that you?" I asked between coughs.

"No, my dear, it's your father. You were dreaming."

"Water. I need water." I sat still rubbing my throat. "It burns."

"Her fever is gone," Dr. Vieira said.

I blinked several times before my vision cleared.

Dr. Vieira was adjusting the IV bag. His heartbeat was sharply distinct, so defined. I glanced at his jugular, up at him, then back to his neck.

"Give her the blood now, Steven," Dr. Vieira said in a sharp tone.

My gaze rounded to my father, and the vein in his neck looked appetizing.

Suddenly, my gums ached. I dipped my fingers in my mouth, and the tip of my forefinger caught the edge of my right eyetooth, which was pointy and longer than the rest. My eyes widened in horror, and I drew in a sharp breath.

Holy Crap! I'm a vampire.

I quickly removed my hands and covered my mouth.

My father handed me a tall glass with a straw in it. "It's okay. It's normal to want blood."

No, it was downright strange that I wanted blood, but I grabbed it anyway. Not certain if I should drink it, I shifted my gaze between him and Dr. Vieira, looking for approval.

They both nodded.

I raised the glass and wrapped my lips around the straw. I inhaled, and the sweet, candied aroma made the flame in the back of my throat burn brighter and hotter in anticipation of that first sip. I released the straw and moistened my lips.

My father sat on the edge of my bed. "Go ahead and drink." He guided the glass towards my mouth.

The first sip slid over my tongue before coating the wall at the back of my throat, cooling the burn and awakening every cell in me. I couldn't drink fast enough. Once I was done, I was ready for more. But I didn't have to ask. Dr. Vieira had another ready for me. Hungrily, I grabbed it and drank, not stopping to breathe. Then one after the other I was drinking glass after glass of the sweet nectar.

Then everything came to a screeching halt when I finished the fifth glass. The room began to spin.

My father had another glass ready.

"No. No more. I'm dizzy."

Dr. Vieira smiled as though he'd accomplished something worth a Pulitzer Prize. "You should be well sated. It's been a long twenty-eight hours. I'm sure you'll sleep well tonight."

I eased myself back onto the pillow. "What day is it?"

My father rubbed his tired eyes. "It's Wednesday evening." He sighed. "Your change is complete. How do you feel?"

I watched him as he studied me, his hand holding mine as if we were best friends. His dull green eyes were pleading, begging me to forgive him. My hatred for him was still there, but I decided to keep it hidden for the time being.

I wasn't sure how to answer him. The pain, the burning sensation, and the vomiting were gone, replaced by... I wasn't sure yet.

"Sleepy right now," I said as I yawned.

"Get some rest. Tomorrow will be another long day." My father crawled in the twin bed next to mine. "I'll be right here if you need me."

Dr. Vieira had left the room—I imagined to get some sleep as well.

I closed my eyes and picked through my brain, trying to take inventory of my body. I lay still, reaching out to every cell within me, trying to find a difference between human and vampire. I couldn't find anything.

As I thought about the blood that tickled my taste buds, I jolted to a sitting position. My gums throbbed, and I winced as my fangs descended. I inserted my fingers inside and touched the tip of my left fang. The back of my throat burned. Suddenly, my skin itched. I wanted—needed—blood. I inhaled and grabbed my pillow, curling myself into a fetal position. I took several breaths in and out. Slowly, my fangs retreated. I closed my eyes, willing myself to sleep. A layer of warmth coated my skin as my muscles relaxed.

Webb had said I was going through vampire puberty, but that was before the change. Now that I was a vampire, what stage was I in? My guess was the bloodlust stage. Whether I was right or wrong, I had a feeling I was one in for one hell of a ride.

26

I awoke the next morning to an audience of people watching me as if I was a caged animal that they were admiring. I wiped my eyes, trying to remove the sleepy crust that glued the corners together. Then I blinked to orient my vision.

Webb leaned up against the sidewall at the edge of my bed, staring at me with those blue eyes that made me mush inside. At the bottom of the bed, Tripp straddled a chair, resting his arms on the back of it, smiling, showing perfect white teeth. Next to Tripp, Dr. Vieira stood with his hands in his lab coat and his head tilted to one side.

I sat up, smoothing my hands over my long hair when a purple color sparkled from the light overhead. I looked down and swallowed hard. From what I could see, my straight black hair had grown an inch and was now hanging down past my breasts. However, that wasn't what had me spooked. I splayed my fingers through the ends of my hair. A mixture of black and purple streaked through the strands.

"Who did this to me?" I demanded in a frantic voice.

Dr. Vieira shuffled up to my bedside. "Interesting. I will have to run more tests." He leaned in and examined the ends of my hair.

"Don't you have enough of my blood?" I tried not to snap at him. But purple hair? I prayed when I looked in the mirror, I wouldn't have warts on my face.

Kate bounced in, happy, smiling as though she found something to play with. "How's my newborn?"

"Don't call me that," I barked.

Like her twin brother, Webb, her blue eyes were bright, and her wavy brown hair was pulled back in a low ponytail. "Wow, what side of the bed did you get up on?"

"Look at this." I grabbed a handful of hair and waved it in her direction.

"Cool," she squeaked.

I wanted to strangle her. It was okay for her to look beautiful, but not me. I was probably getting ahead of myself, but my nerves were on edge. Then something hit me. I touched the scar on my cheek, hoping it was gone. Maybe the change to vampire erased it.

I frowned. The darn thing was still there. I hated my new body already.

My father traipsed in. Tripp jumped off the chair and stood at attention. Webb pushed off of the wall, hands at his side.

"I need everyone in the war room in fifteen minutes," Commander Mason instructed.

Dad was clean-shaven, dressed in tan cargo pants with a navy-blue T-shirt bearing the SEAL emblem in the upper-left corner of his chest. Over top of the emblem in an arc was the word "Jupiter," and under the emblem, in an inverted arc, was the word *Sentinel*. His right forearm was imprinted with some type of hieroglyphs, a series of symbols that looked as if Pythagoras had scribbled a mathematical formula on his arm.

While most of the symbols were foreign to me, one wasn't. The fancy number four overpowered all the surrounding symbols. It was the same one Olivia had on her arm, the mark of the Jupiter Sentinel.

I smirked as I watched him. The most powerful vampire, Commander Steven Mason, barked orders at his troops, while each of them stood at attention, listening to my father's every word.

Kate sat on my bed, talking about something, but I tuned her out. I wanted to hear what my father was saying. As Kate's voice dominated my right ear, I strained my left, trying to eavesdrop on the other conversation, but his voice had dropped to a whisper as he talked with Tripp and Webb. I hoped they were discussing Sam's rescue.

Kate was still jabbering when Dad came over. "Gentlemen and lady, let my daughter get ready."

Everyone evacuated the room, including Kate.

"Everything okay this morning?" He fanned the ends of my hair. "I like the color. It's very becoming against your silver eyes."

"You're just saying that because you're my father."

"Once you look in the mirror, I'm sure you'll agree. You're beautiful." He let go of the strands. "I need you in the war room. I know you probably want to take a shower, so I won't hold you to the fifteen minutes. Kate is going to take you to my apartment." He kissed me on the forehead. "Don't take too long. Sam needs us."

He had his hand on the door when I asked, "So what should I call you?"

A confused look washed over him. "I would love it if you called me Dad, but I know I haven't earned the right. Steven is good for now."

"Um, how's Ben? Can I see him?" I held my breath, hoping my friend was okay.

"Ben is still in a coma. His vital signs have improved, though. I prefer it if you dress first and meet me downstairs. You can see him later."

Before I could protest, he was gone.

Kate graced the doorway. "Are you ready?" she asked.

I pulled off the sheet, unfolded my legs, and planted my feet on the floor. My head spun, making me plop my butt on the bed. *Thank the Lord it was there.* Inhaling, I pushed off and stood upright. My legs wobbled. I stilled for a moment before I tried to move.

Kate leaned against the door watching me. "You need to learn to adjust to your new body. You've been through hell and back. Nourishment is the key, and I don't mean blood. Human food will help."

"Vampires get hungry for human food?" I asked.

"Girl, you have a lot to learn about the vampire

world. My brother was right. You've either watched too many vampire movies or have read too many vampire books."

I wasn't in the mood to argue with her. I was more irritated that Webb had discussed my immaturity about the vampire world with her. Although that wasn't important for the time being. I needed to get my tush in gear and take a shower, but since Kate had mentioned food, my stomach growled.

I managed to shuffle to the door. I was afraid to pick up my feet. My legs were weak, but all my other body parts appeared okay.

Once in the lab, everything seemed so new. My senses were sharp. My vision was crystal clear. I could read the anatomy chart that was plastered on the back wall of the lab. Smells of alcohol, blood, and rotten eggs washed through me. Noises that I hadn't heard before buzzed in my ears. Computers hummed, lab machines beeped, and other noises wracked my eardrums. But one steady beat caught my attention.

I walked over to Ben's room and peered in through the glass. He was still lying on his back, eyes closed, not moving. His chest rose with every artificial breath of the ventilator. Bandages were still wrapped around his neck. I grabbed hold of the doorknob and turned it. The door was locked. I frowned and tried again.

Kate called, "You're not allowed in there. Now, let's go."

I knew my father told me it wouldn't be good for me to see Ben, but he never said to stay out of his room. I peered through the glass one more time then reluctantly met Kate at the double doors.

I was beginning to realize that my father's presence was going to be a challenge.

I smiled. More for him than for me.

STEVEN MASON'S room wasn't just a room but an entire wing of the fourth floor. According to Kate, the fourth floor split into two sections: one half was the medical facility, and the other half was my father's apartment.

My mouth hung open as I surveyed the penthouse of the alpha vampire. The military hadn't spared any expense to make sure that Steven Mason was taken care of. The place was warm and inviting. A tan fabric sofa, two recliners that matched the couch, a square cherrywood coffee table, and pillows galore decorated the living room. The best part was the thick, plush carpeting.

The softness of the fibers tickled my bare feet as I made my way to the windows that lined two walls of the apartment, meeting together in a corner and framing half of the living room. I stopped just out of reach of the sun's rays, which shone through, casting a beam of heat on the floor. I was reluctant to step into the sun's path, afraid that if I did, I would turn into a pile of ashes.

Kate sidled up to me in the sun's beam of light. "It's fine. You won't burn. It actually feels good. While the sun doesn't affect us like you think it does, we can't be out in it for hours on end. Although as you get older, your body will become accustomed to it, and you'll be able to withstand its power longer."

I wasn't ready to test her theory, although she was proof of not bursting into flames.

I pointed to the three buildings that surrounded the courtyard below. "What's in all these buildings?"

She flicked her finger to the building in the middle. "Over there is our base prison. The other two are empty at the moment."

I thought of Jonah and Dr. Case and wondered if they took up residence in a cell. I was also curious how they prevented a strong vampire like Jonah from escaping?

"We have to get moving. Once we get through this mission, we'll have more time for a tour. Your dad's bedroom is in the back corner behind the kitchen. There's also a bathroom in there." She sat on the couch and pulled a magazine from the coffee table.

Before I turned, something below caught my attention. A shadowy figure ran across the courtyard. He kept looking behind him as if someone or something were chasing him. Then he stopped and rummaged around in the back pocket of his camouflage pants and pulled out a cell phone. Then a phone rang in the apartment, startling me. I spun around and looked at Kate.

"Ignore it. It's your father's private line. It will go directly to his cell if he doesn't pick it up in here. Um, shower, clothes, dress—in that order. Hurry, Jo."

I hesitated. I would bet that man was trying to call my father. Maybe he was keeping his commander informed of what he was doing. It seemed logical that all the guards were instructed to do that.

I shrugged and traipsed off, passing the kitchen, which was separated from the living room by a large island. The sounds of the appliances hummed loudly in my ears as I entered the hallway. Every little noise, no matter how soft or loud, drove me crazy and set my eardrums rattling and my head pounding. Somehow, I needed to filter out the background noise, but I didn't know how.

My jaw dropped when I entered my father's room at the end of the hall. It was as if I had stepped into another world—the military world.

It wasn't a bedroom. It was a military command center. The only thing telling me it might not be was the king-sized maps of the United States and other countries hung on the walls. Two credenzas lined half of the right wall. Above them, glass cabinets displayed a multitude of weapons. Why my father wanted to sleep among all these daggers, swords, and guns, especially when there were two empty rooms in the apartment, was beyond me. It was like a military museum.

I trailed my finger along the credenzas. The first cabinet had several different types of daggers. Under each one was a small, typed card explaining the weapon above it. Out of the five daggers, one in particular caught my attention: the *British Knuckle Duster, circa 1943.* It was the dagger that Jonah used to fight Webb. The handle had finger holes with four protruding studs—for punching, according to the card. I wondered if that type of weapon would have really taken out Webb.

As I made my way farther down the line, there were four unique swords in different shapes and sizes. Like the daggers, each of the swords had a card underneath it, explaining its origins, with the exception of one—the Sentinel sword. Unlike the red handle on Webb's sword, the one on display had a camouflage handle, but the blade wasn't exposed. I studied it, trying to figure out where the button to engage the blade was. I pulled on the cabinet door, but it was locked.

When I moved down to the gun section, the apartment door closed. It was weird how clearly I could hear the quiet squeak of the door from such a distance. Whoever came in or went out didn't slam it. They closed it softly, the door clicking in place. Maybe Kate left.

I closed my eyes and tuned out the noises around me to test how good my new vampire senses were.

As I stood there, listening, the doorknob to the bedroom turned. I spun around, adrenaline shooting through my veins. My throat started to burn, and the room around me momentarily vanished then reappeared.

I bolted into the bathroom to find a mirror, not

caring about the intruder. I looked down at my body. It was still me. I patted myself around my cheeks, nose, and mouth—still me. I pulled open a drawer in the bathroom cabinet, and it flew across the room, landing on the toilet. *Jeepers, did I do that? I didn't pull it that hard—or did I? This new body is going to take some getting used to.*

I looked at the contents of the drawer, which were strewn on the toilet lid and the floor below. A compact of some sort lay on the cover of the toilet. *That's weird. Is my father using makeup?*

I opened it, and inside was not only a mirror but also several bullets. *What are bullets doing in a makeup compact?* I jerked my head and flared my nostrils like some type of police dog. The unknown person was in the bedroom. Unlike Kate's cinnamon scent, the intruder had a woodsy scent.

As the bathroom doorknob turned, I jumped to the side of the door. The man walked in, and my animal instinct took over. I grabbed the man by the throat and pinned him against the marble wall near the sink. His hands wrapped around my wrist and tugged, trying to release my grip.

"Let go," Webb said, his voice strangled.

I blinked a few times. His face faded. It went dark for a split second before I could see again. *What is happening to me?* I stumbled backwards.

"You shouldn't walk in on a girl in a bathroom, especially a vampire one."

"I heard a crash. I thought something happened, but I see you've been productive." He glanced at the contents of the drawer.

My cheeks suddenly burned with embarrassment. "I think I'm losing my vision," I blurted out.

"Does the room disappear for a moment then return?" he asked.

I nodded.

"Your eyes were shifting colors."

"But that didn't happen when I was human."

"As a vampire, you're more sensitive to things. I'm sure your vision blurred slightly when you were human. You just didn't notice it. As you grow into your new vampire body, you'll find you get used to things like that." He started to leave. "I put your clothes on the bed. Your father is waiting for you, so hurry up and get downstairs."

I locked the door behind him and leaned against it, breathing deeply, trying to calm my nerves. My heightened hearing, sight, and strength were too much to handle. *Will I feel the same way when it comes to boys? Will my feelings be stronger, sharper?*

Then it hit me. My stomach didn't flutter or do somersaults when Webb walked in. Not like it did when I first met him. *Does becoming a vampire change that? Will I have those butterfly feelings when I first kiss a boy? Or when a boy touches me like Ben did the other day?* I stuff all those questions in a box. Boy problems would have to wait. Hell, I didn't know who I was kidding. A girl like me didn't have boy problems. I would be waiting an eternity for a boy to like me.

Fifteen minutes later, after a much-needed shower, I discovered the clothes Webb had folded on the bed. The jeans looked way too small, and I had my doubts about the short-sleeved V-neck T-shirt. The good news was that my boots were sitting on the floor at the foot of the bed.

I tried on the jeans, slipping in one leg then the other and pulling them over my hips, and shock washed over me—they fit. I wasn't even going to look at the size. Normally, I wore a size ten because of my wide hips. I usually had to get one size bigger in jeans because of it, which caused a huge gap between my pants and my waist. Hey, maybe with my new vampire body, I would slim down—a girl could wish.

I dressed as quickly I could, not wanting to piss off my dad. I was already taking too long. I couldn't do anything with my hair, since I didn't have a band to put it into a ponytail.

Kate was gone by the time I entered the living room. Or so I thought. When I left the apartment, she was waiting for me in the hall with her arms crossed over her chest.

"Are you trying to get me in trouble?" she asked, a scowl forming on her face.

"No. I've been waiting for you," I lied.

She gave me a baleful look as I brushed past her. As we jogged down two flights of stairs, through several hallways, and corridors, I matched her in fluidity. I was surprised by how easy it was. Normally, as a human, I would have been panting for breath after a mile-long jog. Maybe there were benefits to being a vampire.

My dad stood near a podium in the war room when we entered. His head moved from side to side, scanning the crowd. Every seat in the room was occupied.

I leaned against the wall just inside the entrance while Kate took the post on the opposite side of it. I stared at my father, trying to catch his attention and let him know I was there. But he was listening to the people in the front row.

As I waited for my father to speak, I became keenly aware of the subtle noises in the room. I still couldn't get used to hearing the crisp sound of hearts beating, people breathing, stomachs growling, and people yawning, let alone the scents that mixed together, creating a hodgepodge of fragrances that made my nose wrinkle.

Kate leaned in and whispered, "Your father is pissed."

"How do you know?" I asked.

"He bites the inside of his cheek. It's a habit he has. In another second or two, he'll let out a sigh to try to calm himself."

Kate knew more about my father than I did, which set off a spark of anger, igniting a flame of jealousy. My daddy issues were beginning to surface, but I wasn't ready to face them. I started tapping my foot on the floor.

"Like father, like daughter," she said.

"What?" I slid her a sideways glance.

"Stop tapping your foot."

Commander Mason let out a sigh, just as Kate had predicted. He cleared his throat, and the buzz in the room quieted. I wondered what he was so mad about.

"As most of you know, I've been absent for the past two weeks. You've been informed that the Plutariums kidnapped me. While they were the reason I was missing, I won't reveal the full details today. What I would like everyone in this room to know is that we have a very important mission at hand—one that involves my son, Sam. While he may be family, we'll still follow all the protocols that we've learned. I don't want anyone straying from our rules of engagement. With that said, I need everyone to do their job, man their posts, and pay attention to detail. I don't want any screwups. Understood?" Commander Mason waited for acknowledgement.

"Yes, sir," the audience said in unison.

The room vibrated, and I had to cover my ears from the loudness of the deep baritone of collective voices.

"Good. Now, the team leads will report to Senior Chief Cooper and pick up your orders. Once you have those in hand, gather your team and study the plans. As I said, pay attention to detail and know your role." Commander Mason checked his watch. "Okay, we have two hours before we leave. Let's be safe out there."

The thirty or so SEALs started to rise when a siren blasted through the speaker. The pain stabbed my ears, and I thought blood was going to ooze out. I covered them and winced. Everyone in the room froze, looking at my dad and Webb. The alarm stopped, but a red light flashed from the ceiling every few seconds.

"Man your stations," a voice crackled through an overhead speaker. "This is a red alert."

"What's going on?" I asked.

"I've got to run. Go down and stay with Webb."

"Wait," I called as Kate ran out.

Before I could make my way to the podium where Webb was standing, Tripp was beside me. "Jo, come with me."

I followed him down to the side door, which Webb had just exited.

Tripp held the door open for me. "Hurry."

I entered a bustling room full of vampires. It was as if I had stepped into the command center at NASA. Video screens hung from the ceiling, revealing every nook and cranny in the building and around the perimeter. Several desks and tables shaped in half circles were set up with monitors displaying different types of pictures and information. Several large TV screens hung on the back wall just beyond the computers, desks, and surveillance equipment.

The epicenter of the Jupiter Sentinels' headquarters reminded me of a nest of ants. My father stood next to Kate, who wrote on a whiteboard. Her hand moved smoothly, drawing a blueprint of what appeared to be a building. Webb was next to a male vamp, who pointed to a computer screen showing an empty courtyard. One of the bald men who'd sat in the front row earlier stood behind a lady as she typed, her fingers flying across the keys. I shifted my glance from the lady to the TV monitor on the back wall.

A picture of the outside of Highland Memorial Hospital popped up. After a few more keystrokes, the TV screen split into four pictures of the inside of the hospital. *Is that where the Plutariums are keeping Sam?*

I leaned into Tripp, who hadn't moved. "What's happening?"

"We had a breach. Someone hopped our fence and is now somewhere on the property."

I thought about the man I had seen in the courtyard. Maybe I should've said something to Kate or Webb earlier.

A radio crackled in the room. "Echo four, come in."

Webb pulled the radio from his belt. "Echo four, go."

"Sir, we have the intruder."

"Bring him to room five," Webb radioed back.

"Yes, sir. Charlie two out." The radio went silent.

Webb sauntered over to a room in the far corner that was enclosed with a picture window. It reminded me of the one in Ben's hospital room. My father joined Webb as they waited for the intruder to enter.

Kate sidled up next to me. "You should have a seat. This might take a while." She waved her hand at the lounge area, which was another room along the left side of the command center. "There are drinks in the refrigerator. Maybe even some you've had before."

I winged up an eyebrow as my gums started throbbing at the thought of flavored juice boxes.

"You're going to need all the blood nourishment you can get before we head out to rescue Sam," she said.

While the blood sounded appetizing, my stomach growled for human food. I skirted around a few desks and tables before entering the lounge. I made a beeline for the four-foot refrigerator against the counter on the back wall. My gums were hurting just thinking about the Orange Cream flavor I'd had a few days ago as a human.

My choices were limited. I was bummed that the only flavor available was vanilla. Still, I plucked it from the shelf, inserted the straw, and sucked it down. Immediately, my throat lost its burn. I decided to grab another box when my father cleared his throat.

"Don't drink another one," he commanded.

I turned. "Why?"

"For the first few months, it is essential that the only blood you drink is mine."

"But Kate—"

"Kate should know better. I'll have a chat with her later. If you feel the need for blood, you need to let me or Dr. Vieira know immediately." He sounded worried.

"How will I know if I need blood or not?" I was beginning to worry.

"You'll know. I need to talk with you about Sam, but not here," he said on his way out.

I hurried behind him since something in his voice scared me.

The sea of military personnel were busy as they prepared for a mission to save my brother. If it wasn't for Sam, I wondered what they would do all day. I thought vampires were supposed to sleep all day and conduct their business at night. I couldn't help but think about evolution and the vampire. Darcy had told me they were night creatures. But the vampires around me, such as my father, Webb, and Dr. Vieira, were proof that contemporary vampires blended in with humans and the sun didn't burn them to ashes.

I shivered. Just thinking about vampires blew

my mind—and I was one. I pinched myself to make sure I was still alive, even as a vampire, which led to several other questions. *If vampires exist, what other creatures walked among humans? Do werewolves and fairies or witches and warlocks exist? Is there a whole supernatural community I'm not aware of?*

"Jo?" My father nudged me.

I blinked a few times.

"We'll go into the conference room off the war room, where it's quiet."

I was about to turn and follow him when a man sitting in the glassed-in room caught my eye, and I gasped.

"What's wrong?" my dad asked.

"That man." I pointed at the window. "Is he the intruder?" My heart raced.

"Yes. Nevertheless, he's not a threat. Why?"

"I know him. He's a Plutarium. But I thought he was dead."

Everyone in the room raised their heads.

My dad grabbed my arm and pulled me all the way into the conference room. "Sit down."

"Hey, what did I do? Why are you—?"

"Quiet." He paced a few times then scratched his head.

My heart was still racing, and he was giving it

more reason to sprint. "Did I do something wrong? All I said was 'Plutarium.'"

There was something bugging my dad, and it wasn't because I blurted out "Plutarium." It had to be because of the guy sitting in the interrogation room, the intruder—Neil Foster. The man who helped Sam and me. The man I thought was dead. Then it dawned on me. Neil was my dad's source and the friend who owed him a favor. I would bet my life. My dad got the picture of Sam from Neil.

"We need to talk about Sam," my father said.

"He's still alive, isn't he?"

I waited as he paced. I started tapping my foot then stopped, remembering what Kate had said —"like father, like daughter." A rush of darkness washed over me then light reappeared. My eyes must've changed. I pierced daggers at my father, waiting for him to say something, anything.

He knelt in front of me. His eyes had blackened to pools of tar. The outer edges had a silver rim, unlike Webb's, whose eyes took on a red rim when they turned black. He grabbed my hand.

Oh, this can't be good.

I'd been in this same room on Monday, with Webb kneeling to tell me I had to become a vampire to save Sam. I was sitting in the same chair in the same room, about to hear bad news again. A knot formed at the back of my throat. I swallowed, trying to prevent myself from screaming.

"Jo. I don't know—"

"You ass—I don't want to hear it." Tears spilled without hesitation.

"Young lady, you will not speak to me like that. Frankly, I won't have my daughter talking like a truck driver. I'm your father, even if I wasn't there for you. I'm here now, and I expect you to treat me with respect if for no other reason than the fact I'm your elder. Are we clear?" He grasped my hand.

More tears spilled, and I balled my right hand into fist. Fury coursed through me. I'd had enough of people telling me what to do, trying to rape or kill me, bullying me.

Damn the victim, damn the vampires, and damn my father!

"Yes, you're my biological father, but who are you to appear out of nowhere and start barking out commands? I'm not in your military squad, Commander. You told me Sam was alive and that we'd save him. So don't bring me in here and tell me he's dead because—"

The door opened, and Webb ambled in. "Commander, a word please."

Silence filled the room as Dad and I stared at each other.

"We need to leave. It's time," Webb said.

I broke the staring contest and glanced at Webb. His eyes widened. I wondered if there was something on my face. It didn't matter. I wanted to strangle my father, who still glared at me.

"Sir?" Webb called again for my father's attention.

"Give us a minute."

Webb left the room, as my father rose, I braced for impact.

Dad pressed his lips into a thin line. "The purpose of this conversation is to inform you of some ground rules and expectations when we arrive at the place where the Plutariums are keeping Sam. I also want you to be prepared for the worst in the event we can't save him."

"Wait. I didn't become a vampire for nothing. You promised we would save Sam."

He sighed. "He's still alive, according to my source. But he's in bad shape. When we get into the facility, our mission is to remove him first, put him under Dr. Vieira's care, and bring him back here. That's where you come in. You'll need to be there with Dr. Vieira the whole time and you'll need to do everything Dr. Vieira tells you. I don't want any drama, back talk, or temper tantrums from you. I'll explain everything once I know we have completed our mission. Are we clear?" He spoke as if I were one of his soldiers and the biggest bratty kid he had ever met. There was probably some truth to bratty.

I nodded.

Since I'd shed my human existence to save my brother, I had to do everything I could to ensure my vampire life included Sam, even if that meant being the good and proper daughter, stalling my anger for my vampire father for another day. "So I'm going with you?" I asked, looking for confirmation.

"You and Dr. Vieira will accompany us but will stay in the van until we bring Sam out."

It wasn't the answer I wanted to hear. I had a feeling that my brand-new vampire mettle was about to be tested.

27

I sat in the back seat of the van. Webb was driving, and Dr. Vieira sat next to me, behind my dad, who commanded the front seat. The van was set up to accommodate a patient in much the same way as an ambulance. A stretcher was in the back, along with compartments filled with gauze, Band-Aids, needles, and other medical items needed to take care of someone on the road. A cooler sat between Dr. Vieira's legs, and I hated to ask what was in it. I suspected it was my father's blood for me, since I had to give Sam my own blood. I didn't even know how I was going to do that.

I took several deep breaths and gazed out the windshield, trying to keep my mind off Sam. Cars passed, and humans went about their day like any other. If humans knew a person like me, a vampire, lived among them... I thought about Ben. *How is he going to react to my new physical status? Hell, how am I going to react to it? Can I still go to school? Can I still be friends with Darcy?* I let out a breath. I had forgotten about her. I wondered, as the van zipped through the streets of Fall River, what Darcy was doing at that moment. Given her fiery temper, she was probably pulling out her hair, trying to find Ben and me. I prayed I would see her again.

Webb pumped the brakes and slowed for the red light ahead. I couldn't see much of my surroundings since the van didn't have any back windows.

"Jo, remember to stay in the vehicle," my father said.

The last time someone had told me to stay in the car, I was attacked. Webb glanced at me in the rearview mirror, waiting for my response. Then my father turned, pulled down his sunglasses, and peered at me above the rims.

"What?" I asked.

"She'll stay with me," Dr. Vieira assured him.

I snapped my head in his direction, wondering what he was going to do. *Tie me down?*

"Yeah, what he said." I flicked a finger at Dr. Vieira.

My father pulled his sword from his belt. "I warned you about your attitude."

As I rolled my eyes, I caught Webb still staring at me through the rearview mirror, his blue eyes piercing me.

I broke eye contact when the first blade of my father's sword ejected.

Whoa! The shiny blade had a blue hue along its outer edges.

"Just testing it." He ran a finger lightly over the blade. "Don't worry. I'm not testing the second blade."

I eyed Dr. Vieira's waist. He didn't have a sword strapped to his belt. I sensed that Webb had his, as he never left the compound without it. In fact, all the Sentinels wore their swords unless they were sleeping. I made a mental note to ask Kate about the swords—she seemed to be more open with me than the others.

Webb pulled into an alleyway and came to a stop behind a large building. I bent over and glanced up at the back entrance of Highland Memorial Hospital. Then I remembered seeing the hospital on the command center TV screen.

"Is this where they're keeping Sam?" I asked.

"There's an empty wing in the basement," Webb said.

A car door slammed. Then someone knocked on the driver's side window.

Webb pushed the button, and the window lowered.

"We have all sides covered," Tripp said.

"Aren't people going to see you walking in with your weapons?" I asked, frowning as my father wiped down his sword.

Tripp shook his head. "No. The Sentinels standing at the main entrance are in civilian clothes. We're going in through the boiler room, anyway."

"Dr. Vieira, you know what to do," my father said then slid out.

Webb pulled out a pair of black gloves and slid them over his hands. Olivia appeared in front of the van. All four of them were armed and ready to take on anyone who got in their way.

As they walked around the corner of the hospital, a shiver skated up my spine. The tang of blood wafted in through the crack in the window, and it smelled like a pile of decomposing trash. A plenitude of sounds rang around me from car doors slamming shut, horns blowing, dogs barking, and sirens wailing.

"Did you hear that?"

Dr. Vieira nodded as he raised a finger to his lips. "I want you to close your eyes," he whispered.

"Huh?" I glared at him.

"Just do it."

I let out a huff then closed my eyes.

"Now, try and clear out all the background noise you hear and focus on your immediate surroundings. As a vampire, you should have impeccable hearing, as good as or better than the canine species. The sooner you master this, the better it will be for you."

I took a deep breath, thinking that by the time I master this, Sam would be dead. Nevertheless, I did as he instructed, clearing my head and trying to erase all the sounds. The sirens were gone. The faint sound of cars was still there, but the barking dog was ruining my concentration. I shook my head, breathing slowly.

Dr. Vieira placed his hand on mine. "Center on any noise in the van," he whispered.

The only thing in the van I could hear was his heart beating. I counted the beats as blood pumped in and out of his heart, and the other noises began to dissipate.

"Okay, now what?" I asked.

"Do the same with smell. Open up your olfactory senses and concentrate. Try to filter out the weaker scents and bring forth the stronger ones, which will be closer to you."

I inhaled through my nose, smelling trash, some type of rotten-egg odor, and pine, which was stronger than the rest. The blood I had smelled earlier wasn't in the mix. I was curious if this was how dogs ferret out their prey.

"Well?" he asked.

"I smell a combination of things, but the strongest is a pine scent, which I think is coming from you. I did smell blood when we drove up, but it was tangy and had a bad odor."

"Do you think it was human blood?" he asked.

"You mean, you can tell? How?"

"It's mostly instinct, but vampire blood is not as fragrant as human blood. As you get older, it will be second nature for you to smell the difference."

I was only a day old in vampire age, so I imagined it would take me a while before I reached that level.

Dr. Vieira removed his hand from mine when his cell phone rang. He pressed his fingers to his lips again.

All of sudden a metal-on-metal clank whistled in the distance. The last time I heard that noise was when Webb engaged his Sentinel sword. My eyes bugged out of my head.

"They're behind us," I whispered.

Dr. Vieira pulled up his pant leg and grabbed a dagger that was strapped there. "Here, take this." He handed it to me.

"Uh-uh. I'm not using that." I pushed it away, and it fell onto the floorboard. "Can't I just use my fangs and bite?"

Then he reached into a bag at his feet and pulled out a Sentinel sword.

He smirked. "You've got so much to learn. There are two vamps behind us, strong ones. Your fangs aren't going to do anything to them."

"Neither is this dagger if vampires can't die," I added.

"That's not your ordinary dagger, and this isn't your ordinary sword. Both of these weapons are double-edged and made from a base metal of cobalt. Aside from chopping a vampire's head off or burning a vampire to death, the only other thing that can kill a vampire is a cobalt-infused knife or sword through the heart."

"Okay, now I am really confused. You mean I could die today from one of these weapons? And you want me to carry one?" We needed to get the fuck out of there. If I died before we rescued

Sam... I didn't want to think about it. I had already died as a human and returned as a vampire, and I was now living in hell.

"Pick up the dagger," Dr. Vieira commanded.

"I can't do this." My voice trembled as I bent over and warily retrieved the weapon. The leather handle was soft against my palm. I stared at it, trying to figure out how to use it.

"Here's what we're going to do. I'm going to step out on this side. I will distract them. Then I want you to run into the hospital and hide. We can't have anything happen to you. Do you understand?"

I nodded.

"One more thing." Dr. Vieira grabbed my hand. "You're a vampire now. Use your physical strength and your senses to protect yourself. Your father will find you."

"What about you?" I asked.

"I've been a vampire too long. I know how to take care of myself." He grasped the handle of the door. "As soon as I step out, I want you to run. Don't hesitate, or you'll get killed."

Vampire body or human body, it didn't matter. I was scared shitless. I had thought that my predatory instincts would take over, that I wouldn't be afraid, but I was just an ugly, scared, purple-haired vampire. My heart raced, my eyes had already shifted, and my hands were shaking. I couldn't fathom what I had been thinking when I traded my human life for this one.

Dr. Vieira slid open the door and disappeared toward the back of the van. Then he banged on the outside, which was my cue to bolt. I yanked open my door and sprinted around the corner and into the boiler room.

The place was the same as I remembered, but the boiler hummed more loudly now that I was a vampire. Steam filtered out from the grates in the floor, blanketing my skin and causing my cheeks to warm. I dodged the pipes jutting out from above and ran to the back of the boiler, where an exit sign popped into view.

I bent over, placed the dagger in my boot, and prayed it wouldn't stab me. Then I pushed the bar on the door and stepped into a stairwell. I looked up, hesitating for a moment. Maybe the patient floors would be a better place to hide. Maybe that would be the last place the Plutariums would look for me, among a crowd of humans.

I stood in the stairwell, trying to decide if I should go up and hide among humans or down and find the empty wing where Sam was. I needed to stay close to the van, so when my father brought Sam out, I would be there for him. I decided it was best to find my father and his team.

As I climbed down the stairs, a fruity fragrant smell wafted up, tickling my nose. The farther down I climbed, the stronger the smell became. The minute I entered the hallway, the fragrance of human blood overtook me, causing my breath to hitch and my fangs to descend. Dr. Vieira was right. Human blood was definitely distinct.

I looked in both directions. The human smell was stronger to my right, and it tugged at me, pulling me in that direction. Slowly, I shuffled toward the fragrant odor, attempting to resist the seduction of the human scent. But my legs were my enemy. It was as if my body was a magnet being drawn to iron. My gums pulsed, aching to sink my fangs into mortal flesh.

As I approached the end of the hallway to turn left, a shadowy figure climbed up the wall. My pulse quickened, my mouth watered, and saliva coated my lips. I was ready for a taste.

I rounded the corner, and the shadow disappeared. I jogged up to the first door and stood to the side of it. I peeked in through the window, where humans stood behind lab benches with vials of blood in their hands. I tore my gaze away and adjusted my vision to read the sign on the door: Blood Lab.

I'd hit the lottery. I was in vampire heaven. Without another thought, I walked in.

A lady with short black hair looked up from her desk. "May I help you?"

The smell of blood was stronger inside, so much so that I thought I was going to leap across several desks to claim my prize.

"Are you okay, young lady? Are you lost?" She rose from her chair and came over to me.

She kept asking me questions, but all I could do was restrain myself from attacking her.

"Miss? Should I call upstairs and find you a doctor?"

I covered my mouth and mumbled through my fingers, "No, I don't need a doctor. I'm lost. I was looking for my dad. He works in the boiler room."

"Oh. Well, go out here and turn right. Then follow the hallway to the exit on the left. That should take you up one floor," she explained.

I ambled toward the exit and mumbled, "Thank you."

Once in the hall, I sprinted around the corner then stopped. I had to get a grip. I couldn't become a crazed vampire who preyed on humans.

I waited a second to regain my composure then

headed back to the entrance. Since my first choice ended in my almost draining a mortal, my only other choice was to investigate the other end of the hallway.

I jogged. The human scent grew weaker, and my fangs retreated, although I was having a tough time getting the smell out of my mind.

The dim light above me sprayed down, casting a glow, lighting a path that dead-ended at a set of double doors. The room beyond the doors was dark, but my keen vampire vision adjusted, and I could see that an empty room lay ahead. I didn't know if I should go in or not. My choices were limited, though. Either I investigated what lay behind the door or go back. While the humans were definitely more appealing and appetizing, I was afraid of myself more than anything else.

I slowly pushed the door then slipped through the small opening. I hugged the wall to my right as if I was a rat crawling along a perimeter to find food. As I made my way deeper inside, a light illuminated an area on the far side.

My father's voice cut through, pricking my eardrums. He spoke in a different language. I froze, trying to decipher it, when a whistling metallic noise startled me. Then someone grunted, glass shattered, and a door slammed. I'd moved closer to the lighted room and the noise when someone grabbed my arm.

I turned to find Fernando next to me, his mouth stained red. Of all the damn vampires to run into, it had to be the smug and cocky vamp from Ben's house.

"Nice to see you again, Jo, though I'm saddened you're not human anymore," he said as he sniffed the air. "You don't smell as mouthwatering as you did a few days ago."

"What're you? A dog? Get a grip," I countered.

"But I was so looking forward to getting to know you better as a human. In fact, I was hoping when this was all over, we could go out on a date." He stared at me intently, his gaze menacing.

He was asking me out on a date in the middle of a battle between the Sentinels and the Plutariums. I couldn't believe it. "I'm sorry to disappoint you, but I can't say the feeling is mutual. You're such a smug asshole, I'd be surprised if you get dates at all."

His lips curled at the edges displaying a perfect white smile that lit up his tan complexion. "I see you're still a feisty one. I so love that about my women."

"And what woman had the pleasure of your fangs?" I asked, pointing to his mouth.

He squeezed my arm tighter. "That's none of your business."

I cocked my head to one side. An air of danger poured off him.

I thought about what Dr. Vieira had said. *You're a vampire now. Use your physical strength.* I was still trying to understand what those physical strengths were. I'd pulled out a drawer in my father's bathroom that had flown across the room, and I'd grabbed Webb by his throat, leaving him gasping for breath. But that was all I had.

"You're not afraid of me?" I asked.

Fernando laughed. "Afraid of you? You're a newborn. How can you do any damage to an old goat like me?" He laughed again. "I see it this way. You're coming with me. I need redemption to prove to my master that I can succeed, and two human teenagers can't keep me down."

I wanted to laugh. "You mean you got in trouble because of me? I bet you were laughed at for a human getting away from a strong vampire like you."

He smiled again. No matter what I said, it didn't faze him. "I'm growing very fond of you, Josephine Mason."

I cringed at the sound of my name and how he

said it. "Don't call me that. My name is Jo and only Jo."

He frowned and loosened his grip on my arm. That was my cue to run, but instead, I bent over and pulled the dagger out of my boot before Fernando could react. I positioned the dagger in my hand the only way I knew how. I had witnessed Jonah holding one, so I mimicked the way he held it. I wrapped my palm around the leather handle with my knuckles facing up, my palm down with my forearm parallel to the floor in front of me.

In a swift move, I jabbed it at Fernando, but he bent back and laughed.

I had no idea what I was doing, holding a dagger, let alone thrusting it at someone. With my luck, I would hurt myself. A sudden fear rushed through me. My physical being was that of a vampire, but my mind was very human and still sending me signals of anxiety.

"So, little Jo wants to play dirty."

His voice infuriated me, especially when he spewed pet names for me. He pulled out his dagger, and the memory of what he had tried to do to Ben coursed through me. Rage surfaced, and adrenaline pumped through every artery. It was as if someone had injected me with a dose of speed to wake me up. Everything around me became quiet. My vision sharpened. The only thing in front of me was my target, and I was focused.

I took three steps forward, and he took two back.

"You don't want to do this," Fernando said. "You're young and don't know what you're doing. I'm afraid I'm going to hurt you, and I won't be able to ask you out on a date."

I laughed. "Do you think I would go out with you?"

"A guy can hope, can't he?"

I shook my head. He was still trying to pick me up and trying to kill me at the same time. Without thinking I said, "Okay, I'll go out with you. You name the place and the time."

Startled, he dropped his arms, his dagger pointing toward the floor.

I attacked, driving the blade into his left shoulder, just above his heart.

He fell to the floor.

I gasped. *Did I just kill him?*

I'd been stabbed before, so I knew the pain associated with it. I didn't know for sure, but as a vampire I could still feel pain. The blood rushed to my feet. I didn't want to kill him—all I wanted to do was stop him. Dr. Vieira said that the cobalt blade would kill a vampire, but it had to be driven through the heart, not the shoulder.

I bent over to examine my enemy when Fernando pulled the dagger out of his shoulder and grabbed me.

"You can't kill me like that. It burns, but you missed my heart." His smirk turned dark, replaced by hard eyes and a murderous expression. "Now, you're going to pay." He jumped up and threw me against the wall.

My head hit first, then my back, knocking the wind out of me. I slumped to the floor. Before I could get on my feet, he squeezed his fingers around my throat, and threw me again. I landed on a counter, slid off the slick surface, and fell to the floor behind it. I tried to stand, but a pain crept up my spine. So I placed my hands on the floor and pushed myself up. As I uncurled my vertebrae, trying to stretch, Fernando drove the dagger into my stomach.

I lost my breath, but was quick on my feet, yanking the weapon out of me. A burning sensation trickled around the wound. The fall to the floor hurt more than the dagger.

"Have you had enough, Jo?" he asked.

I rolled my eyes. "No, please, hit me some more."

I'd had enough of this asshole.

As he stomped toward me, I slid to the side, closer to the lighted room in the distance.

"Where're you going?" he asked, advancing another step.

When he did, I lunged at him, driving the dagger into his abdomen. I held it there, twisting it, watching as his eyes grew into wide pools of black liquid.

He looked down at me, blew out a breath, and smiled. He was ready to react, when I stabbed him again and again until he collapsed, his body hitting the floor with a thud.

I'd never killed anyone before, but that option vanished when my father's voice startled me. I snapped up my head, searching. I ran toward the back, following the light.

I was several feet away from a set of windowed double doors when an object flew through the air on the other side of it. Webb came into view, two hands wrapped around his sword, blade slanted in the air. He lunged at his opponent, plunging the sword forward. I slid to the side at an angle, peering through the glass to see who he was fighting. Then his ponytailed avenger waved his sword down to his left, turning his wrists over then up again with the tip of the sword pointing at Webb.

It was as if I was watching Zorro. Each fighter was light on his feet, masterful, wielding their thirty-six inches of steel at one another.

"Open it now," my father growled.

I slid to the other glass pane, looking for him. As I placed my hand on the door, a set of hands gripped my ankles. I peered down and found Fernando stretched out, holding onto me for dear life as the rest of his body inched forward like a snake.

I bent my right knee, pulling my ankle upward. His grip was tight. I tried again. Still, he hung on. I tried the same thing with my left ankle. It came loose, and I stepped on his hand. "Let go, or I'll crush your hand," I growled.

He pulled my right leg toward him, and I fell, crashed through the doors, and slid across the tile, stopping when my head hit the marble panel of a lab bench. I grabbed the back of my head. As I looked up, a sword sliced down through the air, toward my foot. I rolled out of the way, but Fernando dove for me, and the sword caught the back of his calf. He screamed out in pain and fell on top of me, crushing my windpipe. I unleashed my vampire strength and pushed him off me. He went flying back through the double doors. My eyes widened. *Do I have that much strength?*

Before I could stand, a hand grabbed me by my

hair and pulled me upright. I stood face-to-face with a vampire who had solid-red irises—I could've sworn I was looking into the eyes of the devil.

Now what? He looked young, but his eyes told me otherwise. Even though I was a vampire and shouldn't have been afraid of anything or anyone, my Spidey sense told me to run. I inched backward, watching the creepy vampire in front me.

"Jo, get out of here," my father commanded.

I twisted my neck to the left. My father was standing in front of a glass room with his right hand clamped around a man's neck. My gaze traveled to rest on the man's face. He had short brown hair, and I recognized him from the photo Webb had shown us in the war room. The man my father had pinned against the glass was my Uncle Patrick.

I turned on my heel and ran to my father. I stopped and glimpsed beyond the two men and into the glass room, gasping for air as my gaze fell on Sam. His lifeless body was lying in front of me with only a sheath of glass separating us. My throat tightened, and tears clouded my vision as anger rose, snaking its way through me.

He looked worse than he had in the picture. His arms were hanging off the sides of the metal table. His cheeks were hollow, his skin pale. I bent over, the room spinning, the light around me fading. I placed my hands on my knees, taking deep breaths, trying not to pass out.

"Jo, get up," my father commanded. "Tripp, get over here, *now*!"

With my hands on my knees, I turned my head, glancing at the red-eyed vampire who stalked toward me. I should have run, but I stood frozen in place. Some vampire I was, standing in the middle of an otherworldly battle with swords, daggers, vampires, and the devil. Panic crept up my spine. I should have been brave, fighting the bastards who did this to my brother. Instead, I was bent over, willing myself not to pass out.

As the red-eyed vamp approached, sword in hand, Tripp came running up behind him.

"Edmund, over here," Tripp called.

Edmund spun around, pointing his sword at Tripp.

"Patrick, open the door. I'm not going to ask you again," my father said.

"That will be the last thing I do, Steven. Do you think I'm going to let your son live? After everything you've done to me since we were kids? Go ahead. Kill me," Patrick barked.

A seed of hatred propelled me upright at the sound of his voice.

"Just break the damn glass!" I shouted. "Do it now. You have to save Sam."

"Look. Your daughter is desperate. And for what? You forced her to change for this, to save Sam's life. You don't really think that's going to work, do you?"

"What's he talking about?" I asked.

"Tell her, Steven. Tell her what she did was all for nothing. Tell her that her immortality was just to satisfy you, so you could make up for all those lost years after you left the twins with your psycho sister-in-law."

How does he know all this? Does my father really know where I was all these years?

"Don't listen to him, Jo. He's just trying to get into your head."

"You still didn't answer me!" I shouted. "What's Patrick talking about? I want to know."

"We don't have time for a family discussion," my father said.

I looked at Patrick, whose face had turned red, his eyes closed as he hung in midair while my father choked him.

I ran to my father. "Get Sam out of there."

I inspected the door to the glass room. An illuminated keypad sat next to it with a dark, square panel just above it.

"You need the combination and his handprint," my father said.

"Just break the glass."

"I can't. It's six inches thick. It would take more than my vampire strength to crack it."

I scanned the room for something to throw at the glass, but I couldn't find anything in the chaos. Webb fought with his ponytailed opponent in one corner of the room. Tripp and Edmund were tangled together. Edmund had Tripp in a headlock not far from where I stood. In the opposite corner to my left, Olivia danced around with another vampire. Karate kicks and punches whipped through the air.

This whole scene was insane. Everyone was fighting, and no one was saving Sam. Behind Olivia, in the far corner of the room, I spied an electrical box. *Would shutting off the power unlock the door?*

I ran to the corner, dodging Olivia's dance moves, and opened the panel. I flipped off the main switch, and the entire room went dark. Machines beeped. The humming of other instruments stopped, including the sound of the swords clanging. Even the vampires stopped in their tracks, their heavy breathing the only sound in the room. Then a small glow of lights turned on. I imagined the emergency power had kicked in.

I sprinted back to the glass room. The door was ajar, and the panel blinked frantically. I wrapped my hands around the edge of the door and pulled with a grunt. It was like trying to move a glacier. I managed to move it several inches before someone pushed me from behind, knocking me to the floor. My body became wedged in the doorway.

I raised my head to look at my attacker. Edmund had a sword pointed my way as he leapt over me and into the glass room. I tried to sit up, but the tip of the sword was pointed at my chest. I froze.

"You don't want to move, little one," he said.

No shit! I wasn't planning on moving just yet. I looked around, examining my options. The good news—I was in Sam's room. The bad news—I had to get away from this red-eyed devil and get Sam off the table, but I didn't know how.

Then as if God granted me a wish, my father appeared at my feet. He grabbed the edge of the six-inch glass door and tore it from its hinges. The door fell to the floor, but it didn't shatter, it just cracked. He towered over me, his eyes sterling silver and his fangs smeared with blood.

I shook my head. It was the first time I had seen his fangs, but it was also weird to see his eyes silver. I had thought all the vampires had black eyes when they changed colors. I made a mental note to ask about that later. For the time being, we needed to get Sam out of there.

"Let her go, Edmund. She is of no use to you," my father said. He placed his left hand on his waist, moving it around.

I imagined he was searching for his sword, which was now in the hands of this Edmund dude, primed and ready to slit my jugular.

Death by my father's sword. What a way to die.

"Steven, my friend, we go back a long way. You know that I wouldn't dream of bringing your daughter into this mess. You know deep down that she doesn't belong in our world." He cocked his head to one side and peered down at me. "My, my, you already turned her. For what? To save your son?" He pointed to Sam. "He's gone. He's not coming back."

Why does everyone keep saying that? I didn't believe it. I couldn't believe it. I became a vampire for one sole reason, and something inside me told me this jerk was lying. Nevertheless, I certainly wasn't going to disrupt the conversation, not with a sword at my throat.

My father stared at the man, not taking his eyes off him. "How dare you lie to me? You know damn well his heart is still beating. Do you think I'm an idiot? I expected more from you, Edmund."

I shifted my gaze slowly between them, trying to figure out how it was going to end. It seemed we were at a standstill, at least until Fernando came stalking up with a dagger aimed at my father's back.

"Watch out!" I shouted.

My father bent down and pulled me toward him. In an instant, he turned, grabbed Fernando, and threw him across the room. A loud bang was followed by a thud. Then my father jumped over me and lunged at Edmund. Both vamps fell to the floor. The sword Edmund had been holding flew into the air, tumbling out of control toward me. I rolled out of the direct line of the falling sword and kept rolling until a large foot stopped me and pulled me to an upright position. I buried my face into his chest before he released me from his grip.

I looked into the eyes of my estranged Uncle Patrick. Anger, hate and disgust surfaced, each emotion fighting to rise above the other. He tilted his head to one side then studied me as if I was one of his lab rats. I closed my eyes and inhaled, trying to unleash my young vampire senses. Then I exhaled sharply and opened my eyes.

"You're still human," I said as I stood in front of him, studying the wannabe vampire.

"Not for long," he replied with an evil grin on his face.

My vision blurred for a second as I rushed him, throwing my body headfirst into Patrick. My anger won—I wanted to tear him to pieces. My fangs descended, and without thinking, I bit into his wrist, my canines breaking through his skin. His heart beat loudly, his pulse throbbing between my lips as I clamped down on his vein. A spurt of blood filled my mouth then slithered down my throat. It tasted bitter, almost acidic. There was nothing good about the taste of his blood.

He screamed and threw back his head.

Arms wrapped around my stomach. Someone was trying to pull me away. I growled then kicked. It was my turn to drain my prey. I wasn't letting go.

"Jo, release him." Webb pulled at me again. "His blood is poisonous. He wanted you to bite him. Now release your grip."

I couldn't stop. I hated this man, my kin, more than anything in the world. He was evil for what he had done to Sam. His blood coated my stomach, and my body started to warm. The world tilted, and a rush of pain clenched my insides. *What is happening to me?* Suddenly, my fangs retreated, and my mouth slid off his wrist. Webb, who still had his arms around me, tripped backward as I fell on top of him. I rolled off, and white foam dripped down from my lips onto the black tile floor. I looked at Webb with my eyebrows pinched together.

"I don't know what it is," Webb said.

I staggered to my feet. Whatever was in Patrick's blood wasn't agreeing with me. I grabbed hold of a chair and sat down. The room began to spin. My lips curled, and I smiled at Webb.

"Oh no," he said.

"What?" I asked.

"He drugged you," Webb said as he ran his hands through his hair.

"I'm fine. How're you?" I laughed.

Tripp walked over. "What's wrong with her?"

"She drank some of Patrick's blood," Webb replied.

"Shit. Drugged?" Tripp asked.

"It appears so," Webb replied.

"Sir, the Plutariums are shackled and ready for transport. The commander is taking Sam back to headquarters," Tripp said.

"Sam? Is... he... okay?" I asked, my words slurred. I shook my head. *What am I saying? Sam isn't okay.* "Where is Sam?" I asked as my body swayed.

Webb placed his arm around me. "Sam is with your father. We need to get you back to headquarters ASAP."

"Why? He'll be dead before Steven has a chance to save him," Patrick blurted out.

His words catapulted me out of the fog I was in. As if someone had touched me with a lighted match, I spun around with superhuman speed and lunged at the mortal monster. *Killing Patrick would be a vampire blessing.*

He sat still as my body blanketed his, tackling him backward, his head hitting the floor. Without another thought, my fangs clamped down on his throat. I began to pull, ripping his skin.

"Get off him, Jo," Tripp growled as his hands grabbed me from behind, pulling me toward him.

"Tripp, she'll rip his throat," Webb intoned.

Now the vamp boys were getting the idea. I wanted to mangle the asshole.

Webb bent down and whispered, "You'll have your moment, Jo. This isn't it. Let him go. He's a human. We don't kill humans."

In my world, Patrick wasn't human. He was a beast from the depths of hell.

"Think of Sam," Tripp said in a soft tone. "We need to get back to him. Time is critical."

That wasn't fair, but he was right. I was wasting precious moments.

I released my bite and looked down at Patrick as Tripp pulled me off him. As he lay there, his feet shackled and hands cuffed, he smirked at me. I wanted to unleash my rage and go another round, but Sam needed me more.

"What are you going to do with him?" I asked. My tongue seemed to be cooperating again.

"We'll lock all of them up in our prison wing and deal with them accordingly."

I drew my eyebrows together. "What does that mean?"

"It means, Jo, that I will be seeing you again," Patrick said.

"Shut up. I didn't ask you," I barked. "The only time I'll see you is when we're lowering you into your grave." My fangs hadn't retracted yet, and I desperately wanted to rip out his heart, no matter how much of his drugged blood I drank.

He laughed. "So young and so naïve," he said as he glared at me.

"What does that mean?" I asked, squirming for Tripp to release me.

"He's not worth it. Besides, we have laws that protect him," Tripp said.

"I don't care about the stupid—"

"Get her out of here. Dr. Vieira is waiting," Webb commanded. "Head back to the compound ASAP. Olivia and I will stay here and clean this up. We'll meet you back at headquarters in an hour."

I didn't need to hold on to Tripp. His grip around me was so tight I couldn't breathe.

"Can you loosen your arm a bit?" I pleaded.

"Not until we are out of here."

"I can't breathe."

"You're a vampire now. You'll be fine," he said as he carried me through the basement of the hospital.

What was that supposed to mean? I might have been a vampire, but I still needed to breathe to live *—or do I? Boy, I have a ton to learn about all this vamp stuff.*

Once outside, Tripp released me. My legs were like rubber, my knees shaking. He walked behind me as I staggered to the van. I took a deep breath. The fresh air was a welcoming relief from the odors and smells that'd had me in a tizzy since I first walked into the hospital.

I was anxious to see Dr. Vieira. I had my doubts when I ran from the van. He said he had been a vampire for a long time, but with two Plutariums against one Sentinel, I wasn't convinced Dr. Vieira would win.

When we reached the front of the van, Dr. Vieira wasn't in view. The area around it seemed eerily quiet. The car that Tripp and Olivia had driven was gone.

"What happened?" Dr. Vieira said as he walked around from the back of the van. He studied me as he pulled my arms to him then examined my wrists. He wiped my mouth with his fingers. "Whose blood is this?" His expression went from concerned to deer in the headlights.

"Patrick's," Tripp said from behind me, keeping me sandwiched between him and Dr. Vieira. "His blood was laced with some type of drug."

I craned my neck and glared at him. "Thanks," I said. The fog from whatever had been in Patrick's blood returned as the adrenaline in me seemed to disappear. My head began to hurt, and with my legs on the verge of turning into Gumby's, I was thankful that Tripp was at least behind me in case I fell.

"I told you to stay hidden. What have you done?" Dr. Vieira dropped his hands from my wrists. "Didn't your father tell you that the only blood you could drink was his for the next few months?" He stood in front of me with his arms crossed over his chest.

"Yeah, but... never mind. Can we just go? Sam needs me."

Dr. Vieira nodded. "I need to get her back so I can somehow figure out how to cleanse her system," he said. "And the others?"

"The commander rushed Sam back to headquarters about fifteen minutes ago. Webb and Olivia will secure the premises. Viking II has taken control of the Plutariums and is taking them back to headquarters as we speak. Patrick is secured and with Webb, who will escort him back," Tripp replied.

"We need to hurry, then. Between Sam and now Jo, I have my work cut out for me," Dr. Vieira said.

I slid out from between them, praying I could at least walk to the passenger side of the van. When I reached the open door, I fell in. A few seconds later, Dr. Vieira slid in and helped me into my seat. Within seconds, the van was moving. I settled in my seat and surveyed my stomach where Fernando had stabbed me. My shirt was stained with blood, but that was it. My stomach showed no signs of Fernando using me as a voodoo doll. I looked at Dr. Vieira then back at my stomach. I shook my head a few times. I remembered the pain when Cliff had stabbed me and how my body took forever to heal. Today—not even a scratch. I didn't know whether to be excited or shocked.

As if Dr. Vieira knew what I was thinking, he said, "It takes some getting used to. I'm surprised, though, that you healed so quickly. New vampires usually take a little bit longer for the skin to heal due to their nutrient levels. But I guess I shouldn't be too surprised since you are a Mason."

I had no idea what he meant by his last statement, but I decided to table that thought for the time being.

I sat back and tried to relax as Tripp drove, but I couldn't stop thinking about Sam and wishing the van would move faster. I was tapping my foot when Dr. Vieira cleared his throat.

"Jo." His nostrils flared, and he looked like he was about to explode.

What now?

"I know that all this is very hard for you. But in the future, if you don't listen to me—if you don't heed my words or warning when I speak—you will not last long as a vampire. In addition, when I tell you what to do when we're back in my medical facility, you *will* listen. Your teenage petulance will not get in the way of my job and saving your brother. Do you understand me?"

All I could do was nod. His words were sharp, his tone unyielding. Sam was the most important person to me. For the moment, I understood what he was saying and would listen to him, but I couldn't promise anything more after he helped save my brother's life.

28

By the time we arrived at headquarters, the effects of the drug had waned. I didn't feel woozy, but just to be sure, I climbed out of the van and took inventory of my senses. My legs weren't shaky, and the fog surrounding my brain was gone. I gave myself the all clear and ran into the building through the heavy steel doors, going directly to the elevator. I banged on the button until the door opened. I couldn't wait any longer.

As the door closed, a hand slid around the edge, forcing it back, and my father slid in. I stared at the panel of buttons, avoiding him. I guess it was his turn to yell at me, to tell me how disappointed he was that I ended up in the middle of a fight when he told me to stay with Dr. Vieira. I could hear all the grown-up words and military jargon he was about to unleash on me.

The elevator began to move, inching up slowly, as if the gears were stuck. He stared straight ahead with his hands clasped behind his back, not even looking at me. I stood still, shocked as silence filled the car. *Now who's being childish?*

The number three lit up, indicating we were close to our destination. Then my father hit the stop button, and the car jerked to a stop. The bell dinged for a few seconds, and the loud, steady buzz stabbed my ears. Suddenly, dizziness washed over me. I hated small spaces.

"I want to speak to you before we go in." His tone obstinate, his posture stiff.

"Um, can we do this out of the elevator?" Drops of perspiration beaded on my forehead, and my hands became clammy.

"We need to do this now," he said.

"Dad, please. I have to get out of here."

He jumped back.

I patted my cheeks, unsure if something odd peppered my face or my appearance changed to prompt his reaction. No, everything seemed normal except the sweat trickling down.

"You called me Dad." A smile split his face, stretching from ear to ear.

My eyebrows disappeared into my hairline. "I did?" A drop of liquid dripped down the bridge of my nose.

He released the stop button. "I'm sorry—I wasn't aware that small spaces bothered you."

"There's a lot you don't know," I said, still panicked. I wanted to be more of a smart-ass, but my phobia kept me from clawing at him. I reminded myself that I had plenty of time—like an eternity—to break out my repressed daddy issues.

When the elevator door opened, I rushed out, and the chilly air breezed over me. I let out a deep sigh and leaned against the wall, wiping my forehead with the back of my hand.

My father followed. "Is there anything I can do?"

Shaking my head, I inhaled as I pushed off the wall. We walked, not talking. The sound of our breathing vibrated with every step, echoing around us. We had at least several minutes before we arrived at the first set of double doors. I dreaded the trek since he had plenty of time to wield his wrath on me.

"Sam is in bad shape." His baritone voice echoed off the empty walls. "I want you to stay calm through the process. An elevated level of adrenaline can be dangerous for you both. It can cause you to go into shock, then we can't extract your blood for him."

I swallowed hard. "He's still alive?" I stopped, waiting for confirmation.

"Um..." He looked down at me.

My father was over six feet tall, and I had to crane my neck to meet his gaze.

As if we were hardwired, I sensed he wasn't telling me something. I searched, looking for some hint, but all I could see was that his eyes had shifted a tint closer to silver.

"What are you not telling me?" I felt my own eyes shift.

"The human body has about six quarts of blood. Draining more than thirty percent causes a human's system to shut down, then death is imminent. Unlike humans, as I explained the other day, those who carry the vampire gene have a little more time. But how long, we haven't figured out. We know Patrick was taking blood from Sam in small vials over the past three days, and today, he started draining his system. I'm not sure how much blood Sam's lost, but his heart is barely beating."

He spoke as if he were my instructor in an anatomy-and-physiology class. After a couple of days with these vamps, I could probably get my medical license.

"You told me that already. You're leaving something out." I started biting my lip then tapped my foot.

He blew out a breath. "I'm not sure you'll... you'll... make it through, either. Sam may need more blood than you can give him. And it's crucial that he receives *your* blood."

"What're you saying?"

"This procedure is dangerous for you. You'll be donating a lot of blood. While you're young and your system can probably handle it, your organs haven't completely developed. Your heart muscle is not strong yet. I'm sorry."

"Sorry? Is that all you've got?" I balled both my hands into fists and glowered at him. I hated him as much as I hated shedding my humanity. "Why didn't you tell me that before I made the change? Why didn't you tell me about all the risks? Wait. Your mission is more important than your long-lost kids, right?" I started jogging, trying to get far away from him. *What the heck does he mean about my organs not being developed yet?*

"We knew this was a risk," he called as I disappeared around a corner and down another hallway.

I turned, and before I could speak, he stood in front of me, his eyes soft.

"No, *you* knew the risks. I didn't." I punched him, releasing some of my bottled-up anger. "I'm not going to die, and neither is Sam!" I shouted.

"You don't know that," he replied. "And you don't have to shout."

I wanted to do more than shout. I wanted to rip out all the other emotions that I had stuffed into a black hole and sling them at him. "And you do know?" I asked in a sarcastic tone.

"I have... special abilities that—"

"That what? Webb told me you can read minds, but that has nothing to do with you seeing the future, does it?"

I didn't know what he was trying to tell me. *Am I going to die?* I thought I had already by shifting my existence into this vampire world.

He shook his head. "I can't see into the future, but I can sense things."

"Then sense this." I stuck out my middle finger and ran. I didn't know what had come over me. It was as if someone was punching keys on a keyboard and hit the command for *raise middle finger*.

"Jo!" His voice boomed and sent a shiver up my spine.

"I'm tired and I don't want to do this anymore," I said in a high-pitched tone.

Emotionally, I *was* tired. While there were some physical benefits to my vampire body, my mind and emotions were still operating in the human realm. I was beginning to regret entering the world of the undead.

I kept running. I wanted to get as far away from my father as possible. Sam was more important than arguing with him. I was grateful when the double doors opened.

Dr. Vieira emerged. "Commander, we're losing precious minutes."

I ran past him and into the lab.

"Same room as last night," Dr. Vieira called.

I made my way to the human changing room, as I called it. Then I blew out a deep breath, hoping to release some pent-up energy as I stopped in front of the closed door. But it was no use. My body began shaking as a slew of emotions coiled through me. My stomach cramped, keeping me rooted to the floor. Maybe my father's senses were right. Maybe there was cause for concern. As I inhaled, trying to squelch the pain, a woodsy scent consumed me.

"Go ahead, Jo. Go in," my father said as he placed his hands on my shoulders.

His voice only made my body shake more, causing me to grind my teeth. I was glad that my fangs were tucked in—otherwise, they would've poked through my bottom lip.

He squeezed my shoulders. "You need to be calm."

I was trying, but his presence wasn't helping.

"He's not in there yet," my father whispered.

I commanded my brain to lift my right foot, but I still couldn't move. I thought I had the courage. But I didn't want to see Sam's lifeless body again.

My dad reached around me, grabbed the doorknob, and twisted it to the right. Then he eased me in gently, pushing me until my feet moved. Same setup inside, except now there were three IV stands instead of one.

"Jo, have a seat on the bed on the right," Dr. Vieira instructed.

"Where's Sam?" I sunk down onto the mattress, taking in steady breaths, trying to still my shaking limbs.

"I'll wheel him in shortly. I need a sample of your blood first. I don't know what Patrick's blood did to you. So, for Sam's sake, I hope it's now clean of any drugs before we begin."

I hoped it was the last time I would be poked

and pricked with needles, but something told me otherwise.

Dr. Vieira inserted the IV into my hand then hooked up the bag. Clear liquid drained through the tube into me, the cold fluid sending a chill up my arm.

"Take a deep breath," Dr. Vieira instructed. "I need your heart to stop racing before I extract your blood."

I inhaled through my nose, released, and repeated the process. After a few rounds, my heartbeat slowed, and my body didn't shake anymore.

Dr. Vieira pulled a vial of blood from me then left the room.

"Lie back," my father said as he guided my legs onto the bed. "I'll be here the whole time, so don't worry."

I wasn't worried. He was the one who should have been worried. I wanted to strangle him. My emotions were one gigantic rollercoaster ride when it came to my father—or maybe it was just vampire puberty in full bloom.

A few minutes passed before Dr. Vieira wheeled Sam in. I gasped as I raked my gaze over his frail, pale body. His hair was greasy, his arms had several puncture wounds from my evil uncle, and his eyes were encircled in shadows.

Dr. Vieira and my dad lifted Sam from the stretcher and carried him to the bed.

I desperately wanted to touch him, hold him, and tell him everything was going to be okay, but my IV wasn't long enough to reach Sam. He looked ready for the morgue, and that made my heart sink as tears rolled down my cheeks. I was helpless as I watched Dr. Vieira insert needles and tubes into him, and when he finished hooking up the equipment, the heart monitor displayed a flat line.

"Is he dead?" *Please say no.*

I blessed myself and silently recited the Lord's Prayer, hoping and praying Sam would make it and my blood would do the trick.

"No, but his heart is extremely weak," Dr. Vieira whispered.

My father came in, carrying four stainless steel containers. I hadn't realized he'd left.

"I need to see if Jo's blood results are complete. Let's just hope your system is clean, young lady," Dr. Vieira said before scurrying out.

Geez, what did I do? I couldn't help it if I wanted Patrick to pay for what he did to Sam. Whether he was vampire or human didn't matter to me. As I thought about him, the words he spat at me when he mentioned he was still human—"not for long"—came roaring back. I didn't know what he'd meant by that, but I had a strange feeling that I was going to find out.

Dr. Vieira returned, jerking me from my thoughts. "Here's how this is going to work. Since Sam has very little blood in him, I'll draw blood from you, just as I did last time. Then I'll transfer your blood over to Sam." He pointed to another IV on Sam's left arm. "I've determined through some loose calculations that he'll need about three pints. What that means is that as you fill one bag, you will need to drink one pint of your father's blood. We'll stop there at first and see how you feel and how Sam's system reacts."

Dr. Vieira slipped on some latex gloves then prepped my right arm, placing a tourniquet on the upper part and patting a vein on my inner forearm before inserting the needle, just as he had done a few minutes before. Then he inserted the spec-imen tube into the holder, and my blood started flowing through the tube and into the bag.

"I take it my blood is clean?" I asked.

Dr. Vieira nodded. "We're lucky."

An ember ignited in me. I didn't like his refer-ence to "we." *Aren't Sam and I the lucky ones?*

I lowered my head onto the pillow, and within fifteen minutes, my gums throbbed, and the back of my throat burned. I sat up. My eyes had shifted, and my fangs descended. I was getting used to the split second of darkness when my eyes changed colors, but the fangs, well, that was going to take longer.

My father handed me a pint of his blood. There wasn't a straw or glass this time. I guessed the honeymoon was over. I opened the steel container and began drinking. The burn slowly eased as the blood coated my throat. It seemed that the more my blood filled the bag, the stronger my thirst for the red, sticky stuff became.

As I took the last swig of the sweet, salty elixir, Dr. Vieira withdrew my bag of blood and hung it on Sam's IV pole. He readied the tube and the other instruments, and my blood started flowing into Sam. Meanwhile, my father had added an empty bag so I could fill a second one.

"Okay, the next thing I need to do is collect your bone marrow. I don't need much, but this part can be tricky," Dr. Vieira said.

"Um, why?" I asked.

"Bone marrow is essential for your body to make new platelets, as well as red and white blood cells. Sam will need a small amount of it to help him build what he's lost," Dr. Vieira explained.

It sounded painful, and his concerned expression gave me reason to be nervous.

"I'll inject a local anesthetic into your hip, make an incision, insert the needle into your bone, and withdraw the marrow. As a vampire, you should heal quickly, evidenced by your stab wound earlier today. Any questions?" Dr. Vieira asked.

Tons of them. Based on the concerned look on my father's face, he had some as well.

"Just get this over with, please," I said.

Time was running out, and my patience was fading. I wanted to be a normal teenager again—as normal as I could be as a vampire. I wanted my brother back so that we could enjoy our relationship. I wanted to hang out with my best friend, Darcy, and I wanted to see Ben. I needed to make sure he was okay. I had been told he was fine, but I wanted to see for myself. A tingling sensation fluttered through me, and I flinched.

"What is it?" Dr. Vieira asked. "Your pulse quickened."

"I'm fine," I said as heat rose, stinging my cheeks.

I didn't want to tell him I was thinking about Ben. Besides, I didn't know what to make of the sudden butterflies inside me. Hell, I didn't know what to make of anything. I was confused about my new vampire body, about still having a heartbeat and a pulse. But I filed my questions away for the time being.

I turned onto my stomach, the needle pricked my skin as if a bee had stung me, and I jerked.

"It's just the anesthetic," Dr. Vieira said.

"It didn't hurt that much," I said, my voice laden with surprise.

"Good. If you feel the incision, let me know."

I waited for the pain from the knife, but I didn't feel anything.

"How are you doing?" Dr. Vieira asked.

"Still no pain," I replied.

"Well, you might feel this," he said.

I caught sight of the long needle, and almost passed out.

"Head down," he commanded.

"Don't move. You have to stay still, or there could be complications," my father barked.

I froze.

A few minutes passed, and I waited, expecting to feel a prick from the syringe as Dr. Vieira inserted it into my bone. I tried to think of anything other than that long needle. The only thing it reminded me of was Jonah and the horse needle, though that was small compared to the one Dr. Vieira was using.

"All set," Dr. Vieira said. "You can relax now."

I eased onto my back to find sweat beading on my father's forehead.

"Are you okay?" my father asked.

"I didn't feel much. A little pressure, but that was it. What now?"

He sighed heavily. "We wait. We'll see how Sam's body reacts to your blood. It may take longer, and Dr. Vieira may need more blood from you. You're doing great."

"Do you still think I'm going to die?" I asked.

"A dad can worry, can't he?"

I guess he had that right. I wasn't familiar with having a dad around, so it was new to me.

After Dr. Vieira left, my father dragged a metal chair near the door over to my bed. "We need to talk, young lady."

Oh boy. I didn't like his tone.

Running his fingers through his black hair, he sat in the chair. "I know you're going through a lot of different emotions. You're in the heightened stages of vampire puberty. I know this is hard for you. I told you the other day that I didn't want this life for you, and I wish I could turn back the clock, but that's not how life works. I lost both of you once, and I don't want to screw this up again. I have a chance to get to know my daughter and possibly my son. So call me selfish if you want to, but don't ever disrespect me again."

His eyes flickered from green to silver as his gaze drilled into me, and his right cheek was twitching. I imagined he was biting the inside of it.

I wanted to pull out the tubes in my arm and claw at him. But something in his eyes scared me. I had a fleeting thought that if he wanted to, he could hurt me.

"Do you understand me, Jo?"

All I could do was nod. Besides, I was tired. As if my inner computer chip kicked in, opening the file on vampire puberty, a pool of emotions consumed me. Tears streamed down my face.

My dad grabbed my hand and squeezed it, which only caused the floodgates to open. I began sobbing.

"Shh. It's okay," he whispered. "This is hard for me too." He wiped the tears away from my cheek with his free hand. "We'll get through this."

He might get through it, but I wasn't sure if I would. I checked on Sam.

As if he knew what I was thinking, he said, "I know you love your brother. I'm praying too."

My mind was swimming with questions. *What*

will happen if Sam doesn't make it? Can I live an immortal life without him? What does the future hold? As if the universe was teasing me, giving me a taste of the future, Sam's body twitched.

"Let me up," I said.

"What's wrong?"

"Sam moved."

My father stood and kicked the chair out of the way.

I climbed out of bed and grabbed the IV pole. My father and I both stood over Sam, examining every inch of his body, looking for movement. A few minutes passed, but nothing more happened. Maybe it wasn't God who'd spoken to me. Maybe the devil was playing a trick on me.

My father wrapped his arms around me. "I'm sorry," he said as he stroked my hair.

I was confused. He'd just reprimanded me but was apologizing.

"Why?" I rested my head against his chest. His heart was beating a steady rhythm.

When he didn't answer, I pulled away. Tears slid down his cheeks. His emotions spoke volumes, and I didn't need a verbal answer.

He kissed me on the head. "We should get some rest. It's going to be a long few days." He got comfortable in the big, cushy chair in the corner.

I sat on Sam's bed and brushed his hair back with my fingers. The heart monitor beeped every few seconds, and the soothing cadence of sound was making me sleepy until Dr. Vieira cleared his throat.

"No change?" Dr. Vieira asked. "Maybe the marrow will help." He inserted it into Sam's IV.

I had hoped that when Dr. Vieira injected the marrow, we would see immediate results. But as time passed, nothing happened.

29

After about ten hours of waiting, pacing, and trying to sleep, I had the jitters. My heart beat as rapidly as if I was on speed. I wasn't sure why. Maybe from not sleeping. I wanted to stay alert in case Sam woke up, but his comatose state hadn't changed at all.

"Can I see Ben?" I asked while I nervously waited. He was awake, according to Dr. Vieira.

The answer wasn't just "no," but "hell no."

My father sat on the edge of the chair in the corner. "He's weak and needs rest."

My wonderfully irritating father was adamant about me staying in the room in case Dr. Vieira needed me, but the adrenaline running rampant through my veins was driving me insane, and claustrophobia was closing in. Another hour of this, and my father was going to have to commit me to a mental institution.

"Damon, should you give her a sedative?" my father asked.

I spun around, curious who Damon was. Then I remembered it was Dr. Vieira. I'd forgotten that he'd told me his first name when he introduced himself over a week before.

Dr. Vieira was checking Sam's heartbeat. "I can, but I'd prefer not to in case we need more of her blood."

"Jo, you have to relax," my father said.

I chewed on a nail. "I can't. Why hasn't anything happened or changed?"

Dr. Vieira wrapped his stethoscope around his neck. "He's improving. His heartbeat is stronger. It's going to take longer than it did for you. Remember, he lost a lot of blood." He tucked his hands in the pockets of his lab coat. "We could try one more blood transfusion. It wouldn't hurt."

As Dr. Vieira prepared the items necessary to draw my blood, I sank down on my bed across from Sam and prayed he would make it. I'd been praying for the past ten hours, but it seemed like no one above me was listening.

I gave more blood, Dr. Vieira attached it to Sam's IV, and I downed a pint of my father's blood. As I was drinking the last drop, a loud bang sounded outside the room. My father flew out of his chair, and Dr. Vieira stopped midstride with his clipboard in hand.

I threw down the blood container and followed my dad. "What is it?"

"Get back," he snapped, opening the door.

I gasped.

Ben stood in the doorway looking as though he'd been through hell. The neck bandages were gone, and a row of stitches traveled from his earlobe down to his collarbone, right along his jugular. *What the heck did the Plutariums do to him?* They didn't bite him—they mangled him. I was pushing my father out of the way to get to Ben when Sam's heart monitor beeped loudly.

Ben cocked his head, shifting his glance to me then behind me. "Jo? What's going on?"

"Um... um..." I had no words.

My father grabbed Ben's arm. "Young lady, I'll take care of Ben. You need to help Dr. Vieira."

Nodding, I inhaled then froze. A blend of burnt sugar and a hint of cinnamon filled the air. Instantly, my eyes shifted and my fangs lowered. The need for blood was overpowering. I swallowed hard, fighting the urge to clamp down on Ben's neck and suck out all his human blood.

My father was talking, but I didn't understand what he was saying.

"Jo? Jo?" Ben's deep voice won out over my father's.

I snapped out of my trance and found Ben had a look of horror on his face. My father had a scowl as he whipped out his phone.

"You need to go with my father," I said. "I'll explain later. Just go with him."

My father was right. I needed to get as far away from Ben as possible. Besides, I needed to help Sam.

I turned on my heel, but Ben grabbed me. "Wait," he said.

"I have to help Sam. Please, Ben. Go with my father." I yanked my arm away and ran to Sam's bed.

"Lieutenant London, report to the medical facility," my dad said into his phone. Then he closed the door.

"Ben is fine," Dr. Vieira said as he lifted one of Sam's eyelids.

"Yeah, I can see that."

I wasn't about to tell him that it was me who wasn't fine—I wanted to drain Ben of all his blood.

Now I understood why my dad didn't want me anywhere near Ben.

"It seems the second bag did the trick. His heart rate is picking up well," Dr. Vieira said.

I pushed out a huge sigh.

Sam's body jerked and reacted to the change. His eyes fluttered open then closed several times as he moaned—the first signs of him losing his humanity.

Dr. Vieira handed me an ice-cold cloth. "Run this over Sam's face and forehead. Keep doing it so he stays cool. I need to get your father in here."

He opened the door, and I caught a glimpse of Webb, Ben, and my dad. Ben was nodding as if agreeing with my father, who was saying something to him.

"Commander? Let Webb handle that. I need your help with Sam," Dr. Vieira said.

My father ran his fingers through his hair, walked into the room, and closed the door.

I was wiping Sam's forehead when he suddenly sat up and inhaled, gasping for breath. It was as if he had awakened from the dead. Then he fell back onto his pillow. He curled his legs up and into a fetal position, grabbing his stomach. My father sprinted into action as if he were a medic working in the ER. He grabbed one of the cloths from the bowl of ice water and wiped down Sam's arms. Sweat poured out of Sam's body, soaking his T-shirt. I lifted it so my father could wipe down his back. We did this for an hour when Sam grabbed his ears.

"Shut the monitor off," my father ordered.

Before I could, Sam was screaming and moaning so loudly that my own eardrums were hurting. I pulled the plug out of the wall. When the sound ended, his body relaxed.

I remembered the pain I'd experienced—seeing it happen to another person was like re-living the process all over again.

"Dad, how much longer?" I asked.

"He should be through the worst in a few hours. Then there will be the bloodthirst," he said.

"Whose blood can he drink?" I asked.

"It will have to be yours for at least the first day."

Jeepers, again? "Do I have that much blood to give?"

"He won't need much. And after the initial thirst, he'll be able to drink mine."

I pinched my eyebrows together. "But you said earlier that you were worried about me not having enough blood."

"You're right. I thought Sam was going to need

a lot more than the two bags, though. Besides, you'll be able to replenish your system with my blood, which helps you to regenerate the nutrients you need. It's crucial for the next few months that your blood sustenance comes from me. You cannot drink any of the garbage we have in the re-frigerators around here. Both you and Sam are too young for that." He stared at me as if waiting for my acknowledgement of his command or a protest.

I nodded. "But where do you get your blood?"

"I still have a good bit of my blood stored for you and Sam."

He didn't answer my question, but I didn't want to push the issue. There were too many things going on, and my curiosity about his con-versation with Ben was pinching me. Since Sam was quiet for the moment, I asked, "Is everything okay with Ben?"

He nodded. "Ben's a little upset."

"Do you think? He's been through hell too."

He let out a deep breath. "I thought you were going to attack him. I smelled your excitement and your trepidation."

"Believe me, I wanted to."

"I'm proud of you. Showing that much restraint as a two-day old vampire is a huge accomplishment."

"A human can't be turned, can they?" Based on everything I knew about natural-born vampires, which wasn't much, I had to be sure.

Ben didn't want anything to do with vampires. He probably wouldn't want anything to do with me.

My dad's eyebrows lifted. "Not unless they carry a vampire gene."

My stomach churned at the thought of having the initial conversation with Ben. "But what if the Plutariums find a way to change humans?"

Something flashed across his face. I couldn't tell whether he was worried or surprised that I'd asked the question. Whatever it was, he didn't give me a warm and fuzzy reassurance.

"Patrick is behind bars," he whispered as he kept wiping Sam's body. "The Plutariums can't follow through on their plan without him."

I hoped he was right. We both continued with our orders from Dr. Vieira to keep Sam cool. My father wiped along Sam's back while I patted his head and chest.

We watched Sam as he went through the pain of the change. Once he finally stopped moving and fell asleep, I plugged the monitor back into the wall on my father's instructions. While Sam slept, it was crucial to make sure his heart was getting stronger, that he was out of danger.

I didn't know how long Sam would be out, but I figured I had some time to clear a few things up with my dad. I made my way to the corner chair then plopped down. My dad was on the empty twin bed.

Except for the heart monitor, the room fell silent.

I listened for voices outside the room—nothing. I guessed Dr. Vieira and Webb were able to appease Ben. While I wanted to see him, I couldn't. I didn't trust myself, and I wasn't ready to have a conversation with him—no way.

"Dad, can we talk?"

"What do you want to talk about?" Frustration rode his tone.

"Who's Neil Foster?"

He blinked a few times. "Not for discussion."

I crinkled my forehead. "Why not?"

"It's classified. When and if the time comes, I'll explain. Until then, he's off limits." He rubbed his eyes.

"What about Dr. Case? Can you talk about him?"

"What do you want to know?" His voice had

softened a bit. Whatever was plaguing him seemed to have disappeared.

"He tried to kill me because he said you killed his sister. Is that true?"

He dropped his gaze. "It was an unfortunate accident. Dr. Case's sister, Ella, was a Navy medic. Both Ella and Dr. Case served under me. They were combat trained, but not as SEALs. During a mission in Afghanistan, things went horribly wrong. She was trying to save one of our team members when she got caught in the crossfire and was shot."

"Did you shoot her?"

My father pulled his hair back behind him. "I didn't, but one of our Sentinels did. It was an accident."

"Why does he think you did it, then? I mean, he said *you* killed her."

"As a leader, I take a lot of heat for what my team does or doesn't do."

"Does Dr. Case know it was an accident?"

He nodded. "He's been looking for revenge for a long time. His only recourse is to take it out on another human close to the Sentinels. He knows he can't kill a vampire. I imagine when you showed up in the hospital that night, he probably thought he'd won the lottery."

"So, wait. Dr. Case is not a vampire, then?" At the funeral home I couldn't tell if he was or wasn't, although his speed seemed to suggest he could have been.

"Affirmative. He knew who we were when he worked on my team. Anyone on my team other than the Sentinels is a human with a very high security clearance. It was unfortunate that Dr. Case chose to leave the military. He's an excellent doctor. But he's made his choice, and now, he's helping the Plutariums. He also knows that any breach of information he secured while in the military will result in death." He yawned. "It's three a.m. I'm tired, and you need to get some rest as well." He rose from the bed. "Sam will be out for a few more hours. Why don't we switch? You take the bed, and I'll take the chair."

Without thinking, we switched.

"Dad?"

"Mm?" he muttered as he reclined.

"What about the people locked up in the prison wing? What are you going to do with them?"

"They'll be dealt with in due time. Don't worry. It's secure, and we have guards stationed in and around the building twenty-four, seven."

I wasn't worried. Okay, I *was* worried. Dr. Case

and Patrick were human, so I didn't believe they could escape—they didn't have vampire powers. But Edmund, Jonah, and Fernando were a different story. Their combined strength could do some damage. I didn't know how they kept a vampire behind bars, but it had me a little concerned.

"So we're safe?" Apprehension oozed as I said the last word.

"Honey, Patrick is still human and doesn't have my blood for his research. Therefore, he is useless. How we punish him is still up in the air. As for Dr. Case, the human military will deal with him. The vampires are a different story, and as you will learn in school, we have laws that are enforced for crimes among vampires. They won't get out. Trust me."

"School? What are you talking about?"

"I want to get some shut-eye before Sam wakes up. We'll talk about school then. I don't want to have to repeat myself."

I yawned. *A vampire school?* I wanted to laugh. Every time I asked a question, five more piled onto the list.

But right now, none of that mattered. My brother was alive, even if it was as a vampire, and I couldn't be happier.

30

I woke up hours later to a suckling sound and tightness in my wrist. I jolted upright and screamed, trying to pull my arm away from the creature that had his teeth sunk into my flesh. Then someone pushed me back down onto the bed. My predatory instinct took over, and I used all my power to sit up, but my dad was stronger.

"Get him off me!"

"Jo, calm down. Please. It's just Sam. He needs blood," my father whispered.

Sam peered at me through hooded lashes while he sucked on my wrist. His eyes were liquid onyx.

I cocked my head to one side. My brother was

alive. *Oh my God!* I wanted to throw my arms around him but....

"It's just gross. Please get him off me." I wiggled, trying to sit up.

"If you move too much, he'll tear your flesh," Dr. Vieira said from a distance.

"What happened to the bag?" I asked.

"He woke up, and you were sleeping. You don't wake a vampire in the middle of a deep sleep," my father said.

Suddenly, my throat burned, my eyes shifted, and hunger so strong rose quick and fast. My fangs shot through my gums.

"A few seconds longer," my father assured me.

"I need blood," I snapped.

"I know, sweetie." Then he nodded at Dr. Vieira who tapped Sam on the shoulder.

Sam raised his head, and I jerked my arm away then grabbed my wrist. Before I could wipe the blood that dribbled out, the puncture holes closed before my eyes. I didn't know if I was more shocked by how quickly I healed or the sight of Sam sucking on my wrist.

"You know, you may not like waking up a vampire, but don't let him do that again. I could have killed—"

Sam jumped on me. "You mean you were going to kill me?" He started tickling me.

"Hey, stop... stop... stop it," I pleaded between laughs.

"Son, she needs blood. I'd get off her if I were you," my father warned.

Sam obeyed as he grinned with blood-smeared lips. His eyes were back to their normal forest green. The black circles beneath his eyes were gone and color had returned to his cheeks.

Tears welled up.

My father kissed me on the forehead. "I know. I'm happy too. Here." He handed me another container of blood. "Drink this."

I downed the blood as Sam and I stared at one another. There were so many questions leaking from his expression, and I had a few of my own. Before I could open the floodgates to ask anything, glass shattered somewhere in the lab.

Dr. Vieira and my father flew out of the room. Sam and I followed. Then my father and Dr. Vieira disappeared into Ben's room.

When Sam and I reached the doorway, my father was trying to restrain Ben.

"I need to get the sedative, Steven," Dr. Vieira said. "I'll be right back." He ran past Sam and me.

"You two, get back in the room and close the door!" my father commanded.

Sam and I didn't move.

"*Now!*" my father growled.

"I want to see her," Ben said. "I'm not going to hurt her." He began squirming, trying to get free from my father's vampiric grip. "Please," he cried.

He was shirtless with sweatpants covering his lower half. His stomach muscles rippled along every ridge, carving out a distinct six-pack. My mouth fell open, and a tingling sensation zipped through me.

When Ben and I locked eyes, confusion and sadness washed over him. He tilted his head to one side, exposing the massive incision tattooing his neck. His pulse beat clearly behind it—not a good move to make in front of three vampires.

I inhaled, and the same smells he'd given off before wafted through the air. I couldn't tell if I was more enamored with his physical appearance or the scent of his blood.

I covered my mouth as my fangs descended. I tore my gaze from Ben and glanced at Sam. He was glaring at Ben as if he didn't know who he was. Then, as if in slow motion, Sam pounced. He leapt into the room as if he were a lion after his prey. He pushed away my father, who landed against the wall. Then he tackled Ben. Both skidded across the bed to the other side of the room, landing on the floor. Sam bared his fangs, ready to pierce Ben's neck. As he dipped his head down, I screamed.

"Sam, get off him!" my father shouted as he tore away pieces of drywall, trying to get out of the hole his body was stuck in.

Dr. Vieira rushed in with a syringe.

But it was too late. Sam had clamped onto Ben's neck, sucking like a newborn on his mother's breast. Ben wailed then stopped.

I ran over to the gruesome scene and beat on Sam to stop.

Ben's eyes were closed, and his body was limp.

"Son, let go. You need to let go." My father wrapped his hand around Sam's arm.

Dr. Vieira pulled the cap from the needle with his mouth then jabbed Sam's shoulder. Within seconds, Sam's knees wobbled, and he slumped to the floor. My father carried him back to the other room.

I bent down, but Dr. Vieira stopped me. "No. Go with your father, and close the door when you leave," he ordered.

I didn't move. Ben's body looked as if Sam had drained all the blood out of him. Dr. Vieira picked him up and placed him on the bed. He wasn't dead. His heartbeat thudded in my ears, although at a very slow pace. "I'm not going to bite."

"You want his blood as badly as Sam does," Dr. Vieira snapped.

"That doesn't mean I'm going to hurt him. I just want to make sure he's okay," I pleaded.

Blood dribbled from his neck as Dr. Vieira placed him on the bed. Then he grabbed an opaque bottle off the side table, opened the cap, and tipped the bottle onto the gauze. Whatever solution was in that container was healing Ben instantly. The puncture holes disappeared right before my eyes. *What the heck? Is that a magic potion? Why isn't it healing the incision on his neck, though?*

"Well?" I asked.

"He'll be fine. But you need to get out of here," Dr. Vieira said.

"No. How did those holes heal like that?"

Dr. Vieira's head spun around, his eyes a penetrating black. "Did you just tell me no?"

"I'm not leaving." I glared back.

He stalked over to me. "Young lady, I told you that when you're in my medical facility, you will obey me. I wasn't kidding." He grabbed me by the arm and ushered me back to my father in the other room. "Steven, keep your daughter in here. I don't want her anywhere near Ben."

My father stood. "We're leaving, anyway. We'll be in my apartment. Inform the team that I don't want to be disturbed for the next few hours unless it's urgent. Are we clear?"

"Yes, sir," Dr. Vieira replied. "It's better for me. I can tend to Ben without being interrupted." He glared daggers at me.

"Both of you, come with me." My father started to leave.

Sam sat on the edge of the bed, staring down at the floor as if he was in shock. I didn't know whether it was from the needle and its contents, or if he was horrified with himself for attacking his best friend. Then again, he was probably struggling with the whole vampire thing. I sympathized with him.

Despite the change in both of us, I hoped this was an opportunity for us to start over—no foster homes, no running, and maybe we could build a life that allowed us to be free of the fear we'd been accustomed to for so long.

31

Sam and I stood in front of the expansive wall of windows in my father's apartment. Neither of us said a word amid the tension stringing us together. We hadn't spoken on our trek there from the medical facility. I couldn't stop worrying about Ben, and I couldn't get the image of Sam attacking him out of mind.

Poor Ben. I had no idea how we would explain Ben's injuries to Mr. Jackson. We couldn't tell him the truth. He would never believe us if we did. I had a feeling we would have to start telling tons of white lies as vampires.

I fixated on the prison building across the courtyard. "Why did you attack Ben?"

Sam's shoulders were hunched as he stared at

something outside. "I don't know. I could smell him, his blood, his fear, and I was still thirsty."

"He's your best friend. You can't do that again." My tone was soft.

Sam regarded me with sad green eyes. "You can't tell me you didn't want to do the same thing. I saw your fangs descend. I know you wanted his blood too."

"You're right. But we need to control ourselves. Ben has been through a lot in the past week. Didn't you see his neck?"

"How much does he know?" Sam asked.

"More than you at the moment. He learned of vampires not long after me when he witnessed one attacking me."

Sam jerked his head at me as anger jumped off him and onto me. "Attacked you?" Sam's eyes bled to black as his face turned crimson.

"It's nothing. I don't want to talk about it right now," I said. "Look, we need to help Ben. We need to make sure he's okay. He hated the idea that I had to change."

He traded his spot next to me for the chaise lounge near the window.

"That building over there"—I pointed to the prison wing—"is where they keep prisoners."

"What prisoners? Is there a war going on?" he asked innocently.

"No war. Just some humans and vampires who were trying to kill us."

He cocked his head to one side. "Is Neil over there?"

I shrugged. I didn't know for sure where Neil was, but I knew my father didn't want to talk about him. "The last time I saw Neil was in a room downstairs. I've asked Dad about him, but he keeps telling me Neil is not up for discussion."

"Stop. You called that man in the back room Dad." He flicked his thumb toward the kitchen. "Why? How do you know for sure he's our father?"

My eyes bugged out. "Have you looked at the man? He looks just like you."

"That doesn't mean shit. He could be one of those bad guys."

I half smiled. "Now there's the brother I know. Paranoid as ever. It's good to see you're still the same person."

He narrowed his eyes. "Jo?"

"Chill. He's our father." I was certain of it.

"And how do you know that?" He knitted his eyebrows together.

"I wouldn't have been able to turn into a vampire if Dad wasn't our father. I needed his blood to change. Too complicated to go into detail right now, but it has to do with genetics. Now deal with it."

He raked his hands through his hair. I didn't think my explanation or lack thereof convinced Sam. I had a feeling the topic would surface again.

"So, back to Neil," I said. "You asked if Neil was over in that building. Why would you ask that? The last you knew, he was dead."

"Sure, but I saw him outside some glass room. I was on a table and kept waking up, but there was never anyone there to help me. Then the last time I remember waking up, I spotted Neil outside the glass wall with a camera in his hand. Then a flash went off, and I passed out."

My mouth fell open. If Neil was there, that meant he was a Plutarium, which would make sense because of the tattoo on his neck. It would also mean, though, that Neil was a mole. That was how my father had gotten the picture and how he'd known where Sam was. Neil *was* actually trying to help us.

"What's wrong?" Sam asked.

"Neil is Dad's mole."

"Mole? He's the janitor at our school," Sam said.

"I don't think so. As far as I know, Neil is a Plutarium, which is a group of ex-Navy SEALs who used to work for Dad. They went over to the dark side. They're trying to take down the government or plan some type of military coup—big stuff. But it seems Neil has been secretly helping Dad, feeding him information about you and where you were."

"So, why is he in that building?" Sam gazed out into the cloudy afternoon.

"Well, to make a long story short—"

A knock sounded at the door. Sam and I both jerked our heads toward it. Then we looked at each other.

My father was in his bedroom. He'd told Dr. Vieira that he didn't want to be disturbed unless it was necessary.

Another rap of knuckles pounded more insistently against the door. Suddenly, I remembered my dad's comment about not waking up a sleeping vampire. I didn't know if he was sleeping, but I didn't want to find out what would happen. But before I could take two steps to answer the door, Sam cut me off.

His eyes were wide, shifting his gaze from me back to the door as if he knew who was standing on the other side of it and was ready to attack. Maybe I'd spooked him about the prisoners.

"Sam, it's okay. We're in a military compound," I whispered. *What am I saying?* I was just as worried, hoping the vampire on the other side of the door wasn't one of the goons the Sentinels had locked up in the building across from us.

The bedroom door squeaked open before my father came into the room. "What's wrong?"

"There's someone at the door," I said.

"Well, why don't you answer it?" he asked as he pulled it open.

Webb stood with his hands behind his back, dressed in tan cargo pants and a blue T-shirt with the SEAL emblem in the upper left corner.

"He's cool," I whispered in Sam's ear. "No worries."

Sam didn't move. He kept his protective stance, keeping his hands behind him, touching my arms.

My father waved him in. "Enter, Lieutenant."

"Commander, a word?" Webb asked, standing only just inside, as if preparing for a quick exit.

"Sam, why don't you shower? My bedroom is down the hall. There are clothes in my closet that should fit you." My father pointed the way.

Sam glared at Webb, not moving. I couldn't tell what he was thinking, but something had him agitated.

I grabbed his hand and guided him toward the

bedroom. "Go take a shower. Webb is a friend," I said.

He looked at me. "Are you sure you'll be okay?"

I nodded. "I'll be fine."

I didn't understand the vigilance. I wasn't hurt. I wasn't fighting for my life like I had been when he rescued me from Cliff. Sure, I was almost poisoned, suffocated in a coffin, and killed by my father's sword, but he didn't know any of that yet. I was beginning to think that the less he knew, the better—at least for the time being.

Sam reluctantly left, and Webb seemed to relax as he made his way into the kitchen with my Dad behind him.

I sat on the couch, curled my legs under me, and snagged a magazine from the coffee table while Webb and my dad began talking. I fanned the pages, pretending to be engrossed in it, when the bedroom door groaned again.

Sam must've showered in two seconds. But when I lifted my gaze, I sucked in a gulp of air.

Sam was holding a gun. His right arm was extended with his hand wrapped around the grip, a finger on the trigger, and his left hand supporting his right. Shock kept me glued to the sofa. My brother lost his mind.

Before anyone could move, Sam aimed the gun at Webb's head.

My father appeared calm with his hands up as if being arrested. "Son, put the gun down," he commanded. "Webb is a friend. He's just here to talk to me."

As my father tried to coax Sam into giving him the gun, I hopped off the couch and jumped over the coffee table, barely clearing it. I ran the short distance to the kitchen and positioned myself next to my dad. I needed to get Sam's attention. Apart from Ben, I was the only familiar face he'd seen since he had awakened as a vampire. He was probably scared and trying to protect me.

I swallowed and blew out a deep breath. "Sam, listen to me. Webb is one of us, a good guy."

He had the gun trained on Webb, hands steady. Sam diverted his attention from my father to me. "You say he's our father, but I still don't believe you. I don't know who these people are. I don't know who I am and what's happened to me."

"I know. I know what you're going through. Please, put the gun down, and I'll explain. A lot has happened to you and me. But, these people"—I wagged my finger between Webb and my dad—"are family. Please, let me explain."

"He's not." He nodded at Webb. "He's here for you."

"Me? What're you talking about, Sam?" I broke eye contact with Webb and regarded my father. If he could read minds, it was the time to help me out.

"He came here to check on you. Don't ask me how I know that. I just do." Sam's voice cracked. "Something doesn't feel right. I'm not even sure you're my sister."

I inched up to Sam. "Look at me."

He kept his eyes focused on my father and Webb.

"Sam," I growled. "I want you to look at me, damn it! I'm still your sister. My hair color may have changed slightly, but look, I have a scar on my face from that night. I'm still Jo. Remember in the funeral home when we talked about some of the physical changes we were both experiencing?" I paused, waiting for him to nod or give me a signal that he remembered. Since he didn't, I continued. "You told me that your eyes changed colors. That was the start... we're not human anymore. We're vampires, but you're still my brother, and I love you. Now put down the gun. Webb isn't going to hurt me," I pleaded.

I wasn't sure if the gun had bullets in it or if a

bullet would kill Webb. Since I was only a couple of days into my new vampire body, I didn't know a whole lot about my species. When Dr. Vieira had explained about how vampires could die, he didn't mention anything about a bullet, but I didn't want to take any chances and find out the hard way.

"Sam, please. Don't do this," I begged.

Webb barely breathed. An electrical charge rose slowly around me, prickling the air. As a human, I'd started to experience weak electrical charges when I was close to Webb, but as a vampire, the charge was astronomically potent, making me squirm where I stood. But this wasn't the time to figure out why. Besides, I imagined I would learn what the charge was all about in vampire school.

"No, honey, you don't have to wait until school," my father said. "The charge you feel is magic—lots of it."

"Okay, that's just wrong. You *can* read my mind?"

As if my father deliberately timed when he could read my mind, providing a distraction from the fact that Sam had a gun in his hand, Webb suddenly bent and slid to the side, clearing the way for my father, who then jumped over the island and grabbed Sam's arm. The gun flew out of my brother's hand, skating across the wood floor, stopping against the cabinet near the sidewall. I ran over to pick it up, but Webb beat me to it.

When I checked on Sam, my father had his arms around him. Then he dragged Sam over to the couch and released him. Sam fell onto a cushion, but just as quickly, he lunged for my father.

I was ready to help when Webb grabbed me. "Let them fight it out," he said.

I didn't want them fighting, but somehow, I knew that Sam needed to release some of the demons he was battling. Sam punched my father in the face then the stomach repeatedly. My father just let Sam use him as a punching bag.

The fight scene reminded me of Sam swinging the bat at Cliff and how he practically beat him to a pulp. There was so much anger in him. I suddenly understood why Mr. Jackson had recommended an anger management class. I hadn't seen it before—after all, my brother's fights had always been to protect me. But as the sound of bone against bone continued, I wondered if all his pent-up madness was directed more toward my father for not being around for all those years.

As Webb and I observed the one-way boxing match, I asked, "Do you know what Sam was talking about?"

"No clue," he said.

"So why *are* you here?" I asked.

"That's classified information," he replied.

Somehow, I knew he was going to say that. The blue-eyed vampire still infuriated me.

After several minutes, my father grabbed hold of Sam and whispered in his ear. My brother dropped to the couch. Then my father retreated into the kitchen, where he and Webb resumed their conversation.

I rushed over to Sam. "Hey, can I sit with you?" I didn't know if he wanted me around, but I braced my heart for his answer. This wasn't how I'd imagined our reunion.

He nodded.

Silence stretched between us. I tried to muster up words of wisdom, but I didn't have any. I was only a teenager—a young, naïve, vampire teenager. I had gobs to learn about my immortal life. We both did. "Do you still believe the man you tried to beat to death is not our father?" I asked.

"He looks like me. I'll give you that. But I want more proof than just looks and what you told me."

It didn't surprise me that Sam needed proof. He wouldn't have been my brother otherwise. He had never trusted anyone. I guess he had my father to thank for that. "What did he say to you that made you calm down?"

Sam looked at me with soft eyes. "He said that he would prove he was my father and that he loved me."

"He actually said he loved you?" Shock waves rumbled inside me. I had to pull things out of him, and all Sam had to do was punch him a few times. It was going to take a supernatural miracle to erase my daddy issues.

My father escorted Webb to the door. "No more disturbances until I give you the signal. Is that understood?" he said to Webb in an unyielding tone.

"Yes, Commander."

Once Webb was gone, my father locked the steel door and joined us as he sunk down into the chair across from us.

The silence became deafening.

I was curious who was going to start the conversation. There we were, the three of us, brought together by genetics and a slew of other weird events, sitting in a military compound as vampires, not sure what to say to each other. The whole scene was surreal.

Finally, my dad cleared his throat, rubbing his jaw. The resemblance between Sam and Dad was uncanny, from the length and color of their hair to their physical build and facial features. From head to toe, I could barely tell them apart, except my father was an inch taller than Sam. The creepy part for me was that Dad didn't look old enough to be our father. I wondered at what age he had become a vampire.

"I'll get to my age at another time. Right now—"

I shuddered. "Get out of my head. It isn't cool."

Sam's features were pinched as he shifted his gaze between Dad and me. "What's going on?"

"Dad is the only vampire in the world who can read minds. At least that's what Webb told me. He's supposed to be the most powerful because of all his abilities that other vampires don't have," I explained.

"Can you read mine?" Sam asked him.

"We'll discuss that later. Right now we have other things to talk about."

32

The clouds rolled in as the sky grew darker, and I wondered if my father would start talking or just stare out the window.

Then he cleared his throat and set his soft green eyes on Sam and me. "Over fourteen years ago when you both were just over a year old, your mother died of leukemia. I'd come home on leave from the Navy to spend the last few months with her and to take care of you. But just after her funeral, I received orders to deploy to Afghanistan. The only family we had was your Aunt Terri, your mother's sister. She didn't want to take on two kids, but she gave in, knowing I wouldn't be gone that long. I hated to leave, but the Navy said the mission would only last two months."

Sam and I glued our attention to him.

Dad's Adam's apple bobbed. "As it turned out, the mission lasted more than a year. During that time, I requested and pleaded with my commander for leave to return home for a few weeks, but that request was denied. They needed me to stay with my team and see the mission through. I'd been in contact with Terri and explained my situation, but during one of my calls home, we had an argument... a nasty one about your mother. You have to understand that Terri was an extremely bitter woman who'd hated me since the day I married your mother. She was the type of woman who relished holding grudges. She decided to call the state foster care system and turn me in for abandoning my children. Her excuse was that she was sick and couldn't take care of you, and that you had no other family. That's when the state stepped in and placed you in foster care." He rose from the chair and ambled over to the window.

Sam and I exchanged a surprised look.

Sam was about to speak, and I shook my head. I wanted my father to finish his story. I was afraid if we interrupted him, he would lose his train of thought.

With his back to us, he continued. "When I returned from deployment, I showed up at Terri's house, seeking answers to find you and take you out of foster care. But the person who answered the door informed me that she had died in a car accident a couple of months before, and they had purchased the house from her estate auction." He tucked his hands in the pockets of his pants. "I contacted the state, but they just gave me the runaround. I provided them with all the necessary information—paperwork, birth certificates, everything—but I kept getting passed from one person to another. I ran out of time before I had to deploy again, and that time, I was gone for two years. I had some of my military friends trying to investigate, but it was even worse for them to get information from the state of Massachusetts." He pivoted on his heel. "I truly am sorry." His forest-green eyes swam with tears.

"I don't believe that you couldn't find us for fourteen years," Sam said in a questioning tone.

Dad eased himself down onto the coffee table in front of us. "After years of trying and between deployments, I was thrown another curveball. It was at that time that Edmund Rain, who is now my enemy, formed a rogue team of ex-Sentinels known as the Plutariums. Edmund wants nothing more than to make me suffer for things he thinks I did to him. I decided then that it was better not knowing where you were. If I couldn't find you, I knew Edmund and his team couldn't, either. It killed me to stop looking for you, but your safety came first. Then he recruited your uncle, Patrick, who also wants to take his own personal revenge against me."

I suspected Sam was in a pool of confusion, not knowing who anyone was. I had been about to fill him in earlier, but then Webb showed up. I didn't want to interrupt my father just yet.

"Come again?" Sam said. "You decided not to search for us because of this Edmund guy? And who is Uncle Patrick?"

I was surprised the name Patrick didn't ring a bell with Sam. After all, Patrick was the one conducting lab experiments on him.

"You don't know who Patrick is?" My voice hitched.

He shook his head.

Dad leaned his elbows on his knees. "Patrick is my half-brother. He's the one responsible for draining you of your blood. In the United States, he is well known as Dr. Patrick Mason, genetic scientist and researcher. He wanted me to help him concoct a serum to turn him into a vampire. His goals became more selfish the older he got, but he lost his chance of immortality years ago. As a human, Patrick had no reason to learn our vampire laws, but they are strict on making the change, becoming immortal. If I helped him, I could've gone to jail, or worse, been put to death. As it is, I'll have to explain to my superiors what happened with both of you and why you two are now vampires." He laced his fingers together and placed them against his lips.

"So why are we vampires?" Sam asked.

Dad gave me a nod, urging me to explain that part to Sam. I wasn't sure that I could remember all the medical lingo. But that didn't matter.

"You were dying," my father replied, "It was Jo's decision."

"I had to become a vampire to save you," I said.

Sam peered at me dolefully, as if trying to tell me I shouldn't have saved him. My heart splintered into a trillion pieces as tears pooled in his eyes.

He grabbed my hand and squeezed. "So," he said to my father, "did your brother get what he needed when he used me as his lab rat?"

"He may have learned a lot by studying you in the short time you were under his microscope, but he didn't get his hands on the final, most important piece," my father replied.

"Patrick needed Dad's blood to complete his experiment," I added, my voice cracking.

"Where is he now?" Sam asked.

"That's what I was trying to tell you earlier. They're in that building over there." I flicked a finger at the window.

There was so much Sam needed to learn and so many questions I had for him, let alone my father. But we mostly needed to bring Sam up to speed on what had transpired during the past week.

Sam listened intently as we explained the vampire genetics, Patrick's motives, the Jupiter Sentinels and their role, our father's role, and the Plutariums. My father explained to Sam that there were vampire laws and that they would all be punished in some way. I filled him in on how Ben had helped me and how he ended up in the medical facility. After a couple of hours of talking, it was my turn to ask some questions, and one for Sam that was burning a hole in my brain. "Do you remember who kidnapped you?"

Sam gnawed on his bottom lip. "Cliff Birch, the asshole who tried... you know..."

I cringed at the name. Oh, I knew. I knew all too well. I traced the outline of the scar on my face.

My father's brow creased. "What did he try?"

Sam jerked his head toward me. "You didn't tell him that part?"

Is he serious? I'd just met the man who was instrumental in bringing me into this world, and while we had a jillion things to talk about, Cliff wasn't the first thing that came to mind. In fact, if Sam hadn't brought it up, I would've stuffed that topic so far down into the earth that the creepy crawlies would eat it, destroying anything related to Cliff and that incident.

I dropped my gaze to the floor as my heart pounded against my chest. I thought back to that night and the pervert's hands on me, and I shivered before I stole a look at my dad.

His eyes flashed silver, his features hard and lethal. I didn't have to ask why his nostrils were flaring. I imagined he had read my mind.

In that instant, my father pushed to his feet, picked up a glass from the coffee table and threw it across the room, where it fractured into minute crystals against the wall. A few more inches, and I was certain that it would have blasted through the window.

I jumped a mile and Sam held my hand tightly. I made a mental note to talk to my brother about it later. I didn't want the topic coming up ever again.

"Hey, Pops, I took care of the creep," Sam said

proudly.

"Not well enough," my father growled. "I want his head on a spike."

I hoped he wasn't serious...or maybe I didn't. "Webb said vampires don't kill humans," I said.

"This human world continues to see more violence every day. And it's humans like him who need to be taught a lesson."

I wanted to laugh then scream. Humans weren't the only ones creating violence in the world. The vampires had their own drama and chaos, which seemed to be out of control.

My father calmed a little, releasing a deep breath. "This isn't over. I will see to it that Cliff is punished, not only for what he did to Jo, but for his involvement in Sam's kidnapping."

Icy chills tiptoed down my spine. I wanted to punish Cliff too. In fact, I secretly wanted him dead. At the sound of his name, my body ached to take my own revenge against him, so he could pay for what he did to me and maybe to other girls. The sole purpose of losing my humanity had been to save my brother, although perhaps becoming immortal might allow me to help humanity and do something substantial in the world—I had an eternity to do it. Maybe it would be my chance to save other foster kids from his disgusting ways.

While the thought of revenge sang to me, it wasn't the time to air my unearthly thoughts on how to punish Cliff. I wanted to change the subject. "Dad?" I said the word softly, afraid he might bite off my head.

He narrowed his eyes, and it looked as if he was going to chew a hole in the side of his cheek.

"You said when Sam made it through, you would explain something about school."

Sam's jaw came unhinged. "We're not going to school. We're vampires now."

I laughed. "You don't think vampires go to school?" I laughed again. "I know why you don't want to go back. You don't want to go to anger management class."

His eyes shifted, losing their brilliant green color. "Shut up."

My father dropped his jaw. "Is there something you're not telling me, son?"

"After I strangle my sister, there's a lot you and I need to catch up on, Pops." Sam glared at me with liquid-onyx orbs.

Vindication was a sweet thing. "Now you know how it feels," I said.

"What did I do?" Sam asked so innocently.

"Never mind. So what about school?" I looked at my dad.

"Once I clear up a few things around here, I'll make the appointment for us to visit St. Anne's Academy, which is here in the city. Your first year as a vampire is going to be rough, especially around humans, and St. Anne's is a school designed for young vampire teenagers who have made the change early. Plus, both of you have to learn about our species and the laws we live by," he said.

Sam and I burst out laughing.

"You both think that's funny?" my father asked.

"Do you realize the weirdness of vampires going to a school with the word 'saint' in it? Is this some sort of Catholic school?" Sam asked.

I still couldn't speak. All I kept thinking about were uniforms. The name implied so much more than just "Catholic." Plus, I wondered whether there were that many vampire teenagers in Fall River. I shook my head like a dog shaking off water. No way. I refused to believe any of it. *What about the school we used to go to?*

"Sorry, sweetie, public school with all those humans is not a place for you or Sam to be, no, no, no." My father was shaking his head in a deliberate side-to-side motion.

"Please, stop reading my mind!"

"I'm actually surprised I can read yours,

though. I usually can't read anyone's mind unless I'm touching them. I've only been able to read one other person's mind without touching them." He raked his hands through his hair then rubbed his jaw.

"And me?" Sam asked, taking in a deep breath.

"I can when I touch you, son. But with Jo, it seems I don't have to touch her."

"That's what every teenager wants to hear," I blurted out.

"No need to panic," my father said.

"Easy for you to say. I don't want to be mind violated every time I see you."

"Jo, that's a bit of an overstatement," my father said.

"Yeah, Pops. Hands off me," Sam added.

"Look, you two. Usually, I'm good at controlling when I read someone's mind. But—"

"You said there was one other person's mind you could read without touching. Whose is it?" I asked.

"My father's... and he was stronger and more powerful than me."

He was starting to scare me. "What does that mean, Dad?" I asked.

Telepathic connections, now mind reading—what's next?

"I need to make a few phone calls. There's human food in the kitchen. If you need blood, let me know. And don't leave the apartment. And one more thing. Webb said Ben is going to be fine. You'll be able to see him tomorrow." He stormed down the hall then disappeared into his bedroom.

I sat, stunned by the shakiness in his voice, which made my blood stop for a second. I was confused about his father being more powerful than him. Did that mean there was a correlation between my grandfather and me?

Sam waved a hand in front of me. "Hey, are you alive in there?"

I blinked. "I was just thinking."

"So Ben is going to be okay," Sam said with a hint of sadness in his voice. "Do you think he'll forgive me?"

"I'm not sure. Ben has had a hard time accepting that vampires exist." I didn't want to lie to Sam and tell him Ben would forgive him. With Ben's moodiness, I couldn't gauge how he would react to Sam attacking him, let alone the fact that Sam was a vampire. Ben hadn't wanted me to change, so I had my own issues with smoothing things over with him. "We'll talk to him tomorrow."

Silence filled the room as I sat next to Sam,

staring out the window, thinking about how our lives had changed in just two weeks, how our journey began because of a mortal creep like Cliff. *Should I thank him or kill him?*

I closed my eyes and shook my head a few times. The person I needed to thank was Neil. He was the one who'd really saved Sam. If it weren't for him, we would still be searching. I squeezed my brother's hand and silently thanked God for his return, even though it was as a vampire.

I stood to stretch my legs when Sam grabbed me. "I still have one more question for you." His voice was sullen. "If you had a choice to stay human, why didn't you?"

The blood rushed to my feet—I didn't know how to tell him that I came really close to staying human, which would have meant that he wasn't sitting in front of me and asking me that question. I wasn't sure I could explain how I'd struggled with my decision. I had sacrificed my belief in humanity, in growing old and living life as a human and not drinking blood as my main meal. My legs quivered, so I eased myself down to the coffee table.

"Well?" His gaze burned through me, watching my lips, waiting for an answer.

"I did it to... save you," I replied as I looked

down at the carpet.

He touched the bottom of my chin, guided it up, and studied me.

"You don't believe me?" I asked.

"I know how you hated anything to do with vampires, especially the blood part. So, yeah, part of me believes that you were forced. Maybe for his benefit." He tipped his head toward the hallway.

It was as if someone had driven a knife through my heart. "I promise you, I did it for you, for us. In fact, I waited too long to make my decision. You were dying by the time the Sentinels rescued you, a heartbeat away from a human grave."

"Then you should've let me die," he whispered.

"I won't lie. I wanted to stay human. I didn't know what you would've wanted me to do, if humanity was something you cherished or not. But when I saw a picture of you in that glass room, I wanted to die. My whole world imploded. I didn't realize until then that life meant nothing without you in it, vampires or not. Then the more I got to know the vampires around here, the more I thought it wouldn't be so bad. Maybe we could do some good in the world. But more than anything, I knew if I were lying on a table in a glass-walled room, fighting for my life, you would've saved me." I smiled weakly, waiting for a response, confirmation that he accepted the decision I had made for him.

He pulled me into a bear hug. "I just needed to make sure we were connected. You're right. I'd do anything to protect you, and I'll always be there for you. I love you, Jo," he whispered.

I snuggled deep into his chest, relief washing over me as he whispered those last words. I didn't want to move. I wanted to stay wrapped in my brother's protection for a long time.

There were still a lot of unanswered questions about our uncle, the Plutariums, Ben, Neil, our father, and school. But immortality meant lots of time to figure out the answers.

Maybe Sam and I had a new life to begin, albeit a vampire life, which meant new laws, new rules, new skills, and vampire manners that were a prerequisite before we could exist among humans. But none of that mattered. I had my brother back, and I wasn't letting go.

Thank you for reading On the Edge of Humanity.
Book 2 - On the Edge of Eternity is now available
in Ebook and paperback formats.
Turn the page to read a sample

On the Edge of Eternity - Sample

My first kiss could be my last...

I once dreamed of high school dances and my first date. Now, as a newly formed vampire, I'm navigating a new world with an animalistic hunger I must learn to control.

A human boy wants to date me. Another wants to kill me. And a Navy SEAL vampire keeps sending me mixed messages. Yet as I adjust to my novel powers and battle to restrain my vampiric urges, an enemy is closing in...

I thought I had my bloodlust in check...

Until I'm kidnapped and left in the middle of a storm-tossed ocean with the human who has a crush on me.

Can I get us both to safety before the sea swallows us whole? Or will I lose myself to the dark pull of my ravenous thirst?

Chapter 1

I always believed a little piece of heaven would have my name on it when I died. I wasn't so sure anymore. I was only sixteen on the day I became a vampire, and I hadn't imagined my life as one of the undead. I didn't want that life, but destiny had pulled me to the edge, where one step, one word, and one person had erased my humanity, changing my life forever.

It had been two weeks since I made the change. I sat on the chaise lounge in my dad's suite on the Navy SEAL compound, staring out the window. I'd dubbed it a penthouse, though it was far from being the Ritz Carlton. My father, Steven Mason, was the commander of a vampire SEAL team within the Navy known as the Jupiter Sentinels, so he had the largest living quarters on the military base.

Yep, not only was I the daughter of the most powerful of all vampires, but my dear old dad was in charge of some badass secret military vampire unit. *Go figure.* While my human life had hardly been heavenly, the window to my new world was in question, but it was too early to tell whether it would be better or worse.

From where I sat, I had a picture-perfect view

of the prison building, where the SEALs kept vampire convicts behind bars. Given their superhuman strength, my curiosity beckoned me to visit the creepy place and see how they kept them locked up. My father had said it was off-limits. In fact, my brother Sam, who was also a vampire, and I weren't allowed out of the open-plan apartment because of some vampire law about newborns and their bloodlust, which my father had yet to explain. The legal side of it was a mystery, but I understood the bloodlust. My throat burned with the need for the sticky red liquid almost all the time.

For the fourteenth straight day, I had nothing to do. My routine was the same. I drank my fill of Dad's blood, which he had stored in stainless containers, slept, and brooded. While the world outside of *my* prison was alive, I was dying inside. My thoughts were my enemy. I pined to see Ben, my friend who was my last link to the human world. I was uncertain what he thought of me as a vampire —he hadn't wanted me to change. He believed in mortality, the human race. The last time I saw him was the day Sam woke up as a vampire and attacked him, sinking his fangs into his best friend.

I sighed for the umpteenth time. I had an inkling that talking to Ben would have to wait a bit longer, especially since Sam's action had rattled my father. Hell, it scared the bejesus out of me too. I wanted to do exactly what Sam had done.

"Jo?" The familiar voice was low and soft.

I tore away from gazing out at the dreary day. It had been raining nonstop for over a week. I'd always thought April was the month for rain and May was the month for flowers, but Mother Nature was a little late.

"Everything okay?" My father strode over and sat down next to me, kicking out his feet on the chaise lounge.

It was the first time in two weeks that Dad had spent more than an hour in the apartment. He'd said he wanted more time with Sam and me to discuss topics he felt were important as we began our new life as vampires, but the events surrounding our change and the new prisoners on-site had meant a ton of paperwork to complete and countless phone calls to make, thanks to both military and vampire protocols.

I nodded. "Why are you asking? You mean you're not reading my mind today?"

My father's mind-reading abilities usually only worked when he touched someone, but for whatever reason, he could read mine without physical contact. He'd probably read my thoughts as he walked into the room, which would only have reinforced his decision to keep me away from humans, especially Ben.

He put his arm around me. "Sweetie. I don't do it all the time."

I wanted to believe him, but I was on edge whenever he walked into the room—we had relationship issues even beyond the mind reading to work out. We were still getting to know each other as father and daughter.

"You know they aren't getting out." He nodded toward the prison. "That building is heavily guarded."

The past two weeks had been tense for a whole host of reasons, including worrying that my Uncle Patrick would escape. My father tried to assure me I didn't have anything to worry about, but he'd seemed nervous the past few days. Not only was his brother responsible for trying to kill Sam and me, but also my dad's ex-best friend, Edmund Rain, was now his outright enemy and in charge of the Plutariums, a rogue team of vampire ex-SEALs. Edmund was locked up, too, though I imagined them in separate cells—Patrick was human, though he had threatened he wouldn't be for much longer.

"Patrick and Edmund aren't going anywhere," he whispered.

I glared at him. "You're doing it again, Dad!"

"I'm sorry."

I relaxed against his chest. His heart beat slowly, thudding in my ear. "Dad?"

"Hmm?" he muttered.

"You mentioned something the other day about my organs not being completely developed yet as a vampire. What did you mean?"

He kissed my hair. "You have so much to learn. And I want to be there when you experience everything."

His tone intimated that he might not be around to see me do much. Dad and his team were concerned about the Plutariums. After all, his ex-best friend was trying to build an army of vampires to overthrow the government and to get back at Dad for personal reasons.

"You'll learn about our species in more depth once you're in school, but like humans, we have evolved over many centuries." He took a breath. "There was a time in our existence that we were creatures of the dark. All those myths that humans believe to be true of vampires were actually real.

"Now, we can go out in the sun. Our hearts do beat. Our organs do function. Sure, we're not human in the sense that we don't age, and our diets are different, but we still breathe. Our heart rate is very slow, much slower than a human athlete in great shape. As vampires, we have even better endurance and strength, which means we can run faster and longer than any human. So, when I say your organs haven't yet developed, I mean your heart muscle and other organs are still adjusting to the change. Over time, they will become stronger. Your heart rate will be hard to detect. If a human were to check your pulse, they would be hard-pressed to find one. You can only hear mine because of your acute hearing."

I placed my right hand over my heart. It definitely beat faster than my father's. I glanced up at him, searching every inch of his fairly young features. "You never told me and Sam how old you are."

"I'm not sure you're ready to hear my story or know how old I am," he replied.

"You said there's a lot to learn. And I want to learn more about you."

He wasn't getting away that easily. I had signed up for a life of eternity, and if I was going to build a relationship with my father, I wasn't waiting any longer to start on either the road to a life of bliss or one of hell. Regardless, I needed to know who I was traveling with.

"You're right, sweetie," he said. "I was twenty-two when I became a vampire. That was over a hundred years—"

A low whistle filled the air. I sat up to see my twin brother, Sam, sauntering toward us. His inky-black hair grazed his bare shoulders, and his forest-green eyes had a sparkle to them.

A smile ghosted across my face. It had been a while since his eyes sparkled.

As he approached in jeans that hung low on his hips, dimples dented his cheeks. "Pops, how come you don't have gray hair? Shouldn't you be walking with a cane?" He snorted.

My father ignored his comment. "Do you want to hear the story or not? I'm not repeating myself."

Dad and Sam had a volatile relationship. My brother still doubted that Steven Mason was our father, but Dad had promised he would provide written proof. He was waiting for our birth certificates to be delivered from the vampire government. According to Dad, the vampire government wasn't any better than the human one.

The one thing that had me perplexed was why Sam called him "Pops" if he didn't believe he was our father. When I'd asked, Sam had said that it slipped out the first day they met and just stuck, but that didn't make sense. When I probed him even more, he just said he didn't want to talk about it.

Sam sat on the floor with his bare back against the windowed wall, his long legs extended. His normal attire since turning vamp was jeans and no shirt. He said it was too hot to wear any clothes.

I adjusted slightly in my seat while Dad shifted his arms encircling my waist.

He released a sigh. "It was the early nineteen-hundreds. My father—your grandfather—was a vampire, an immensely powerful one. Far more than me. He wanted me to change, to become immortal for the sole purpose of continuing our family heritage. I valued my humanity, so I decided against immortality. But fate or destiny has a funny way of changing your life." He paused.

He was correct about fate. It sure did have a way of disrupting things.

"I was a rising baseball star in 1905. We didn't wear batting helmets back then. Anyway, I was at bat, and the pitcher threw a fastball that hit me just above my left earlobe. It knocked me out completely. I was rushed to the hospital. My brain was swelling, and I had internal bleeding. A week later, I woke up as a vampire. My mother told me afterward that she had to beg my father to turn me."

My father's bottom jaw dug into my scalp as he swallowed.

I glanced at Sam, whose mouth hung open. Sam loved baseball and had even played for the high school team before he lost his humanity. He and Dad had something in common. I hoped that would bring them closer together. Sam's eyes suddenly lost their brilliant green color. As vampires, our eye color shifted when our emotions changed, which meant that Sam might have had a connection with Dad.

I'd felt mine shift when my father's heartbeat sped. My skin prickled with his power, which floated in the air like a thousand bolts of lightning peppering the room. I still wasn't used to the electrical charge—or magic—vampires emitted.

The three of us sat there, not saying a word.

Dad's voice finally broke the silence. "My mother was extremely happy, and my father, well... he got his wish of me carrying on the family heritage. Now, here I am, over a hundred years later."

"So, you were twenty-two in 1905?" Sam asked.

My father nodded.

"Whoa!" Sam shook his head, rolling his eyes around. "That means you were born in 1883! No freaking way. You're old as crap, Pops."

I was just as shocked. While he looked young, there were signs that made him seem older. The area around his eyes had a smattering of creases. Nothing too deep or pronounced, but the lines were still there. His forehead also had a few worry lines. But aside from his physical appearance, it was his mannerisms that really gave away his age, with his prim-and-proper nature and how he was a stickler for manners.

"Are all the Sentinels your age?" Sam asked.

Great question. I'd been wondering how old they were. They all looked around our age, including the drop-dead-gorgeous Webb London, Dad's second-in-command.

"Well, let me put it this way. All the Sentinels turned vampire between the ages of seventeen and nineteen. It's a requirement for the vampire SEAL program. We like them young so that we can mold them into good soldiers."

"Didn't you tell me that Webb was twenty?" I asked.

"I might have, but he was nineteen when he turned. I recruited him a year or so later."

"What does it matter, Jo?" Sam asked. "They all look as young as we do."

"Not Dr. Vieira," I replied.

"You're right, sweetie," Dad said. "Dr. Vieira

turned in his twenties. But... he is a doctor and not a Sentinel."

"Pops? Did you start the vampire SEAL program?" Sam asked.

Dad's cell phone rang. "I did, with the help of a few people with the human military." He slipped out from behind me. "I'll explain it to you someday." He dug his phone out of his pocket.

I sat there thinking about age. There were only a few ways natural-born vampires could die and growing old wasn't one of them. As I'd learned recently, I could die if someone beheaded me, burned me to death, or drove a cobalt blade through my heart. None of those options sounded like a party.

"Go," Dad said into his phone, walking toward the kitchen. Halfway there, he stopped mid-stride. "They can't be. They're not expected for a few more days. I thought I had time to explain it to them. *Merda!*" His tone dropped to a low growl.

Uh-oh—my father sounded irritated. I didn't recognize the last word, but I imagined it was a curse. I opened my mouth to speak.

"Sam? Jo?" Dad said.

We jerked our heads in his direction.

"Why don't both of you come and sit at the bar? I need to talk to you about a few things."

I didn't like the sound of that. Sam and I glanced at each other, and he shrugged as if he could read my mind. We made our way to the bar and pulled out two high-backed chairs. Dad stood on the other side of the counter, biting the inside of his cheek, confirming my suspicions. He did that whenever he was irritated or worried about something.

Sam slid onto the stool with ease, given his six-foot height. I had to step up on the bottom rail to climb onto mine.

"First, I know I haven't spent time with you like I wanted to. As you know, I've been busy with all the government bureaucracy. I wanted to discuss school and other things, but it seems I won't have time today either." He let out a sigh. "There are a few reasons, which I've mentioned, why you've been confined to this apartment. The critical reason is your bloodlust phase. As the two of you have experienced, the bloodlust period is difficult. You *cannot* be around humans while trying to get your hunger under control."

I thought of Ben as he mentioned humans. I could still smell his burned-sugar scent, which seemed to be glued to my brain. My mouth watered at the thought.

Dad quirked an eyebrow my way. "Problem, Jo?"

I shook my head vigorously. I had to remind myself that Dad and my brain didn't mesh well. His mind-reading talent was trouble with a capital T.

"To continue," he said, "our world has laws and a process that governs who can make the change. It's not like you decide one day you want to be a vampire and then you are."

"I didn't decide anything," Sam said bitterly. "And you didn't give Jo much of a choice, either, did you?"

Dad stared at the counter. It seemed my brother had hit a nerve.

"I'm sorry about that, son," Dad said, lifting his gaze to Sam. "I truly am."

"Dad, are you trying to tell us something?" I asked before the two of them got into it.

Dad blinked. "Yes. I thought I had more time to explain a few of our laws, but..." He placed both hands on the counter. "I don't know what's going to happen or what they have in mind, but I want you to listen and obey."

I had no idea what he was saying. My heart picked up an extra beat, and I started tapping my foot on the bottom chair rail.

"You're not making any sense," Sam said. "Why are you so nervous?"

Dad closed his eyes and pinched the bridge of his nose with his thumb and forefinger. "Like humans, our laws are in place to protect our society, our people." He opened his eyes. "If we didn't, vampires would run rampant around the globe, doing whatever they wanted. There are some laws you'll learn soon enough, but I was hoping to at least have the opportunity to explain the Eternal Protection Law. It governs the rules and regulations involved when natural-born vampire children decide to become full-fledged vampires." He glanced at Sam then at me.

My nerves were doing some kind of tap dance in my stomach. I'd seen my father extremely pissed once before, but he didn't look as mad as irritated, as if whatever he was about to explain was out of his control.

"The Council of Eternal Affairs mandates the laws within our world," he said.

A choked laugh hung in the back of my throat. As I deciphered Dad's words, Sam snorted.

"What the fuck are you trying to tell us?"

"Son, I've warned you about your language. I don't want any swearing under my roof," he said, glowering.

The room became quiet as a church. They both stared at each other again. Black threaded through Sam's green eyes, and silver dominated Dad's emerald orbs. I had yet to get used to their ego-trip staring contests. They were so much alike in many ways, yet so different in others. Their relationship reminded me of pouring oil in water. It just never mixed well. I prayed every day that they would work out their differences. I guess I shouldn't have expected miracles, since we'd only been together as a family for fourteen days.

"Dad? Council of Eternal Affairs. Remember?" I asked, trying to prevent an argument.

He broke eye contact with Sam. "Because I didn't get prior written consent from the council for both of you to become vampires, we have to explain and justify what happened."

I didn't like his reference to "we."

"So? That should be easy, right?" Sam asked.

"Well... yes and no." Dad raked his hands through his jet-black hair. "The Eternal Protection Law is a law that the vampire government is extremely strict about. There's a lot of paperwork followed by a hearing, then a board of vampires analyzes each case. If all goes well and they approve someone to become a full-fledged vampire, then you're admitted to Grayson Manor to make the change. Afterward, there are restrictions and steps you must follow during the bloodlust period before they will allow you around humans."

A knock sounded at the door. As always, Sam grabbed my hand, stood, and planted his body in front of mine. I adored his protectiveness, but his smothering love was getting a little out of hand. We were in a secure facility and in Dad's apartment, no less.

I glanced at Dad, who was looking at his watch with his eyebrows drawn together.

Before I could ask him if everything was okay, he strode to the door then opened it.

I peered around Sam to find Webb standing in the doorway. I had to keep my mind from wandering—Dad would surely have had a cow if he read my thoughts about Webb. But every time I saw that gorgeous vampire, I couldn't control the racing of my heart. My body had a mind of its own. I gave myself a stern lecture to keep my thoughts G-rated.

He looked handsome as ever, with his wavy brown hair tied in a low ponytail. His SEAL uniform fitted his body to perfection, especially the black T-shirt that stretched across his toned chest. But what always had my belly fluttering were his cobalt-blue eyes. He looked past Dad, searching the room. When he found me, he slanted his head and gave me a captivating smile that caused instant goose bumps.

Sam growled as though staking his territory.

"What're you doing?" I asked in a tone only Sam could hear.

"Nothing," he replied.

"Bull crap. You don't have to protect me from Webb."

"Oh, yes I do. There's fire between you two," he shot back.

I laughed then pushed him. "What's that supposed to mean?" I was beginning to think that maybe it wasn't my father I had to worry about.

"Enter, Lieutenant London," Dad commanded.

Webb followed Dad's order. "Sir, they're here. We should go."

"Why are they here two days early?" Dad asked.

"The council has a pressing matter with Lord James that suddenly came up."

My father's eyes widened as both he and Webb walked over to the bar.

"Christ. I can't even take one day off without something happening." Dad looked at Webb. "What's going on?"

"Sir, I'm not sure. Regardless, we must take

care of this matter with the twins today, if at all possible."

My gaze volleyed back and forth between Webb and Dad. "Lord James" didn't sound like military personnel.

As Webb placed his hands on the bar, Sam stood, blocking me from Webb.

"Son, stand down. Webb isn't going to hurt your sister."

"See, I told you." I pushed Sam out of my way.

My brother's relationship with Webb—well, it was nonexistent. A couple of times during the past two weeks, Webb had visited Dad for his signature on military papers. Each time was the same. If Sam was in the room, he would hover around me, watching every move Webb made. When I asked Sam why he kept trying to protect me, his answer was always, "There's something about him. I can't put my finger on it. Until I figure it out, I don't want him near you."

If I ever went out on a date, I would be in serious trouble—no, scratch that. My date would be in serious trouble. Between Dad and Sam, any future boyfriend didn't stand a chance. Nevertheless, that would probably be a very long time in the future. Most boys never liked me as a human. As a vampire, it would snow in hell for anyone to like me.

"I barely scratched the surface of the Eternal Protection Law when you knocked. I guess we'll see what they have to say."

"What's so urgent?" Sam leaned back against the chair.

"The Council of Eternal Affairs is on the premises," Webb said. "They're here to meet with your father and both of you."

"Why are they here now?" I glanced at Dad.

"When I filled out the paperwork last week," Dad said, "they set a date for the hearing, which was six months out. When I explained the situation and that you'd already become vampires without their written consent, they moved us to the top of the list."

I bit my lip. "And why do you seem worried?"

"Because we didn't follow protocol, and I'm not sure what they're going to do." Dad ran his hand through his hair.

I didn't get it. "We're already vampires, Dad. Why would any of this matter now?"

"Well... they can rule to have both of you sent to Grayson Manor for the duration of your blood-lust quarantine."

I raised an eyebrow.

"In simple terms, it's our vampire hospital," Webb said. "All new vampires spend six weeks there, between the change and getting through the bloodlust period. As you know from your time in the apartment here, it's critical in the first few weeks."

Sam blurted out, "I'm not going down there and meeting with them. And I'm not going to any vampire hospital. This wasn't my choice."

My father's eyes silvered again as he glared at Sam.

"You will meet with the Council." Dad's tone hadn't left any room for arguing.

My brother had issues with authority and especially the law.

"And if I don't?" Sam argued.

I cringed. *Here we go again.* Anger dripped from Dad, spilling into the air.

"Then I'm afraid they'll take you into custody," Webb offered.

"You're going with me, Sam." I punched his arm. "We're family. I know this wasn't your choice, and I'm sorry. But you're not leaving this place without me."

"We didn't do anything wrong." Sam's voice dropped an octave.

"You're right, son. You didn't."

"But you didn't follow the law by changing us into vampires now, did you?" Sam taunted.

Dad reached over the counter.

"Sir." Webb lightly touched Dad's arm before he made contact with Sam.

"Stop it, Sam. We've been through this." My tone was soft, trying to calm him. "Why are you so worried about us going to Grayson Manor?" I asked Dad.

He was leaning against the counter, eyes liquid silver and a snarl etched on his face.

"You're safe as long as you're on this base," Webb responded as he guarded the raging vampire.

"The Plutariums are locked up," Sam countered.

"There are more Plutariums than those we captured. They could use both of you as leverage to get their leader out of prison. The council doesn't care about our problems. They follow the law and our traditions with no exceptions." Webb held out an arm, still keeping Dad at a distance.

"Grayson Manor or any place outside this base is not safe for you," Dad added, his vampire eyes slowly changing from silver back to green, indicating that his anger was dissipating.

"Look, Sam, let's just listen to what they have

to say," I told him. "I lost you once. I'm not going to lose you again."

I had no idea of the full details of the Eternal Protection Law or what the restrictions were for new vampires. I loved my brother, but his resistance to authority and his anger often clouded his vision. Regardless, we were in it together, and I would do anything to make sure we stayed together.

On the Edge of Eternity is available in Ebook and paperback formats.

ABOUT THE AUTHOR

Bestselling author **S.B. Alexander** is an independent author with over 20 titles to date. She writes paranormal, new adult, and sweet romances that feature hot heroes stealing hearts.

S.B. or Susan as she likes to be called is a navy veteran, former high school teacher, and former corporate sales executive. She's a lover of sports, especially baseball, although nowadays you can find her glued to the TV during football season.

When she's not writing, she's a full-time caregiver to her soul mate of twenty-two years who got a bad deal in life when he was diagnosed with ALS. Her motto: "Life is too short to waste. So live every moment like it's your last."

You can connect with S.B. Alexander in the following ways:

Reader Group: https://sbalexander.com/beastsandbitches
Author Website: https://sbalexander.com
Newsletter: https://sbalexander.com/newsletter
Email: susan@sbalexander.com

NEVER MISS A NEW RELEASE:

Sign up for her Author App
iTunes: https://bit.ly/sbalexanderitunes
Android: https://bit.ly/sbalexanderandroid

facebook.com/sbalexander.authorpage

twitter.com/sbalex_author

instagram.com/sbalexanderauthor

amazon.com/author/sbalexander

bookbub.com/authors/s-b-alexander

goodreads.com/sbalexander

ALSO BY S.B. ALEXANDER

MAXWELL SERIES

Upper Young Adult/New Adult Contemporary Romance

Dare to Kiss

Dare to Dream

Dare to Love

Dare to Dance

Dare to Live

Dare to Breathe

Dare to Embrace

THE MAXWELL FAMILY SAGA SERIES

Young Adult Sweet Romance

My Heart to Touch

My Heart to Hold

My Heart to Give

My Heart to Keep

THE VAMPIRE NAVY SEAL SERIES

Paranormal Romance

On the Edge of Humanity

On the Edge of Eternity

On the Edge of Destiny

On the Edge of Misery

On the Edge of Infinity

STAND-ALONES

New Adult Contemporary Romance

Crazy For You

Unforgettable

Holding Onto Forever

Breaking Rules

Rescuing Riley

THE HART SERIES

New Adult Contemporary Romance

Hart of Darkness

Hart of Vengeance

Visit https://sbalexander.com/all-books/ to learn more about S.B. Alexander books and future releases. Please note release dates are subject to change based on reader demand and the author's schedule. Subscribing to the author's newsletter or following her on Facebook is the best way to stay updated with planned new releases.